# THE VAZIEN PARADOX
# SINCLAIR V-LOG Q890/M

## Merita King

Published by Merita King

Eastleigh

United Kingdom

Cover photo – SF Covers via SelfPubBookCovers.

ISBN 978-0-9928491-5-3

# CHAPTER ONE

This is V-Log reference Q890/M data log reference point 4136902/614. Detective Samelan Sinclair-Vaylo reporting.

Hi there, it's been ages hasn't it? Sorry about being away from the V-Logs for so long, I've had so much shit going on I've hardly had the time to sit and breathe, let alone record any logs. Some of it will no doubt find its way into future V-Logs, so I won't go into it in detail here. I was sick for a while and spent some time in a medical centre out on Atilos 4 after being stung by a mature Ganeda Weed flower. It was my own fault, I'd been warned about the inconspicuous tiny yellow flowers that grow everywhere on that planet, but I guess my concentration lapsed just long enough for me to sit on one and regret it instantly. Yeah, I was stung on the ass. Go on, laugh, I deserve it.

I don't remember much after the pain swept up through my left ass cheek and into the small of my back, but I must've been with it long enough to get an emergency call out because I was quickly rescued by a couple of detectives from the local Law Enforcement Agency outpost and taken to their medical centre. The problem for me was that I was stung in just the right place for the poison to quickly make its way to my spinal column and up into my brain. I came round three weeks later paralysed from the neck down and had to endure three further months of treatment to wash the poison from my system so my body could function again. All in all, it took six months to get back to normal and by the time I was deemed fit to return to work, I was climbing the walls. The one good thing to come from it is that I'm now immune to the poison, which is a definite bonus in my job as it has its devotees among the criminal fraternity who sometimes use it to kill their victims.

There's been a lot of personal stuff going on too, major changes to my life and it was during this time that I found true love and allowed my real self out at long last. I had been wrestling with the growing realisation that I was not who I always believed myself to be, for six years by the time this case happened, but I'd avoided dealing with it. I was finally forced to face the issue by falling in love and making a commitment. They say falling in love is a life changing event, don't they? Well this truly was life changing, you'll see, a little later. I found love, lost it, then found it again, thought I'd lost it a second time, then found it again. Complicated just doesn't cut it.

# The Vazien Paradox – Sinclair V-Log Q890/M

There was a time during this case where I believed some people I trusted were not the law abiding and loving friends I'd come to know, that they might be responsible for much suffering and illegality. This caused me a lot of personal pain as I truly loved my friends, looked up to them, and strived to be like them. To suddenly find evidence that they were criminals, frightened and dismayed me to a degree that some might believe was out of proportion. It was made worse by the fact that I was already deeply in love with one of them when it happened.

Hi there, this is Commander Byron of Drycenia here. I'm First Officer and Chief Engineer to His Majesty King Lomas VII of the Drycenian Nation, on his Battle Cruiser DBC1. I thought it prudent that I add a few words here before Sam continues with his V-Log. Wow, this feels weird talking to a machine, but never mind. As he has hinted above, this case had a very high personal cost, for Sam especially, but also for the rest of us who were with him. There was a time when I doubted my ability to cope with the loss and I was plagued with very negative thoughts. When I look back now, with a more balanced perspective now that the passage of time has calmed the raw emotion, I can see that every moment of all our lives brought us to those brief few weeks when everything changed. Through it all, the danger, the anger, the tears, the loss and recriminations, the one thing I've learned is never to waste a moment. You never know how important memories are until they are all you have left, so make sure you fill each moment of your lives building good ones. Now, back to Sam and this case.

This is one of those cases that seemed straight forward at first, despite the personal anguish it caused me. As time went on, it became something different, and far more sinister, and for the first time, I truly doubted my ability to sort it out. I was not meant to become involved at all, it was sheer chance that I found myself on site when it went down. The promise of a few days relaxing after weeks of chasing an annoying and well known scammer, lured me to the Tyrrin System where I knew a well run Agency outpost operated. It was not the nearest system but I had an Agency colleague there who I knew would ensure I had a good time. After depositing my prisoner and going through the usual legal stuff to hand him over, I took a room at the Headquarters building and looked forward to checking out the nightlife with my old friend and fellow Detective, Tip Danso.

I heard the smile in his voice when he answered my Unicom call. "Sam, how are you? It's great to hear from you."

"Hi Tip. I've just dropped off Falmer Rawlings at your headquarters and thought I'd take a few days here to relax."

"Falmer Rawlings again? He couldn't have been out long. That old fart is a thorn in all our backsides. So, you're here on Tyrrin?"

"Yeah, and I thought it would be nice to get together and have a drink when you're free."

"Absolutely. Where are you staying?"

"I've taken a room at Headquarters, room twenty-three."

"Okay, don't unpack. You're staying with me. I'll see you shortly after six."

The apartment was large and enjoyed a nice view over the city from its seventeenth floor situation. After unpacking in the spacious spare bedroom and taking a hot shower, we sat on the balcony with drinks and talked for hours. In less than an hour it was as if we had been together every day since our first meeting a few years previously, on Deep Space Refuelling Station Zeta 12. Tip was a different man in those days, in every sense of the word, and I smiled as I looked at him.

"That seems like a lifetime ago," I remarked and saw him become introspective for a second.

"It might as well be," he replied. "I'm a new man now, a man I can respect for the first time in my life. That's a good feeling and it never gets old."

I looked at the huge muscular frame and jet-black eyes that marked him out as Lilean and remembered someone else. "Are you still in contact with Vincent and the Drycenians?" I asked.

"Yeah," he grinned. "They're all fine and ask about you from time to time."

This pleased me and I couldn't help but grin. "They do?"

"Of course, why wouldn't they?"

My mouth flapped. "Well I umm, I don't know, I guess. I'm just a cop who did a job for them. It's not like I'm family or anything. I'm neither Drycenian nor Lilean and don't have your, umm, gifts."

Tip's eyes glazed for a moment as he seemed to look right through me. I knew what this meant and allowed him the time he needed without interrupting. When he blinked and looked at me, I raised my eyebrows questioningly.

"Leon and Syra send you their love and assure you that Vincent knows we are spending time together again. They say you're to take the opportunity the next three days offers you to relax your mind and body fully. They say they're happy you're now fully recovered. Were you sick?"

I nodded and relayed the story of my six month recovery after the Ganeda Weed poisoning. I was happy to know that our mutual friends Vincent and the Drycenians were doing well, happier than I would have expected to be and this surprised me. I allowed my thoughts to settle on the subject of Leon and Syra and frowned. This aspect of life for my Lilean friends still baffled me.

Tip saw my frown. "What's up?"

"Oh nothing really. It's just, well this thing you Lilean folks do still seems odd to me, in an awesomely cool kind of way."

Tip laughed aloud. "I guess it is awesomely cool. I remember my first time with it and how quickly it became normal. I sometimes forget other people don't have it."

"I often wish I had it," I admitted and realised that I was feeling envious. I blushed, cursing this uncontrollable habit that had always plagued my life.

Tip pretended not to notice. "I admit it is a definite advantage in our line of work."

"Do they tell you everything?" I asked. "You know, when you're working a case. Do they give you all the details and save you the leg work?"

"No," he grinned. "They only tell me what is necessary to keep me on my pre-destined life path. Come on, Sam, you know this already."

I nodded. "Yeah I guess I do. Sorry to sound like a sceptic. It's been a while since I spent time with any Lileans. It's difficult to understand what it must be like not being totally on your own."

"You're not. You just haven't developed the ability to know that." I sniggered at this remark and Tip grinned. "Yeah I know that sounds awfully convenient but it doesn't change the fact that it's true. You get those moments of insight when your brain seems to leap to just the right conclusion despite there being no evidence to confirm it as such, don't you?" I nodded and he continued before I could argue. "You're famous in the Agency for your people reading skills, but do you really know where that insight originates and how it finds its way to your consciousness? Why don't all our Detectives have those same skills? Why just you?" I shrugged. "Maybe it comes from outside of yourself, Sam, have you ever entertained that notion?"

I had to admit that I hadn't. "No, I guess I haven't."

"Have another beer," he said as he handed me a bottle and raised his own. "A toast to you, Sam. Giving me the opportunity to live a good life and make amends for all that has gone before, is a gift I can never repay. Everything I have now, every good thing I have a chance to do, every achievement, is down to you and thank you will never be enough. If you even try to deny it, I shall throw you from this very balcony."

We laughed together and drank and I allowed the warmth of friendship borne of mutual struggle to take hold of my heart for the first time in ages. When I said earlier that Tip was a different man when we first met, I meant every word. He was a criminal back then and spent his life in thrall to a really twisted sicko. Without going into too much detail, he turned his life around and I helped him get a job with the Agency. No one but me, the Drycenians, and the other Lileans I worked with on that case know his past, who and what he was back then, but despite the chance I was taking on him, the secret has never been a burden. Not even Tinnias, my adopted father and Boss, knows anything about it and never will unless Tip decides he wants him to. It is part of what binds us as friends despite the distances in time and space that often separate us.

I heard a distant clock tower strike three in the morning before we decided to go to bed, and it was then that something struck me as odd. As it came to the forefront of my mind, I realised it had been bothering me since Tip first mentioned it hours before but I'd not understood the significance of it.

"By the way, Tip. You said that Leon wants me to relax for the next three days." He nodded. "But I was planning on staying for a week while my ship is serviced and my armoury restocked. If I'm only going to get three days in which to relax, what's on the cards for the others?"

He shrugged. "I haven't a clue."

"Can you ask Leon?"

"It doesn't work like that, Sam. I can ask until I'm blue in the face but if they don't think it right, they won't tell. Besides, he's not here anymore and Malea just smiles and shakes her head when she wants me to stop pushing."

"Okay, never mind."

"It could be something good y'know," Tip grinned. "Don't always assume it means trouble."

I laughed aloud. "When you've been at this game as long as I have, you'll have the same difficulty, believe me."

"Sleep well, Sam. I'll probably be gone by the time you wake up so help yourself to anything you want. There's a spare key in the bowl by the door so you can come and go as you please. I'm not much of a cook so you should probably eat out or go shopping if you want to play housewife."

"Right, good night."


The sun shone through the large windows as I padded to the kitchen. I was naked and fresh from the shower and enjoyed the chance to feel real air on my skin after weeks of the recycled stuff in my ship. Don't misunderstand me, my ship has everything I need to be comfortable for months at a time if necessary. It has to be, it is my home as well as my transport when I'm away from my home world on Sigma Prime, which is most of the time. The demands of being a chase, catch, and deliver guy with the Inter-Galactic Law Enforcement Agency are great, so I spare no expense in making sure my ship is homely as well as functional. The only things it can't give me that I miss, are fresh air and real sunshine, so when I am planet bound, I make the most of the opportunity and often stroll around with very little on. My morning routine doesn't change much unless the job demands it. I wake, have a specially formulated nutrient drink, then spend at least two hours working out.

After struggling back to health for six months, it felt good to be at full strength again and I enjoyed every moment of the martial art that was my daily practice. I had been taught by my best friend, Ren, and it was during this daily workout that I felt closest to him. He was a Damiklonian and their martial art is shrouded in mystery. They guard their culture very closely and it is almost never heard of for a non Damiklonian to be taught their martial art. We met when we worked undercover on a case, one that ultimately cost him his life and I knew I would never fully recover from the loss. Although I had come to a healthy peace with it, the void he left ached constantly. I found that if I allowed thoughts of him to accompany me through my daily workout, it hurt less for the rest of the day. Don't think I'm being maudlin or anything like that, I don't go around in deep mourning all the time, but I do miss my friend and have no desire to lessen my love for him by denying the pain his loss causes. He made me laugh and see life in a totally new way and I remember those aspects of our friendship most of all. He taught me that the best way to honour a loved one is to remember the good in them and strive for that in ourselves. I hoped, as I hope every day, that he was proud of me.

The city was an eclectic mix of old alongside new, the home grown sharing space with the exotic, but despite this odd mix, it looked and felt pleasing as I strolled along. Smiles greeted me everywhere I went and I quickly understood why Tyrrin 4 is known as happy central. For the next three days,

I explored the city, chatted with total strangers, laughed with guys in various bars and cafes, and bought far too much stuff I probably would never use or need. On the third day, I decided to go and catch a movie. After spending a couple of hours in a modern vidicom movie theatre, I looked around for somewhere to eat and settled on a little place that sold food I had at least heard of before. I was halfway through a delicious fruit based dessert when my Unicom rang.

"Hi, Son. How's things?"

"Hey, Dad. Everything is fine. I handed Falmer Rawlings over to the Agency guys on Tyrrin 4 a few days ago."

"I'll bet they were pleased to see their old friend again," he laughed.

"Extremely. Is it okay if I take a few more days off? I might as well make it a whole week. I'm staying with Tip Danso."

"Sure, take all the time you need. How is he? You've always had a soft spot for him, haven't you?"

"He's great, and yes, he's a nice guy. This place is lovely by the way, everyone is very friendly. No wonder they call it happy central."

"I spent some weeks there years ago when I was a young Detective," he said. "I broke my arm there when I slipped over in a store and everyone was very helpful. The store owner visited me daily in the medical centre and promised me that I would never pay for anything in his store ever again."

I laughed. "Really? What's the name of it, I'll pay them a visit and see if they remember."

"Don't be mean, they might be struggling to make ends meet."

"I'm kidding. They probably sold up by now anyway, after all you're so old the store owner might not even still be alive."

"Watch it, Son," Tinnias barked, the laughter evident in his voice. We spent a few minutes catching up and I told him to give my love to Grellina and Ambella. He then asked me when I would be home.

"I'm planning on staying here for a week, then if nothing comes up job-wise, I'll make my way straight home. If all goes to plan, I should be with you in three weeks, give or take."

"Okay, that sounds good. I've managed to get a table at the Sky Diner in five weeks' time. It'll be good to have the whole family together."

"Wow whose ass did you have to kiss to get a table that quickly?" I asked. "I hope you're not walking funny."

I heard him laugh. "I may be old but I still have some power you know."

"I'll know I've made it big when I can get a table at the Sky Diner," I said.

"Dream on, Son, dream on. You take care now; do you need anything?"

"No, I'm fine thanks. I'll see you soon."

"I love you, Sam. Be safe."

"Always. I love you too, Dad."


The next day, I decided to go shopping for gifts for the family and ended up buying myself all sorts of stuff that would no doubt end up shoved to the back of a dusty closet. Struggling to turn the key while my arms were full of my purchases, I stumbled into the apartment and turned to shut the door behind me. As I reached to push the door, something dark fluttered to life deep within me and my hand froze in mid air. Reaching instinctively for my laser pistol with one hand, I put the bags down and looked around. The hallway was a small space, with doors leading off to the two bedrooms on the right, and the bathroom to the left. Ahead to the left was a spacious cupboard, and directly in front was the door to the large living area with the kitchen leading off. Ignoring the warning bells that screamed within me to run and never come back, I forced my mind into as calm a state as I could and analysed what I was feeling.

The home felt violated, as if someone had been here without being welcome. It was akin to the feeling of hands running over my body to whom I had not given the invitation to touch, to feel my private places. Nausea swept into my gut and I fought the urge to rush to the bathroom to vomit. Forcing myself into working mode with the greatest effort of will, I made my way around the apartment and found it empty. Nothing seemed obviously out of place but then it was not my home and I had no way of knowing if anything was missing or moved. After checking my own belongings and finding nothing missing, I locked the windows and doors and carried the bags of shopping into the kitchen.

The thought that maybe someone was trying to get to Tip in some way was first in my mind as I prepared to make dinner for us both. I made up my mind to question him about whatever case he was working on as soon as he returned. Looking through his music collection had me shaking my head in horror, and I made up my mind to return to my ship for a supply of music chips with which to keep myself company. After eventually choosing something I could at least hear the words to, I cranked it up and found myself jigging along to the beat. Maybe this stuff wasn't so bad after all.

The smell of burning had me cursing aloud when I realised I hadn't heard the timer over the loud music, and I was forced to begin my preparations again. It was then that something occurred to me that had me racing to my bedroom to rummage in my belongings. It was the loud music you see, not being able to hear anything over the loud music made me realise that someone might be listening. Two hours later, I sat down and looked at the small pile of components that lay on the table before me. Five listening devices and two cameras, none bigger than my thumb nail, had been placed at strategic places around the apartment and I frowned. No wonder I felt weird when I came back from my shopping excursion. I must've missed the culprit by mere minutes.

The two cameras had been placed in the hallway and main living area, with the listening devices placed one in each of the rooms.

"What the hell are you involved in, Tip?" I said aloud, confident that no one could hear me anymore. I thought it best I ring Tinnias and let him know, just in case I found myself involved in something that would delay my home coming. He was incensed.

"What the fuck? Did you get them all?"

"Yeah, I swept the place twice. There's nothing more here now, but they now know I'm onto them of course. I disabled them all and have them bagged and tagged. I'll put in a couple of my own so I can see if anyone else comes visiting without an invite. I don't know what this means but it's probably connected to whatever Tip is working on. I'll talk to him tonight."

"Do you want me to go official on this and report it?"

"Not yet, let's keep quiet for now or we might scare them off. I'd rather catch them than frighten them away."

"Okay. I guess there's always the possibility that it was ordered by the Agency. Maybe they're checking up on Tip. Maybe they're checking up on you."

"Does that happen?" I asked.

"Sometimes. After what happened with Detective Rime the Agency is being ultra careful about what their personnel might be involved with. It's understandable I suppose, but annoying never the less."

"I guess so. Tip wouldn't be involved in anything bad, I'm happy to stake my career on that, and I'm sure as hell not either."

"I'll stake mine on that," Tinnias said. "No. You're right. It must be connected to whatever case Tip is working at the moment. Talk to him and see what he says. If you want, I'll get in touch tomorrow and let the Outpost

Commander know that I want you put on the case alongside him. As Senior Detective you'll automatically be given superiority over him so you'll have access to all the case notes."

"Okay, that sounds good to me. I'll let you know if and when I think that's our best option," I replied. "I'll update you the moment I know more."


"It's a pretty run of the mill case really," Tip said as we ate. "Some money was stolen from one of the local banks. Of the employees that were absent from work right after the money disappeared, two are still unaccounted for. A man and a woman. We're assuming that they've done a runner with the money to live a life of luxury somewhere. That's all we know at the moment."

I knew he was telling the truth and I felt my soul relax deep inside my body. Those few hours spent wondering if the man I had taken such a chance on had got himself involved in something unsavoury, were the worst I'd endured for a long time. The relief I felt is indescribable and it must've showed for he glared at me.

"You didn't think I was involved in anything untoward did you, Sam?" I hesitated for a moment too long before answering and he knew without being told that for a while at least, I had worried about him.

"It's not that I doubted you," I replied. "I was worried that someone might be trying to get to you. I was concerned for you, not doubtful of you. Ask Tinnias yourself, I told him I would happily stake my career on you being stain free. He suggested that it might be the Agency's doing, checking up on you, or me, or both of us. After that Rime business they're being extra careful."

His eyes glazed over as they had done the previous evening and I knew he was communing with his spiritual kin. When he once again met my gaze, he nodded. "Of course, I'm sorry. I didn't mean to leap down your throat like that."

"No problem."

"I'll hand them in tomorrow and see what my boss says. If it is the Agency, they should admit it now that we've found the stuff. They won't want me adding it to the case evidence if it doesn't belong there. It could fuck everything up in the long run."

"Okay. Do you want the benefit of my many years of experience?" I asked and he nodded. "Pre-empt them on this by adding it to the case evidence first. Don't make a thing about mentioning it unless they ask about it. Do the paperwork and then hand the stuff over to forensics like any other bit of evidence. If it is the Agency's doing, they'll be falling over themselves to sort it out. If you just hand it over to them, it might mysteriously disappear without a trace and you could find yourself never getting an explanation. Act dumb and they won't think you're a threat. That's what I'd do anyway, but it's your case."

He grinned at me and nodded. "I'm very glad you stopped by, Sam. Very glad indeed."

After that moment of difficulty passed, we enjoyed the rest of the evening and exchanged stories of our various exploits since we last met and I was glad to learn that Tip was becoming an experienced Detective and not the green rookie I had wet nursed for six months when he first joined the Agency. For the first time I was able to look upon him as almost an equal rather than a pupil.

"I'm surprised your umm, y'know, your friends, didn't warn you of this," I said.

"I told you, they don't control every moment of my life," he laughed. "They probably didn't have to, with you here to discover the stuff, they might've felt no need to tell me about it. Maybe they didn't warn me because they already warned you, and you acted on that warning and got the job done."

"How do you mean they warned me?" I frowned. "I heard nothing, saw nothing."

"How did you feel?"

"It was weird actually," I admitted. "I knew the moment I came in that something was wrong, although there was nothing to show why I should feel that way."

"And it was like a heavy ball of darkness right inside here," Tip said, pointing to his solar plexus.

"Yes, just like that. How did you know?"

"That's how it is for us too, when they want to warn us of danger. I know I'm probably preaching to the converted, but whenever you feel that way, never ignore it. Always go with your instinct when that happens. Promise me."

"I always do," I said. "It happens pretty regularly and has saved my skin many times."

"Promise me." Tip said.

"I promise."

We spent the rest of the evening watching a couple of decent vidicom movies before going to bed. I had been asleep for no more than a couple of hours when I was shaken awake by Tip, who yawned widely as he sat on the side of my bed.

"What's up?" I asked, awake immediately. Instinctively I reached for my pistol.

He laid a hand on mine and shook his head. "Relax, nothing's wrong. Do you know someone who had very large oddly round eyes of a strange watery blue grey, long fangs, and peculiar marks on each side of his neck?"

My eyes widened as tears sprang to the corners unbidden. My mouth fell open in shock and I nodded. "Yes," I hissed emotionally. "You saw him?"

"Briefly. Malea allowed me to see him for but a moment so I could give you the answer you seek. I didn't get his name, I'm sorry, but the love he has for you is immensely strong, it covered his energy in a thick blanket."

A strangled gasp of emotion escaped me as I listened to Tip's explanation of my best friend. "Ren. His name is Ren. He was my best friend. He was killed on a job we were working."

"Oh, I believe I heard about that on the rumour mill. I remember someone saying you lost a partner on a case. A Damiklonian if I remember rightly."

I nodded. "Yes. It's just like him to want to look after me. I should've known."

"You can talk to him you know. He will hear you, even though you might not realise. The more you accept and work with it, the stronger it will become. It's like a muscle, it needs to be worked to become strong and dependable."

"Thank you so much," I said. "You've no idea what this means to me."

"Oh yes I do, my friend. I remember the first time I saw and heard Malea after living for years with the brain dysfunction that prevented me from being like other Lileans. I know exactly what it means, and how much joy it brings your soul when you know that love survives and continues with us." With another yawn, he got up and shuffled sleepily towards the door. "Sleep well. See you tomorrow. I'll ring you and let you know if anything is said about the new evidence."

## CHAPTER TWO

After breakfasting lightly, I spent the next couple of hours installing some tiny security cameras into Tip's apartment. I put one facing the front door which should give me a good full face view of all callers, good enough to be used in trials. The Consoria P41 cameras I use are no bigger than my fingernail and can be hidden almost anywhere. The picture and sound quality are amazing and I've had several cases that resulted in successful convictions purely on the evidence these little babies can deliver. I have loads of them and wouldn't remove them from my basic kit bag for anything.

I put two more in the main living space, one facing the kitchen area and one facing the door to the hallway. Both views covered the entire living and kitchen space and would ensure I could see everything that happened. One more in each of the bedrooms had the whole apartment covered and I felt more secure knowing my own trusted equipment was now looking after me. I set up my vidicom to record the feeds and made myself a hot drink.

Having chosen not to reveal to Tip that I intended to wire his apartment with Consorias, I pondered as I drank on why I had made this decision. Tip was someone I always regarded as a friend and totally honest guy, so why the subterfuge? The only explanation I could come up with was my own need for self preservation. Maybe I've been doing this job for so long that I've become selfish, I don't know but instinct told me to keep it to myself, at least for now.

Tip's household Unicom rang and I picked it up. "Danso residence," I answered. Several seconds of silence ensued. "Hello? Who is this?" I demanded. The barely audible click told me whoever made the call did so from a hand held personal Unicom rather than another household unit. When the same thing happened a couple of hours later, I rummaged in my belongings again and had the Unicom wired within ten minutes. I frowned at this new development and registered a small knot of unease come to life behind my navel. Tip said the case he was working was a simple bank job and I had no reason to disbelieve him. This kind of case is our bread and butter and makes up a good seventy percent of our time on the job. Thefts outweigh other crimes by several hundred percent, confirming my long held conviction that people galaxy wide share one important trait no matter how alien they might be from one another. Humanoids are, above all else, greedy assholes.

Any law enforcer can find themselves being surveilled by the criminals they are charged with investigating. It's happened to me more than once and although a nuisance, it has no bearing on the character or motives of the law enforcer. I was not at all surprised that Tip should be in this position and if this was all it was, I would not be frowning into my rapidly cooling drink. The Unicom calls put things into an entirely different perspective and it was these that occupied my thoughts.

Let me explain my thought process here, so you know how my brain operates sometimes. When I call someone on my Unicom, I do so because I want to speak with them and hope they want to speak with me. I call them because of something that connects us, either an emotional bond or something to do with my job. I might be calling a medic to make an appointment to have my excessive flatulence sorted out, or I might be asking a possible witness to allow me to pay them a visit, it could be anything. What I'm getting at here, is that a Unicom call symbolises the desire for a connection of some sort.

The next weird thing was why the caller, or callers, did not appear to want to talk to me. If I'm being overly cautious, answer me this; why didn't they ask for Tip when they heard a strange voice answering their call. A simple, "Is Tip around?" would be the normal thing to say, wouldn't it? It's what I say when I call people. You must've had similar calls yourself. Someone calls for a family member who is out when they call. It usually goes something like this.

"Is Samelan there?"

"Sorry, he's out at the medical centre getting his excessive flatulence sorted."

"Oh okay, sorry to have bothered you."

"Can I give him a message when he gets back?"

"Tell him to call me when he has the time. My name is Shitface and my number is…"

You see where I'm going with this? The fact that our mystery caller did not wish to engage with me told me a couple of things. Firstly, he didn't want me to know who was calling nor the reason for the call, and secondly, he wasn't expecting me to be there. This second point was not a huge surprise as Tip had only invited me to stay a few days before but still I noted it down inside my mind. Not wishing to make something out of nothing, I was aware of the possibility that the caller had simply got the wrong number and was too embarrassed to speak to a total stranger when they might have been expecting someone they knew. For this to happen twice in as many hours though, either with the same caller or two different ones was too weird.

I was officially worried and called Tinnias. I could almost hear the frown in his tone.

"Hmm that's odd. You want me to quietly look into what Tip's been up to recently?"

"Yes please, that would be helpful."

"No problem. My advice would be do what you've probably done already. Record everything for a few days and see if you catch anything interesting."

"That's what I was planning. What else is there to do when I'm not yet sure anything is wrong? Despite the evidence pointing towards something going on, there's not enough for me to act officially yet. I'll just hang around here and scratch my ass until something, or nothing, appears on the recordings."

"I agree, Sam. I can't advise anything more than that if you want to remain on the right side of the regulations, which is advisable if this becomes an official case later. I know I'm telling you what you already know so I'm sorry for the lecture. I'm your boss as well as your dad remember."

I grinned. "I know, Dad. I'd rather you reminded me of something I haven't forgotten, than don't remind me of something I have. If something wrong is going on here, we can do without silly mistakes."

"Exactly. Keep me fully informed on this. Call me regularly. Even if you've nothing specific, we can always bash ideas off each other."

"I will."

"Do you need anything? How are you for money?"

"I'm fine. I might well end up not making that dinner you booked though. Sorry."

"There'll be another time for that, don't worry. Be safe, Son. I love you."

"I love you too, Dad. Give my love to the family."


Feeling much more at ease after sharing my concerns with Tinnias, I worked out for a couple of hours, showered, dressed, and went out for a walk to think. What worried me most was not that it was happening at all but that it was happening to Tip. With his background and no doubt the dubious connections that went with the life he led, the possibility that someone from those days had found him and was maybe blackmailing him was all too real. I wondered what I would do if it happened to me and found myself a little surprised that after twenty years as a law enforcer, a similar experience had so far eluded me. There was no doubt that I would involve Tinnias from the outset. As my adopted father and boss, there is nothing I wouldn't trust him with and I have every confidence that he would move mountains to help me sort it out.

Tip doesn't have the benefit of someone like Tinnias in his life though. He is effectively alone, his change of identity at the time of his turnaround making it imperative that everyone he knew back then believe him to be dead. I knew he kept in regular touch with Vincent Domenico and his family, the people involved in the case I was working when we first encountered the man who Tip used to be. I wondered whether it might be worthwhile giving Vincent a call, just to catch up of course. Also obvious was the knowledge that the Drycenians kept in touch with Tip, at least once a year anyway, to supply him with the drugs he needs for his brain dysfunction.

The Drycenians were also involved in the Domenico case and their memory always makes me smile with genuine affection. They are a mysterious race who deliberately keep themselves apart from interaction with other races. They were one of the very first races to get into space and have the most amazing technology and knowledge. Their name is greeted with gasps of awe by everyone and they are the subjects of many a fireside tale and legend. When I say their technology is advanced, I mean it more than you could ever imagine. What they can do often defies belief, I've seen some of it with my own eyes and Tip owes his life to just such an amazing advancement. During the Domenico case, Tip was one of the bad guys we were chasing and as the chase reached its climax, he died. The Drycenians, themselves having gotten involved by then, have the technology to bring back the dead and Tip is an example. If you ever meet him, you'll notice a silver coloured metallic plate attached around the back of his neck. This is the only visible effect of having been through the Drycenian process and is what keeps him alive. As far as I remember, it's called a Brain Stem Regulator and keeps his brain functioning normally.

It was while they were caring for him that they found out about a dysfunction in one part of his brain. On Lilea, this illness is incurable but the Drycenians were able to provide a drug to combat the effects. I wondered how often they meet him and wished I had the means to give them a call. Like I said, they keep themselves very much to themselves and apart from a very few non Drycenians, no one ever gets to meet them that often. I cursed as I was forced to realise that I was not one of the favoured few. It wouldn't hurt to mention them, ask after them perhaps, during conversation or over dinner. He might open up about how often he sees them and I can maybe express a vain wish to meet up with them again to say hello. I didn't hold out much hope but hey, if you don't ask you don't get, right?

Back at the apartment, I put down my purchases and went to prepare dinner. Resisting the urge to interrogate Tip about the recording devices I found, I kept the conversation light for as long as I could. After an hour, I knew I would burst if I didn't say anything so I jumped right in.

"How did it go today?"

Tip shrugged. "There's nothing new on the whereabouts of our missing thieves, unfortunately. The boss thinks we should hand it over to a chase, catch, and deliver guy to find them."

I nodded. As one myself, I was confident that one of my fellow freelance law enforcers would track them down within a couple of weeks at the most. Most thefts leave a money trail, especially those involving large amounts. Only hardened career thieves know how to control themselves when they come into possession of huge amounts of money. Novices and opportunists tend to go a little crazy and the money trail is easy to follow. I have contacts all over the galaxy and I knew I'd have little trouble finding them if I was given the job.

My official title is Detective, Senior Grade, Freelance but we are known throughout the Agency as chase, catch, and deliver guys because that is what we do. Unlike office bound Detectives, our patch is out there in the cold void of the inter-galactic shipping lanes, the planetary systems both large and small, the races both recognisably humanoid and less so. This is where we work and spend much of our daily life and I wouldn't change it for anything. I began my career behind a desk at the Agency headquarters building back home on Sigma Prime and worked the streets of my home city, Alimenika, for over eight years. One morning as I did yet another report, I realised I was bored and needed a change. It was not the job that bored me but the regulations I was bound by. After a lot of thinking, I decided I had two choices, resign or go freelance. I've never regretted my decision for a moment.

As a chase, catch, and deliver guy, I am given a specific target to find, apprehend, and deliver into the hands of the relevant arm of the Law Enforcement Agency. It is not my job to ascertain the guilt or innocence of my target, just to find them and give them to those whose job it is to judge such matters. Over the years I've been doing this job, I've acquired a lot of contacts whom I call my eyes and ears, on many different worlds in many different systems. I make a point of contacting them all on a regular basis, just so they know I still value them, for without their indulgence, my record wouldn't be a quarter as impressive as it currently is. I knew without a doubt that Tip's absconders would not evade me for long.

"Good idea," I nodded. "A freelancer would find them quickly if they've left a trail."

"Yeah, but I like to see it through to the end sometimes. Handing it over to a freelancer always seems like admitting I've failed somehow."

"Come on, Tip, you know how this job is. It's a team effort. We're all working towards the same goal. It's not a competition you know."

"Yeah I know it's silly and most of the time I'm happy to give the leg work to guys like you. Just now and then though, I'd like to do the whole job from start to finish."

"That's not how the Agency works," I replied. "No one ever does the whole job. It's done that way to avoid mistakes or misdeeds by law enforcers. When there's a whole team on a job, it's more difficult for one dirty law enforcer to hide something. You must've had this lecture during your training at least once."

He nodded. "Several times, and yes, I understand and agree. I guess I'm hankering after some glory, a medal or something silly like that."

"Medals are just something more for your cleaning woman to dust. They mean nothing. I'd rather have the security of a team I trust working with me and backing me up, than a medal and a moment of applause from the office staff that will be forgotten by lunch time."

"When you put it like that, I sound like a glory hunter."

"I'm sorry," I said. "I didn't mean it like that. I guess I'm just surprised it bothers you."

"Oh it doesn't, not really. I guess this case has got to me. It's just a couple of thieves but they've managed to evade all my efforts to find them. It should be a simple case, as you say yourself, the money trail should be easy to follow. I shouldn't be having such a hard time apprehending them. I guess they were lucky and slipped away under our noses."

"It happens sometimes. It won't be the last time so you better get used to it. The bank will be insured anyway so they'll get it all back and pass on the expense to their customers by raising their fees."

Tip sniggered. "Yeah. Every time my bank raises its fees from now on, I'll be cursing law enforcement."

We laughed together and I brought the subject back to the recording devices I found. "Did you hand those recording devices in?" Tip nodded. "Any reaction?"

"Nope. At least not to me directly. Forensics have them now and say I should have them back tomorrow afternoon."

"You noted where they were found on the file?" I asked.

"Yeah."

"And no one asked about it?"

"Nope."

"That's odd," I frowned. "Don't you think?"

"Maybe they're busy with other cases," he said.

This reply astonished me and I almost burst out laughing. I managed to control myself enough to issue a mere, "what the fuck?"

"Well I don't know what it's like on Sigma, Sam, but here on Tyrrin 4 it's busy. Visitors to our world hear the talk about this being such a laid back place, happy central where everyone walks around with an inane grin on their face and wishes everyone else peace and love. They think we're an easy target and crime by off worlders here is high. Thankfully our arrest rate is equally high."

Tip's voice now had an edge that signalled his annoyance and I was taken aback. Not knowing whether to respond with equal assertiveness or back down, I hesitated and he took advantage by digging further.

"Of course, there is always the outside possibility that my boss trusts me to do the job without feeling the need to look over my shoulder or question my every move."

This outburst of aggression could easily have angered me into a screaming match with my friend but I knew better. I have a well-deserved reputation as an expert reader of people and I knew that his angry response was an act designed to divert me from a path he didn't want me to go down. Having taken no more than a nanosecond to decide not to be drawn away, I went for the jugular.

"What have you got yourself involved with, my friend?" My voice was calm, the question slow and deliberate so as not to be taken as an attack.

Tip sighed, pushed his plate away, and looked at me. "Nothing. It's just that you haven't been here for five minutes and you're questioning my actions. I'm thinking perhaps you wonder whether I am a good guy after all. Maybe you think there's still some Andrew Midship in here somewhere huh? I'll always be grateful to you for helping me when I turned my life around, but I think you doubt me more than you'll admit to. I guess I'll never quite win your trust after all."

"That's not true," I replied. "I admit I worry that someone from back then might find you one day and try to use what they know against you, but I've never doubted your honesty or determination to leave your old life behind. I never think of you as Andrew Midship anymore, ever. He died and good riddance to him. You just seem a little …" I began, struggling for the right words.

"A little what?" he glared at me.

"A little evasive, I guess. I think you're hiding something and I want to help."

Several seconds of silence passed between us, during which his jet-black eyes looked into my brown ones. As I gazed at those eyes, I saw a light go out and I knew our friendship had been damaged, perhaps permanently and I was saddened.

"I think perhaps we've evolved in different directions, Sam," he said finally, continuing with his meal. "We don't seem to have enough in common for our friendship to be worthwhile fighting for."

My eyebrows shot to the top of my forehead as I realised he was telling me our friendship was over just because I expressed concern over the case he was working on. Without waiting for the indignancy of being thrown out, I rose from the table. "I'll go pack my stuff and be out of your hair in a few minutes."

"You'll be wanting these," he said and I turned to face him.

He nodded towards the centre of the table, on which he placed a small package. I walked over and picked it up to find all the cameras and the Unicom bug I had so carefully installed around his apartment.

"I came home earlier to pick up something and found them. I knew you'd probably have put some in after what you found. I'm saddened that you neither asked my permission to bug my home or told me you had."

"I just wanted to keep you safe," I offered.

"I'm a grown man," he replied. "This is my home and I don't appreciate you coming in here after I offer you my hospitality and bugging the place within the first couple of days. I'm a law enforcer, not a criminal. I know you're a chase, catch, and deliver guy but I'll thank you to remember I'm not your target."

"I'm sorry, Tip. I know you don't want to hear it but I do want to help you if you let me. Whatever has happened, you have my word I'll do whatever I can. You have my number, call me anytime and I'll be here for you."

"Goodbye, Sam."


An hour and a half later, I was signing the paperwork and receiving the key to room twenty-three again back at the headquarters building. The desk clerk nodded to my thanks and handed me a list of the canteen opening hours. Once I had unpacked and taken a shower, I called Tinnias and told him of my afternoon.

"I'm sorry, Sam. That must be upsetting for you. I know you liked the guy."

I nodded despite knowing he couldn't see me. "Yeah, I've not much of a record where friendships are concerned, have I? They either get murdered or they quickly come to hate me. It's a good job I've tried to be a little detached with people or it could upset me."

"Oh, Son," Tinnias sighed, seeing through my veneer of indifference immediately. "It's not you, it's the job. It has the same effect on everyone's personal life. Listen, why not come home now? There's nothing there to keep you gainfully employed and if Tip has moved his life away from your mentorship, just wish him well and get on with your own. We love you and miss you and you've lots of people who like and respect you here."

"I'm sorry for my attitude," I said, embarrassed at my negative outburst. "It's just so unlike Tip to behave this way. I'm convinced he's got into something he doesn't know how to handle. I think I should hang around and do some digging, on the quiet of course, and see what I find."

"Okay, is there anything I can do to help?"

"Did you dig into his cases like we talked about the other day?" I asked.

"I did and there's nothing that stands out as odd. I'll keep looking though and ask around. Don't worry, Son, you're not the only one with a good network of contacts. This old timer's still got it you know."

I sniggered. "Thanks. I'll make a few calls myself and we can compare notes."

My contact in finance and banking answered my call on the fourth ring and I detected a genuine smile in his tone. We hadn't spoken for a couple of months and I was glad he seemed pleased to hear from me. After being unceremoniously dumped by Tip, it felt good to know at least one other person liked me.

"Hey, Sam, how ya doing buddy?"

"I'm in an odd situation actually, but personally I'm well, thank you. How's the family?"

"They're good, thanks for asking. The youngest got married a few weeks ago, much against my advice I might add. She'll do okay though; the guy is a little slow but he's a hard worker and adores her."

"You mean that little kid with the scar on her shoulder that looks like a heart? She's married? Shit, where does the time go?"

"Don't ask, Sam, it scares me too. Now how can I help you?"

"There was a theft recently from a branch of the Schilgaard Bank on Tyrrin 4. Thirty-two thousand galactic credits were stolen. Two of the staff at the bank failed to return to duty right after the theft, a man and a woman and both haven't been seen since." I gave him the address of the bank and the names of the two missing people.

"And you're convinced it was an inside job?"

"Well it's not exactly my case," I hedged. "I'm helping a colleague and he has indicated that it has been accepted as an inside job, yeah."

"Okay. The reason I ask is that Schilgaard Bank is known as being one of the big sources of finance for Gaht."

Gaht is the name of a very large and very powerful network of gangs whose territory stretches over five different systems, the Tyrrin system being one. This surprised me and only served to increase my worry about Tip. If he was involved with Gaht, his job as a law enforcer was definitely a conflict of interest and I would have a duty to report it.

"Oh fuck," I sighed. "I didn't know that. Is there any way you could find out if this theft had anything to do with them?"

"Sure, I have several contacts within the network. Give me a day and I'll make a few calls and see if I can't call a favour in."

"Before you go, can you also find out if a particular person is involved with Gaht? Like if they're working for them for instance?"

"I can try. My contacts might not have access to the records of every gang in the network but I'll do my best. What's the name?"

I hesitated before answering. "He's a law enforcer, so umm …" I began.

"So you want this handled with discretion."

"Yes please."

"You have my word."

"Thank you. His name is Tip Danso. He's a Lilean and works here on Tyrrin 4 at Agency Headquarters."

"I'll call you tomorrow. Keep your Unicom nearby."

Despite my worry for Tip, I felt better knowing I was actively doing something to help me understand what might be going on and I decided the first thing I needed was information about Gaht. First on my list of things to do for the next day, was find a library and spend a while on one of their research consoles. My preference for a library console was deliberate, despite there being the most up to date and comprehensive research facilities right there at headquarters. In order to use a law enforcement console, I would have to log in my name and badge number, which would be easily traceable in the event of anyone wanting to know who'd been snooping. At this point in time, I had no desire for Tip to have any idea what I intended to do with my spare time, so the anonymity of a library console was ideal. Satisfied that I had at least the bones of a plan, I went to bed early and slept soundly.

There were several libraries in the city, so I chose the one that seemed the busiest and booked a couple of hours. There was a reason for my choice; staff in a busy place would have less time to do much in depth checking of customers, which meant less likelihood of anyone peering over my shoulder while I read up about a major gang network, an act that could mean me being questioned by the local law enforcers. Not only would that be embarrassing, but Tip would no doubt hear about it and I was not yet ready for him to know I was checking on him. I smiled at the pretty girl who handed me back one of my many fake identification documents and followed her to the back of the room.

"Are you familiar with the use of library consoles, Sir?" she asked in a voice that would not sound out of place on a seven year old.

"Yes, I'm an old hand," I assured her.

"Okay then, don't hesitate to ask if you need any help," she smiled and walked away.

I sat down, switched on the modern console and fished for the gadget in my pocket that would ensure my searching would be instantly wiped from the machine's memory bank. As nonchalantly as I could, I attached it to the docking port on the side of the machine and began to type. For two hours I searched and made copious notes, preferring not to print anything that might alert the staff. Writing everything in my own Sigma language, it was as safe as I was able to make it in the circumstances.

Gaht started life as the largest gang on Niruvan Prime, which is still the location of its centre of operations. Originally concerned with the terrible crime rate on the planet, the gang initially concentrated its efforts with protection rackets, quickly bringing the crime rate down to a fraction of its former level. Once word of the punishments dealt out by these new vigilantes got out within the criminal fraternity, a new peace fell upon the major cities of Niruvan Prime. After turning their attention to their neighbouring planet, Niruvan 3 and having the same effect within ten years, those in authority began to take notice. Although their methods were questionable, the results were impressive and people in positions of some power started to become involved.

Despite the distances between systems, word somehow gets around this galaxy of ours and when people in neighbouring systems heard about Gaht, they wanted a piece of it for themselves. Those who ran the network at the time decided that the expense of operating in different systems would be prohibitively high and would necessitate them committing crime themselves in order to combat crime, effectively biting the hand that feeds them. Although they committed crimes, they were for the most part, limited to beatings and threats. They got their money from the protection rackets, seedy restaurants, and gambling houses they ran. Knowing that there was no way this income would pay for them to expand to other systems, they decided to adopt the more successful of the local gangs to operate under their own banner, as satellites. A group would be sent in to train the local gang leaders in Gaht methods and ethos, and when running successfully as a fully-fledged satellite, they took a cut of their earnings.

The system seemed to work very well and Gaht spread to cover five systems within fifty years. As the operation grew, so the money earned did too and they began to use banks to launder their money. There were several high profile killings claimed by Gaht, all of whom were high ranking criminals who somehow stepped on Gaht's toes, thereby sealing their own death warrants. The current boss of the entire operation is a man named Belotan. On his fifth marriage and with twelve children he admits to, he is said to be a stickler for gang etiquette and regards any flouting of the accepted dogma or standards of behaviour, as deeply insulting. He is rumoured to have had a man beheaded for failing to call him, Sir.

Just as I was about to read about the gang's rumoured financial turnover, my Unicom beeped. It was my banking contact.

"Hi, Sam. I can confirm that the theft was not carried out by members of the Tyrrin 4 Gaht satellite group but was in fact ordered by a rival gang network called The Dankera Collective. Your missing thieves are now back on Dankera 7 under the protection of the gang's leadership. I can also tell you that during the past eight months, eleven other bank thefts on Tyrrin 4 alone were likely ordered by Dankera. All were apparently carried out by two employees who disappeared right after the thefts. None have been apprehended. The amounts stolen were relatively small when taken as individual thefts, between twenty and sixty-five thousand credits apiece. When taken together though, it's a considerable sum."

I was shocked and it showed in my reply. "Fuck. So there's a spat between gangs going on."

"It would seem so."

"Any idea why?" I asked.

"Sorry. Finance is my area not interpersonal dynamics."

"I'm very grateful for this. Thank you so much."

"There's something else too."

"Oh?"

"Your man, the law enforcer?"

"What about him?"

"He joined Gaht five months ago as a law enforcement leak."

## CHAPTER THREE

"I suppose there's no chance your contact is wrong?" Tinnias asked after he stopped cursing.

"None I'm afraid."

"Oh shit. Please don't let this be another Detective Rime thing."

"Well according to my contact, he's apparently acting as a leak, so I guess he won't be getting involved in any violence. I know it's no consolation but it's not another Rime."

"A dirty law enforcer is a dirty law enforcer, Sam. Okay we have to be careful here. Gaht is a powerful operation so we must tread carefully or we could both lose our kneecaps. The first thing for you to do is get out of there and come home. Once you're safely out of the way, I'll make an official report. Can you come up with anyone who will testify? The word of an anonymous contact won't be enough."

"My contact won't testify, I can tell you that for free," I replied. "As for those from whom he got his information, he told me they are serving Gaht members, so I doubt they'll be willing to take the risk either."

"Hell, I'm getting too old for this shit."

"Listen, Boss," I soothed. "I've been thinking about this since last night and I'm not totally without options here. I'm not sure how much effect I can have, but there is something I can try."

A sigh from Tinnias conveyed his frustration. "Okay, talk to me, Son."

"Well, you know the Lileans have that umm, spiritual stuff."

"So?"

"I happen to know, because he told me the other night, that Tip's in regular touch with Vincent Domenico."

"How can he help?"

"I don't know if he can, but if Tip still thinks of him as a friend, maybe he can talk to him or something, get information maybe, I don't know. It's worth a shot isn't it?"

"I guess it can't do any harm," Tinnias agreed. "If nothing else, at least you'll get to catch up with how the family are doing. Another thing too,

Vincent might be able to use his umm, spiritual thing, to help or find out what's going on."

"That's what I'm thinking," I said.

"Do you have Vincent's Unicom number?"

"I have one, although I don't know if it's up to date. It was six years ago. Could you check it for me?"

"I'm doing it now." Tinnias relayed the number to me and I was pleased to know it was the same one that was logged into my Unicom.

"I'll do it right away and get back to you."

"Or you could go there and turn up on his doorstep."

"You mean go to Lilea, now?" I asked.

"Well I'm thinking that as they're friends, Vincent could just hang up on you or say he'll look into it and call you back but then not bother. If you go there and bang on his door, you can look him in the eyes and tell if he's lying. There's also the added benefit of being in the right place to look into Tip's background, his family life etc."

I had to physically restrain myself from blurting out everything I already knew about Tip and his dubious background, his change of heart and subsequent spotless record, but having given my word that I would never divulge what I know, I held my tongue. This put me in a spot I found uncomfortable and I mentally writhed in anguish at having to lie to Tinnias. Never before had I lied to him and I didn't like how it felt. Not once had he ever done me wrong in all the thirty or so years I'd known him; he'd guided my career, advised me on personal matters, and welcomed me into his family by asking me to adopt them as parents. Now I was to repay his love by lying to him? This didn't feel good at all and I squirmed inside the turmoil of my mind. There was no denying that I had given my solemn vow six years ago that I would never tell anyone what I knew about who and what Tip used to be. I gave my word not only to Tip, but Vincent and his family, and most importantly, to the King of the Drycenian Nation. Up until this moment, the secret has caused me no problems. Now here I was having to choose whether to betray the trust of those people or lie to my father. There was no question where my loyalties lie when my back is against the wall and having accepted the situation I was now in, my decision was easy and decisive.

"Dad, I don't suppose you can get here can you? I have to speak to you before I do anything else in this case."

"What's wrong, Son?"

"I can't, not over the Unicom. It must be in person. If I'm to fly to Lilea, maybe we could meet halfway." There was silence and I knew Tinnias would be wearing deep creases across his brow at the sudden cryptic nature of my reply. "Look, never mind. I'm coming home right away. I'll talk to you first, then go back to Lilea and meet with Vincent. I'll see you in a couple of weeks." I hung up and grabbed my bag. Within ten minutes I was packed and racing back down to the desk clerk, who looked at me like I'd grown another head when I again handed back the keys to room twenty-three a few hours after having taken possession of them.

"You're not having a good day are you, Detective?" He said and I shrugged.

"Sorry buddy, shit happens, usually to me. Today is that day."


After leaving Tyrrin 4 airspace, I gunned the engines and set off into the void at maximum speed. My ship has had a few enhancements over the years and she can now cruise comfortably at half light speed. The journey home to Sigma Prime was still going to take me thirteen days though, so I decided to use the spare hours to call more contacts and see what I could find out about Gaht's relationship with the Law Enforcement Agency, how it used its agency leaks, and for what purpose. Seeing that we are in the business of crime fighting and bringing criminals to justice for their misdeeds, I assumed that Agency leaks would most likely be asked to lose evidence here and there, alter someone's record perhaps, maybe even alter witness statements or conveniently forget a witness exists at all. This seemed the obvious and best use of an agency leak, at least to me. A high-ranking member of the Law Enforcement Agency has access to a large amount of highly sensitive information about a lot of people, information that might be of great value to an outfit such as Gaht. Anyone can be trained to mete out beatings, killers can be hired from any street corner, but valuable information like that contained within the Agency's records is not so easily accessed by those outside the Agency.

Another few calls to some contacts confirmed it. Law Enforcement Agency collaborators are always used as gateways to information and evidence and statement tampering. They are never used as killers or for anything of a violent nature that could endanger their position within the Agency. A detective who gains a criminal record, especially one of violence, would lose his job immediately and an unemployed ex law enforcer is of no use to Gaht. This information made me feel much more at ease for although I knew without doubt that Tip was going to lose his job, maybe even do some time in prison for his connection to Gaht, it pleased me to know he was keeping to his word and not going back to being the thug that he used to be when he was Andrew Midship.

I took advantage of the endless hours of space travel to give my ship a thorough clean and did a complete inventory of everything aboard. All my firearms were cleaned, power cells recharged, and I made a list of everything I needed to restock my supplies locker. Everything from hand cleanser to the foul-smelling stuff I use to clean the emitter heads of my laser rifles, it all went on my shopping list. Next time I called into an Agency headquarters for more than a couple of days, I could spend some of their money for them to make my life more comfortable.

After the first week, I was passing the halfway point and my ship was looking, and functioning, better than she had in a long time. I'm not a mechanic by any stretch of the imagination but I know enough to keep her running safely. We have to; it's part of the training for Freelancers like me. We must be proficient in basic tasks such as oiling moving parts, replacing certain components, running diagnostics and things of that nature. I was more than capable of handling an emergency should my engines fail, a fire, and even a hull breech, so I took the opportunity to do a few checks and get my hands dirty. After adding the three components I had used from my supplies to replace the worn ones I found inside the life support unit and the rear hatch mechanism, to my shopping list, I took a shower. The smell of oil thankfully gone, I dressed in fresh clothes and went to get something to eat.

Staring out through the cockpit window, I felt a frisson of fear snicker up my spine and nodded. This always happens to me when I look into the endless blackness of space. It may seem glamorous to be flying a spaceship between systems, especially if you're a fan of science fiction movies as I am, but there is no more dangerous place to be than out there. The frigid void takes no prisoners. Believe me, the threat of a horrible death is ever present and if something goes wrong, help is a very long way away. I never take space travel for granted and I always acknowledge the risks I take every time I gun my ships engines. That familiar frisson of fear is something I never try to ignore, for I reckon it keeps me sharp.

Acknowledging that fear always helps it settle into a relatively comfortable position in my mind, and I sighed as I ate my tasteless Nutri-Vend meal. When I was finished, I decided to go to my small bedroom and watch a vidicom movie, so after a final check of the cockpit's guidance system and auto pilot readout, I headed to the small space in which I sleep. Just as the beautiful but brainless female was once again putting the handsome hero in unnecessary danger due to her inability to follow simple instructions, my comms gave a crackle.

"SC257 please respond."

I leapt from my bed and raced to the cockpit, to see a huge Agency battleship before me. I grabbed the headset from the hook and flipped a switch.

"This is SC257 acknowledging your hail. Detective Samelan Sinclair-Vaylo commanding. Please state the reason for your hail."

"Son? This is your Dad here."

"Dad? You came?"

I heard a snort through my earpiece. "Of course I came. When my son says he needs me, I get my ass off the chair and go see what's wrong. Now get your ass round to the shuttle bay. Someone is sending you the docking beacon. Switch your auto pilot off would you? These guys like to be in control."

I switched off the auto pilot and allowed the battleship's crew to take control. When the bay doors closed and the siren sounded to let me know it was safe, I leapt from the side hatch and embraced Tinnias, his face etched with worry and I knew he probably had not slept at all well since our strange conversation a week previously. The relief that flooded through me is indescribable, save to say that for a few moments, I struggled to contain my emotions.

"Come to my cabin, Son, and tell me all about it."

"I'm sorry for our last conversation. I didn't mean to cut you off like that."

"Don't worry about what's past. Let's concentrate on the here and now."

I followed him down corridors until he stopped outside a door marked with his name and rank. With a swipe of his Agency key card, we were inside a reasonably sized room. Every time I had been a guest on an Agency battleship, I'd been given a room no bigger than my firearms locker. I guess rank has privileges everywhere. He sat me down and opened a bottle of some dark brown liquid whose label was in a foreign language I was unable to read.

"Drink it all down in one go," he said as he handed me a glass.

"Shit," I said as I coughed and wiped away the tears that streamed from my eyes. "What the fuck is this?"

"It's illegal is what it is," he laughed. "It'll make you feel comfortably relaxed so you can tell me what's on your mind without being anxious. Now, what's up?"

I blushed, then launched into Tip's story. I held nothing back and explained the reason for having kept it secret for the past six years. I assured him I hadn't done so out of mistrust of him, but because of my promise to the Drycenian King. For twenty minutes, I talked and not once did Tinnias interrupt. He nodded from time to time, frowned a couple of times, and poured us each three more drinks by the time I stopped talking.

"That's the whole story, from start to finish. Please don't be mad at my secrecy, be mad at my having got an ex criminal a job as a law enforcer if you want, but don't be mad at my reasons for not telling."

"I'm not mad at you, Sam, for anything."

"But I'm going to get into a great deal of trouble for having helped a criminal change his identity and then got him a job at the Agency. I could lose my own job for this and as my father, you'll be embarrassed, both professionally and personally."

"No I won't."

"Yes you will. Detectives talk, stories get embroidered and embellished. You'll lose their respect, maybe even their obedience."

"No I won't. Trust me, Son."

I looked into his eyes and saw a look I hadn't seen before. That look told me he knew something, had his finger on a pulse I probably hadn't known existed, and not only did he have his finger on it, but he was probably miles ahead of me in this situation.

My eyes widened as I realised my dad just might have got one over on me. "What's going on? Come on, I know what that look means. You know something, don't you? I've been worrying for nothing, haven't I? Have you known about Tip all along?"

He shook his head. "No, not all along. I found out a few days ago."

"How?"

"I got a call. A couple of hours after you and I last spoke. I was worried about you. I've never known you to be so cryptic and obviously worried about something and you've never begged for my help like that before. I knew you were deeply troubled about something, so there was no way I was prepared to wait for you to get home. I was arranging passage on an Agency battleship when my Unicom rang. I thought it was you, but it wasn't."

Tinnias reached into his pocket for his Unicom and dialled a number. After a few seconds, I heard faint mumblings from the other end. "You can come in now," he said and hung up.

I frowned and looked at Tinnias, who smiled in that way someone does when they know they have everything under complete control.

I struggled to know how to react, so I settled on a rather inadequate, "what the fuck?" and watched as the door opened. A gasp leapt from my throat as I looked into those eyes and realised what was going on. The emotional burden floated away as those overly large bright yellow eyes gazed at me. Those eyes were just as mesmerising as I remembered, they held me for long moments. The man stood no more than five foot six and smiled at me.

He walked to me and took my hand. "Hello Detective Sinclair-Vaylo. I am Shuttle Commander Mautaq and I bring you greetings from His Majesty King Lomas VII and the entire Drycenian Nation. I am here to shuttle you to the Battle Cruiser where His Majesty awaits your arrival. Shall we, Gentlemen?" he indicated towards the still open door and stepped aside.

I looked at Tinnias, to find him smiling at me in a way that said he'd got one over on me and was delighted to have surprised me in this way.

"Lomas will explain everything, Son. Be patient a little longer."

"But, how did you … I mean … I don't even know how to … so how did you …?" I sighed, unable to even formulate an understandable sentence.

"He didn't," Mautaq replied. "We did."

"Come on, Sam," Tinnias said, encouraging me towards the open door with a hand to my back. "We'll explain when we get there. One of the Troopers will fly your ship back."

I followed the Drycenian along corridors and entered the shuttle bay behind him, Tinnias bringing up the rear. Ahead, sitting on a pad waiting to depart, was a Drycenian shuttlecraft and I smiled as the years rolled away to those few days on Regnor Prime when I first met these wonderful people. The Drycenians have a sense of style that I've not encountered in any other race. They have this innate ability to understand that function doesn't necessarily have to override aesthetics. I remember someone telling me during that case six years ago, that curves and circles are important to them somehow, but I can't remember why. Everything they build has sinuous, almost alluring, curvaceous lines and you can't help but reach out and touch. Everything about them, that I saw anyway, is stylish and beautiful.

A group of a dozen Troopers stood to attention beside the open hatch and I noticed a couple smile and nod to me.

"Good to see you again, Detective," said one.

I smiled back. "You've no idea how happy I am to see you guys again."

"Oh yes we do," said another. "That's why we're here."

Knowing we were going to be boarding the battle cruiser very soon made my heart flip, but for a decidedly non work related reason and I found myself both excited and nervous at the prospect of our imminent meeting.

We sat and waited for the shuttle bay to depressurise and as the huge bay doors opened, I looked out into the void and felt a thrill rush through me. The huge leviathan sat at anchor several kilometres away and I let my eyes caress her lines as we approached. The mere presence of this craft, and the people living and working within the safe confines of her protective body, gave my soul a feeling of calm and my heart, hope. I suddenly wished very much that my best friend and ex-partner, Ren, was here to share this moment with me.

The shuttle bay doors closed silently and I thought back to the irritating squeak made by the doors of the Agency battleship. Why the hell can't anyone oil them? It's a few minutes out of someone's day for fuck's sake.

Turning to Tinnias, I voiced my frustration. "Hear that?" He frowned. "The bay doors are silent. Is the Agency on a money saving drive or something? Can't they buy some oil and have someone give up three minutes of their day to take care of that grinding squeak?"

Tinnias grinned. "It's already on my list."

"You have a list? Is there much on it already?"

"I have a list, yes, and it's already quite long. I've not wasted these past few days, Son. Our hosts and I have enjoyed some most interesting conversations."

This intrigued me and I longed to ask for details. At times such as this, I have to force myself to remember that Tinnias is my boss as well as my father, and as such, there'll be stuff he can't tell me. It sucks but I understand and respect his position. The fact that he was here meeting the Drycenians at last made me very happy. Many times over the previous six years since the Lilean case, I'd relayed my story to him and although he wouldn't admit it, he was envious that I'd got to meet them. I knew without him having to admit it, that this would go down as one of the coolest moments of his life. The fact that I was the one sharing it with him made it even more awesome for us both, despite the gravity of our reason for being there.

When it was safe and both ships were safely locked onto pads, we exited the shuttle and descended the ramp into the enormous, spotlessly clean shuttle bay. Several shuttlecraft sat on pads around us, several had panels removed and hoses snaked across the floor in all directions. Mechanics in pristine white overalls toiled at them all, some buried head and shoulders within the engines and bodywork. Those who could do so, looked over at us and I noticed several hands raise in greeting. I smiled and nodded at them all, despite my embarrassment at not remembering each of them individually. I hoped that my respect and love for them as a people would make up for this failing.

"The agency's repair and maintenance division is going to be making some serious changes to their methods," Tinnias said as he looked at me. I grinned in response.

"If you'd like to follow me, Gentlemen," Mautaq said, "I'll take you straight to the Observation Room where His Majesty waits to greet you. The Troopers will see to your belongings."

We followed him along spotless corridors and as I looked at the stylish decoration that adorned the walls and noticed the gently curved ceilings, it all came flooding back. For a few days when the Lilean case finished, I lived within this very ship, walked these corridors and marvelled at the attention to the finest of details that turn something functional into something that is also beautiful. Elevators whisked us silently upward and I grinned as I saw Tinnias run an appreciative hand along an elegant handrail, his fingers caressing the spirals, whorls, and loops of the intricately carved design that covered its surface. He saw me looking and sighed deeply, then shook his head. I frowned.

"Why do I suddenly feel that the gulf between these people and us is hundreds of millennia wide?"

"Because it is," I replied. "They were already exploring space when we were just learning to build crude earthen huts to live in."

Another sigh from Tinnias, another quick glance at the handrail. "I feel like an uneducated savage all of a sudden."

"Please don't," Mautaq interrupted. "We weren't always refined and technologically advanced, Commander Vaylo. Please believe me when I tell you that in our ancient history there is far more savagery than you could ever imagine. Perhaps it is because we have that legacy to overcome that we are as you find us now."

"I meant no offence, Sir," Tinnias replied, contrite.

"And none is taken, my friend. I am simply pointing out that you have no reason to feel less of yourselves than you do of us. Ahh, here we are, deck five. After you."

It was some time before I realised that I had yet to notice Mautaq's fangs, the tips of which were visible whenever he spoke. I smiled as I realised that this aspect of their physiology no longer struck me as odd, that I now accepted it as normal. My best friend, Ren, had fangs. Very long ones with which he was able to deliver a venomous bite, but his were retractable, unlike our Drycenian friends, whose own were fixed and therefore, always visible. I wondered how Tinnias felt about them and grinned. I was brought out of my musing when we stopped outside a door, a plaque upon its surface covered in Drycenian writing, which they call Script. I knew this was the Observation Room because I had spent many hours in there during my previous stay, not because I was able to read their language. The door opened with a swish and Mautaq stepped aside, his extended arm inviting us to enter.

"Samelan, how wonderful to see you again after all these years." King Lomas swept towards me, his arms open wide to embrace me and I couldn't help but grin.

"Your Majesty, it's a privilege to meet you again. You haven't changed a bit, it's as if we met only yesterday."

After a surprisingly strong embrace that belied his reduced stature, he grasped both my hands in his and looked me right in the eyes. "I am so sorry for the loss of your friend, Ren. Know that we shared your pain and although you were unaware, we kept a close watch on you during your time of grieving."

Emotion sprang to my eyes unbidden and I struggled to contain myself. "Thank you, Sir. It warms my heart to know that."

He smiled and I saw, and felt, the deep wisdom flowing from those enigmatic yellow eyes. This man, more than any other I have ever met, has the power to make me feel safe by his presence alone. If there are indeed such things as gods, this man is the closest to one made flesh that I have ever encountered.

Walking over to Tinnias, he shook his hand warmly. "Hello again, Tinnias. It is our pleasure to host you for our meetings this time. I want you to know that your son is a very dear friend of the Drycenian Nation and it pleases me beyond measure that he chose you to be his father and guardian."

"Thank you, Your Majesty. He makes me proud every moment of every day." He looked at me and winked and I couldn't help but grin back.

Looking at me once again, Lomas stepped back and with a sweep of his arm, indicated a small group standing behind him. "Come, Samelan, reacquaint yourself with old friends. Commander Byron, my son and heir, Prince Toma, Doctor Jam, come on, don't stand there grinning, say hello."

Byron stepped towards me, his eyes fixed on my own and both hands outstretched, a grin splitting his face in half. "How ya doing, Sam. And your ship, how's she these days?"

I shook his hands and grinned back as my heart leapt and danced in my breast, making it difficult for me to breathe. He was here at last and it was with some difficulty that I restrained myself from falling into his arms. "Your modifications are awesome. I can't tell you how useful they've been. Thank you so much."

"No problem. I'd like to take a look at her sometime, if I may." He held my gaze with those lovely yellow eyes and I was surprised that it didn't feel awkward.

"Hey, anytime you like," I replied, holding his gaze. "You don't have to ask."

Prince Toma edged himself in. "Come on Byron, I'm royalty, step aside now and let me say hello." Byron laughed and Toma grinned. "Hello again, Sam. I've been looking forward to catching up with you. You owe me a battle board rematch, remember? I intend to thrash you this time, so prepare to lose spectacularly."

We laughed out loud. "I'd forgotten about that. You'll win, no problem at all. I haven't used a battle board since I was last here, obviously."

"Don't worry, you'll have time to practice. It's not sport if I have you at a disadvantage, is it?"

"If you're going to be battle board racing against Toma, then you might just be needing my services before too long." Doctor Jam stepped around Toma and embraced me. "Blame me for this, Sam. It is I who nagged His Majesty to get involved this time."

"Thank you, Jam, for everything," I said quietly as I gazed into the eyes of the kindest, most compassionate man I've ever met. Jam has been through a great deal of his own pain and yet hasn't lost his ability to love and care deeply for everyone. Never have I met a man so devoid of anger, hate, and the need for revenge that plague the rest of us. I strive constantly to be like him and fail completely to get anywhere near. He was very good to me during our last meeting and helped me to come to terms with everything I had experienced and witnessed, and which troubled me more than I would have anticipated.

"You will be spending some time with me in the Medical Bay, Sam," Jam replied. "As will Tinnias. Lomas will send you both along when there is time. I look forward to catching up."

King Lomas clapped his hands together and smiled. "Now that we are all together, let's get some refreshments and talk about this unfortunate business with Tip Danso. Come everyone, sit and be comfortable."

I'm going to take a break here for a while to make a few calls and have something to eat.

This is Sinclair V-Log reference Q890/M data log reference point 4136902/615.

## CHAPTER FOUR

This is Sinclair V-Log reference Q890/M data log reference point 4136902/616 continuing report.

Before I continue further about what transpired during my time revisiting with the Drycenians, I need to explain about something that will, no doubt, seem incredulous to you. It did to me when I first encountered Lileans and learned of their spirituality, or more precisely, how they practice it. You may be forgiven for thinking I've finally, irrevocably, lost my mind but I assure you I'm as sane as the day is long. Incredulous or not, explain it I must for to launch into the rest of the story without doing so would render it nonsensical.

Six years previously, I was given a job by the Inter-Galactic Law Enforcement Agency, my esteemed employers, which I readily accepted. My target was an escaped inmate from a maximum security psyche facility in the Diamond Heart System. It's named the Marramuir System but everyone calls it Diamond Heart for reasons that are unnecessary here. Due to a long history of bad blood between my target and his adopted brother, Vincent, it was suggested that I secure his assistance in tracking him down. It was thought that Vincent's presence in the chase might lure the escapee out so I could detain him.

Vincent's first reaction was to turn me down when I called on him at his home and I assumed that I would be doing the job on my own, as usual. Before I left Lilea to continue with the hunt, Vincent's baby son disappeared and it was assumed by everyone, myself included, that the brother, Wesley, was to blame. After this unfortunate development, Vincent and his wife, Farra, decided to accompany me on the chase after all. It was during the following days in which I spent all day every day in their company, that I learned about their unique spiritual beliefs and practice. I was every inch the sceptic at first but emerged from that case a believer. I hope I can explain it clearly and in a way that doesn't make me sound like I need a rubber room.

Every race, on every world I know of, has some sort of belief in life after death. It seems to be one of those intrinsic humanoid things which crosses all known boundaries of race or creed. Some have a vague hope of something after they die, while others have a detailed and complicated belief system. The only thing everyone, even sceptics, agree on is that no one knows for sure. Well, we do know for sure. I know for sure and the Lileans know for sure. The Drycenians know for sure, due to their extended connection with Vincent, and because of Doctor Jam, whose story might come later, if it becomes necessary. I can assure you with complete authority that life, that is, consciousness itself, does indeed continue after the body ceases to function. Some of the process can be proven scientifically, the rest I can attest to by my own experience. It's all down to what is called by scientists, the conservation of energy.

To make it as simple as I can, it needs to be for me to understand it, the conservation of energy means that energy can neither be created nor destroyed. It remains constant and merely changes its form. I could get very scientific here and go into the various forms of energy and how they change but you would probably fall asleep and I would end up talking to myself. You can go onto the galactic web network and look it up easily. Put simply, energy, in whatever form, cannot be destroyed. It merely changes to some other type of energy. The clue is in the name, conservation. The universe conserves the total amount of energy, keeping it constant but ever changing.

Our bodies give off electrical energy in the cells. The atoms and their various components give a measurable electrical charge all the time they are alive and working. The food we eat is chemical energy, which our bodies transform into other types of energy to fuel its various needs. Our brains give an electrical charge all the time they are functioning, consciousness itself is energy and like all the other bodily systems, this can be measured by the most sceptic of scientists.

The body is, however, a biological entity and as such, decays over time and will eventually cease to function, as is the way of all things biological. When it can no longer function, the bodily systems cease, but the conservation of energy means that the energy from that body, that consciousness, cannot die. If it cannot be destroyed, it must go somewhere, change somehow. The consciousness of our loved ones, not being able to be destroyed, must therefore survive intact. Lileans can communicate with those surviving conscious energies, due to them having a slightly different brain structure. Something in their brains that is concerned with consciousness and awareness is much larger than the corresponding gland the rest of us have and this gives them an easy awareness of the life essence of their kin who have died.

I'm telling you this because those incorporeal Lilean energies came into the case at this point. They had valuable input, albeit given in an annoyingly cryptic manner, and to not acknowledge them for their input would be unjust, in my opinion. The Lileans, and Doctor Jam too, all have what they refer to as a guide or spiritual helper who see their role as one of companion rather than leader, guidance rather than dictatorship. Ask them and they will always say their role is to keep their charge on their predestined life path and nothing more. They help when they deem it necessary to prevent the person from straying from this path, but they don't intervene all the time. They don't prevent suffering, injury, nor even death, if they deem it to be in the person's destiny and they don't pass on information if they don't regard it as important to do so. You can ask until you're old and grey but if they don't think it right, they won't tell.

"So Samelan," Lomas began. "Tell us everything you know. We will then do the same. Once we know how our respective information converges, or otherwise, we might be able to formulate something resembling a plan."

I nodded. "Okay, well it's not much really. I had just finished a job and decided on a whim to stop into Tyrrin 4 and say hello to Tip, maybe take a few days off if he was around and open to spending some time with me. Everything was fine at first. I called him and he seemed his usual self. He invited me to stay at his apartment rather than take a room at Agency Headquarters, so I readily agreed. That first evening was good. We caught up, laughed some, gossiped plenty, and generally had a good time. For the next three days, while he was at work, I went out to explore the city and do some shopping. On the fourth day, when I returned to the apartment, I knew something was wrong the moment I stepped inside the door. My gut told me something was just, off. I searched the place but there was no one around and nothing seemed out of place, so I assumed I was just on edge after the last job. Later that afternoon, I prepared to make dinner and burned the vegetables due to not hearing the timer. I had put some of Tip's music on rather loud you see and I didn't hear the beep. It was this that gave me the idea that maybe someone had been in to bug the place. I swept the entire apartment and found several recording devices and cameras."

"They could've been Tip's own," Byron suggested. "Perhaps he's security conscious."

I shook my head. "He seemed as surprised as I was when I showed them to him. He told me he was going to put them into the evidence chain of the case he's working. The next day, I decided, unwisely as it turned out, to put in a few of my own, just so that if anyone returned, I'd have the evidence. His Unicom rang twice that day, and both times the caller rang off without saying anything when I answered. I put a recording device into it so I could record his calls, just in case he was into something bad. Again, like the day before, I went out into the city and then returned to the apartment to check the recordings. No one had been in or called, according to my … holy shit."

"Excuse me?" Lomas enquired. "And just what is your holy shit?"

"I'm sorry, Sir, for my language. Please forgive me. Something has just occurred to me that hadn't previously."

He waved away my apology. "Do tell."

"My cameras recorded no one in the apartment while I was out, yet Tip told me he returned to the apartment and found my devices while I was out. He removed them and gave them back to me when we argued that evening. If he was telling the truth, my cameras would have seen him enter and remove them, but they didn't. Either he tampered with my vidicom, which I doubt as I have extremely tight security measures to prevent just such an occurrence, or he lied."

"He's obviously lying," Tinnias said and everyone nodded.

"But why?" Lomas asked. "That is an important question for which we must seek an answer."

"Even I can work that out," Doctor Jam said, sending everyone into silence.

"Ahh, here we go. Doctor Jam is about to crack the case for us. He does this sometimes you know. He'll sit and listen, sometimes for hours without saying a word. Then quite suddenly he'll say something that turns out to solve the whole case. You're quick off the mark this time, Jam. Sometimes you keep us chasing our tails for days before helping us with your insight."

Jam grinned and blushed. "Can't you see? It's obvious really."

"Then enlighten us dimwits please," Lomas said with a smile.

"Okay, stop me if it gets complicated. You put cameras into the apartment to keep watch on the place, didn't you, Sam?"

"Yes."

"Tip said he went back to the apartment but you were out. True?"

"Completely."

"He also said he somehow found your devices and removed them."

"He did."

Jam threw up his hands and shook his head. "As you have just said, why isn't it on your film? Surely your cameras would've seen him enter, search the place, and remove the devices one by one."

"So he must've tampered with your vidicom," Tinnias said. "He will have erased that portion of it containing himself inside the apartment."

"No. I'm sorry but that's impossible. There is no way anyone can get through the security I have on that vidicom. Anyone aboard is welcome to try."

"But he had to," Toma said. "There's no other explanation. Your film doesn't show anyone in there, yet he obviously was in there as he gave you back the devices. He must've somehow tampered with your film."

Jam sighed loudly and slapped both hands onto his knees. The room fell silent as every face turned towards him. "I'm sorry for my outburst but it's so obvious it's killing me listening to you all not getting it." I heard several sniggers before Jam continued. "You're all making it too complicated when it's really simple, so simple that no one is considering it."

"Jam," Lomas said sharply. "Get to the point before I grow a beard, please."

There were several more sniggers, my own amongst them. Tinnias looked at me and grinned. I knew he was going to like these people. "Sorry, Sir," Jam looked at me and continued. "He didn't give you back your own devices, Sam. He gave you new ones."

"Fuck," Tinnias said quietly.

"Indeed," Jam replied.

There was a pause, during which everyone tried to digest this new information. Then Lomas bade me continue. "Continue please, Samelan."

"Well, we argued. He was offended that I'd been asking questions about the case he was working. He assumed I was automatically thinking he was not being honest and kept saying I thought he was still Andrew Midship, that I obviously didn't trust his honesty. He wouldn't listen to reason and said our friendship was over. I went to pack my stuff and just as I was about to leave, I told him to call me anytime and assured him I would be there for him if he ever needed me. He then handed me a package containing my cameras and yelled at me for bugging his home without telling him. Despite me telling him I was looking out for his safety, he said it proved I didn't trust him. That's everything. I left and returned to Headquarters where I rang you, Dad. During my trip to meet you, I called some contacts who told me he is a law enforcement leak for Gaht."

"What is the nature of the case he's working?" Byron asked. "If you're allowed to tell us. No problem if you can't, we understand."

"On the surface, it seems like an ordinary bank job. Thirty-two thousand credits were stolen from a local branch of Schilgaard Bank. Two employees of the bank, a man and a woman who were among those staff members away right after the theft, have since disappeared without trace. They seemed the likely initial suspects. During my journey here, my contact told me that during the past eight months there were eleven other bank thefts on Tyrrin 4, all apparently carried out by two employees who disappeared right after the thefts and none of which have been apprehended. The amounts stolen were relatively small when taken as individual thefts, between twenty and sixty-five thousand credits apiece."

"And you're assuming they're all connected?" Toma asked.

I nodded. "Yes. My contact told me that particular bank is known for being under the thumb of Gaht, as are many other banks all over the five systems in which they operate. They use the banks to legitimise their money trail. We assumed at the time that the two employees must be members of Gaht, but my contact was able to tell me that they are in fact, members of The Dankera Collective and are at present back on Dankera 7 under the protection of the Collective."

"Wow. That puts a different face on things doesn't it?" Lomas said and everyone nodded.

"So Dankera are stealing from Gaht," Byron said.

"It would seem so," I nodded. "That's as much as I know. What about you? How much do you know?"

"Not much actually," Lomas said. "Jam came to me a couple of weeks ago and asked me if I would arrange for you to visit with us. I said yes of course I would, as soon as I was less busy. Over the next couple of days, he became insistent that we meet with you and finally came to me and begged for me to order the ship to come and get you. He said you were going to need our help, that we should rush to your aid and help you in any way we can. I believe our first port of call is Lilea, is it not, to meet with Vincent?"

Jam nodded. "Yes. You see, Sam. My guide, Arshad, told me that I was to do whatever is necessary to get Lomas to order the ship to come and find you and bring you aboard. He wouldn't tell me why though, despite my asking and begging for his reasons. All he will say is that you need our help and that we should give it. I am still asking him for more information but he just says he cannot give me anything further, that I should trust him and do as he suggests."

"Lomas got me to find you and I tapped into your Unicom call to Tinnias," Byron said. "That's how I knew you were heading home to Sigma, so as we were nearby there at the time, we called Tinnias and asked him to come with us to pick you up."

"You can imagine how I reacted when I answered that call," Tinnias said as he grinned at me. "I didn't believe for a moment it was actually the Drycenians calling me. I believe I might have been a little rude, forgive me, Your Majesty."

"If my memory serves me correctly," Lomas said, "you called me a weird ass crank who really needs to get a life and stop being a jerkoff."

Everyone in the room roared with laughter and Tinnias blushed. "Oh shit, I'm so sorry."

"No need, I have a sense of humour despite my great age. Anyway, Sam, due to my inability to convince Tinnias of our authenticity, I decided the best course of action would be to wait until he was safely aboard the Agency Battleship, then meet them mid-flight. Our identification details proved satisfactory to the Battleship's Captain, and we were able to assure Tinnias of our intentions. After securing the Agency ship to a towing line, we rushed to meet you."

"During the trip," Tinnias said, "we had a few meetings aboard the Battleship and I told them of our conversations concerning Tip. They told me about Tip's past, about his involvement with the Domenico case, his turnaround, and of your part in securing him honest employment. I investigated his record since joining the Agency and I can assure everyone that he has carried out his duties in a most exemplary fashion. I have no reason to put any stain upon his spotless record, until now anyway."

"Tinnias told us of your suggestion to visit Vincent and we agreed it seems like a good idea in the absence of anything better, so that is where we shall go until such time as circumstances dictate an alternative course of action. Are we all agreed?"

Everyone nodded and Lomas smiled. "Good, then I shall show you both to your quarters so you can settle in. Your ship should be aboard by now and I know Byron is anxious to get his hands on her. We will all meet again at dinner. Come, my friends." He got up and led us to the most sumptuous rooms either of us had ever stayed in. "Everything is voice controlled," he told us. "We've programmed everything with the Sigma Language so just ask when you want something." He demonstrated by turning the lights on and off, the air conditioning, the shower controls, and the entertainment unit. "You'll find hundreds of vidicom movies in there, plus millions of books, magazines, and articles covering every subject you can think of and several you can't. If you wish for someone to come and help or you need anything, the intercom is by the door. You have the run of the entire ship, Gentlemen. Make yourselves completely at home and explore all you want. If there is anywhere you're not supposed to go, it is for your own safety and you'll find the door locked. If a door opens, you're welcome to enter. I'll leave you to settle in. Dinner is at eight. Do you remember the way to the dining hall, Sam?"

"Deck three?" I asked and he nodded.

"Jam wishes you both to visit him at your earliest opportunity. You can choose who goes first. The Medical Bay is on Deck four."

"Thank you for helping me," I said. "So many times I've wished I was able to call you for help, and I often think about you all. It's so good to see you all again."

Lomas took my hands in his own and smiled. Wisdom poured from his eyes and I drank it in. "You have been through much in your life, Samelan, but through everything you've suffered, you never lost your compassion or your determination to do the right thing. Never doubt that our lives are enriched by your presence in our hearts. You are family, Sam, part of the Drycenian family and we are honoured to call you friend."

I had no words to reply to such a statement, so I nodded and smiled. I didn't admit that not only was I relieved and happy to be meeting them again to receive their help, but also to be spending time with Commander Byron again. I guess it's time for me to explain about that, isn't it?

When the Domenico case finished, I spent some time aboard the battle cruiser and got to know the Drycenians a little. During this time, I experienced two strange meetings with the handsome Chief Engineer and First Officer, which brought up an issue I'd been ignoring for years. The first time I saw him, he was surrounded by a bright glow and his eyes were holding my own. I couldn't tear my gaze away and despite not yet even knowing his name, I knew immediately that it was important I get to know him. A couple of days later, a similar event happened in the Obs Room. I was getting myself a drink when he walked in. I turned to see who had entered and our eyes met, held each other for long moments as something ethereal passed between us, before the spell was broken. Since that moment, I've spent the intervening years facing the question I'd been ignoring. Over and over I examined myself, my life, my beliefs about who I am and finally accepted that I was not who I had spent most of my life trying to be. I tried my best to make sure I spent as much time as possible with him and by the time I left their company, I had fallen in love. Every day since that time, I thought about him, wondered how he was doing, wanted him. I knew the chances were good that he was a straight guy and accepted, albeit reluctantly, that we were unlikely to end up together, but my heart refused to be silenced and called for him every day. It was agony. I had gone from being a commitment phobic, to hopelessly in love with someone who was likely never to be mine. Shit and fuck!

Lomas turned to Tinnias and shook his proffered hand. "Thank you, Tinnias, for being both friend and guide to Samelan. I couldn't wish for anyone better to look after him."

"It has never been anything but a pleasure," Tinnias replied.

After taking a couple of wrong turns, I eventually found my way to the Medical Bay and greeted Doctor Jam, who looked up and smiled with genuine affection when he saw me.

"Hi Doc. Reporting as ordered," I grinned.

"Ahh yes, hello there, Sam. Come and sit up here for me would you?" He placed a hand on the edge of an examination table, so I wandered over and made myself comfortable. "This won't take long. I just want to ask a few questions. Your answers will help me decide if you need my help further. Tell me about your health since we last met."

"Well I'm pretty healthy really," I began. "I now work out for at least two hours each day, which has made a positive difference to my strength and endurance. I lost quite a bit of extra fat and gained some muscle as a result."

"What sort of workout do you practice?"

"The Damiklonian martial art," I replied. "Ren taught me."

Jam raised an eyebrow and I could tell he was impressed. "That is an excellent way to keep yourself strong and flexible without becoming too bulked up with muscle. How about your appetite, do you eat enough?"

"I take more care to choose wisely when eating," I replied. "I seem to eat a lot more vegetables and fruit than I ever used to, and I've noticed that meat doesn't seem to excite me as much as it did. I'm not exactly vegetarian but I don't eat a lot of meat anymore. I used to have a big appetite, it got out of control for a while, but I'm on top of it now."

"Is that purely because you've gone off the taste of it?" Jam asked.

"Mostly," I nodded. "I have noticed I get indigestion sometimes, especially if I eat a lot of meat in one go."

Jam was nodding and making notes as we talked, tapping furiously on his medical console. How are your bowels? Have you noticed any changes in that department?"

I blushed, cursing myself for being unable to control this irritating and embarrassing habit. "Well yes, actually. I seem to umm, produce a lot more. I still go every day as usual, but there's more of it. I am eating a lot more vegetables though, so I'm not surprised."

Jam probed embarrassingly deep into my bowel habits and I found myself discussing in intricate detail the colour, consistency, odour, and frequency of this intimate and unsavoury bodily function. Why are doctors so interested in shit? Just as I was beginning to visibly squirm, he found another way to increase my discomfort.

"How's your sex life, Sam?"

My mouth flapped a few times before I found my voice. "Well I umm, I'm too involved in work most of the time these days. It's not such a driving force anymore." I was not yet prepared to tell him that I was no longer interested in sex with the opposite gender because I was in love with Commander Byron, so I left it at that.

"Any problems?"

"Not that I'm aware of."

"Do you wake in the mornings with erections?"

"Sometimes."

"Has the frequency of this changed at all?"

I thought about it and realised that it had. "Umm, well yes it has. I never thought about it before. It was always a daily occurrence, every single morning without fail. I guess over the past year or so it's slowed to maybe, three times a week, four perhaps. Hmm, you're going to be giving me a complex now, Doc."

Jam grinned. "Don't worry, Sam. It happens to us all as we get older. When you went to Deligon 2, you were shipped out there in cryo sleep for two months, is that correct?"

"Yes."

"When they woke you up, you experienced a bout of cryo sexual syndrome for a day or so."

"Don't remind me," I replied.

"It's nothing to worry about, Sigma men often experience it."

"That's what the doctors aboard the troop carrier told me at the time," I said as I remembered.

"Okay, that's enough of the embarrassing stuff," Jam said. "I see you were stung by a Ganeda Weed recently and had quite a severe reaction."

I nodded. "Yes. I sat on the damn thing and got stung on the ass. The poison went right up my spine and straight to my brain. I was paralysed for a while."

"I notice from your medical record that you had the standard cellular flush treatment and were rehabilitated to full health in six months." I was nodding as Jam relayed the details of my most recent health scare. "Have you noticed any change to the way you feel since getting back to work?"

I frowned. "Changes? I don't think so. I guess the changes to my eating habits happened since then, but surely that's just my own conscious choice to eat healthy, isn't it?"

"Probably," Jam nodded. "It doesn't hurt to make sure though, since you're here and I'm able to be a little more thorough than your own doctors." I nodded; he had a valid point. It would be silly not to take advantage of the Drycenians' advanced medical skills and knowledge. "I'd like to take some blood and do a body scan and general work up, if you're happy to indulge me," he smiled.

"Sure," I replied. "Knock yourself out."

Two hours later, I was redressed and hearing news that knocked the wind out of me. I had no idea of the chain of events, nor the direction my health was heading, and found myself happier than ever that my friends had come and found me when they did.

"I'm so glad Arshad insisted we crossed paths with you again," Jam said.

"So, you're saying I'll be dead within a year," I hissed, my voice rapidly deserting me.

"No," Jam shook his head. "I'm saying that if we had not come to meet you today, you would have a year, two at the most. As it stands now, I'll have you back to full health in no time at all."

"So, I don't have a condition as such," I asked. "I don't have a particular disease?"

"No. It's one of those million to one chance things. It's a combination of three things. The infection you suffered when attacked by the dragon on Dracunya Prime shortly before we first met you. The Ganeda Weed poison, and a mutated gene within your DNA."

"But how?"

"Okay, I'll try to explain. Stop me if it gets too complicated. When you were attacked on Dracunya, the infection passed into your system from the Dragon acted upon the mutated gene you carry in such a way as to make you doubly vulnerable to mutagenic poisons. They are poisons that cause mutations. Because the gene affected already has a mutation, it meant that should you ever encounter any mutagenic poisons, you would be more at risk than other people. The Ganeda Weed poison is one such mutagenic. The moment it entered your system, it found your already mutated gene and latched on, enhancing the effect of the mutation, thereby speeding up the rate at which this effect becomes life threatening to you. Are you with me so far?"

"Yeah," I nodded.

"The particular gene concerned is one that is involved with your immune system, the major organs' ability to resist infection, and also the speed of cell turnover, the rate at which your cells age, die, and replace themselves. As your immune system gets weaker and your cells die quicker, the major organs begin to suffer and you find it more difficult to recover from infection and viruses. Your body, in an attempt to strengthen itself, demands more energy from your food in order to try and sustain itself at optimum. During this phase, your appetite often increases and you find yourself constantly hungry but unable to fully satisfy that hunger. There comes a time when the energy provided by your food is not able to sustain your organs satisfactorily and your immune system fails. You find your appetite suddenly decreases or changes. This is the reason for the changes in your appetite, why it seemed to be out of control for a while and why it is less now. That is why you've found yourself not wanting to eat as much meat and seem to crave vegetables and fruit. As the body begins to shut down, the demand for input of energy decreases. Add to that, the increased rate of cell death and your body's reduced ability to replace them, and you have a disaster waiting to happen. The most minor of infections become deadlier for you with each passing day."

"So my body is shutting down?" I said, my voice a mere whisper now.

Jam nodded. "Yes. Your organs are struggling, Sam."

"Shit," I replied. "How the heck am I supposed to process this? How do I get my head around this?"

"Listen to me, Sam," Jam said, gazing right back into my eyes as he spoke. His voice now had an authoritative edge that seemed comforting to me as I tried to hold my emotions together. "I can fix this easily. You can be as fit as you were twenty years ago within a couple of days. If you decide you want my help with this, I'll begin right away. If you don't wish me to intervene, I will do everything I can to keep you comfortable in the time you have."

I gaped at him. "You're offering to do nothing? Seriously?"

"I have to," Jam replied. "Not everyone wants medical intervention. Some people wish to let things take their natural course. It is my ethical duty to offer you all choices, not just those that feel comfortable to me."

"I don't want to die yet," I replied immediately. "I don't have a problem with dying but I'm not ready to do it just yet. My life is good now, better than it's been in decades and I want time to enjoy how it feels to be happy. I have a family now, parents again and I enjoy knowing I'm not alone any longer. I still enjoy my job too; it fulfils me as much as it ever did and I'm good at it. This job allows me to make a positive contribution to the universe. I've only just realised that I'm in love too, for the first time in my life and I haven't even approached him yet. I can't die before finding out if there can ever be anything between us. I'll know when I'm ready, but it's not today."

Jam smiled and nodded, put down his medical console and stood. He pressed a call button on the wall and a nurse came through, smiled at me, and looked at Jam. "Yes Doctor. How can I help?"

"Prepare the DNA repair module please, Sam will be spending a day or two with us."

"Right away," she smiled to me and left us.

"Come with me, Sam. You'll be in a room just off the main Medical Bay where I can always be close by".

"Will I be in one of those tank things?" I asked.

Jam sniggered. "No, don't worry. You're going to be hooked up to a machine that will repair the mutated gene in your DNA and then I'll be able to fix the damage done to your internal organs. You'll be asleep for most of the time so you won't be aware of much discomfort." He took me to a small room off the main medical bay. "Take off all of your clothes and take a shower in the cubicle over there. You'll find a tube of cleanser on the shelf, use all of it and scrub every inch of your skin and hair. Don't dry yourself afterwards. I'll wait here for you."

"I'd like to tell Tinnias first," I said, "before anything else happens. I promised him I would never keep any secrets from him."

Jam nodded and pressed the intercom button by the door. "Tinnias Vaylo to the medical bay immediately please." Looking back at me, he smiled. "I'll send him through and wait in the medical bay until you're ready."

Less than ten minutes later, Tinnias entered, red faced from rushing, worry creasing his face. "Sam? What's wrong, Son?"

"I'll be just outside if you need anything," Jam said and left us alone."

Trying hard to remember all the facts correctly, I told Tinnias what Jam had told me. When I finished, a moment of silence hung between us and I saw a tear trace its way down his cheek.

"It's your choice, Son, but just as you've been honest with me, I'm going to be honest with you and tell you that I want you to take the treatment. I can't lose you, not like this, because of some random chance DNA thing. Hell no. Get killed by some Merc while chasing a serial killer, that I can cope with. It's the job you do and I've always accepted that there's a chance it'll be the job that takes you from us, not this DNA shit."

"Oh I'm taking the treatment, no hesitation on that."

"Thank the Gods for that. I thought maybe you weren't sure or something."

"No, not at all. I'm just wanting to share everything with you. I'm never keeping secrets from you ever again. Okay, the Drycenians told you about Tip before I did, but I kept it from you and I feel bad about that now. It's also kind of, cool knowing someone will be worrying about me until I get better, so I'm being a bit selfish too you know."

"Thank you for telling me. It's nice having someone worry about you isn't it? I guess I take it for granted because I've had Grellina and Ambella. You had no family for so long and didn't have the luxury of anyone worrying for you. I wish I could go back in time and change that so you didn't feel so alone for so long."

"Everything happens at the right time," I said. "And that is my profundity for today. Jam says I'll be asleep for most of the treatment, so I guess I'll see you in a day or so."

"Would you like me to pace the corridor outside and wring my hands every few minutes?" Tinnias grinned. "Or would a more manly daily visit do?"

We laughed together and embraced. "I'm sure you'll choose wisely," I replied.

## CHAPTER FIVE

My awareness of the following couple of days is patchy, but there were periods of lucidity. During these brief episodes, I was aware of some discomfort that seemed to emanate from deep within my bones and seep through every cell in my body. Once, I became conscious enough to realise I was trembling violently and heard Jam's voice far away, soothing my discomfort despite my inability to make out the words. Another time, I awoke and found myself being transferred to a wheeled trolley and covered with a warm blanket, then returned to my bed where darkness embraced me again. Jam later told me that I had been violently sick, a natural effect of such radical treatment, which necessitated the cleaning of my bed and almost the entire room, such was the force with which my body expelled the nutrient rich solution being pumped into me. A couple of times, I became lucid enough to realise someone was holding my hand and once felt a touch on my cheek, lips against my skin and then darkness again.

I awoke in the early hours of the third day and knew I was finally back to full consciousness. My body felt surprisingly good given the experience I had just endured, and I smiled as I gingerly moved my extremities and found them strong; each cell feeling vibrant and alive in a way I had forgotten was possible. Several tubes connected me to machines placed around the bed and soft beeps echoed in the small room.

The door opened and Jam entered in his nightshirt, yawning widely so I got a good view of his long fangs. "Welcome back, Sam. How do you feel?"

By early afternoon, I was up and exercising under Jam's watchful eye and after breakfast the following morning, he declared me fit enough to discharge me from the medical bay.

"I want you back here every day after dinner, for a few tests and to monitor your recovery. If all goes to plan, I can declare you fully recovered by the time we reach Lilea."

"I'm seriously grateful to you for this, Doc," I said. "I don't know how I'll ever repay you for the care and kindness you've given me."

"You're doing that already by calling me your friend. Don't underestimate how precious a gift that is, Sam."

"Now I understand what Vincent meant when he said you're a special guy," I grinned. Jam hesitated before answering and I guessed I'd touched upon a delicate subject. "I'm sorry, Doc. I can see that makes you uncomfortable. Forgive me."

"No need to apologise, Sam. Vincent and I shared an experience once that brought us close as friends. It's difficult to put into words really. Sometime later, He was accused of a crime and everyone thought he was guilty, the evidence seemed clear. I reported having found his DNA and he was charged, found guilty, and sentenced to be executed. What I didn't know was that it was a hologram that went through the execution, not his real body. I felt responsible for his death and tried to kill myself. The guilt was too much and I made a bad choice. The fallout tested that new and deeper friendship. It served to give us both a very deep understanding of the power of connection that two souls can have. That's why I say to never underestimate how great a gift your friendship is."

I was shocked by this admission and was unsure how to reply. "Wow, I'm so sorry. Can I admit something too?"

"Of course."

"Since I first met you all, I've admired you, Doc. Your unwavering compassion is tangible, it never wavers and always makes me feel safe. I strive to be like that myself but fail to do it with as much authenticity as you do. Thank you for being the way you are. I'm in your debt."

"Thank you for your words. There is no debt between friends. We believe that when two souls are bonded in friendship, what each does for the other, gives the other, is given freely and without need of repayment. There is as much joy for us in giving as there is in receiving. When someone allows you to give of yourself for their benefit or wellbeing, it is an unspoken declaration of your worthiness to provide that aid, that no one else is deemed worthy to provide it. We regard it as a huge honour to be deemed so worthy."

"There is no one else I know of who can do what you've done for me, Doc," I said truthfully. "My own doctors never told me, so I guess they don't even know about it. You're amazing and I feel honoured to be allowed to receive the benefits of your knowledge."

"Then we are even, aren't we?" Jam smiled and extended his hand, which I shook.

"We are indeed," I nodded. "By the way, I hope you don't mind me asking, but do you have a dermal optimiser aboard?"

By the time I left the medical bay, Jam had fixed me up so I would never need a dermal optimiser again. My face looked almost ten years younger, my hair would grow thick, and I would have a permanent light tan, all with the aid of a minute nano particle. I was delighted and amazed.

The journey to Lilea took a further eight days, even at the top speed available to the Drycenians' battle cruiser. During those long days, Tinnias got a full health check by Jam and after a couple of minor interventions, was given a clean bill of health. Commander Byron thought it prudent that we both learn to use the Battle Board in case any situation should arise that might require us to travel quickly where a shuttle or ship is unavailable. Both of us agreed that it was the most fun either of us could remember having in years, and it was lovely to get to spend a whole day in Byron's company. Toma did indeed thrash me in our battle board rematch and it was great fun despite having lost.

The Battle Board is a unique mode of personal transportation the Drycenians have at their disposal. It is an oval shaped board on which a person stands and by use of a simple joystick, allows travel at three to four feet above the ground in terrain where a ship would be at a disadvantage. Travelling at considerable speed whilst weaving in and out of thick forest or rocky mountainous terrain takes skill, but once mastered, the board proves its usefulness and has saved countless Drycenian lives. Byron and a group of Troopers gave up their spare time to coach me and Tinnias in the basics, after which they challenged us to races in order to hone our burgeoning skills. I remembered using a Board when the Lilean case was being concluded and after less than an hour at the joystick on my own, quickly knew I wanted one for myself. Knowing the Drycenians would never allow any such advanced technology out of their sight, I sighed sadly but determined that I was going to become as proficient as the time available allowed.

I tried my best to find reasons to seek Byron's company and found him more than willing to indulge me. Either he didn't realise my motive, which was likely, or he was being polite, which was also likely. His laughter lifted my soul, his eyes hypnotised me, and his smell was intoxicating. I managed to work the conversation so that I found out he was still single and my heart leapt in relief.

"All of the guys aboard who are into guys are already in relationships," he said nonchalantly. "That doesn't really bother me, none of them are my type anyway."

I almost gaped open mouthed at that remark but just stopped myself in time. So he was into guys after all? Wow, this was getting better by the second.

"What is your type?" I grinned.

"I've never been attracted to Drycenian men. Not because of physical appearance, I'm not quite that shallow. It's weird I know but our typical personality isn't something that attracts me, despite knowing I'm like them in many ways. I find a different personality more attractive than one like my own."

"You like them extrovert and assertive," I sniggered. "You like to be dominated huh?"

He blushed and laughed. "Something like that. There was a time when I thought the reason I was so consistently unsuccessful in finding anyone was maybe because I was, well, barking up the wrong tree, so to speak. Anyway, I met a woman and she was everything like in those movies we all hate. Pretty, funny, strong, sexy, you know the type. I thought I was getting attached but then she went and committed to someone else so I decided to concentrate on work and forget about getting involved. It wasn't a total loss though; it did teach me that I was wrong to doubt myself. Looking back now, the thought of … y'know … with her, or any woman, is not a pleasant thought. To think how close I came to contemplating it, and the potential for problems later on if anything had happened between us made me wary of contemplating an attachment to anyone for ages. Sorry, I'm rambling. You don't want to know this shit."

"You ramble all you want," I replied. "Thank you for trusting me enough to share."

His eyes held me and for a moment it felt like his soul was reaching out to grasp my own. "I've never told anyone that shit before. Thanks for making it easy."

My next dilemma was whether to tell him I was into guys too or not, but he took the choice out of my hands, much to my relief.

"How about you, Bro? Now that you've found your identity, have you found anyone?"

"How the hell did you know? I blushed and laughed, shaking my head in disbelief. "I've not told a soul."

He sniggered at my red cheeks. "Another man's man can always tell. You'll get to realise too, as time goes on. It might take a while as you've denied your identity for so many years but you'll understand one day. Was it a struggle for you, realising who you really are I mean?"

"No, not a struggle at all. It was an education, but it felt so right that I never felt I wanted to fight it."

"Do you have anyone?" he asked, moving closer and leaning in conspiratorially.

"No. I've … well it's sort of … there's …" I finally gave up trying to explain and he sniggered.

"There's someone you like but you're too shy to do anything about it?"

"Something like that, and in my defence, I didn't know for a while if he was into guys or not."

"Is he?"

"Yeah, and he's single, but for the first time in my life, I'm scared to act. That's never happened to me before, I was always happy to let a woman know I was up for it if she was, but now I'm frozen. Maybe it's because it's not just sex anymore but feelings too."

"Probably," he nodded. "Have you had any relationships with men yet at all?"

"No," I shook my head. "Like I said, I'm not after just a fuck anymore. Feelings are involved now and that makes me hesitant to act in case I mess it up. Then I'll have not only this massive change to get used to, but a broken heart to fix too. Why does life have to be so fucking complicated, Bro?" I looked into his lovely hypnotic eyes and we laughed together.

"Maybe it isn't complicated at all. Maybe his feelings mirror your own and he's just as scared of messing up and losing you as you are of losing him. Maybe he can read you like a book and just needs to know there's a chance before he finds the courage to reach out."

"How the hell do I get that across?" I asked, "without actually saying, hey, Bro, I'm crazy in love, wanna hang out?"

Byron roared with laughter and the cargo bay echoed with our guffaws. "You always make me laugh, Sam. That's one of your greatest assets."

"It also gets me into trouble sometimes," I admitted.


The evening before we were due to arrive in Lilean airspace, a meeting was called in the Observation room to discuss the coming meeting with Vincent Domenico, its possible outcomes, and any further options that might be open to us. I was convinced that Vincent's loyalty would lie with Tip first and any enquiries by ourselves would be unwelcome. The Drycenians disagreed and although we didn't argue about it, the debate was lively. Lomas, and especially Jam, kept on about Vincent being such a good guy who always does the right thing, even when that means considerable discomfort for himself. To be truthful, the way everyone around me, except for Tinnias, kept on about what a wonderful guy Vincent is became more than a little nauseating, and went against everything my own years of experience had taught me about people. One thing above everything else annoyed me and there came a time when the pain in my gut was too painful to ignore. I had to say it or I'd explode.

"Listen," I snapped, a little too harshly but which served to quieten the entire room immediately. "I'm not ignorant of the guy. I spent days with him and his wife during the case six years ago. Please don't treat me as if I don't know what I'm talking about. Yes, I agree they're both nice people. We had a few laughs and I got along with them fine. They were secretive though, and it was noticeable from the start that they were a little closed off to me. They didn't trust me and although they treated me nicely and were never rude or dismissive, I could tell they were waiting for me to let them down. Vincent himself kept referring to me as a Merc for fuck's sake."

Mercs are an annoying hazard in the job I do but one we are forced to put up with. I am officially registered, licensed, and accepted by the Inter-Galactic Law Enforcement Agency and have documentation to prove it. I operate under their guidelines and am subject to their rulings and decisions. I get a salary from the Agency, whether I catch my target or not and I am not allowed to collect any reward money or bounty that may be on a target's head. Mercs are unlicensed and not recognised by the Agency. They do the job for the reward, the bounty, and have no code of ethics governing how they do their job. Anyone can set themselves up as a Merc as they have no Agency documentation. They mistreat their prisoners, often bring in a dead prisoner when a live one was required, and sometimes bring in lookalikes to get the money and take off before the Agency notices. However many of these insects we bring in, there are always more to take their place. They give all of us registered Freelancers a bad name and although I do understand that the general public might not know the differences between us, I find it annoying and insulting.

"I'm sorry for my tone," I continued. "Look, I've been doing this job for over twenty years and I'm an expert at reading people. Vincent is Lilean, Tip is Lilean, they're buddies. That case brought them close, closer than the normal friendship two guys usually share. And before anyone says anything, I ask you to remember that I spent every minute of six entire months with Tip when he joined the Agency and I've kept in touch ever since. He talks about Vincent as if the guy is some sort of semi deity or something and if the guy feels anything approaching the same level of connection to Tip in return, you can all take it from me that they will look after their own interests before confiding in off worlders like us. Well, like me anyway. You people are special to them so you're probably higher up their ladder of acceptance than mere Mercs like Tinnias and I. Forgive my candour but I think maybe your affection for them might be clouding your discernment."

I looked down at my drink and waited for the fallout. It was regrettable that I had allowed myself to be so openly expressive when these kind people whom I always looked up to had put themselves out to help me, especially in front of their King but, well you must know me by now. Honesty is my middle name and I'm aware that sometimes honesty must be expressed at inconvenient moments. Knowing I would be apologising to Tinnias before the evening was over, I mentally rehearsed a suitably contrite speech that I hoped would save me suffering the shame of having him yell at me.

"You have our sincere apologies, Samelan," Lomas said. "At no time have we wished to make you feel bad in any way. Having shared so much with our Lilean friends, we do tend to assume that we know them better than anyone else. I did forget that you have spent time with both Tip and Vincent and will have valuable insight. Your relationship with them was and still is, different to the one we share and as such, will have gleaned experience that ours hasn't. This serves to increase everyone's knowledge of them, as our experience with them must also do to yours."

I was somewhat surprised by Lomas' quick apology and happy that he had the skills to defuse what could have become an awkward disagreement. He had a valid point too, one I had also not considered, up until now. "Thank you, Sir. It will be of more use to us to combine all of our knowledge and experience of them, don't you think?"

Lomas nodded. "Indeed I do. We must be aware that Vincent might choose to keep his mouth closed when asked about Tip. I feel sure however, that if he should choose to do so, it will be because he feels it right for the situation and not because of any lack of trust between himself and all of us."

Every Drycenian head in the room nodded in agreement with Lomas and I registered the feeling of isolation returning to my gut. Realising that getting these people to accept my experience as worthy of note was a battle I couldn't hope to win, I changed the subject.

"So how are we to approach him? Do we just turn up on his doorstep and claim to have been in the neighbourhood or what?"

"We have to be honest with him," Jam said. "We call him and tell him we wish to speak with him about something important."

"He's bound to ask what it's about though," Tinnias said. "He could use the time it takes us to get down there to do anything."

"What sort of anything?" Jam asked.

"Like calling Tip and warning him we're poking our noses into his life," I said.

"Or calling him to ask what he should tell us," Tinnias added.

Jam shook his head and I noticed several other Drycenians doing the same. "No," Jam said. "Vincent could never be so, so dishonest."

I sighed audibly and I noticed Toma look in my direction. By now, I didn't care whether I was offending them or not, I was annoyed and finding it hard to appear calm. "Why? Because he's a nice guy with spiritual beliefs? I've known many people who claim strong faith and spiritual awareness and seventy five percent of them are now in jail."

"How many of them were Lilean, Sam?" Jam snapped in reply. Everyone in the room looked at him, astonished to hear him raise his voice. It seemed as if I had achieved something few were able to do, annoy the fuck out of him.

He had me there. None of them were Lilean and my hesitation, together with my stinging cheeks answered for me. Fuck, I'm so sick of blushing. Can't anyone cure that shit?

"None, actually," I answered truthfully. I saw a hint of a smile tickle the corners of Jam's mouth and I lost it. "Oh, you find that amusing huh? You enjoy catching me out do you?" I stood, vaguely aware of Tinnias' hand on my arm but shook it away. By now I was incensed and any thought of holding back was out of the question. Whatever my punishment was to be, I was going to speak my mind. "I've always looked up to you people since the last time I met you. You're legends, mysterious and enigmatic figures no one ever sees and I believed the hype for years. Since meeting you, I thought of you as wise and godly people who long ago evolved passed the need for the egotistic and negative emotions the rest of us insects are subject to. I was delighted when you showed up here. I was confident you'd help solve this shit that's going on with Tip, because he's a friend and I was worried. I put myself out for him, put my job and reputation on the line, committed an offence to help him out and I knew that if anyone could help, it would be you people. Well you know what, Doc. You're no more evolved than me after all, you're just cleverer than me. That stupid smirk gave you away, buddy."

As I breathed to try and calm myself, I noticed Byron had stood and moved next to me, his hand resting on my arm. I looked into his eyes, the love I felt was painful and I longed for him to hold me and tell me everything would be alright. He nodded and blinked slowly and I knew he understood.

"Breathe, Bro," he whispered. "I'm here for you. Take a breath for a moment."

"Let's take a break and have something to eat," Toma said after a moment of intensely awkward silence. "Everyone needs time to breathe and relax. Sam, remember I mentioned about sampling a very special drink?" I ignored him and closed my eyes and I tried to relax my mind. Toma continued anyway. "Good, let's go and sample some now. I'll bet you a hundred it makes you cough. Are you man enough for a small wager?"

I knew he was trying to get me away so the others could express their annoyance at my behaviour and despite my first instinct being to remain and let them all squirm, I allowed myself to concede to his suggestion. "Sure, why not? A drink sounds like a great idea."

"Son," Lomas called to us as we headed towards the door. Toma turned and smiled at his father. "If you're planning what I think you're planning, please take care. Our friend here probably hasn't experienced Tiche Rammei before. We want him back conscious, please."

"Trust me, Father," Toma replied. "I'm eighty-seven years old, not eighteen. Have some faith."

"I have every faith in you, Son. I also remember that security guard from Laminos 2. Oh the shame."

I heard several giggles and Toma made a face. "You're never going to let me forget that are you?"

"Why should he?" Byron replied. "It was hilarious."

Toma's quarters were sumptuous, as befitting his status as Royal Heir and I sank into a deep blue chair that hugged me like a lover in all the right places. Toma walked to the opposite wall and pressed his foot onto a small plate in the floor. I watched in awe as a portion of the wall slid back to reveal what looked for all the world like a generously proportioned balcony.

"What the fuck?" I exclaimed as I rose from the seat and strode over. "A balcony? But this is a spaceship, how is this possible?" I glanced around at the potted plants, their yellow flowers that smelled so sweet and sighed. There was even a warm evening breeze that brushed my face.

"It's an invisible force field," Toma replied. "It's amazing isn't it?"

"So this is really outside the ship?" I asked as I pointed to the void that surrounded us.

He nodded. "Yep, really outside."

"Shit, it's incredible. I would love something like this. It would make the months of space travel this job requires, that much more comfortable."

Toma laughed, pleased that he had impressed me. "No matter how long we spend aboard, this never ceases to be amazing. Now, come with me and try to win yourself that hundred." I followed him back inside to a small cabinet from which he took two bottles of spirit. One held clear liquid while the other one's contents were golden. He poured a small measure of the golden liquid into a glass and handed it to me. "This is called Tolompka. We reserve it for the most special of occasions. It is expensive and the production process takes a very long time so we must be disciplined with it. Try it."

The golden spirit warmed its way down my throat and I nodded appreciatively. "Nice," I replied. "Very nice indeed. Warm and smooth without a hint of bite."

He smiled, pleased at my response. Taking up the bottle of clear liquid, he removed the cap and I noticed it had a dropper attached to the underside. Using this dropper, he measured a single drop into my now empty glass. After refitting the dropper cap to prevent accidental spillage, he measured another quantity of Tolompka into the glass and swirled it gently. As I watched, the golden liquid turned clear, after which he handed it to me with a smile.

"That bottle is called Mundil and this mixture of the two is known as Tiche Rammei. Drink it all down in one go. If you cough, I win a hundred. If you don't, you win. Okay?"

I nodded. "Okay," I grinned and knocked it back. At first, I was not aware of the liquid having any taste at all. It was as if I had drunk water and I was about to say so when I became aware that my stomach seemed to be on fire. It was no more than a slight warmth that quickly became a volcano that took my breath away. After a further few seconds, the volcano obviously decided it was time to erupt, as the searing lava flew upward to my throat and out of my mouth. I fully expected to see flames licking at the opposite wall and was somewhat surprised when they did not. The lava, having lost none of its heat, seared its way around to the back of my neck and raced up my skull. I was convinced my hair was being burned away and gingerly ran a hand over my head to check. Expecting to feel my skin melting, I was relieved to feel my own hair still in place. The flaming tide continued down my face and sprang from my eyes in tears of liquid fire that I was sure would be melting my corneas. It was at this point that I became aware of a slight desire to cough but resisted. I know it's silly but I'm quite competitive when I'm in the mood and I had no desire to allow these people to make me feel even more of an inexperienced idiot than they had already done. The more I held on, the worse the need to cough became and in less than a minute I was in pain and hugging my chest.

Toma was bent double, his guffaws filling the room and I wanted to punch him for finding my distress so funny.

"Asshole," I hissed through my pain.

This served to make him laugh harder and I noticed tears running down his cheeks as he held his sides with the effort. "Cough, Sam. Go on, you know you want to."

"Never," I hissed.

"The pain will stop if you cough," he declared between guffaws.

"Fuck you." I was about to add to the insult when I felt my stomach give a lurch. This meant one thing and I mentally groaned at the knowledge that I was about to puke liquid fire. "Oh shit I'm gonna puke."

I felt strong arms grab me and haul me towards a door in a corner of the room, which opened to reveal a bathroom. Toma dragged my considerably larger frame with ease towards the toilet and dumped me down on the floor. It was all over with a couple of heaves and I felt better straight away. The liquid did not, thankfully, burn its way up but felt like I was puking clear water. Within a couple of further minutes, I felt as good as new. After taking the opportunity to wash my face and hands in the swankiest bathroom I had ever seen, I returned to the room to find Toma still grinning.

"I'm impressed, Sam," he said. "You're the first one in ages to beat the game. Here, you earned it." He held out a galactic credit card and I took it.

"Thanks. That's the hardest won hundred of my entire life. I apologise for being rude to you by the way. I was in pain, if that's any excuse."

He waved away my apology, the grin still fixed upon his face. "I forgive you, absolutely."

"Was that really just one drop of the stuff?" I asked.

"Yes. Just one."

"Where do you get it?"

"It's from a plant back home. It's a defence mechanism. Animals won't eat it because of that fire."

"So why do you?" I asked.

"Because it has medicinal properties first and foremost, but also because despite our apparent godly wisdom, we do like to drink and have fun, take silly risks and behave like idiots sometimes just like everyone else."

I wasn't sure whether that statement pleased or dismayed me. I had always regarded the Drycenians as special in a way that no other people could ever be special. To me they were wise, almost god-like figures with the knowledge and skill to make anything and everything all right. I constantly wished to meet them again and hoped that somehow, as if by magic, some of what made them so special would rub off on me. That evening taught me that although they were wise and had technology and knowledge way beyond anyone else's, they were just like the rest of us in many ways. Suddenly, in the time it took to have a disagreement, they lost some of that mystery, that godliness and became a little like me, ordinary. It was akin to a death having taken place and I felt the grief as clearly as if a loved family member had died. I realised that Toma had taught me a valuable lesson; that his people are just like me, but no less worthy of respect and admiration because of it. In those few moments, he stopped being a young and rather reckless royal with little actual purpose in whom I found little worthy of note. I found myself seeing him in a different light, a young man waiting to bear the burden of Kingship, who hid his considerable wisdom behind a mask of youth. I had underestimated him.

Unable to put my feelings into words, I painted on a fake smile and nodded. "Glad to hear it."

"Let's get back shall we? We still have to decide how we're to proceed once we've met with Vincent," Toma suggested.

## CHAPTER SIX

I followed Toma along corridors and was aware that I felt awkward. Then a memory fluttered to the front of my mind and I frowned.

"Hey, Toma. You said you're eighty seven. You don't look a day over twenty. Was that some sort of family joke between you and your father?"

He laughed aloud. "No. I really am eighty seven, Sam."

"That's impossible," I laughed. "You're tugging my chain."

"We're a very long lived race," he explained. "Without giving you a long lecture, it's a result of the experiments the Transmortals did on our ancient ancestors. Those experiments had a permanent effect upon their brains and their DNA. One of the results was a greatly lengthened life span. If we remain healthy, we can live to over four hundred years old. Father is three hundred and twelve. Byron is eighty five, and Jam is two hundred and four."

"Jeez," I hissed. "I can't imagine having to live that long."

"You make it sound like it would be an unpleasant thing."

"It would in many ways," I nodded.

"I guess it does have its down sides," Toma agreed. When we reached the Observation Room, he held the door open for me. "After you."

Cheers and applause greeted our arrival and Toma laughed.

"Are you a hundred richer or poorer, Son?" Lomas asked.

"Poorer," Toma replied. "Sam won his hundred admirably."

"Congratulations, Samelan," Lomas grinned. "That's quite an achievement for a non Drycenian. You can feel justly proud."

"I do," I grinned back. "I earned every single credit, believe me."

"We have a couple of possible outcomes from our visit tomorrow," Lomas continued. "Why don't we take each in turn and discuss the pros and cons, does anyone disagree? Okay then, who wants to start?"

"He could have all the information we need," Byron said. "He might happily give it to us so Sam can then decide his best course of action."

"Believe me," I said. "I've been doing this job for over twenty years and I can count on one hand the number of times that has happened."

"It's no doubt the rank outsider," Byron agreed, "but it's not impossible."

"If so, then Tinnias and I will know how we're to proceed." As I looked at Byron, I noticed his eyes looked as if he'd been crying and I frowned at him. He smiled and nodded back at me.

"Even if Byron's scenario does happen, we could find ourselves with a lengthy case on our hands," Tinnias replied. "It will depend on what the information tells us."

"He could claim he knows nothing," I remarked. "Which could either be the truth or a lie."

"What do we do if that happens?" Lomas asked.

"We could approach both Gaht and Dankera and tell them we know they have a situation between them, and ask them to take it elsewhere," Toma said.

"If we did that, we'd either lose our kneecaps or be ignored. Or both," Tinnias replied.

"I could go undercover and join Dankera as a law enforcement leak," I offered.

Tinnias nodded slowly. "It's an option. Not one I'd like you to take, but it's an option we must be aware of. It could end up being our only one."

"That's far too dangerous," Byron added.

"What other possible scenarios are there?" Lomas asked. "Or is that it?"

"He could be angry at us for approaching him with this," Jam said.

"Which would be the same as him claiming to know nothing, in effect," I replied. "Whether he's angry or not, he could claim to know nothing. He might truthfully not know anything about it. Being angry won't change anything. I guess there's always the possibility that he could be so angry he decides to ask Tip about it, which will alert him to us poking around in his business. That could be awkward."

"Maybe it could be a good thing if Tip found out about us poking around," Tinnias said. "It might frighten him into leaving it alone or coming to us with it."

"So now we have some insight into what could happen as a result of tomorrow's conversation with Vincent, how do we proceed once we know?" Lomas asked.

"The way I see it," I said as I scratched my chin. "We have just two outcomes. He either gives us information or he doesn't. If he does, we will know our next course of action. If he doesn't, then umm, I guess I go undercover."

"Or I alert his Commander and let him have the problem and we go home," Tinnias said.

I nodded. "Yeah, we could do that too."

"We won't know for sure until tomorrow, so I vote we all try to get a good night's sleep. The more refreshed we are, the better will our decision making processes be," Lomas suggested and everyone nodded.

Everyone got up and started to wander off to their respective rooms.

"I'm going for a swim before bed," Tinnias said to Byron and I. "Would you two like to join me?"

"No thanks," I said. "I'm going next door to smoke and think about everything."

"Fancy some company?" Byron asked.

"Sure."

I was glad to find we had the smoking room to ourselves and lit a cigarette, then offered Byron one, which he accepted.

"Are you okay?" I asked. "You seemed upset when Toma and I got back. Was there any grief about me?"

"This business is worrying," he said. "Not just because of Tip and the illegal stuff. I was worried our friendship might be falling apart and the last thing I want is for you to hate us."

"I could never hate you people," I replied. "I was just angry at the way everyone seems to worship Vincent. It's as if his presence makes everyone but me lose all ability for discernment and common sense. That annoys the fuck out of me. He's a guy not a god, just a guy with big muscles and a superiority complex."

Byron sniggered. "I can't believe Jam, snapping at you like that. I was shocked."

"So was I. I'd never peg him as a guy who would yell and lose his temper. I guess he's head worshipper."

"That's true."

"I'm sorry for yelling. You must think I'm an annoying fuck who doesn't like his opinions challenged."

"Not at all," he said quietly. "You've no idea how wrong you are."

"I'd like to know," I said boldly, expecting to get my face slapped. To my surprise, he blinked slowly and smiled.

"There you go. You did it at last. That wasn't painful was it?"

"Huh?" I frowned.

He grinned. "The other day, in the cargo bay, we were talking about you finding yourself at last and you asked how to let someone know of your willingness to accept their approach."

"I remember," I nodded.

"I said maybe he just needs to know there's a chance so he can find the courage to reach out to you."

"Yes, you did."

"Those four words make the difference, Sam. Did you mean them?"

I gave a deep sigh and nodded. "Yes, every one. Holding this inside for all these years is killing me. I need to know so I can either be happy or move on."

He bent down and put out his cigarette, took mine from me and put it out, then took my hands in his own and gazed into my eyes. The hands made their way slowly up my arms to my shoulders and to my complete surprise, my own found his waist and held him. He drew me to him and I willingly allowed myself to be drawn in until I felt his chest against my own. The hands moved up to my neck, fingers caressing my hair as my arms encircled his waist and hugged him close. His lips were soft and full and my mouth tingled at their touch.

"I love you," I said when our lips parted. "Since Regnor. I haven't been able to think about anything else."

He nodded. "I remember seeing you down in that mine and knowing one day we'd be here, that I'd be kissing you and telling you how much I love you. These past six years have been agony."

"For me too."

"Whatever happens in this case, however things turn out, promise me you'll not lose that love," he asked.

"I promise. Even if all the others aboard end up hating me, promise me you'll still love me."

"I promise."

I pulled him close and kissed him, all fear now gone. I was in love and he loved me. I was happy despite the gravity of the case.

Tinnias and I talked late into the night and although we didn't argue, we disagreed.

"Y'know, Dad," I began. "These past few days have been a real education for me."

"How come?"

"I now have a much healthier view of the Drycenians than I did before."

"You did rather idolise them," he agreed.

"Yeah but those romantic dreams are gone for good. My eyes are wide open now."

"Just because of a lively debate and difference of opinion?"

"No, not just because of that," I shook my head as I stripped and climbed into bed.

"Then what?"

"I don't trust them all of a sudden."

Tinnias gaped at me. "Why ever not? I would have thought these people above all others in the galaxy would be the ones you wouldn't hesitate to trust."

"So would I until tonight," I replied. "Now though, there's something about them that's making my gut churn. To be totally honest with you, I'm having to fight the urge to get as far away from them as possible. They scare me and I want to run away."

I could see Tinnias was having a problem putting his reaction into words, so I nodded at him. He hissed through his teeth and ran both hands through his hair. "I don't know what to say, Son, except that I'm beside you whatever you decide. Promise me you'll never think I'm taking anyone's side against you. Whatever you feel you need to do, I'm with you. Promise me."

I nodded. "Thank you. I promise. I was worried. I thought maybe you would take their side if I seemed to react against them."

Tinnias looked shocked at my confession. "What? Don't you ever doubt my loyalty to you, Sam. Even if you're dead wrong in your choice of action, my place is beside you and that's where I intend to stay."

"I'm sorry, I guess I'm feeling cornered and defensive. Too many years working alone with only myself to count on."

"You're not alone anymore, you got that? If I turn around and find you've run off without involving me I'm going to be very angry. Worried to fuck but angry too. I may be an old fart who sits behind a desk and gives orders, but I'm not a relic just yet. I was young once. Hell, I've even fired my sidearm, how about that?"

I grinned, my mood lightening immediately. "Wow, Dad, I never knew you were such an action hero."

"What was that drink like?" Tinnias asked, changing the subject.

"Awful. It nearly killed me. It started out like plain water for a few seconds and then quickly turned into a volcano. I puked my guts up, but I didn't cough and that's what matters apparently."

"Don't you think it a little odd that halfway through an important discussion about how to proceed with this case, Toma suddenly asks you to go and drink with him?"

"I thought it was weird when it happened," I nodded. "I assumed he was going to warn me to mind my manners or something, threaten me perhaps, but he really did just want me to try that drink. The only conclusion I came to about it was that it was some sort of attempt to bolster my self-esteem after I made it obvious to everyone that I was disappointed in them."

Tinnias considered this before nodding. I noticed the nod seemed half hearted and knew he wasn't sure. "I guess it could be. It's just like them to do something like that. They regard feelings and emotions as important, or at least they seem to. I get the impression that offending people is something they try to actively avoid."

I shrugged. "I guess so, yeah. Did they say anything to you while I was away?"

"Nothing specific. They just talked about Vincent and how they hope he's with us on this. I was expecting them to ask me to control you or something, but they acted as if nothing had happened out of the ordinary. It was a bit weird actually, like the turd in the corner everyone can smell but no one wants to comment on. The only unexpected thing was that Byron got a bit emotional and was worried about losing your friendship."

I nodded. "Yeah, he told me about it in the smoking room. He's the only one of them I'd trust right now and whatever happens, even if they all hate me, I'll be keeping in touch with him."

"He's very fond of you, Son. If I had to stick my neck out, I'd say he's formed an emotional attachment to you."

I smiled. "I know."

"How do you feel about that?"

"I'm ecstatic about it."

"Is there going to be a connection? A personal connection I mean."

"Yes, there already is."

"So, my Son has finally chosen someone huh? I thought it would never happen. I'm happy, and proud of you."

"Thank you. I'm relieved you approve. I'm worried that if we fall out with the Drycenians over this case, it will make a relationship difficult."

"We'll do our damnedest to ensure nothing gets in the way of your love. I'll fight beside you, Son."


Early afternoon the following day saw the battle cruiser arrive in covert orbit around Lilea 4 and we gathered in the observation room to listen to Lomas call Vincent and ask if we could visit with him. I admit that I was a little nervous about it; it had been six years since I spent time with him and we never became real friends as such. His insistence on referring to me as a Merc told me that he regarded me as being on an entirely different level and lower social strata than himself. Despite my confidence that he would welcome the Drycenians like old friends, I would not have been at all surprised if he refused to entertain me.

The call was answered on the third ring. "Domenico residence."

"That voice can only belong to Vincent," Lomas smiled.

"Lomas?" The surprise in the voice that replied was genuine and warm.

"Hello, my friend. How are you all?"

"We're fine. Kyle and I were only talking about you last night. Is there a problem?"

"We most certainly hope not, but we would like to visit with you if you'll have us."

"Of course, you're always welcome here. When will you be arriving?"

"We're already in covert orbit. Shall we come to you or do you wish to come here?"

"You're here already? Wow, okay. Well I've just got our ship back from having a refit so it wouldn't hurt to take her for a spin and see how she's going. I can be there in an hour or so."

"We look forward to welcoming you aboard again."

We made our way to the shuttle bay after a drink, during which we all decided to let Lomas begin any discussion. I had to reluctantly agree that since Vincent feels a strong bond of friendship with him, he would be best placed to put him at ease. A small ship entered the shuttle bay and I noticed that although much smaller than my own, it was obviously a top of the range model that would no doubt give my own a run for her money in a race. I registered a flutter of envy rush through me and struggled to dismiss it for a few moments. Once the bay doors shut and the room safely pressurised, we entered. Lomas led our little party towards the descending hatch.

The years fell away from my mind as the huge, bald headed man jumped down and approached Lomas with a grin, his arms outstretched to embrace him. He was just as I remembered, he hadn't aged a day and I felt the same intimidation at his sheer bulk as I felt six years previously. Unsavoury as it was to my ego, I was forced to admit to myself that I was in awe of the man for many reasons. It wasn't just his physical size, although as a guy myself, that stuff is important. Everything about him seemed to put my own existence to shame and I hated myself for allowing him to destroy my self-esteem. Knowing what little detail I did about his life, his single handed defeat of the dreaded Transmortal Army, his fight with the most feared beast in existence, the Zaltoid, and even his cosy family life on the most beautiful planet I had ever visited, made me feel like a Stankid Worm.

After their warm embrace, Lomas indicated the rest of our party with a sweep of his arm. "You know all but one of us here. We have Samelan Sinclair with us, together with his Boss, Commander Tinnias Vaylo. Vincent nodded and greeted each of the Drycenians warmly. Man hugs abounded, accompanied by affirmations of friendship and declarations of having missed them all terribly. When Vincent stood before me, he smiled and offered me his hand, which I shook.

"You're looking well, Mr Domenico. How's the family?"

"They're great. Thank you for helping us find Gabriel. We are always grateful."

"Just doing my job," I smiled. "I'm happy it turned out well for you all. We couldn't have wished for a better outcome, given the circumstances."

Vincent moved on to Tinnias and exchanged the usual pleasantries. I noted with some dismay that not only had our re introduction lacked the warmth of his greetings to the Drycenians, but he hadn't asked how I'd been since our last meeting. Not even a simple, 'how have you been?' was offered us.

"Let's go to the Observation Room and get some refreshments shall we?" Lomas smiled.

As Tinnias and I trailed along at the back of the line, my gut twisted itself a little tighter and I groaned in the silence of my mind. So gentle that I almost didn't notice, a decision was made that I knew I would be powerless to change. It was not made consciously for I had no active part in the decision making. It was more of a deep inner knowing that this was the only course I could take. Not only for the case, but for my own peace of mind. Knowing I was soon going to piss everyone off mightily, I sighed. Tinnias heard and looked at me quizzically, his eyebrows raised as if to question me. I shook my head sadly in response. I was sad not only for the case and how the coming event would affect it, but also how it might affect my relationship with Byron. I reluctantly had to accept that it would likely be ended before it had begun. I could've cried.

Once drinks were handed round and plates of food arranged on the tables between us, Vincent looked at Lomas.

"It's great to see you guys again. What are you up to these days and what brings you to this arm of the galaxy?"

To my utter amazement and complete annoyance, Lomas got right to the point. "We've come to ask you about Tip Danso."

I almost cried out in horror. I had assumed that Lomas would have the sense to work his way around to the crux of the matter gently, maybe even tell a white lie or two to put Vincent at ease before digging the knife in. How wrong can I be? He just comes right out with it and gives Vincent the perfect opportunity to get his defences up and clam up.

"What about him?" Vincent asked and I noticed a frown crease his brow.

"I'm led to believe you and he have kept in contact, is that correct?"

Vincent nodded. "Yeah, we talk on the Unicom now and then and we met up once on Tyrrin 4 when I took the family on holiday. What's the problem? Is he in trouble? Please don't tell me he's gone back to all that shit he left behind."

Lomas shook his head. "Not as far as we know, but he does seem to have got himself into something that is a worry. We're hoping he confides in you about things and that we can persuade you to confide in us about it. You know us well enough to be sure we wouldn't be asking if it weren't important."

Vincent's eyes glazed over, as if he were looking back over his life in search of something and I hoped that what he searched for would be information I could use to help Tip.

"As far as I can remember, our conversations have all been benign, at least they seem that way to me. He's never come right out with anything that has worried me. What sort of something has he got into? Can you tell me about it?"

Up to this point, I was happy to be a bystander, but this question almost made me leap off my chair. I had to get in before Lomas ran his mouth further. Besides, the way he made me feel made me less than willing to share what little I knew with him.

"I'm sorry, we can't. If this becomes an official matter later, the fact that we discussed it with you could jeopardise our chances of getting the right outcome."

Vincent's eyes went cold as he turned them on me and I knew he was annoyed by my response. Tough shit, I thought to myself as I held his gaze to let him know I was not about to be intimidated by him anymore.

"He's my friend," Vincent said. "What we went through six years ago, if you remember, means his wellbeing will always be uppermost in my mind."

"That's precisely why I can't tell you," I replied. "If it should turn out that he's committed a crime, your loyalty to him could encourage you to act against our attempts to bring justice where it's due. And for what it's worth, which I realise is probably nothing to anyone but me, he's my friend too."

"Then why are your loyalties not as questionable as mine?"

"Because I'm a law enforcer," I replied, "as is he. Because my friendship with him is tempered with my desire to see right be done. Because I have my Boss here with me to make sure I don't step out of line, and because my friendship with Tip is not as umm, personal, in the same way yours is. I don't have the same personal debt of gratitude to him that you do."

Vincent rose from his seat and for a moment I thought perhaps he was intending to get violent with me. Relief flooded through me when he began pacing the room and I guessed he was fighting to resist the urge to punch me. No one in the room said anything and several seconds of intense silence hung over us as we all watched the big man pace, back and forth, back and forth. After the fifth journey across the Observation Room, Vincent sat back down and looked at me.

"I understand your point, Mr Sinclair, and I accept that the law requires certain rules to be adhered to in order for things to conclude in the right way. I can assure you, and your Boss, that I would never stand by and allow Tip, or anyone I care about, to fuck up their lives after having had such a monumental struggle to change it as he had. I am also aware that you've no way of knowing that, seeing as how you don't know me that well. Believe me or not, if he's done something wrong, I'll be first in the queue to let him have the full force of my anger, friendship or no friendship."

"I can assure you that it is entirely safe for you to believe Vincent's word, Sam," Jam said.

"My belief, or lack of belief, in anyone's word means nothing to the Law Enforcement Agency," I replied. "Unsavoury as that fact is, I have to live with it just as everyone else has to." I was getting more than a little annoyed that Tinnias had yet to jump in and show solidarity with me, so I shot him an angry glance, which he greeted with raised eyebrows.

"I'm sorry we can't give you any details," Tinnias said, having understood the meaning of the look. "Believe me, if we could, we wouldn't hesitate. We are fully aware of your connection with Tip, that's why we're here asking you for help. There is no joy to be gained in having a law enforcer commit a crime, you can believe that both Sam and I understand that better than anyone alive. Neither of us wishes to make a mistake that could cost lives."

"Neither do I," Vincent replied. "I also understand that as his father, you have a bond equal, if not stronger, than the one Tip and I share." The two men stared into each other's eyes for long seconds before Lomas' voice cut the silence.

"Please, friends, let's not make enemies of each other so soon. Everyone is aware that this is an issue that is easy to cloud with emotion. It calls for us all to be strong to avoid succumbing to those emotions, or the actions we might take under their influence."

Vincent sighed and looked at Lomas. "I'm sorry, Sir. I had no desire to insult your hospitality. You are my best friends and I have nothing but love and admiration for you."

"It is that friendship that prevents us from being insulted by your honesty, Vincent," Lomas replied. "Now, despite Sam's inability to fully inform you of the details, has Tip ever said or done anything that could hint at his being involved in anything untoward? Please take all the time you need to think."

Vincent shook his head. "He always says he loves his job and is aware of the opportunity he was given, the chance he now has to do good and make amends for everything he did as Andrew Midship. Rather than do anything wrong, I'd say he's a little fanatical about being as good a law enforcer as possible. I can't think of anyone less likely to commit a crime. If I remember anything, I'll tell you of course. Is there no doubt about him having got himself into something? Could you be wrong?"

I shook my head. "Unfortunately not. My information is beyond reproach. I only wish it were wrong. You can choose to believe me or not, but I find the knowledge that my friend has most likely got himself into something awful, most distressing."

"How awful?" Vincent asked.

"Pretty awful," Tinnias answered for me. "This could put him away for a long time. It's a serious crime."

I was somewhat pleased to see Vincent's tanned complexion visibly pale at Tinnias' words. "Has he hurt anyone?"

Tinnias hesitated before answering. "Probably not directly. Not with his own hands, so to speak but maybe as an effect of his actions."

"Shit," Vincent hissed and ran a hand over his bald head. I wondered what I would look like bald but dismissed the idea immediately. There was no way I wanted anyone to think I was copying Vincent. "I was so pleased when he said he wanted to become a law enforcer. I thought it was the best way for him to move forward from all that stuff that went before, to immerse himself in the right side of the law would be the best medicine. Now it seems it's just made him go back to where he was. Great idea getting him that job turned out to be. Well done."

Vincent glared at me and my shock momentarily numbed my tongue, preventing me from replying. When I found my voice, Vincent's size did nothing to quell my anger.

"Excuse me?" I snapped. "You think it's my fault he couldn't handle being a good guy after all? How dare you accuse me. What did you ever do to keep him on the straight and narrow huh? You admit you only saw him once in all those years. I make sure to spend time with him at least twice a year, just to let him know I'm still there and care about how he's doing. You sit down there with your nice family in your cosy house and just because you exchange a couple of calls a year, you think you have the monopoly on caring about him? How many of those calls do you initiate? Well? How many?" Vincent shifted his gaze momentarily to his feet before glaring at me again and I knew I'd hit the spot. "I thought so. I always call him before he calls me, I turn up at Tyrrin and ask him if he wants to get lunch or a beer, so don't lecture me about your bond, asshole."

Vincent stood, sending his chair scooting back several feet and Lomas leapt from his seat. "Now gentlemen please let's take a breath here for a moment." Vincent went to step around him and I dutifully stood. Whatever was to transpire in the next few minutes, I would meet it like a man despite knowing that I could be going to bed that evening in considerable pain.

Lomas looked at Tinnias. "Some help would be welcome, Tinnias."

Tinnias put an arm around my shoulder and steered me over to a plate of sandwiches. "Come on, Son. Let's take a moment to compose ourselves shall we?"

## CHAPTER SEVEN

Tinnias stayed close as we ate some of the delicious sandwiches and although I was aware of people milling around, I chose to ignore the hubbub of conversation. I would never have expected this first meeting with Vincent would so quickly become such an angry exchange and I placed most of the blame firmly at Lomas' feet. Wise and well loved he may be, but his interrogation skills left a lot to be desired. His position as not only King, but as Captain of the ship on which Tinnias and I were guests made my position as Detective, rather awkward. I was acutely aware that for this case to move forward in a way that suited the Agency, Lomas and I would need to have an uncomfortable conversation. Tinnias met my gaze and we both sighed.

"Stay calm, Son. No good can come from losing it with these people, however infuriating their behaviour might be."

"He didn't even wait," I hissed. "He told him right away that we want information about Tip. No preamble, no gentle approach to the point. I thought these people were more evolved than the rest of us morons."

"It looks like their investigative skills haven't evolved alongside their technological abilities," Tinnias replied, his voice a whisper so as not to be overheard.

"You can say that again."

Tinnias sniggered. "The look on your face when he said it was priceless."

"It was funny," a voice beside me whispered. I turned and looked into the gorgeous eyes of Byron.

I nodded and we both laughed as quietly as we could. "We need to have a conversation with Lomas," I said, "and soon. There's an awkward conflict going on and it's getting in the way."

"How do you mean?" Tinnias asked.

"He's in charge of this ship, and he's the King of these people. He's used to giving the orders and being obeyed without question. As guests here, we are obliged to be gracious and do as he says. He's not in charge of this case though, at least I hope he's not." I gave Tinnias a grave stare and he shook his head.

"Of course he isn't. We're the Detectives around here and we're in charge of anything to do with this case."

"I don't think he realises that," I replied. "He's used to being the head guy and taking his natural inclination to look down on the rest of us as uneducated savages who don't know our arses from our elbows. He's assuming he knows best and is trying to take over. I know there's a whole royal protocol minefield we're in here, but I'm quickly becoming extremely hacked off. I'm almost tempted to let him have the case and fuck off home. I don't need this pissing contest when my friend's safety is in danger."

"Please don't go," Byron said.

Tinnias moved between us and put a hand on each of our shoulders. "Now, boys, don't worry. Whatever happens here need not interfere with your personal life. You just need to decide that no matter how it goes, you're staying together. Don't let the case cross into areas of your lives where it doesn't belong okay?" We both nodded. "I know it's becoming awkward and I agree it needs to be discussed openly."

"Another thing too," I continued. "All this competitive stuff about who's a better friend to Tip, who knows him best, who has his best interests at heart. What the fuck's that shit about? I thought I was his friend too. Maybe I'm mistaken. I'll tell you something for free; I'm going to be a lot less free about giving my friendship to anyone from now on. People can get fucked, I'm going to live in a cave and be a recluse." Tinnias and Byron sniggered and I grinned. "I mean it."

"That means you'll be growing a beard, not washing, and wearing animal skins," Byron replied. "Oh, and shitting under a bush, don't forget that."

"Better make sure you don't sit on another Ganeda Weed," Tinnias added, "especially if you're buck ass naked under that fur pelt. You may be immune to the poison now but you're not immune to the pain of getting stung on the balls." I winced at the thought, then all three of us burst out laughing at the mental imagery of me, clad only in an ill-fitting animal hide, beard down to my chest, hopping around in agony with my balls on fire. Try as we might, we couldn't keep our laughter quiet.

"I'm delighted to see you back in good humour again," Lomas said. We turned and saw him standing behind us.

"Sorry, Sir," Tinnias said between sniggers.

"Don't apologise, Tinnias," Lomas smiled. "Humour is a great healer and I often think that if there were more of it, there might be less aggression. Are you ready to rejoin the debate?"

We sat and the discussion continued for a couple of hours. Throughout it all, Vincent continued to deny any knowledge of Tip being involved in anything untoward. Lomas and the rest of the Drycenians continued to believe Tip incapable of any criminal activity and Vincent of any deceit. Despite my anger at the way Lomas was handling the situation, I had lost the desire to fight and held myself back from the entire debate as much as I could. Quickly realising that it seemed I was losing interest in the case altogether; I chose not to argue even the most trivial points and kept my mouth shut. Only when specifically asked for my opinion did I bother to reply at all, and I kept my responses to a non committal shrug or nod of the head wherever possible. The most the party got out of me was an agreement that the level of weirdness was quite high. Byron had chosen to sit next to me and as my anguish grew, I felt his leg press against my own and it gave me considerable comfort. I pressed my own back in response and it helped us both to relax. Tinnias took his cue from me and mirrored my responses with similarly bland ones of his own, and I was pleased that I had two allies amongst this group.

As the voices droned on, I made a decision that I knew would do several things quite quickly. Firstly, it would undoubtedly piss the Drycenians off, which was fine by me. Secondly, it would enable me to get on and do something proactive, which was also fine by me. Third, it would allow me to do the job I'm good at, make the decisions I know are the right ones, and not have to spend hours debating weirdness levels with people who look down on me as nothing more than a troublesome insect. This was also fine by me and I decided to tell Tinnias when we went to bed. There was little doubt in my mind that he would be with me, he'd promised me his allegiance already, but even if he did go back on his word, I'd do it anyway. It was the right thing to do, for this case and my own sanity. Byron's reaction was a worry and I decided to make sure he knew and was confident in my love before I acted. He would still hurt, as would I, that was unfortunately unavoidable, but he would know I still loved him and our relationship had a chance of surviving.

My train of thought was interrupted by Lomas standing before me. I looked up to see him bending down, a glass in his hand.

"Are you still with us, Samelan?" He asked.

"Oh yeah, sorry, I was miles away."

"Some liquid refreshment? I promise it won't hurt."

I heard Toma laugh and I couldn't help but grin. I took the glass, looked at Toma, and made a show of raising the glass high and downing it in one. He roared with laughter and I heard several sniggers from around the room. When everyone finished their drink, Vincent looked at Lomas and smiled.

"Your Majesty, Farra and Kyle made me promise under threat of a painful death to invite you, Toma, Jam, and Byron to dinner this evening. I understand you're busy, but for my own safety I have to ask."

Lomas grinned. "We would be honoured to share your evening meal. Thank you for asking us. I'll let the chef know the four of us will be absent this evening and follow you down in a shuttle. Shall we meet in the shuttle bay in thirty minutes?"

"That sounds fine, Sir," Vincent replied.

I gripped Byron's hand and hoped no one else noticed. He squeezed back and I smiled into his lovely eyes.

"I love you," I mouthed silently. He smiled and nodded in response.

I turned to Tinnias, the grin that fought to split my face in half difficult to suppress. He caught the look and frowned.

"Perfect," I hissed. "That's one problem avoided." His frown deepened and I gave in to the desire to grin. "Fancy a swim and a sauna, Boss?"

He shrugged. "Sure thing."

I stood and cocked my head to the side, indicating for Tinnias to follow. He dutifully stood and we headed towards the door. Lomas was busy talking to the kitchen staff via the intercom and smiled as we approached.

"Sorry to leave you alone for the evening, my friends."

"No apology necessary, Sir," I replied. "Tinnias and I are going to make use of your swimming pool and sauna if we may."

"By all means, make yourselves completely at home. I've instructed the Chef to serve dinner at nine."

"Enjoy your evening. See you again soon."

I saw the barest hint of a frown threaten the King's brow, but a call from Toma interrupted before he could question me further. He turned towards his son and I took the opportunity to lead Tinnias out through the door and down the corridor. When we were safely back in our quarters, I sighed with relief.

"What's going on, Sam?"

"Pack your stuff," I commanded, then remembered that Tinnias is my boss as well as my father. "Sir."

"Pack?" he frowned. "Why? Are we leaving?"

"Yes. That's exactly what we're doing. At least that's what I'm doing. If you feel awkward about it and want to stay, that's up to you but I'm out of here the moment they've gone."

Several seconds of silence hung between us as we stared at each other before Tinnias nodded firmly and yanked open the cupboard door behind which were our cases. Within ten minutes, we were packed and sat down to wait for the King and his party to leave. I put my now full case back into the cupboard and told Tinnias to do the same.

"Just in case someone decides to come and visit before they leave. They don't need to know until they return from their little soiree."

"Talk to me, Son. I'm with you but I want to be informed. Hold out on them if you wish," he jabbed a thumb towards the door, "but don't hold out on me. We're a team, okay?"

I nodded. "Absolutely. I don't like all this debating about how they can't believe Tip would commit a crime, and as for all that shit about who's been a better friend, well I can certainly do without that. Maybe I have been deluding myself for the past six years and Tip and I aren't friends at all. I don't know but what I do know is that I'm going to be pulling back from him after this. I'll do the right thing by the Agency, first and foremost and friendship can go fuck itself. I don't need it and no longer want it."

"Please tell me you're not doing this just because your nose is out of joint," Tinnias said.

"My nose is out of joint, a little," I admitted. "But no, that's not why I'm doing it. I'm doing this because while they're sitting on their over entitled asses debating, I'm going, we're going, to be out there asking questions, finding shit out, and hunting down the truth. All this jockeying for position is getting in the way of solving this riddle. He can flounce around being profound all he wants, but he's not telling me how to do my own job and he sure as hell isn't taking charge of this case. No fucking way."

"Is this why you switched off during the second half of the meeting?" Tinnias asked.

I nodded. "Yeah. I made the decision within five minutes of sitting down after our break, so I couldn't see the need to take part and make him think I'm okay with what he's doing."

"I admit that it was beginning to worry me too," Tinnias said. "I was scared at the thought of the conversation I knew would have to happen soon. Who the hell wants to offend the Drycenians for fuck's sake?"

"Right, but we're law enforcers, Dad. Our priority is working this out according to Agency regulations not spending days listening to that lot debating about who has been a better friend to Tip Danso."

"There's something else pertinent to this, Son. Officially, you haven't been given this case. We could just go home, report what's happened, and leave it to those higher up the chain than me to make the decisions."

I pondered this point. He was right of course; he wouldn't have achieved such a high rank if he didn't have the ability to see things from as wide a viewpoint as possible. My law enforcer's instinct told me to get stuck in and work it out, but then realised that I had misread the depth of friendship I thought Tip and I shared. Knowing I had been taken for a fool tempered my instinct to sort out whatever trouble Tip has got himself into. He was no longer a friend in my eyes and as just another possibly dirty law enforcer who didn't even work at the same Agency outpost as myself, there would be other law enforcers closer to him who deserved the chance to bring him in. Another possibility occurred to me and I looked at Tinnias.

"We could head home via Tyrrin 4 and report this to the local Headquarters Commander. Tip is under his jurisdiction and his fellow law enforcers will want to be involved in bringing him in, if indeed he is dirty. We would've gone nuts if another outpost had tried to take control of the Rime case. We owe it to them really."

Tinnias thought about it and I allowed him the time to work out the legal protocol without interruption. Finally, he looked at me and nodded. "That would be the best thing to do, if we want to go strictly by the book with this."

"Which we should," I replied. "If we have a dirty law enforcer on our hands again, everything needs to be done right. The entire trail needs to be spotlessly clean or he could get off."

"The only thing that slightly bothers me about this course of action is what if he's not the only leak at Tyrrin 4 Headquarters? We could find ourselves reporting everything we know to someone who is also involved."

"And that someone would then know we know," I added.

"And we could lose our kneecaps."

"Once we're safely away from this ship, I'll call one of my contacts and ask him to find out if any other Tyrrin law enforcers are involved with the gang network. We'll know what to do then."

Tinnias nodded. "Okay, that will be useful to know."

Through the large porthole in the wall of our room, we watched the shuttle follow Vincent's ship down towards the surface of the beautiful green planet below us. I stood and yanked open the closet door.

"Time to go," I said, "after I've written a letter to Byron." I struggled with it for nearly a half hour until I finally decided I was satisfied. I read it to myself a couple of times to make sure I'd said everything I needed to say.

'Byron, My Love, hey, Bro.

Tinnias and I will be gone by the time you get this but please try not to worry. I must sort out this case, for my own sanity if nothing else and all this jockeying for position is getting in the way. Vincent is no help; I know that now and his attitude is really getting my balls in a knot. I need to tell you that no matter what the rest of Drycenia ends up thinking of me, I'll always love you and I beg you not to hate me. We promised each other and I intend to keep that promise. I hope our love doesn't cause problems for you with your colleagues, but if it does and you find you cannot cope with it, I'll try to understand. I'll be thinking about you every day, don't doubt that for a moment. When this is over, please call me, even if it's to tell me you never want anything more to do with me. Be safe, be happy, be sure of my love, always.

Sam.'

Tinnias took up his own case and followed me out of the door and along the corridor to the elevator.

"I hope the shuttle bay crew don't give us any trouble," he said as the elevator door closed silently.

"They can't imprison us here," I said. "We're the law, remember?"

Tinnias grinned. "It's a long time since I was a chase, catch, and deliver guy," he grinned. "This is the most fun I've had in years. I feel years younger already."

"Maybe you should resign your rank and team up with me then," I grinned back.

"Can you imagine how Grellina would react?" he replied. "She'd have my balls for breakfast."

The elevator door opened with an almost silent swish and we entered the shuttle bay waiting area. Several men in pristine white overalls stood together, studying a digital console readout and all looked surprised to see Tinnias and I, cases in hand, demanding our ship be prepared for take off.

"His Majesty didn't tell us you were leaving, Mr Sinclair."

"He's had a lot on his mind, with all the recent developments," I lied. "You know how distracted he gets when he's flustered."

The hint of a grin tickled the corner of his mouth and he nodded. "I wondered why you were not joining them for the trip down to Lilea."

"You'd make a great detective," I grinned. "Is she ready to go?" I nodded towards the door that led into the huge shuttle bay. "Time is of the essence."

"Of course, forgive me," he said and opened the door. "Go right ahead and I'll have you on your way within a few minutes."


The battle cruiser shrank and disappeared as I flipped my ship into auto pilot and headed her away from Lilean airspace. Relief flooded through me as I looked around my ship and allowed her humble and familiar energy to re energise me.

"Thank the gods we're away from them," I said. "Any longer and I'd have gone stark staring mad." Tinnias laughed and I grinned. "Come on, I'll make up the extra bunk for you. It's not as swanky as the Drycenians' ship but it has everything we'll need to be comfortable."

Once Tinnias was unpacked and his bunk made up, we got ourselves a drink from my Nutri-Vend and sat down to make the call to my contact. He answered on the second ring.

"Hello again, Sam. Is everything okay?"

"I'm sorry to bother you again so soon but you're the only one I can call on for this."

"Hey, no problem. What are friends for huh? What do you need?"

"I need to know if there are any more leaks from the Tyrrin 4 Law Enforcement Headquarters. Especially within the higher ranks."

"Right, give me an hour and I'll get back to you."

"Thanks a lot." I hung up the call and looked at Tinnias. "Now we sit and wait until he calls back."

"I'd love to be a fly on the wall when the Drycenians get back and find us gone," Tinnias grinned.

"I hope Byron doesn't hate me," I said sadly.

Tinnias put an arm around my shoulders. "Now, Son, give him some credit. He's a grown man and wouldn't have told you how he felt if he wasn't sure about it. As you now know, once you're in love, you can't just switch it off."

"I guess you're right," I admitted. "It's just so new. I've waited years for him and now this could fuck it up before it's had a chance to begin."

"And he's waited for you just as long. Trust him, huh? I would love to see Lomas' reaction when they return though."

I laughed at the mental image. "Yeah that would be a laugh. Lomas would flap his arms around like he does when he's stressed, his robes fluttering behind him as he races along the corridors yelling our names." I got up and demonstrated and Tinnias roared with laughter.

"He'd be like, Samelan, Tinnias, oh where are you, my friends? What have we done? We swore to be at their side in their hour of need, we must race after them. Show us the meaning of haste." Tinnias' impersonation of Lomas' voice was almost perfect and I laughed so hard my stomach ached.

"I never knew you were such a good mimic," I said when I had some control over my laughter. "That's fucking brilliant."

Tinnias grinned. "I have many talents, Son. Stick with me, boy, and you might just discover a few of 'em." His voice now had a guttural quality that was vaguely familiar and I frowned.

"That's from a movie, I'm sure of it," I said as I searched my brain.

"The Monster From The Black Hole," Tinnias announced. "The old guy with the walking stick."

"Of course," I grinned. "I love that movie. That talent could come in mighty useful in this job you know," I said. "I might just be asking you to make a few calls before this business is sorted."

"If it can help, then sure thing. They're bound to call us you know. The Drycenians I mean. Once they return and find us gone, they'll be begging us to go back."

"Not if I block their numbers," I said, fiddling with my Unicom. When I was finished, I smiled. "There, now they'll just get 'number unidentified' when they try to call. If they can't call me, they can't trace us … oh shit."

"What's up?" Tinnias demanded.

"What do you bet they fitted some kind of tracker while we weren't looking?"

Tinnias sighed, then rose from his seat. "I'll take the cargo hold and shuttle bay, you do the cockpit and other areas. We'll do outside together. Where's your gear?"

Three hours later, we struggled out of the space suits and got ourselves a drink. Between us we tore the ship apart and found several components I knew didn't belong. One was attached to my auto pilot, which I guessed would tell them our route. Another was attached to the covert stealth modulator which allows me to remain invisible to scanners. I realised this was probably placed in order that their own scanners could detect me even when the unit is functioning. What looked like high-end cameras were placed in several locations, and some sort of locator beacon had been attached to my communications aerial on the outside of the ship. I was relieved to notice that none of them appeared able to record audio. At least they hadn't heard our conversation so far.

Tinnias looked at the haul of components and blew out a breath. "Wow, they're thorough, I'll give them that much. They're obviously determined to know what we're up to. I wonder why that should be."

"It does seem unlike them," I replied. "From the little experience I had of them last time, they came across as being unwilling to get involved to such a proactive degree. When they do get involved, they were efficient and thorough, but they fixed their attentions on the bad guys. Why are they going to such lengths to surveil me? That's the bit that's odd."

"It's as if we're the bad guys here," Tinnias remarked and I nodded.

"Which we're not, obviously," I replied. "Unless of course they're more involved than they're letting on."

"Involved how? Like involved in finding Tip or involved with the gang network?"

I shrugged. "I don't know. I would hope it's not the latter, but I'm not going to assume anything just because of the legends and myths surrounding them. There's always the possibility that they're not quite as benign as they make themselves out to be. However unlikely, it could all be an elaborate cover."

"Imagine the public furore it would cause if it got out that the Drycenians are really leaders of a galaxy wide gang network."

I couldn't help but laugh at the thought. "It would certainly make our careers."

"Or seal our death warrants," Tinnias replied. "They're powerful people despite keeping themselves private like they do. Their technology alone puts them in a position of advantage. If they do turn out to be the bad guys, the galaxy is screwed."

"Come back Transmortals, all is forgiven," I remarked and Tinnias nodded.

"Indeed. At least they were open about their evil intentions. Everyone knew where they stood with those assholes. The Drycenians though, they're in a different league entirely and we are justified in being terrified of their true intentions."

Before I could reply, my Unicom beeped. I checked the screen before answering and was pleased to see the familiar number of my contact.

"Sam?"

"Hi. Do you have anything for me?"

"Yes. I've found three law enforcers based at Tyrrin 4 Headquarters connected with the gang network. Two of them, Tip and a guy named Detective Anhil Lyemark are Gaht leaks. Senior Detective Moyd Barak is allied to The Dankera Collective. There could be others too of course, but these are the ones I've found."

"Shit," I hissed, dismayed at this news.

"There's something else you might want to be aware of, Sam."

"What's that?"

"The head guy there, Commander Ranil Taiko, was kidnapped late last night while on his way home from work."

"Holy fuck," I exclaimed and shot a look at Tinnias who sat open mouthed before me, his wide eyes unwilling to accept this grave news. "Who took him? Do we know?"

"No one has claimed responsibility yet. His wife called his office when she woke up this morning and noticed he hadn't returned home. A warrant was issued and a search ensued. They found his hover car abandoned behind a disused vehicle refuelling stop. This news hasn't got to the media yet by the way. I have a civilian contact there who told me about it."

"Thank you for this, I appreciate you putting yourself out for me. Give my love to the family."

"I will, and you must come to dinner when you're in the neighbourhood."

"I'll look forward to it."


Tinnias and I discussed this grave turn of events for hours before mental exhaustion forced us to bed. We decided to avoid returning to Tyrrin 4 and possibly giving valuable insight and information to the wrong people. There was no way either of us felt it right to return home to Sigma Prime and leave the situation alone. Our problem was what we should do. Both of us felt there was no one we felt comfortable trusting and the weight of the problem became all the heavier because of this new and frightening loneliness.

I was of the opinion that the obvious thing to do was go undercover but Tinnias wasn't keen. He felt the dangers were too great, especially as we were both working the case unofficially and could therefore expect no back up from the Agency. We argued about it for a while, but our discussion ended peacefully when we agreed that, so far at least, it was our only option. Due to Tip's involvement with Gaht, I suggested we concentrate first on staking out The Dankera Collective. The two law enforcement leaks didn't know either of us and our cover would be relatively safe. Tinnias reluctantly agreed and suggested we make like tourists, at least until we knew our way around and had some firm leads to follow.

"I don't suppose you brought any fake identification with you, did you?" I asked.

"I never travel without it," Tinnias smiled.

"Wonderful. I'll lay in a course for Dankera."

"I'll do some research about the place so we know what tourists usually look for," Tinnias said. He got up and went over to my research console. "Okay, let's see what we can find. Let's hope the weather is good this time of year. Okay, here we go. The place has quite a presence on the Galactic Web, there are plenty of articles and advertisements."

"Advertisements?" I frowned. "For what?"

"Water sports mainly. It seems Dankera is famous as a centre of excellence for water sports. There's only one landmass on the planet so most of it is ocean. The Dankerans decided long ago to devote their time, energy, and resources, into finding ways to make use of this resource and have got quite a name for themselves for their water sports centres and their floating cities too."

"Floating cities?"

Tinnias nodded as he continued scanning the screen. "They are renowned for their expertise in the design and building of floating platforms of all sizes and for many different uses. Their fusion reactors are all built on floating islands, as are all manufacturing plants over a certain size. This keeps the landmass from becoming marred by ugly buildings and allows them to keep it for residential purposes."

"Sounds sensible to me," I remarked. "If you have such a large amount of open ocean, why not make use of it if you can?"

"They have a large floating city called Coma Sita, which is being used as a continuing and ongoing working experiment. People live and work there just as normal, and their scientists continuously monitor how the building functions, test its safety features, check for damage etcetera. If the monitoring proves satisfactory after fifty years of continuous use by the population and no ill effects from the ocean are apparent, they intend to build more and have set up a committee that will be available to those on other worlds who might want to do something similar. The experiment has another eighteen years to run."

"Sounds like they're sitting on a fortune," I said and Tinnias nodded.

"It's late Autumn on Dankera at the moment, so the weather will be windy with frequent showers."

"Not ideal for water sports enthusiasts like ourselves, is it?" I said. "Don't they have any indoor touristy stuff?"

"Not especially. There are the usual things like museums and art galleries, concerts and dances but nothing that would be a draw to anyone from across the galaxy."

"Why don't we rent a place and if anyone asks, say we're just finding out what the place is like as we're thinking of buying a place for you to emigrate to when you retire."

"That's a good idea," Tinnias replied as he read yet another advertisement. "Oh wait, it seems this company here, Dankera Painters Cottages, hires out little places for people who like to paint. There's quite a little industry in fine art and it's quite well known amongst the painter crowd as being good for landscapes. Apparently, the trees are quite something."

"Oh well," I smiled. "I guess we're learning to paint."

"How long until we get there?" Tinnias asked.

"Forty six hours at top speed."

"Then I vote we start practicing first thing in the morning. Do you have any paints aboard?"

"I do actually. I took some stock from a guy in lieu of payment for services rendered. He didn't have the money so I kept the stock, intending to sell it on. He was quite an artist but was found out as a forger of famous artworks and had to disappear quickly. That's why I didn't get my money, he left town before paying up. There's all sorts down in the hold."

Tinnias grinned. "Services rendered? Dare I ask what kind of services you provided?"

"Get your mind out of the gutter, Dad," I laughed. "He was a contact and sometimes, when his artwork sales slowed, I would go on to the Galactic Web posing as a gallery owner and fine art dealer and express great interest in his stuff, a willingness to pay whatever he asked for a particular painting, shit like that. It got people interested and his sales often went up. It was my way of repaying him for the time and help he gave me."

"You realise that's a crime, don't you, Son?" Tinnias grinned. "Oh the shame," he placed a hand dramatically across his brow and sighed. "My son, a criminal. What will I tell his mother?"

I'm going to get some sleep for a few hours. See you in the morning. This is Sinclair V-Log Q890/M data log reference point 4136902/617.

## CHAPTER EIGHT

This is Sinclair V-Log Q890/M data log reference point 4136902/618 continuing report.

The wind on Dankera was relentless. Icy daggers found their way inside our clothing no matter how many layers we put on. The continuous frigid torment had my ears frozen almost solid within twenty minutes and drove tears from my eyes which stuck my eyelashes together into a solid line of ice. By the time we'd walked from the parking lot to the shabby hotel room we were forced to rent when we found out all the cottages for hire were booked, both of us were shivering to our bones. Having tossed a coin and won the shower, I wound the gauge up to maximum and stepped in. Tinnias filled the bath and sighed with pleasure when he climbed in and sank up to his neck.

"I thought you said it was autumn here," I said.

"That's what the tourist information said on the Galactic Web," he replied.

"I dread to think what the winters are like here then."

"I sincerely hope we don't have to find out," Tinnias grinned. "It's cold enough here to wither your ball sack in ten minutes flat. It's a good job Grellina and I don't want any more children."

Our guffaws echoed in the tiled room and I decided that despite the gravity of the situation we had found ourselves caught up in, having Tinnias with me was going to lighten the mood considerably. I had never worked a case with him before, the closest I ever got was when we were working the Rime case back home on Sigma Prime. That was a different situation though; we were on our home ground, based in the headquarters building and several other detectives worked the case with us. Here it was just him and me on our own and I knew it was not only going to be fun but would strengthen the bond we share. It sounds a bit weird but having him working the case with me also made me acutely aware of how lonely my job can be. I knew it would take me a while to get used to working alone again when this case was over and done with. Once back to normal, I'd have to go back to being the anti-social chase, catch, and deliver guy that nobody wants at their party. There's always a price to pay for happiness and I realised that there really is no such thing as a free lunch. Even if my relationship with Byron did survive this, I still had to work and so did he. There would still be long periods of time spent alone and missing him.

During our journey from Lilea 4, Tinnias called a couple of his own contacts and discovered that there had still been no claims of responsibility for Commander Taiko's kidnap. We both knew this was odd, given our combined experience that told us those responsible almost always make their claim known within a few hours. Another contact furnished him with the address of the Dankera Collective's base of operations and what little was known about its leader. We decided to act like tourists while we scoped out the area and got to know the lie of the land. Having to hole up in the hotel room meant we were in the city centre, which was not conducive to staking out the Collective's base, which was in an isolated location to the North East of the city. A quick shopping trip furnished us with not only warm hats, scarves, and gloves, but also a map of the city and its environs, which we studied for an hour before going to the hotel diner for a meal.

"I reckon it's a couple of mile hike from here to the boundary of their base," Tinnias said.

I nodded. "Easily. Shit, we could be sitting out there for days."

"Want to go back to that store and get some thermal underwear, Son?"

We laughed, and I seriously contemplated doing just that.

Tinnias pointed to the map. "What's that symbol mean?" I looked at the area within the Collective's boundary and frowned.

"I've no idea," I replied as I looked at the map, the X topped with three wavy lines. "It could be anything. Wiggly lines could mean water I suppose. Maybe there's a river there."

Tinnias shook his head. "The map doesn't show one. It could mean steam too, perhaps there's a volcanic blow hole."

I laughed aloud. "They smell like sulphur don't they? So, we're going to be frozen solid and stinking like rotten eggs. Nice. It looks kind of like a Heinan's asshole don't you think? Maybe there's a herd of them there."

Now it was Tinnias' turn to roar with laughter. "Isn't there a list of symbols on the back somewhere?"

I turned the paper over and grinned. "It's a campfire symbol. It's obvious when you think about it."

"There's a camp ground there." Tinnias exclaimed. "So, we hire a pitch and watch from there."

I nodded. "First thing in the morning, we go back to the ship and do a bit more research on my console. We can find out what there is for campers up there."

"Good thinking, Son."

We agreed that it would sound more plausible if we booked a pitch for a couple of days ahead rather than say we wanted one right away. The cost was reasonable, so we booked for two weeks starting from two days ahead. This would give us time to get stocked up with food and any other essentials we would need to make our stay comfortable. The ship would give us warm shelter and a reliable bathroom, but we would need to cook on an open fire unless we were prepared to live on Nutri-Vend.

We made several shopping trips and stocked the cargo hold with food, several changes of warm clothing, and some weatherproof panelling units that would make a semi enclosed outside area to shield both of us and our fire from the ever present horizontal wind and keep us dry should it rain. We paid extra and got the deluxe insulated panelling units with integral windows and lockable screen door, at Tinnias' insistence. He paid and would claim it on expenses when we got home.

The night before our relocation to the camp ground, we checked our inventory and discussed our plan of action for the stakeout.

"We need a cover story," Tinnias said. "We're bound to get talking to our camping neighbours and they're bound to ask about us and our lives. We need to agree a back story."

I nodded. "Okay. How about the two of us are going into business together? We're going to start our own security for hire company and are scouting several planets looking for the ideal place to base our new company. We're both ex-military and security, and with me being single and you recently widowed, we decided to start afresh with something new. We can't share a military history but we could share a work history in security."

"I was your Supervisor for the security firm we worked for," Tinnias suggested and I nodded.

"Right, and with our combined savings, together with the results of wise investments, we found ourselves with enough money to branch out on our own."

"Sounds fine to me, well done, Son."

We were allocated a camping spot situated on a slight rise that conveniently overlooked what we were told was the campsite owner's private compound. Thankfully screened by a stand of trees to the rear, we were sheltered from the worst of the wind. Our nearest camping neighbours were a hundred metres or so away, so we didn't feel too overlooked. I parked the ship between ourselves and the view of the compound so as not to be obviously spying and arranged one of my ship's external cameras to do the spying for us. With the weather being a little inclement, remaining inside the ship to monitor the camera's feed was not a problem. With a few clicks on the console, a motion detection module in the camera's mounting bracket would notify us when anyone was moving around down there. This would save us the need to watch the screen day and night.

During our first evening, our nearest camping neighbours sauntered over and introduced themselves and despite it being something of a nuisance having to do the social thing when we had a job to do, they were a nice couple and gave us some interesting information.

"Have you met the manager yet?" the husband, a small thin man named Deetling asked.

"Not yet," Tinnias replied.

"You will do soon. He always comes and introduces himself to new campers within a day of their arrival. He's a nice enough guy, if a little nosy."

"Nosy?" I asked.

"Yeah," Deetling nodded and exchanged a look with his wife, a waif like creature called Aflanka. Both grinned. "He always seems very interested in your background, how you earn your living, your general belief system etcetera. If you don't want him to know your shit, just lie. We did."

"Thanks for the warning," I said. "We can have some fun with him I reckon."

"How so?" Deetling asked.

"I'll fire a few pointed questions of my own and see how forthcoming he is about himself. Either that or I'll make sure my answers are a little strange. That usually sorts out the nosy ones."

Our new friends exchanged another grin. "I can't wait to hear how that conversation goes," Deetling smiled.

Sure enough, when Dankera's twin moons were high in the sky, Tinnias spied a figure approaching. "Looks like the interrogation is about to begin.

Remember we're here to do a job so don't put yourself across as too weird or he's likely to kick us out."

I sniggered and went to meet him. "Hello there," I said as I extended a hand and smiled broadly.

"Evening gentlemen, I trust you've settled in okay." He looked to be in his early thirties and appeared what you might call, a little rough around the edges. He was friendly enough, dressed in smart casual attire, but there was an overall sense of him being the type who always manages to look a little unkempt. His hair was a little too greasy, his chin a little too stubbly, and I noticed the knees of his pants were wearing thin.

"We have, thank you," Tinnias smiled as he too, extended a hand.

"I'm Lunde, the campsite manager. I have a couple of documents for you here." He handed over two small pieces of paper. "One is a list of general rules and regulations, nothing too awful I assure you. Just the usual sort of thing to make sure we keep our licence and don't fall foul of the authorities. The other one is a list of what's available to tourists, both here on site and in the local area. We have a social evening once a week during the season to which all campers are welcomed. There'll be a bar and some food laid on, some music and dancing if you're into that sort of thing. It's only ten credits per person. Just pay on the door if you decide to come along. It starts at eight and goes on until everyone looks bored or drunk. The details are on the sheet."

"Sounds like fun, thanks," Tinnias replied.

"So what brings you to our humble world?"

"We're going into business together," I replied, "and we're taking some time out to scout around for the best place to set up as our base."

"What business are you in?"

"Security. We worked together for years, for another company of course and we decided that we wanted to be our own boss for a change, so we pooled our resources and here we are."

"Security eh?" Lunde replied. "Reliable security for hire is a good business to be in. You shouldn't find it too hard to make even a reasonable success of it. It depends on where you decide to set up shop of course. Where else are you planning to visit?"

"We've considered Lilea 4," Tinnias replied, "but that wasn't suitable as they like to sort their own security, and premises are very expensive for off worlders. Nice place though, beautiful. We also looked into setting up shop on Sigma Prime, but there are already a lot of security firms there all vying for the same customers. We don't mind where we go if it means the pickings are easier. We went to Tyrrin 4 and almost decided there and then but someone told us the place is quite tightly controlled by a gang network. We don't want to have to deal with any of that shit; neither of us is getting any younger and we just want to run a successful business for a few years, make a handsome profit on our outlay, and retire in comfort. We're probably going to visit Deligon 2, Solar 3 and 4 are maybes, Regnor Prime is a definite candidate, and Corroptima 8 is a possible. After that, if we don't find something that grabs us, we'll do some more research and extend our list."

"You went to Sigma?" Lunde asked and we nodded. "I visited there once. Nice place."

"So how long have you been here?" I asked. "Have you always worked in tourism?"

"I'm Dankeran by birth," he replied, "although much of my childhood was spent moving around rather a lot for father's work. I always wanted to be the boss of my own company but I could never decide what sort of company that would be. When father settled back here and opened this site up, I asked if I could help run it and he thought it was a good idea. He can enjoy the benefits without having to do any of the work and I get valuable experience in a managerial position. I'm still young enough to have that company one day."

"Very sensible way of doing things," Tinnias remarked. "If you have enough passion and drive, you'll be surprised what you can achieve. It's never too late to realise a dream."

"Exactly," Lunde smiled. "Well it's a pleasure to meet you both and I hope to see you at our little gathering. Goodnight."

"Goodnight," Tinnias and I chorused.


We spent over an hour trying, and failing, to find details of Lunde on the Galactic Web but were surprised and dismayed to find nothing. This was very odd and put us both on alert immediately. Everyone has some kind of presence on the Web, even just a birth notification but not Lunde.

"It's as if he doesn't exist," I said.

"Which means either he employs a very talented computer hacker who has erased him from every digital media in existence, or he's using twin aliases."

"Lunde is obviously the non existent twin, used for verbal communication, so no wonder it's nowhere on the web. It might not even be a name, it could be Dankeran for fart, or he could've just made up the word."

Tinnias sniggered and nodded. "And we've probably little chance of finding out the name of the live twin, which might even be his real name. We need one of those computer geniuses you mentioned."

"I happen to know such computer geniuses do exist," I replied. "I have one as a contact."

"Would he be able to find out if Lunde has been erased from the web?"

"There's only one way to find out," I said, reaching into my pocket for my Unicom. The call was answered quickly and I recognised my contact's voice. "Hi, it's Sinclair. Is it convenient to talk?"

"Sam? How ya doing, man? It's been ages."

"I'm still alive and kicking. How about you?"

"Me too. How can I help my favourite law enforcer today?"

"Is it possible to tell if someone has erased all their details from the entire galactic web?"

I heard him blow out a long breath and guessed the prospect seemed unlikely. "Wow, that's one heck of a task but yeah, it's achievable. Unlikely but doable."

"Why unlikely?" I asked.

"Because it's a very long and complicated job; one that would cost a king's ransom. If someone wants to disappear from public notice, it's far easier and cheaper to assume a new identity. Fake documents are easy to come by, anyone can have a new identity within a few days. The sort of job you're talking about would take weeks and would need constantly updating."

"How come?"

"Because everywhere we go and everything we do is monitored these days. We give a DNA and retinal scan when we travel, buy a home, get married, go to hospital, get employment or start a business. Our photograph is taken every time we enter a store, a public building, use public transportation, or have a beer in a bar. You can't move without being monitored in at least two ways. The results of that monitoring are held on computer systems, many of which are shared with other public safety bodies, law enforcement, you name it, your name is on it. I would have to re scan the entire network on a weekly basis and continually erase all those entries. I can erase everything about you from the day you were born up until now but the moment you enter a bar tomorrow, make a Unicom call from an unsecured line, use a galactic credit card, or anything else we all do every day, you're back on the web."

"Okay, that makes sense. Our guy is obviously using an alias then. But then how come the alias doesn't appear on the web? Surely everything you've just told me would mean he can hide his true identity but not his alias."

"There you have me at a loss, Sam. That is weird and the only thing I can think of is that he's using twins. Give me his name and any details you have and I'll see what I can come up with. I can't promise it'll be much though."

"Thanks, I appreciate this," I replied and gave him what little we knew of Lunde. "Anything at all is more than we have."

"In case I need more information, are you likely to be meeting this man again?"

"Yeah, why?"

"Do you have any micro monitoring devices you could use when you see him again? If you can get a photo or a recording of his voice it opens up another couple of avenues for me."

"No problem," I replied. "We'll be seeing him again the night after tomorrow at some kind of social get together. I'll call you right after and send you what I get."

"Okay, that would be helpful. By the way, just out of interest, who is, we?"

"Oh sorry, I have my boss with me on this case. Tinnias Vaylo."

"Okay that's fine. If you trust him, I know I can. I'll work with what you've given me and wait for you to send me some photos or a voice recording in two days."


Never had I been so keen to attend a party and do the social thing as I was on Dankera 7. Tinnias and I spent several hours the next day working out as much of a plan as we felt able, given the unknown nature of the event. We each exchanged a shirt button with tiny cameras that would record audio as well as vidicom footage. I would also carry a small device I was given by a contact, that can 'see' the energy signals given off by security devices, cameras and the like. The feeds from these would be relayed back to my ship and recorded, for us to peruse later. We would arrive together, then split up and mingle, visit the bathroom, talk to as many people as we could, and see as much of the environment and buildings as we could.

"It says on the sheet Lunde gave us that no weapons are allowed. We're to be given a pat down on entry," Tinnias said.

"We could strap a small weapon to the inside of our thighs," I said.

"Son, walking like you've shit yourself may look cool on actors in those movies you love, but not for middle aged law enforcers. Besides, you may be happy to drop your pants in order to defend yourself, but I'm certainly not. Have you ever tried running away with your pants around your ankles?"

Despite the stress of the situation bearing down upon us, we laughed at the mental imagery Tinnias' comment brought to our minds and we spent the next few minutes demonstrating the problem to each other and roaring with laughter.

"I could just see the news broadcast now," Tinnias said. "Law Enforcement Commander caught with his pants round his ankles at a party organised by The Dankera Collective."

"Ouch," I replied and winced. "I get your point. I guess if it comes to a fight, we'll have to talk our way out of it or resort to using our fists. How long is it since you punched anyone?"

Tinnias looked thoughtful for a moment, before I noticed a smile tickle the corners of his mouth. "About eight months, give or take."

My jaw dropped in shock. "So recently? What was that about?"

"You, actually."

"Me? How?"

"Someone made a disrespectful comment about you adopting us, being the boss's pet, you know the sort of thing."

"Who was it?"

"Never mind that. It was a fellow law enforcer, that's all I'm going to say. I told him if he wanted to make something of it to meet me outside of work. Truthfully, I wasn't expecting him to but he did so we sorted it out the old fashioned way."

We looked at each other without speaking for long seconds before I could formulate a suitable reply that would accurately convey my feelings. "Thank you, for defending me, us, and I'm sorry our relationship caused a problem."

Tinnias shook his head. "It isn't a problem, then or now or at any time in the future. We both went back to work the next day and had a long conversation. I told him a few home truths and he admitted to having some unresolved shit from his own family environment. We shook hands, declared the matter closed to our mutual satisfaction, and moved on."

"Wow," I exclaimed. "I never expected that, although I probably should have. People are bound to think you give me preferential treatment."

"I do," Tinnias laughed. "But not to the detriment of the job, and not overtly. I don't flaunt you in front of anyone, but I refuse to be extra hard on you simply because I'm now your Dad. That would serve only to make you resent me and I'd rather our colleagues resented me than you did."

I nodded. "I have wondered why you don't seem to be extra hard on me in front of our colleagues. I guess I expected it. I hope I would handle it in a healthy way but I know myself well enough to be able to say with some conviction that I'd find it difficult not to bite back."

"We can do without personal stress adding to our burden. The job provides enough on its own."


The night of the social event arrived and we set off towards the compound. A few other campers sauntered ahead of us and I was glad we would not be the first to arrive. A gate separated the campsite from the owner's compound and a couple of burly security guards patted us down before allowing us through. Another two stood across the main path that led through another gate and in to the main compound and herded us across to a large barn ahead from which we heard music and excited chatter. Scanning the area as we walked, it looked like the main compound was fenced off from the barn by wicked looking laser fences, beyond which I saw what looked like a house and several large outbuildings. I couldn't see what lay beyond the barn but I supposed the fence carried on around to completely seal it off from the main compound. We were delighted to notice several seating areas outside the barn, a couple of which already had occupants and I decided that at some point in the evening, we would want some fresh air. This would give me an opportunity to scan the compound for anything interesting. Thankfully it was a warm evening.

The barn itself consisted of one huge room with a bar across one end. A dancing area occupied the very middle of the room and tables filled the space around. At the other end were four bathrooms, a medic's office, and a security room marked, No Entry – Security Personnel Only. Reaching into my pocket, I switched on the little gizmo that would notify me of the presence of any security devices and leaned in to Tinnias.

"I'll take the two left hand bathrooms, you take the two right hand ones."

He nodded. "Beer? Better stick to something light. We don't want to be blind drunk."

I grinned. "Beer is fine. They probably won't have Kambino, so I'll have whatever you're having."

The beer tasted suspiciously like it had been well watered down and I tried not to make a face.

"No chance of getting drunk tonight then," Tinnias hissed in my ear and I grinned.

"Not a chance in hell."

"Okay then, one drink then we split up and mingle. I'll take the area from the bar to the dance floor, you take the back end up to the bathrooms."

"Then we go outside for some fresh air," I suggested and he nodded.


With a nod to Tinnias, we split up and went to mingle with our fellow campers. There was quite a crowd by this time, so I was not short of choice. For the next two hours I listened to life stories, relayed my own fake one, looked at photos of people's kids, ex-spouses, deceased relatives, holiday homes and feigned interest in their jobs and beliefs. A few were regular visitors and one man had been holidaying at this campsite every year for the past fifteen. He told me that some of the people at our little soiree were from the main compound and warned me to watch out what I said around them.

"Have you seen the little green badge some of the people are wearing?" I hadn't taken that much notice so I shook my head. "Those are compound folks. Between you and me, I reckon they're here to recruit for a cult or something."

"What makes you say that?" I asked with genuine interest.

"Because they'll latch on to someone sometimes, spend all evening with 'em and not talk to anyone else. They buy 'em drinks and then they'll go off somewhere together. The next year I come back and that person is now wearing a green badge and pretending to mingle, much like you're doing only not as well."

He looked me right in the eyes, raised one eyebrow, and smiled. My stinging cheeks let me down yet again and he sniggered. I couldn't help but snigger along with him to disguise my embarrassment. "Why do I always meet someone like you at times like these?" I asked.

He laughed aloud. "Because you're blessed, Son. Now tell me, where are you camped? I'll drop by tomorrow and we can compare notes."

The bathrooms provided me with little of interest other than a couple of Greenies, as I decided to call them, both of whom stopped talking when I entered and watched me intently as I thoroughly washed my hands, checked my hair, and adjusted my shirt before leaving. As I left the second bathroom, I passed a pretty young woman who sported a green badge pinned to the low neckline of her dress. Thinking quickly, I smiled at her and said hello, allowing my eyes to linger a moment too long to let her know I found her interesting if she was up to a fumble out the back of the barn. To my complete surprise, she grinned back and looked me up and down, the slight twitch of her eyebrows telling me she approved of what she saw.

It took me two drinks to get her out the back and up against a tree and by the time my hand found its way inside her panties, she was telling me I should stay on Dankera and find work so we could, 'get together at weekends.' The fumble was as reasonable as could be expected, hurried as it was by the threat of discovery and the difficulty I had manoeuvring through those tight panties, but there was no way I would emigrate here just to feel her up. Before the Domenico case, I would've happily fucked her to get the information but now the thought horrified me. Not only did it serve to teach me just how committed I was to Byron, but it made me realise that I had indeed been trying to be someone I wasn't designed to be.

"What is there here for me, apart from you?" I asked, kissing her hard on the lips in an effort to make her believe she would be enough.

"You could join us, join our group. You being here would make it much more fun."

"What group is that? What do they do?" I hissed as her body began to convulse.

She was too busy with her orgasm to answer me.

# CHAPTER NINE

"I'll bet you a hundred your finger didn't help us as much as the half hour I spent dancing with that wrinkled old bag in the purple," Tinnias grinned.

"You're on," I laughed. "That gal told me we should join their group. When I asked her what the group does, she said they're an unofficial crime fighting group who use political pressure and peaceful demonstration to effect changes in the law. The leader's name is Yanit and his dream is a unified and peaceful Dankeran System. Just to be sure we were talking about the same group, I asked her if her group had a name and she said it's called The Collective."

Tinnias nodded and grinned. "Get your hundred out, Son, you owe me."

I laughed. "Oh come on, I worked hard for that. It was like beating a dead fish. I deserve a medal."

"It's good, but not nearly good enough. Wrinkly told me that the owner of this site, a man called Yanit, wants us out of here by first light."

This stunned me and it showed by my wide eyed expression and the way my mouth flapped. "What the fuck?"

Tinnias nodded. "Apparently, he knows we're law enforcement and our real names. He assures us that he had nothing to do with Commander Taiko's kidnap, and he feels that our presence here might be viewed by Gaht as a provocative gesture, should they find out. He is convinced they will find out too; apparently, they have spies everywhere. He asks us, politely, to leave by first light and assures us that if we do so, we'll not encounter any hassle from them. If we remain here, we're fair game."

"Shit," I exclaimed. "You win. You'll have your hundred." I sat down and ran a hand through my hair. "What are we to do? Do we leave or stay and fight?"

"I think we should wait until we hear what Yanit has to say for himself, don't you?"

"What do you mean?" I frowned.

"He's coming here to meet with us; he should be here within the hour." Tinnias saw my puzzled expression and grinned. "I told old wrinkly that I think it only polite that the man in charge comes and tells us himself. She disappeared for a few minutes and when she returned, she confirmed he would come here at one o clock in the morning."

"Dad, I'm seriously impressed."

"Makes your fumble up against a tree seem a little lame doesn't it?" he grinned.

"Totally, I replied.

Before he could reply, a shadow stepped into view a little way across the campsite, flanked by two other shadows a little behind. Tinnias and I exchanged a look.

"He has two heavies with him," I said quietly.

"I'll take the left one if need be," Tinnias said.

"Okay. What are you carrying?"

"Number three sedative darts, you?"

"The same."


I was a little surprised at the man who stepped into the pool of dim light that spilled from the hatch of my ship. He looked young, despite being in his early sixties and so clean looking that he could've just stepped from the shower. His skin shone and I got a mental image of a little boy of eight being forcibly scrubbed by an irate mother. The inch or so height advantage I had over him afforded me a good view of his hair, which had been slicked back with some cream. It was a harsh look and did him no favours, but I supposed it was a deliberate attempt to look harder. Having what some describe as a vain streak myself, I had to admit that there are some places where looking young is a disadvantage. I found myself wondering what his cohorts thought of being ruled over by something resembling a pre-pubescent child.

"Yanit, I presume?" Tinnias said as he extended a hand.

The man smiled and shook Tinnias' proffered hand. "Commander Vaylo." He then looked at me and extended a hand, which I felt compelled to shake. "Detective Sinclair-Vaylo."

Tinnias indicated towards the open hatch. "Come on in and have a hot drink."

"Thank you."

Once the initial pleasantries were out of the way and hot drinks served. I leaned forward and addressed our guest. "We've been led to believe that you wish us to leave."

He nodded. "Yes, I think that would be a good idea. Don't get me wrong, Detective, this is not a personal slight to either of you in any way. What with the way things are between ourselves and Gaht, for us to be seen to be entertaining law enforcers who aren't here on official business could be seen as a provocative move. I have no wish to start a gang war. My ultimate desire is to unify the larger gang networks into a single, unified force all working together as overseers of government policies and as a focus of unification for the ordinary man in the street who often feels he has no voice."

"Did you kidnap Commander Taiko?" I asked.

"No. Such an act would not serve the aims and objectives of The Collective at this time."

"Do you know who did?"

"Not for certain. Oh the rumour mill even reaches to these grey distant hills, but nothing definite."

"Was it Gaht?"

Yanit looked me right in the eyes and I noticed a new sharpness to the creases that played at the corners. He was annoyed at me pushing and would not be forthcoming with anything more of value. "I don't know, Detective. Like I said, I know nothing but rumours and I'm not one for passing on what may turn out to be an untruth that could, ultimately, cost lives."

Although we had nothing to go on but his word, I knew he was telling the truth when he said The Collective hadn't kidnapped the Commander. Remaining on Dankera 7 any longer would be a waste of time. "I understand completely," I smiled. "Thank you for taking the time to explain this personally. We'll be gone within the hour."

Yanit smiled and I would swear in any court in the galaxy that he sighed with what I can only describe as relief. "Thank you, Detective. I'm very happy that we see eye to eye on such a delicate matter." He put his cup down and motioned to his heavies. One came over and they exchanged a few words in Dankeran. The heavy nodded and reached into his jacket. For a moment I thought we were about to be shot and my hand instinctively reached for the pistol at my hip. Yanit held up a hand in a placating gesture.

"Relax, Gentlemen. I have a gift for you, that is all." The heavy held out the small bottle and I took it from him, nodding my thanks. "It's a powerful spirit we produce here on Dankera and this is one of only fifty bottles of such quality. Be careful with it or you will be very sorry indeed."

"Thank you very much," I replied. "We appreciate your kindness."

Yanit rose and headed for the hatch. "I bid you safe journey and success in your endeavour."

Dankera 7 faded into the black void as my ship raced away from the system and headed towards a barely used minor shipping lane. Once safely switched to autopilot, Tinnias and I sat and discussed our position in light of Yanit's visit. It took us several minutes to get over the shock before we were able to discuss the matter with any clarity but once we did, we wondered how he'd known who we were.

"I never told anyone where we were going," Tinnias said. "We went there directly after leaving the Drycenian ship, in fact as far as I remember, we didn't even decide what we were to do until after we'd left."

"Correct. We were intending to return to Tyrrin 4 but weren't sure whether that would be a good idea. I was going to call my contacts before we made a final decision."

"If our room was bugged, they'd be thinking we'd returned to Tyrrin," Tinnias continued. "As it turned out, we didn't."

"Which leaves us with the problem of how Yanit knew us," I said.

"I suppose we did sweep the ship for bugs thoroughly, didn't we?"

I sighed and ran a hand through my hair. "Well I thought so. I guess it wouldn't hurt to do it again just to be sure."

Two hours later, Tinnias and I sat down with hot drinks and sighed. Neither of us found any further bugging devices, cameras, or tracking equipment of any kind and as I sipped my drink, I swore.

"Fuck. I'm at a complete loss. As far as we know we're not being bugged and neither of us told anyone else of our plans, yet we're still unable to answer the question of how Yanit knew us."

"Unless of course," Tinnias began but hesitated. "No, that's ridiculous, they wouldn't."

"Come on, Dad, don't hold out on me here. We've exhausted all the probable solutions so crazy is all we have right now."

"Well I just thought that maybe there's a leak within the Drycenian ship."

"But that still wouldn't explain how they knew we went to Dankera 7. We didn't decide to go there until after we left their ship. Leak or not, it doesn't answer our problem. Either one of us is lying and secretly calling someone with our plans, or there's a tracking device we missed. Those are the only possible explanations I can come up with. Do you have any other ideas?"

"No, I'm afraid I don't," Tinnias sighed. "Shit. The ship is clean as far as our combined knowledge and skills can tell and they've no other way of tracking us other than fitting some device to the ship. Byron had open access to it since the moment we boarded the battle cruiser. There's no other way that ..." he began but stopped mid sentence and I saw a look of horror wash over his face. "Oh fuck."

"What?" I demanded.

"The doctor."

"What about him?" I frowned. "He didn't have access to the ship and anyway, he doesn't have the skills necessary to fit a device so expertly that neither of us could find it."

"True, but he did have access to you and I would be happy to bet that he has more than adequate skills to fit a device inside of you."

I felt my insides sink somewhere dark as my mind received this information and for a moment, I thought I was going to pass out. "Holy fucking shit, that has to be it. Damn that asshole. What the fuck are we to do now? Everywhere I go, I'll be telling them where we're going?" My voice trembled as the first flutter of panic and revulsion reached for my mind. The knowledge that someone had violated my insides and put something inside me that didn't belong, sickened me. It wouldn't have been so bad had I been asked for my permission. It wasn't the presence of the object that bothered me, it was the secrecy I found difficult to process. I felt as if I'd been raped.

Tinnias, hearing the rising panic in my voice, took control in the way that only a father can. "Now, Son, don't panic. We'll sort this out, I promise."

"How?" I screeched.

"By heading for the nearest Deep Space Refuelling Station and booking you into its infirmary, that's how. My rank will ensure the doctors' obedience and their own code of ethics and regulations should ensure they keep their mouths shut."

I nodded, pleased beyond belief that a possible solution was ahead. "But what if it's in my brain or something and they can't remove it without turning me into a vegetable?"

"I don't think Doc Jam did anything to your brain, Sam. There'd be a scar on your head, you'd have been shaved or something. There's no such marks on you that I can see."

"I guess that's true," I nodded. "He couldn't just zap me with a laser beam or something because he had to put something in me, a physical object. That requires opening me up, doesn't it?"

"Right," Tinnias nodded. "Now where is the nearest station?"

"Unidentified vessel, this is Deep Space Refuelling Station Omega Twelve. Please send your identification beacon and state the nature of your visit."

I flipped a switch and nodded to Tinnias. "Deep Space Refuelling Station this is SC257, Commander Tinnias Vaylo of the Inter-Galactic Law Enforcement Agency commanding. I request permission to refuel, resupply, and my fellow crew member needs urgent medical attention under Inter-Galactic Regulation 83868463/A12 Sub Section 374658."

"Come around to Shuttle Bay Nine, Commander. Please switch off your auto pilot and open a remote command port; we'll bring you in. The duty medic has been called and will meet you at disembarkation point four."

"Thank you," Tinnias replied as I flipped a switch that would allow the station's pilots to remotely pilot my ship into the shuttle bay and onto a landing pad. "You have control."

Once the shuttle bay had refilled with air and the siren sounded, I opened the hatch and saw a young man running towards us, a digital console in his hands. Without waiting to be invited, he leapt into the ship and looked at us.

"My name is Shole and I'm the duty medic. Where is the patient?"

"That would be me," I smiled as I held out a hand, which he shook.

"Ahh, walking wounded, that's good. What's the nature of your medical emergency?"

Tinnias smiled as he leaned down towards the small man. "Inter-Galactic regulations prohibit me from discussing the details with anyone other than a Doctor, qualified to level three or above. Do you have such a person in your medical facility?"

"We do, Sir. Is the patient able to walk or shall I call for a travel bed?"

"I can walk just fine," I said. "Lead the way."

"Doctor Mavdip at your service, Commander Vaylo. Here are my identification documents."

Tinnias took them, scanned them into his personal console, and handed them back. "Thank you, Doctor, now if I can have a retinal scan, we can get on with the matter at hand. Tilt your head back a little for me."

"Of course, no problem," the Doctor replied.

Once Tinnias was satisfied the regulations had been properly adhered to, he sighed. "Thank you for your compliance, Doctor. We are in quite a predicament here and you're our last hope."

The Doctor indicated for us to sit. "Okay then. Start from the beginning and tell me what you need."

Tinnias sighed and nodded. "Without going into details of the case, we have reason to believe that a Doctor inserted a tracking device of some kind inside my colleague here whilst operating on him for another medical problem. We need two things from you. First, we need to confirm its presence. Second, we want it removed, so long as removal doesn't cause harm to my colleague's health, obviously. If it can't be removed, we'd like help in stopping it from working. A laser burst or something."

The doctor looked shocked. "A tracker implanted into his body, are you sure?"

"Well no," Tinnias replied. Obviously our first job is to find out if it is there or not."

"It's the only explanation," I added. We've swept my ship, almost torn it apart twice. There's nothing more aboard other than what we found on our first sweep. It has to be inside me."

"Finding out is no problem at all," The doctor said as he got up. "Remove all of your clothes and lie down on this bed."

Five minutes of beeping, blinking lights, whirring, and clicks later, I redressed and sat down next to Tinnias as we waited for the scanner to give us its findings. I noticed the doctor's eyebrows lift and knew he'd found something. A mixture of revulsion and relief swept through me.

"If you'd like to come over here, Gentlemen," the doctor said. We both leapt up and raced around the bank of machinery to find ourselves looking at a digital display of my insides. Veins, arteries, bones, and organs all looked perfectly normal to me, as someone of almost zero medical knowledge that is.

"Show me, Doc," I said. "I can see that's the inside of a body, which I'm assuming is mine, but I can't see anything out of the ordinary."

"See this?" he pointed to a spot below my left lower rib and tapped the screen twice. The image enlarged and I saw it. A small oval shadow right below my lowest left rib. "That shouldn't be there."

"But that's just a solid shadow," Tinnias said as he squinted at the screen. "Can you get a bit more definition?"

A few more taps on the screen and the image enlarged so that the mysterious oval now filled the screen. Two more taps and both Tinnias and I exclaimed aloud.

"Holy fuck," Tinnias hissed.

"Shit," I countered. Then my stomach gave a lurch and I knew what was coming. I put a hand to my mouth. "I'm really sorry, I'm going to puke." Doctor Mavdip just managed to get a metal bowl into my hands in time and put a hand on my shoulder as I heaved. Once I was done, he took the bowl from me and loaded it into a large machine for sterilisation, then prepared a glass of pink liquid for me and sat down, scratching his head in disbelief. "Drink this, Detective. I admit to you both, I've never seen anything like this before. I've had similar experiences with other law enforcers a few times, but I've never seen a device like this. This is higher than high end stuff. If we weren't bound by regulations, I'd beg you to tell me where it came from."

"I'm not in the least surprised you haven't seen this before," I said. "If it's any consolation, neither has any other doctor in the galaxy, other than the one who put it there of course."

"I'm going to need a recording of this, Doctor," Tinnias said. "Can I dock my console with your machine?"

"Of course, the docking port is just here. Now let's see if we can't learn a little more about it before opening you up. A holographic display might give us more definition still." He tapped a few more times and the digital image disappeared, to be replaced moments later by a three dimensional hologram of my insides. The detail was amazing and when the doctor enlarged the portion containing the device, it was so clear I felt I could reach out and touch it. It was smooth, with no visible lumps or bumps, no buttons, nothing interrupted the smooth lines of the oval device before us, other than a short vertical stem that stuck out the top. We could even see the barest hint of decorative Drycenian scrollwork etched upon its surface.

"That's incredible, Doc," Tinnias said. "Can you let us see it from every side?"

"Sure." More taps and my holographic body began to turn slowly clockwise. When we got to a full rear view, the doctor exclaimed aloud and stopped the display mid spin. "Damn."

"What?" Tinnias and I demanded in unison.

The doctor tapped again and the hologram enlarged still further. "See that?" he said, pointing to a spot on the lower rear portion of the device. We both nodded. "Let's see where that wire goes." With gentle practiced fingers, he moved the greatly enlarged image inch by inch, following the wire which he told us was approximately a third the width of a hair. "Ahh, we might have a problem here."

"How?" I asked. "Come on, Doc, talk to me. This shit is inside me, I deserve to know."

"And keep it simple, please," Tinnias added. "We're law enforcers not doctors."

The doctor nodded. "Okay then. As you are both no doubt aware, any device needs to be powered in order to function." We nodded. "This device is no different. The wire we're looking at has been attached to a lateral cutaneous branch of one of your thoracic nerves. The nerves are what make your muscles work. They fire off little jolts of power and your muscles use those jolts to fuel their movement. Are you still with me?" We nodded. "This device is doing the same thing. It's using the power conducted by the nerve to fuel itself so that it can continue doing whatever it is that it does."

"I see," I replied. "So why did you say, damn?"

"Because I don't have the skills to remove that wire from the nerve without damaging the nerve itself. Nor do I know of any doctor alive today who does have the skill. This is amazing work, whoever attached this inside you is a genius."

"Does this mean you can't remove it?" Tinnias asked.

"I can remove the device itself. That's not a problem. I can simply cut the wire as far back as I dare and lift the entire thing out. What I can't do is remove that part of the wire that is attached to the nerve. That portion will have to remain in place."

"Will it have any effect?" I asked. "The bit you leave inside me I mean."

"It shouldn't do. It's just a millimetre or so of wire that won't be attached to anything and I'll encapsulate the cut end in Permabond which should prevent any current getting through from the cut end and giving you pain."

"What sort of effect would damaging the nerve have?" I asked. "If I said to cut it out as best you can, how would the damage you predict show itself?"

"You'd have pain for a start, involuntary muscle spasms or loss of feeling possibly, maybe even partial paralysis. There's also the threat of loss of bladder or bowel control, difficulty or loss of gaining and/or sustaining erections, the list of possible effects is quite long," the doctor replied. "This particular nerve is one branch of many that power all of your abdominal muscles both front and rear and no one really knows the full extent of every single muscle fibre's influence. The area of the branch the wire has been attached to is what we call, a sub cutaneous nerve, which means it's just under the skin. Damage to this part of the nerve would result in abdominal pain, which could be anything from mildly irritating to debilitatingly painful. You'd be forced to receive local anaesthetic treatment for the rest of your life. After a while on such treatment, you'll probably find your body becoming attuned to the anaesthesia, rendering it a less effective treatment as time goes on. Such pain would affect your ability to move around freely, which would no doubt have a negative effect upon your ability to do your job. Then there are all the other possible effects, some of which could be treated, others which can't. I wouldn't recommend it."

"You're sure you can fix the wire so it doesn't zap him or anything," Tinnias asked.

"Absolutely. That's no problem at all."

Both men looked at me and despite the gravity of the situation, I blushed. "Okay, do it."

"Right, remove your clothes and put on this gown."

"You're okay with me witnessing the procedure?" Tinnias asked. "I have to I'm afraid, for the regulations."

"No problem, Commander. Follow me and I'll show you how to scrub up."


"Here it is, Sam," Tinnias said, holding an evidence pouch towards me.

I took it and peered at the tiny object within. "It's tiny. I know it's too late to question it now, but what if this thing is part of the treatment Doc Jam gave me."

"I thought of that already. From what I remember of our conversation with him at the time, he told us that he was going to repair your damaged DNA and the damage to your organs. At no time did he tell you this treatment would involve placing a device inside you, wired to one of your nerves."

I nodded. "Yeah, I remember. If this thing was part of the treatment, he'd have to tell me and get my permission, wouldn't he?"

"Yeah, he would. Besides, when all this is finished and we get home, we'll get your DNA and internal organs checked out, just to make sure."

"I'm glad it's out of me. I know it probably wasn't harmful but just knowing he put that thing inside me without telling me gives me the creeps. I know it's silly but I feel violated, like he raped me or something."

"It's not silly at all," Tinnias smiled.

"When can we be on our way?"

"The doctor wants you here overnight and if you're okay, he'll discharge you in the morning. I'll organise a refuel and resupply with any stock we need. Let's make a list, there's everything you could imagine on sale here."


"SC257 you're clear to leave the shuttle bay. Thank you for your custom."

"Thank you for your hospitality, SC257 out," Tinnias said as I lifted the ship off the pad and headed out through the huge gaping maw into the void beyond. The moment we were beyond the official safe zone, I gunned the engine to maximum and engaged the covert stealth modulator.

"I'm not taking the risk of them seeing us," I said. "They probably have the technology to see through my covert mode anyway, but we have to try."

"Where do we go now then?" Tinnias asked.

"We have two choices as far as I can see. We can go to Tyrrin 4 and dig for some information or we could go to Niruvan Prime."

"The Gaht home world?"

I nodded. "Yeah. We could stake them out and see if they have Commander Taiko. At the very least we should be able to find some sort of information on Gaht itself. Hell, we could kidnap its leader and demand a trade like in those old vidicom movies."

"That would be fun," Tinnias grinned. "Unfortunately, it would put us on the wrong side of the regulations and we'd have no case. Damn, now I begin to understand why you went freelance."

Now it was my turn to grin. "I know the regulations are there to ensure everything is done properly so crazies don't get away on stupid technicalities, but they are a royal pain in the ass. It seems like we have just those two options. Which is it to be?"

"We now have a third thread in this case," Tinnias said. "The Drycenians are obviously involved. What we don't know is how or why. We could go there and see what we can dig up."

I laughed aloud and he frowned. "No way, that's a ridiculous idea. Not only are they extremely secretive about themselves, they do not allow anyone to visit Drycenia without royal permission. They live in enclosed mountaintop communities that would be impossible for us to access without being discovered. Besides, it's not as if we could exactly blend in, is it?"

"I guess not. Those eyes and teeth give them a rather unique appearance don't they? I can see why Byron appeals to you, on a purely physical level I mean. Okay so I vote we try Tyrrin first. We do some discreet digging, maybe interview Taiko's wife and even take a look around Tip's apartment. If we find anything that points to Gaht, we go there."

"I agree. We can't go in tooled up for a fight without having firm facts behind us. We have to remain in the right or we're fucked."

"Good, we have something resembling a plan then. How long until we reach Tyrrin 4?"

"Three days and a couple of hours at top speed, why?"

"Slow down a little and make it five days would you?"

"Whatever for?"

"So we can grow beards. Do you have any hair dye?"

"You've been watching too many vidicom movies, Dad. You could always shave your head. Now that would be one heck of a disguise."

Tinnias laughed aloud and I couldn't help but join in. "Can you imagine how our colleagues back home would react? I'd never live it down. Not one of your better ideas, Son."

Although the case was proving difficult to understand let alone solve, being with my father was like a balm to my soul. Spending time with him deepened our bond and mutual respect and I began to realise for the first time just how lonely I had been for the past couple of decades. There was always a nagging worry that he might come to harm, but then I realised that he must carry that same worry every moment I'm away from home working. When I mentioned him joining me and us working as a team, I hadn't been joking and although I knew it was impossible, a part of me had dared to hope. His presence also helped stop me from sinking into melancholy about being separated from Byron so suddenly and the worry about his reaction.

Once we knew the Drycenians would not be able to track us anymore, we both felt a measure of relief, but so many questions remained and we had answers to none of them. We talked them over and over as we journeyed to Tyrrin 4 but got no nearer to a plausible solution. We still did not know how Yanit got his information about us and this bugged me more than anything else. The obvious answer was that there was a leak somewhere but try as we might, we could not identify a possible source. The problem was that no one knew we were going to Dankera 7 because we didn't decide to go there until after leaving the Drycenian ship and neither of us told anyone of our plans. I was unwilling to entertain the possibility that Tinnias was running his mouth to anyone, but the problem of the leak went unsolved. Now we felt reasonably sure we were no longer being tracked or bugged, we ought not to find further progress hindered.

## CHAPTER TEN

Five days after leaving the refuelling station and with a healthy growth of beard each, we entered the Tyrrin System and headed for the fourth planet. Having already decided to keep as far away from the Law Enforcement Headquarters as possible, we booked into the shabbiest hotel we could find on the far edge of the city. Our clothes, having been deliberately slept in for the previous two nights in order to render them crumpled, gave us a nicely dishevelled appearance which helped us blend in with the locals in this poor neighbourhood. My ship was parked a couple of miles away in a secure lock up facility, so we planned to say we travelled to the city by public transportation should anyone ask. Our aim was to appear to be poor travellers doing a planet wide tour on the cheap and I reckon we looked the part perfectly.

A bit of research on my ship's computer console gave us the address of Commander Taiko, along with the names of his wife and three daughters, so after changing into smart clothes, we set off to interview them. This could not be done in any official capacity of course. We were not officially given the case and as we had been tracked, bugged and who knows what else, pretending to be the investigating law enforcers would render any information inadmissible. Our cover was to pose as private investigators and offer his wife our services, for free of course, due to the Commander being such a well respected member of law enforcement.

The house was large and set within its own landscaped gardens to the rear and one side in which flowering trees wafted their scent into the light morning breeze. The other side of the building was attached to the house next door. The front door loomed at us from atop a flight of six extravagantly wide stone steps, flanked by stylish metal handrails. The number sixty adorned the door in silver paint and a plaque was fixed below which read simply, 'Taiko.'

"Swanky pad," I hissed as we climbed the steps.

"Tyrrin 4 law enforcers obviously earn more than we do on Sigma," Tinnias replied.

"But they don't have the view we've got."

"That's true."

I rang the bell and adjusted my jacket while we waited. Four attempts later, we had to admit that the Taiko family obviously weren't at home and turned to leave. Halfway down the steps, I heard a voice.

"They're not in you know."

I looked up, resisting the urge to say, 'you don't say' with some difficulty and smiled. An elderly woman was leaning from an upstairs window of the house next door.

"Any idea when they'll be back?" I smiled.

"Not exactly. They just said they would be away for a few weeks and weren't sure when they'd be returning."

"Oh, so they've gone on holiday or something?"

She nodded. "Yes. She said they were going to visit friends."

"Where exactly? Did they say?"

"Oh yes, they've gone to visit friends on Lilea 4 while the Commander's away. I know for sure because I commented to them about the time I visited there when I was a girl. I told them to make sure to see those beautiful trees, the ones that talk."

"Whispering trees," I remarked with a smile.

"Yes, that's the ones. You've seen them?"

"Once, yes."

"So beautiful they are."

"They are indeed. Well thank you for your help, we appreciate it."

"You're very welcome, Gentlemen, anytime."

We walked away, our faces like thunder.

Around the corner, we found a small area of parkland and sat down on a seat by a small river and watched the water birds sail past as we discussed this latest bombshell.

"This means Domenico is obviously involved," I said.

Tinnias nodded. "That means the Drycenians are obviously involved too, but then we guessed that much ourselves."

"No wonder we didn't get invited to dinner," I remarked.

"We have to think about what we're to do next. Where do we go from here?"

"It would be silly not to take the opportunity to check out Tip's apartment while we're here," I said. "After that, I'm not entirely sure. If we go to Lilea on a rescue mission, we will have both the Lileans and the Drycenians to fend off. With their combined abilities and technological advances, it would probably be a suicide mission. Our only real option is to go to Niruvan Prime as we planned and stake out Gaht's headquarters."

"I agree, unless we can think of anything better. Let's go back to the ship and turn back into filthy street bums, then go and rummage through Tip's underwear drawer. Better bring the detector kit; he probably re installed his own cameras and bugs."

"I'm assuming that Commander Taiko has actually been kidnapped," I said. Tinnias frowned. I shrugged. "It's just a thought. What with Domenico and the Drycenians probably being involved, I just wondered whether there's something totally different going on that we're not aware of."

"But if they had rescued him, why not bring him back or tell the media he's safe at least?" Tinnias replied. "Before they bugged us, lied to us, and led us astray, I might have believed the idea was valid but not now. Not after the run around they've given us. If they're so helpful, good, wise, and benign, why did they not take us into their confidence?"

"Why meet with us at all," I said. "I can't get my head around the fact that they took the trouble to meet with us and then they refuse to tell us what they're up to, lie to us, slice me up and put a tracker in my guts, and who knows what the fuck else they're doing. None of that explains why they made the effort to meet us in the first place. Doesn't that seem odd to you, Dad?"

Tinnias nodded. "Very odd. I guess Doc Jam could've been telling the truth about wanting to ensure your medical health was maintained. Maybe they somehow got wind of Tip being involved with Gaht and decided to get involved. He's Domenico's friend after all so Vincent would've wanted to help him get his life back on track."

"That's another odd thing," I said. "They told you all about Tip's past, which is very sensitive information that could ruin both his and my careers, yet they hold out on us about whatever else is going on. This is getting weirder by the hour."

Tinnias shook his head and sighed. "It is indeed a paradox, Son. At this moment in time, I have no idea how we're going to sort this shit out, nor even if we can. I'm tempted to say let's just go home and crack open a bottle of green wine, sit on the verandah, and talk about old times."

"If you did, I'd be tempted to agree," I replied. A thought then occurred to me and I grinned. "We could of course be very naughty boys, just to stir things up a little and see how the ripples spread."

"What do you mean?"

"Well look, the media reports all say that no one knows anything about where Taiko is, who took him, or why. We could leak it to the media that he might be on Lilea hiding out and that the Drycenians are involved in it all."

Tinnias' mouth gaped and I grinned. "Oh, Son, we couldn't. Do you think we should? The fallout would be horrific. You have Byron to think of now remember."

"True, then how about we say Lilea is most likely involved in it? Blame it on that brainless thug and give him the single finger."

"Let's think about it, at least until we've turned over Tip's apartment. I suppose there is always the possibility that he organised Taiko's kidnap by Gaht. That would explain Vincent Domenico and the Drycenians being involved, at least partially. It still doesn't explain why they've been giving us the shit stick, but it's more than we've had up to now."

I nodded. "It's certainly possible, although I hope with all that I have that it's not true. Come on then, let's get back into street bum mode and do some breaking and entering. We can sit in the park across the street from his apartment block and watch for a while, just in case he's at home."


Leaning back against the wall to the side of the door, I poked my arm around and waited for my detector to tell me if any detectors were ahead. Sure enough, it registered the presence of a camera ten feet ahead and eight feet off the floor. I turned to Tinnias and nodded.

"Camera inside, ten feet ahead and eight feet up. From what I remember of the layout, it's above the door to the main living area."

Tinnias nodded and fiddled with the gadget in his hands. The laser burner sends out laser pulses of varying frequencies which disrupt the power supply to all manner of electronic gadgets. "I've set it to maximum," he said as he handed it to me. "Try a single burst of three seconds first; we don't want to set the whole block on fire."

It took us seven minutes to disable every device in the apartment so we could search without being seen by whomever was watching through those cameras. We would have to be quick as there was the risk that they would call law enforcement the moment they saw their devices go down. I knew they would probably assume it was me, but there was no need to make it too easy for them to identify one of the intruders. Like the professionals we knew we were, we'd swept the place, emptied the safe I found hidden behind a false wall panel, copied everything on his computer console, mobile console, and the two Unicoms I found under his mattress, and locked up behind us within another fourteen minutes. As we calmly strolled back to my ship to examine our haul, Tinnias sniggered.

"That was the most fun I've had in years. The adrenaline rush is awesome. It's moments like this I miss being on the street."

I laughed. "We're going to be laughing about this for years to come."

"I'm going to be telling the grandchildren about it, if Ambella ever gives me any that is."

"You'd make a good burglar, Dad," I grinned. "You turned that place over with more precision than I did, and I do it several times a week. How long is it since you did something like this?"

"Several years. Not since I got promoted to Commander. It's like swimming, once learned, you never forget. When I joined the Agency, we were given a set of lock picks each. We had nothing like the electronic gizmos we have now. Breaking into a place took skill in those days, Sam."

"Really?" I gaped in awe. "You still have 'em?"

"Yeah, why?"

"You have to teach me, you have to."

He grinned at me. "Okay then, it'll give us something to do on the journey to Niruvan Prime."

Back at the ship, we changed into our scruffy clothes and got ourselves a snack from my Nutri-Vend before sitting down at my computer console. The files provided nothing of any interest apart from one file that refused to open without a password. I used every word combination I could think of that Tip might choose but nothing worked.

"Shit and fuck," I hissed.

"Take a breath, Son. Don't you have a contact who could advise you?"

"I do, a couple actually but they'll probably be unable to do anything unless I send them the file, which I'd rather not do just yet."

"They might be able to talk you through the process or tell you where to purchase a gizmo that could do it for us. It's worth a try at least."

"The Agency guys would be in there within ten minutes," I said.

Tinnias nodded. "Less than that, probably. We can't run the risk of this getting lost though. This business with gangs has got me paranoid about the guys I work with. Anyone could be a leak."

"When this is over, I'll get my contact to look into the workforce at Sigma Headquarters and see if we have any leaks," I said. "At least you'll then know, even if you can't do anything about it."

"That would be helpful, Sam, thanks."

My contact answered on the very first ring. "Hey, Sam. What can I do for you?"

"I have a computer file here that won't allow me access without a password."

"And you're wanting in?"

"More than anything. Can you talk me through opening it?"

"Okay, stop me if I get too technical. Now then, look up at the top right corner of the screen. You should see a clock icon."

fifteen minutes later, the file opened and I grinned. "I'm in. That's awesome. Thank you so much. I owe you one."

"My pleasure, Sam. Would it be rude of me to redeem that now?"

"What do you need?"

"I'm running short of Holdex DigiMax Transducer couplings, the four point two type. There's a rather annoying little regulation about who can buy them and with my slightly less than spotless record, I'm having difficulty finding a supplier."

I turned to Tinnias and mouthed, 'sorry' but he grinned at me and nodded. "How many do you need?"

"Fifty would see me through a couple of months."

"You'll have them," I assured him.

"Always a pleasure doing business with you, Sam. Call me, anytime."

Before I could examine the now opened file, Tinnias grabbed his Unicom and dialled a number. While he waited for an answer, he shoved a piece of paper at me. "What's your guy's address?" I wrote it down and shoved it back just as he was exchanging pleasantries with someone he called, Omni.

"Hey Omni, it's Thud Thud here." Several moments of silence passed during which a smile crept across his face. "Yeah, too long, man. How's the family?" More silence and I tried to supress a snigger at the thought of Tinnias having such a funny alias. This was obviously a contact of his, someone in the digital supplies market I presumed. Tinnias confirmed my assumption as his conversation continued. "I'm hoping you can help me out with something. I need fifty Holdex DigiMax Transducer couplings, the four point two type. Can you lay your hands on them for me? Wonderful. I'd like them couriered to this address. Thanks. Now, about those traffic violations you were so worried about."

When he finished the call, I grinned at him. "Thud Thud? You have to explain that one to me, Dad."

He grinned. "When I first joined the Agency, everyone said they could hear the thud of my footsteps a mile away. They called me Thud Thud after that. Several of the guys taught me how to tread softly, but the nickname stuck. I broke my ankle when I was eight and I've always had the habit of thudding that foot down a bit hard because the bones didn't set quite right. And if I ever hear you call me that, you'll be very sorry."

I laughed aloud. "I won't, I promise." I didn't know if he realised that by telling me that story, he'd told me his contact was probably an ex law enforcer, but I wasn't about to question him about it.


We worked our way through each document in the file and the more we read, the more astonished we became. There were a lot of photographs; many of which showed men meeting, shaking hands, and passing packages over. A few showed couples kissing and two displayed a couple having sex in what looked like an empty building. There were a few of me inside Tip's apartment, making food, watching the vidicom, and the usual boring stuff one does when home alone. We didn't recognise any of the men in the photographs, but we assumed they were either law enforcers or Gaht members, or both. We turned our attention next to the vidicom clips, which showed similar stuff to the photographs and I saw with some annoyance, a vidicom clip of myself walking around inside the apartment. Tinnias grinned when we watched the clip of myself walking around with my detector and disabling all the devices.

One document contained a list of two hundred names, many of whom were law enforcers. There were also bankers, politicians, a few celebrities, and some company owners. Alongside the names, were addresses, Unicom numbers, bank details, and details of all family members. Our first thought was that this was either a list of leaks or a hit list. We were relieved to see that the list contained no names from Sigma. To have another bad law enforcer to deal with after the Rime business would have been too much to bear. The wound Detective Rime caused all of us at the Sigma Headquarters would forever be raw and we had no desire to have to go back to similar territory again so soon.

The last document was a list of eighty-one banks in five planetary systems. Alongside the names and addresses of the banks were the names and addresses of all staff, together with full accounts of the banks going back from between ten to thirty-two years. I guessed these banks were ones used by Gaht to launder their illegally gained funds.

"I wonder why some only go back ten years, but others go back thirty or more," Tinnias said.

"Maybe that's when each of the banks began working for Gaht."

"Oh yes, that would make sense."

After copying everything to a spare data chip for our own records, we bagged and tagged the original chip and locked it away in a secret compartment I built into a dark corner of my ship's cargo hold. Then we looked at the contents of Tip's safe. The first thing we found was a bundle of galactic credit cards with a total balance of three hundred and seventy-two thousand, four hundred and ninety credits.

"Shit," Tinnias exclaimed. "I wonder if they want a leak on Sigma."

I laughed. "Think of the fun we could have with this lot at our disposal."

The next item was unrecognisable to us, other than its obvious connection to the Drycenians, as displayed by the now familiar fancy scrollwork and symbols etched into its entire surface. It looked like a rather fancifully decorated metal cube but I guessed it had some definite purpose, although what that use might be evaded me.

"I'll bet this opens somehow," I said as I turned it over in my hands and allowed my fingers to brush along the edges, feeling for any irregularities.

"Probably," Tinnias nodded. "Knowing the Drycenians, opening it is probably way beyond our abilities."

A couple of spare laser pistol cells came next, along with Tip's Agency Pledge certificate. Two Unicom handsets were next, and I noticed that one had received calls but not made any, whilst another had made calls but not received any.

"That's weird," I said. "He's making calls on one of them and receiving calls on the other. He's really covering his tracks; I can't help but be impressed with his thoroughness."

"You taught him well, Son."

"A little too well it seems."

The last item was a set of hover vehicle keys. We could see right away that they weren't for any of the Agency vehicles, and I knew Tip didn't own one. Living so close to his workplace meant he could forego the extra expense of upkeeping a vehicle, parking charges, and fuel etc, so which vehicle those keys should fit, eluded us. We bagged and tagged the lot and stashed them all away for safe keeping. Then we discussed what to do next.

"I guess our options now are to go to Niruvan Prime and stake out Gaht headquarters or stay here a day or two more and tail Tip," Tinnias suggested. "It's a shame we didn't fit a bug to his household Unicom."

"I thought about it but if my previous experience is anything to go by, he'd find it quickly and we'd give away our presence here. I reckon for the time being at least, it's best he doesn't know we've returned."

Tinnias nodded, then scratched his chin and grimaced. "I'll be so glad when this business is over. I'm hating this beard, it's so itchy. I'm gagging for a shave."

I grinned. "Me too, and a decent shower, we both stink like a Bannidge Beast's arse."

"Yeah, I'd be hopeless as a street bum."


We tailed Tip for two whole days, during which he went to work, went home, went out for dinner, and did all the normal boring stuff we all do every day. He shopped, banked, visited a vidicom theatre where a new release was being shown, worked out in a local gym, visited a whorehouse twice, and spent both evenings sitting on his balcony drinking beer. As darkness fell on the second night, both Tinnias and I were bored out of our skulls and I thought back to a case I worked on Deligon 2 several years previously. I found out I was being tailed and was so incensed that I deliberately went and sat in an art gallery for two whole hours, spent another hour reading every food label in an entire store, then another couple lying in the sun in the local park before returning to the apartment my friend Ren and I were sharing. It was as I was reliving this funny memory that something occurred to me that turned my smile into a frown.

"Fuck," I hissed as we made our way to the grubby hotel.

"What's up?"

"I've only just this minute realised, how stupid. Jeez I can be thick sometimes."

"What?" Tinnias demanded again.

"Tip is Lilean."

Tinnias frowned. "I was aware of that. How is that relevant?"

"He has one of those Lilean spirit friends hanging out with him all the time."

"Well yeah I guess he has," Tinnias said. "But I still don't … oh. I'm with you now."

"I'll bet she's been telling him we're tailing him."

"Is that Lilean spirit shit on the level? Isn't it just a belief system or something?"

"It's on the level," I nodded. "I've seen it in action and I know they actually do exist and tell them stuff."

"I guess our cover has been blown since we got here then," Tinnias said. "But then why weren't we disturbed when we broke into his apartment? You'd think he'd be delighted to catch us committing a crime."

I nodded. "Yeah, that's odd. I guess when she's with him, she can't be with us. We were probably lucky to choose a time when she was with him long enough for us to get in, do what we had to do, and get out."

"I wouldn't mind betting that either she or Vincent's one will be blabbing about where we are and what we're up to. The Drycenians probably still know everything we're doing despite not having the tracker inside you anymore."

"It's entirely possible," I replied. "And I don't know of any way to remain invisible to them. That's way beyond my capabilities I'm afraid. We could spend some time researching while journeying to Niruvan Prime."

"It wouldn't hurt. Although unlikely, you never know what we might discover. Some kind of scanner wave that interferes with their energy frequency maybe."

"You could have a point there, Dad. It's bound to be something to do with an energy frequency isn't it? If we can find out what frequency the Lilean spirits operate at, we could find an alternative frequency that could block it. I've got a couple of contacts that could make something for me, if we can give them the relevant frequencies."

Tinnias grinned. "We could make a fortune and become famous inventors. I can see the vidicom ad now, 'Are you troubled with annoying spirits haunting your home? Well suffer no more with the patented Vaylo Spirit

Shield. Only one hundred and fifty credits, plus admin charges and shipping."

We were still laughing when we entered our filthy hotel.

The sun was not yet up when we awoke and packed our few belongings. With a six day journey ahead of us, we wanted to be on our way and try to at least gain some understanding of whatever this weird situation was even if we couldn't fix it. Back at the ship, we showered and dressed in fresh clothes and felt much better. Our beards remained though. We might be glad of a disguise on Niruvan. After shoving our dirty clothes into the incinerator and watching them burn, I paid the parking attendant and nudged the engines. As Tyrrin 4 shrank into the void behind us, I punched in the co-ordinates for the Niruvan system and flipped her into auto pilot.

"Right," I said. "Let's go and do some scientific research."

After two hours of searching the galactic web network, the information consisted of nothing more than supposition and belief. Frustratingly, there was a plethora of opinions and ideas on how to increase one's perception of and interaction with, various spiritual entities but almost nothing on how to keep them away. It seems everyone wants a pet ghost these days. The only thing that remotely connected to our search criteria, were weird pseudo-religious practices consisting of visualising bubbles of white light surrounding us and other such nonsense. One article that made both Tinnias and I roar with laughter, said the best way to keep unwanted spiritual attentions away is to yell, 'go away, you're not welcome here,' at every possible opportunity in as commanding a voice as possible.

"If you think I'm walking down a street with you screaming 'go away, you're not welcome here,' every few seconds, then you've lost the plot," Tinnias said, his face purple with the effort of laughing so much. "We'd be in a psyche facility before the end of the week."

For the rest of our journey to Niruvan Prime, one or other of us would periodically leap up and scream, 'go away, you're not welcome here,' and send us both into fresh fits of laughter. I knew that this memory would forever bring a smile to my face no matter how grave a situation I should find myself in. I was grateful to be forming happy memories with my new father that would entertain the whole family for years to come. It made me feel truly a part of the family and I looked forward to a time in the future when I would be able to say, 'do you remember that time when…?' Shared memories can be either terrible or wonderful. They can torment your mind or lift you to the heights of joy. We give so much importance to having those memories to call upon whenever we need them that we forget they need first to be made, built from experiences lived moment by moment, borne from times of trauma and happiness. Only then can they be available for company in the dark lonely hours. I have many memories of my natural parents, most of them good, but I had no idea how important those moments were to become when I was experiencing them. The eight year old me had no insight into the memories I was building that would be my companions for the rest of my life.

As a man, with a new father, I was able to make sure those moments shared with him would be the most blessed and comforting of companions in the future. I hoped with everything I had that I would also get the chance to make memories with Byron.

During the journey to Niruvan Prime, I called a couple of my contacts to see what information they could give me about Gaht that would help us in our quest. The galactic web network had provided the basics but what we needed was the stuff that would never find its way to the web or media outlets. The most important thing to know was the address of its home base, its headquarters. An easy place to stakeout would be wonderful, a nicely isolated farm with outbuildings, surrounded by woodland ideally, even a walled in city based compound would be doable.

Some idea of the layout would be good too, a floor plan would possibly be accessible from the local Residential Records Office, if Niruvan had such a thing. The problem with this was that making such a request would undoubtedly alert Gaht to the fact that someone was snooping and that could be troublesome for us. High ranking public officials such as those running a body like a residential records department of a city government would quite likely be Gaht puppets and wouldn't hesitate to inform the gang bigwigs of anyone asking about the group. The same likelihood applies to neighbours, if there are any. Having people like Gaht officials living and conducting their shady business next door might very well make people frightened to speak out for fear of reprisals. That is of course, if they're not already working for them.

I am always quick to acknowledge the importance of having a good network of contacts and I am especially blessed to have the most awesome bunch of what I call, eyes and ears, in law enforcement. Yeah, I know every law enforcer says that, but mine really are incredible and have helped me crack cases time without number. Their information has saved my hide many times and I'm always sure to give credit where it's due. I couldn't do this job without them and many of them put their careers, safety, and sometimes their liberty, on the line every time they speak to me. I try to return the favour as often as I can, by turning a blind eye, helping obtain something they need but can't get hold of, and giving a bit of information back from time to time when asked. I would never give them any information that would compromise another case or help someone hurt another person though. I have a code that goes beyond Agency rules and regulations, a personal code that I endeavour to stick to in everything I do. My code is simple really, I want to be able to look myself in the eyes when I shave my face every morning and not be ashamed.

## CHAPTER ELEVEN

My two Unicom calls did little to make either Tinnias or myself happy. It wasn't the lack of information that irked us, but the content. We learned much of value from those two calls, most of which I hadn't been able to glean from my earlier research. As I said before, what we needed was the kind of stuff that never finds its way to the galactic web or media and that's what we got. It was what that information told us that made our hearts sink.

The head guy at Gaht was a guy named Belotan. As I already knew from my earlier research, he was currently on his fifth marriage and admits to twelve children with his five wives, despite there being many rumours of several more resulting from liaisons with various mistresses. These rumours put the number of children at anywhere between fifteen and twenty-three. At seventy-seven years old, he has been at the helm since starting Gaht with three friends over fifty years earlier and has lost none of his ruthless need for power and absolute control. Four of his sons work as his personal bodyguards, two more handle the financial side of the operation, another three train the elite branch of what they call field operatives, who are nothing more than armed killers who do a bit of martial arts to keep fit. Of the three remaining, one is said to be his chosen heir to take over the helm of Gaht when he dies and does practically nothing other than follow his father around to learn how to be the head of such an organisation. The last two have no interest in their father's work and have paid the price for their disrespect.

Both had businesses of their own but accusations of illegal dealings, rumours of predatory sexual behaviour with children, even talk of a couple of killings, quickly made them about as popular as a sun baked turd pile at a society wedding, and they both went out of business within two years of setting up their companies. One spent five years in jail for fraud when some evidence magically appeared out of nowhere that incriminated him. Both were regularly waylaid in dark alleyways and beaten, one had all his fingers and toes broken and spent weeks in a medical facility learning to walk again. The younger of the two turned to drink as a way of coping with the mental stress and his marriage quickly suffered as a result of his drunken rantings. His wife disappeared one night with their three children and was never seen again. After losing his livelihood, his wife, and his children, he found he was unable to support himself financially and lost his home and was forced into life as a homeless street bum, begging for coins and sleeping in doorways.

"We have to find him," I said, glaring at Tinnias should he dare to disagree.

"We'll do our best, Son, I promise you that much. We might have to wait until all this business is finished with so we can have access to Agency resources, but we'll do our best."

The other one of the two shot himself in the head after finishing his treatment for his broken fingers and toes and finding himself landed with a huge medical bill he had no hope of paying. During his three months stay in the facility, his wife took to selling her body to make enough to feed their two children and pay household expenses. When he came out and discovered what his wife had been doing and then getting the medical bill for his own treatment, he shot himself in front of her, in the kitchen of their home. My contact told me that all indications are that she continued selling her body now that she had no man around to help with the financial load, and quickly gained a drug habit in a vain effort to alleviate some of the mental stress.

"She should be easy to find," Tinnias said, pre-empting my request to help her too. "Once we find her, we can get her into a treatment facility to clean up."

"Thanks," I said quietly. Having been blessed with the most loving of parents twice over, I have a big problem coming to terms with the horrendous shit some poor souls must deal with at the hands of parents who should never have been allowed to breed in the first place. It breaks my heart and stains my soul if I know about it and not try to help. For me, knowing and not helping is the worse crime of all. Call me an old softy if you want, I'll wear the label proudly. Okay, so I'm not made of stone, fine, sue me.

Gaht's base of operations was in a disused spaceport that was built for the sole use of the once thriving port that now lay in ruins at the far eastern edge of the city. Situated on a three mile wide river that leads to the ocean, goods came and went by water borne craft for local distribution and by space shuttle to orbiting freightliners for off world trade. A financial crash a couple of decades previously ruined the city's import export trade and the port fell into ruin. After lying dormant for ten years, it was bought for peanuts by Belotan, who spent a lot of money on it and used it as Gaht's headquarters, training base, and staff accommodations. The space port allowed them to come and go with ease, without the worry of the public seeing what they were carrying or knowing where they were going.

My contact supplied us with a basic ground plan of the site, which showed half a dozen large warehouse sized buildings, the old spaceport building, the jetty where water craft once anchored, and a large open area of ground that used to be a parking facility for the port's large workforce. Although we had no idea what lay within each of the buildings, nor how they might have been refitted, at least we now had some idea of what we were dealing with. The entire site was located on a small spit of land that stuck out from the mainland, making a discreet approach almost impossible. Access from the city side was via a permanently guarded fifteen foot high gate. Within the gate was a fifty metre long access path, flanked by ten foot high walls on either side. Another guarded gate at the end gave access to the main site, which was entirely enclosed on the ocean side by twenty foot high, five foot thick stone walls. Guard towers were situated every fifty feet along the top of the wall, making access from the water impossible to achieve unseen.

"Shit," I hissed. "How the fuck are we to get into the place?"

Tinnias shrugged. "He certainly knows how to protect himself."

We also found ourselves with photographs of Belotan and the nine sons who work for him, so at least we would know if we happened to bump into any of them. My contact, who was still on the Unicom discussing the layout with us, gave us another interesting piece of information that we felt might offer us a chance to get into the place.

"There are several homeless hostels in the surrounding streets and Belotan regularly offers the odd day's work here and there. For the men it's normally along the lines of cleaning up the outside areas, sweeping floors, washing vehicles, unloading supply deliveries, and restocking the supplies store, basic maintenance of the buildings and upkeep of the grounds. The women do laundry and clean the living quarters, prepare fruits and vegetables for storage in stasis units and all those indoor type tasks. They're given a good meal, shower facilities, and there's even someone willing to cut hair and shave the guys if they want. He may be a violent psychopath but he's allegedly very kind to the local homeless in the area who welcome the opportunity for a decent meal and a wash and are willing to keep their mouths shut in exchange."

"Looks like we're back to being street bums again, Son," Tinnias said and I laughed.

"Better sleep in our clothes from now on then," I grinned. I heard my contact laugh and thanked him for the information. "I appreciate it, this is a great help to us."

"My pleasure, Sam. Sellina says hello and sends you a hug by the way."

"Give her one back from me," I grinned.

Belotan was an unpleasant looking man. His hair showed no signs of thinning, but it was greasy and hung limp around his ears, from each of which sprouted a clump of black hairs that had me grimacing with disgust. His skin was coarse, with large open pores and many small spots that were crying out for an hour in a dermal optimiser. His obvious preference for over indulgence was further illustrated by the large belly that strained against his belt, the creases in the crotch of his pants telling me they were either his only pair or he seldom changed them. I opted for the latter, given everything else I'd gleaned from his photograph and knew I wasn't wrong. His lips were so thin as to be almost non existent and gave him a mean look which didn't surprise me in the slightest. I would happily have bet my pension he got off on violence.

The four of his sons working as his bodyguards could not have been more different from their father. They had the sort of clean but tough appearance often favoured by young men these days. If their father was old school, these four young men were the new world order and knew how to use a pleasant physical appearance to their advantage. Belotan ruled by fear, whereas these four wanted you to like them before they kneecapped you. They obviously made use of the usual tricks to achieve the look; the daily workouts supplemented by muscle building drugs, shaven heads, and sharp suits would impress the younger generation and ensure a plentiful supply of future Gaht supporters.

The two financially minded sons were typical sharp suited business types obviously comfortable in the high stakes' world of dodgy business and like their four hulking brothers, kept themselves immaculately, but did it with far more panache. I imagined expensive men's fragrance and rare skin creams gracing their bathrooms, hand stitched shoes made from the illegally killed hide of some critically endangered creature, and as usual, the obligatory expensive jewellery. Of all Belotan's sons, if I was a man of business, it is these two I would fear the most, for I knew from experience that they would have extensive knowledge of financial law that would ensure not only that Gaht got away from any accusation of illegal financial dealings, but the accuser would be ruined for daring to speak against them.

The next three on the list oversaw training what Gaht humorously calls, Field Operatives, which is a way of saying killers without it sounding scary or illegal. These three were dirty versions of the four bodyguards, dressed in what they thought passed for off duty military garb, and shaved their hair to half an inch to further enhance the look. I've met these types by the thousand during my career and they're all essentially the same. They want to be soldiers but couldn't take the discipline so they dress the part, work out, do a bit of simple martial arts, and shout a lot. Don't get me wrong, these guys are no pushover but they lack any real intelligence or flexibility that would enable them to think quickly to rapidly adapting situations. They like the routine of working out, weapons training, marching up and down, and contrived combat exercises and that's where they operate best. They may not be very capable in a real combat situation but they know how to turn eager young men into killers.

The future kingpin was the next son whose photograph I examined and he had an intense gaze that told me not to underestimate him. Although he spends much of his time watching over his father's shoulder and doing very little, I knew there was much going on behind those eyes that he confided to no one. If I wanted to stick my neck out, I'd say he was hatching a takeover plan for some time in the not too distant future. I could foresee his father suffering a tragic accident before too long. This made me uncertain of his motives and that made me uncomfortable. If I couldn't rely on predicting his actions and reactions to a given situation, if Tinnias and I should reach a point where we felt it prudent to make a scene in order to achieve our goal, his unpredictable nature could seriously fuck things up.

The last two photographs showed the two dissenting sons, obviously taken before being ostracised from the family. One had what I can only describe as a look of foreboding in his eyes, whilst the other just looked emotionally drained. Knowing a little of what lay in store for them since those two photographs were taken made me angry for them, and I silently vowed to do my utmost to get justice for them. The mental imagery that flooded my mind as I thought of having all my fingers and toes deliberately broken, no doubt slowly and as painfully as possible, gave me a knot of tension in my gut. However much a man should disagree with his family, no one deserves that sort of treatment. It reminded me of the darker side of family life that many endure and I felt grateful that I had not experienced similar in my own lifetime. I've seen the results of such family disharmony in my job, so I'm not totally without understanding and I hoped the empathy would aid me in bringing this crazy paradoxical situation to some sort of satisfactory close.

We spent the rest of the journey formulating as much of a plan of action as was possible with what little concrete information we had managed to glean. Our first priority was to become homeless and take up lodgings in the nearest hostel to the Gaht compound. We would stake out the exterior of the place whilst waiting to be offered work in the hope that we might discover a more discreet way of gaining entry or escaping if need be. Once inside, whether by invitation or subterfuge, we could then plant a few cameras that would enable us to monitor activities on the days we were not hired as casual employment. Further plans would have to wait until we could see what those cameras might catch, if anything. If we should see Commander Taiko, we could either formulate our own rescue plan or anonymously report his whereabouts to the Law Enforcement Agency.

Even if we didn't see Taiko, we might hear them talking about their plans for him, where he was being held, or even other plans they might have for the future which would be useful information for the Agency's substantial file. Even if we saw and heard nothing of value, or if we should find out they're not in possession of the Commander, it would be useful to know, if troublesome. This last point was the subject of a lengthy discussion between Tinnias and me during our evening meal on the last night before our arrival at Niruvan Prime.

"What do we do if we find out they definitely don't have Taiko?" Tinnias said. "What's the plan then?"

I blew out a long breath and shrugged. "I haven't the faintest idea. If Gaht don't have him, I suppose Dankera is the obvious suspect. I don't fancy having to go back there after our last encounter, do you?"

Tinnias shook his head. "Not in the slightest. They know us now, know who we really are I mean. It would be stupid to go back ourselves. We wouldn't last a day. That camping place is isolated enough to make hiding out without being discovered, difficult. We can't go undercover again so soon; they'd recognise us straight away. It would be suicide."

"I agree. Do either of us have any contacts willing to take such a job? I don't think I do. My eyes and ears are willing to tail someone or listen in to Unicom calls but they're largely information gatherers not field operatives. How about yours?"

"Same here," Tinnias replied. "We can't even call in the Agency troops either, since we're not officially on this case."

"There's a strong possibility that a solution to this case is going to elude us," I said. "We could easily reach The Wall on this one."

"I know, I've been thinking about that possibility myself. It's going to eat at me forever but we have to accept we might not win this one."

Most of the cases I get involved with do end with some sort of definite conclusion. Either I catch my target and he gets what's coming to him, he dies while trying to evade me, or he gets off on a technicality due to some stupid Agency error. Whether satisfactory or not, most of my cases are solved. Just occasionally though, we get a case we're not able to solve. Either through lack of enough information, my target being clever enough to evade me completely, or because the target is powerful enough to frighten anyone into leaving them alone. Whatever the reason, sometimes we must admit defeat and back off. Have you ever had those dreams where you're going somewhere but suddenly the path ends at a high wall and you can't go forward? It's too high and too vertical to climb and you can't go around because it stretches into the far distance in both directions. You can't go back because maybe there's a monster chasing you, or you have one of those irritatingly urgent appointments you're always late for in such dreams. Whatever the reason, you can't go back but you can't go forward either. You're stuck and it makes you angry and panic stricken and those feelings sometimes hang around with you all day until the dream fades far enough into the mist to release its hold on your emotions. When a case reaches a point where we cannot progress with it no matter what we do or what we know, we call it The Wall because it's just like that wall in those dreams and affects us just as much.

I ran both hands through my hair and sighed. "Fuck it, fuck them, and fuck everything they stand for," I snapped. I never cope with the prospect of The Wall very well.

"Take a breath, Sam. We're not there yet. Even if we do get there, we've gleaned plenty of useful information to add to the files on both The Dankera Collective and Gaht. It won't have been a wasted journey."

I nodded. "Yeah, and the information about Belotan and his family might one day be useful. Those sons of his will come to the Agency's attention one day and what we know about them might help us then."

"That's true," Tinnias nodded.


We were up early in preparation for our arrival at Niruvan Prime. While I was studying a map of the city that was our destination, Tinnias' Unicom rang. I watched as he furiously wrote notes and allowed myself to hope that he was receiving information that would help us. After thanking the caller profusely, he hung up and looked at me with something I realised at that precise moment I hadn't seen in many days. His eyes shone with hope.

"I have the last known address of the street bum son."

I grinned. "That's awesome. We have a possible ally, even a possible witness."

"Let's hope for that huh. That hope will sustain us for a while," Tinnias replied. "On the first day we don't get hired to work in the compound, we go and look for him. He's still on Niruvan, in a large city a few hundred miles south from our destination."

I nodded. "Even if he won't actively help us, he might tell us something helpful. Even if it's just his opinion on his father's motives, it'll help us get to know Belotan a little better. The better we know him, the more chance we have of out manoeuvring him."

"After what he's been through at Belotan's hands, I would dare to guess that the opportunity for revenge would be too much to resist," Tinnias said. "It often is in such circumstances."

You often hear me talk about my need to understand people, to predict their behaviour. I've learned a lot about the workings of the mind during my years as a Law Enforcer and my constant striving for psychological understanding has never been a waste of time. People tend to be driven by their emotions, often taking the wrong path because their emotional need drives them that way. People are seldom able to put their emotions aside and act objectively and this is something I'm glad about. Such people, rare though they are, are the most dangerous of criminals because of that very ability. The absence of controlling emotions allows them to act coldly, to plan the most heinous acts in meticulous detail, and then to carry them out without their emotions telling them that what they're doing is wrong. They aren't bad because they've been driven to it by years of abuse or a life of poverty, they are bad because they believe it is right. One thing I knew for certain was that when you've been driven to the very edge of your endurance by the cruelty of someone powerful, when you've lost everyone and everything you held dear to your heart, and when you reach a point where you no longer care whether you live or die, the opportunity to strike a blow in your own defence at last and hurt your abuser, tends to be irresistible.

I nodded. "If he's reached the limit of his endurance with what he sees as a cursed life, he will be happy to tell us all about it, even if he doesn't want to get actively involved."

Tinnias banged a fist down on the back of the pilot's seat. "Damn, a ray of light at last. I thought we were doomed."

"Let's hope he gives us something we can use," I said. "Now let's find a place to land and lock up the ship. I have a city plan on the screen now."

The city was of moderate size, with the port situated on a spit of land that stuck out from the western coastline. To the north, it met the southern edge of another, much larger city with no more than a narrow strip of green land dividing the two. Along the western edge was a large manufacturing area, with mines, power plants, and factories. On the south western point were several tourist campsites dotted around the edges of four large lakes. A nice area of woodland separated this area from the outskirts of the city, so we decided to set up camp there. It would be far enough away to avoid our cover as street bums being blown, a short walk through the woodland would bring us to the edge of the city where a couple of hover bus rides would get us to within a mile of the port area easily. On the days we didn't manage to secure work within the Gaht compound, we could come back to the ship for some decent food, fresh air, and no threat of unwanted visitors while we watched and listened to the devices we planned to plant within the grounds of the compound itself. If we should find ourselves targeted or our cover blown, we could hide out back at the ship in relative safety, safe in the knowledge that my extensive on-board armoury would enable us to defend ourselves effectively. Both of us have enough years of experience to be able to shake even a well trained tail, a job that is easier within bustling city streets. We were confident we would not be showing any undesirables the way back to our camp.

"Okay, let's go camping," Tinnias said as I punched in the co-ordinates to my scanner. "Better blow the engine core filters before we arrive or everyone will know who we really are."

I flipped a switch, then pressed a button and we heard the dull pop deep within the engine core. My ship has been upgraded a few times, the last time by the Drycenians. She now has an extremely efficient Trans Flow Sub Wave Core Element. This gizmo is a miracle of Drycenian digitonics that gives the existing engine core four hundred percent more power output for the same amount of fuel input. She is now capable of cruising at half light speed without raising a sweat and can even give me sixty five percent light speed in two hour sprints. Byron told me when he fitted it, that it would give me twenty three minutes of eighty percent light speed before blowing up, should my life ever depend upon it.

Part of that fantastic upgrade was the engine core filtration system they fitted. The new gizmo gives off particles that need to be filtered out so they don't adhere to the core emitter nipples and clog everything up. Every so often, I just press a button and the system blows away the accumulated particles into the void of space, where they disperse harmlessly in the vacuum. Before fitting the filters, they added a system of jets situated on the outside of each nacelle. If needed, I can flip a switch before blowing the filters and the resulting blast will coat the outside of the nacelles with a film of black dust. This coating nicely resembles a recent engine fire and conveniently hides my ship's registration number that the law requires me to display on each nacelle. My ship is SC257 and is also the reason I affectionately refer to her as Essy. The registration tells anyone who wants to know, where the ship was registered, the letters SC telling them it was registered in Galactic Sector 834835. The numbers refer to the planet within that sector, 257 being my home planet, Sigma Prime. I sometimes joke with people who ask that it stands for Space Cop 257. Anyone can then call up the records for all ships registered on Sigma Prime and find that SC257 was registered to Samelan Sinclair, Freelance Law Enforcer with the Inter-

Galactic Law Enforcement Agency. This information is not secret, it is available to everyone who may wish to know and because of this, gives me away as a cop. Before the Drycenian upgrade, I was forced to get into a suit, go outside, and physically paint on an oily coating before landing, which was a proper pain in the rear end, believe me. Although fully qualified in a suit, not having to faff about in one is always a relief.

Happy now that our true purpose was hidden, I checked the covert modulator that would ensure our arrival would not be noticed by the authorities and headed down towards the surface of Niruvan Prime. Both Tinnias and I allowed ourselves to hope that the next days would bring us an opportunity to rescue our captured comrade, to find out the extent of the Drycenians involvement, to understand how Vincent Domenico fitted into the situation, and to help my friend Tip from becoming the man he used to be, the man he left behind in the dark days of the Domenico case, the man we all hoped was dead forever.

The first rays of weak dawn sunshine filtered through the trees as we landed in our chosen, fairly secluded spot and began to unpack and make like camping tourists. My research told me it was late spring here on Niruvan Prime, so the early mornings were a little chilly before they gave way to pleasantly warm days. We picked a spot on the south shore of the largest of the four lakes, a long rather than wide body of water that was no more than a half mile wide at most and probably at least two in length. Four bridges spanned the lake, affording quicker access to the smaller ones than walking around. Four runners puffed their way around the lakes, using the bridges and paths to break up the monotony and change direction I supposed. I envied them; if I had been there on holiday, I'd be joining them at least once a day, normally twice. The three smaller lakes lay at evenly spaced intervals beyond the opposite shore and we spied small boats bobbing in the gentle swell. The middle of the three was for the sole use of swimmers and had a jetty from which they could dive. The largest lake on whose shore we were camped had moorings for larger boats and hover vehicles and several very impressive craft waited patiently for another day of fun spent, no doubt, in trying to impress fellow campers.

Now I must break for a while. I must go and visit a couple of witnesses. I'll be back with you this evening. This is Sinclair V-Log Q890/M data log reference point 4136902/619.

## CHAPTER TWELVE

This is Sinclair V-Log Q890/M data log reference point 4136902/620 continuing report.

The complex of buildings at the entrance to the site sported a row of shops, laundry facilities, bar, Vidicom theatre, and restaurant for those who weren't that keen on roughing it too much. Tinnias unpacked my hover bike and roared off to buy something for breakfast while I got a fire going and set out some comfortable seating. Twenty minutes later, he returned laden with enough food to ensure we could eat well for several day's meals.

"There's meat in this packet here," he said as he handed me a large bag. "A huge hunk of some dark red meat that looks like it will probably need cooking long and slow. There's a couple of fowl in there too. One should be enough for the two of us for each meal. There are some vegetables in this bag, and fruit in this one. I got some eggs, bread, and a couple of bottles of local beer." He handed me two more bags and grinned. "I also got you a gift, since you like the stuff so much." Reaching into his coat pocket, he drew out a small bag and handed it to me. From the feel of the pack, it contained some kind of powder but the label was written in a language I didn't recognise, so I opened it and hoped I would know what it was. I racked my brain to think of what sort of powder I might be a fan of but it wasn't until the smell hit me that my face split into a huge grin.

"Coffee," I sighed as I sniffed long and hard. "Thanks, Dad. It's been ages since I've had this."

"You're welcome. They also had bottles of Green Wine, the good stuff too not the cloudy muck."

I stared in horror. "You didn't buy any, did you?"

"What, and give us away as Sigman so soon? Credit me with a little sense eh, Son."

"Sorry," I replied. "I didn't mean to doubt you. It's one of those things people do without thinking, one of those little mistakes that make my job easier. You see something you love and buy it without thinking someone clever like me is on your tail."

"I know, don't worry. No offence taken. The worst that can happen is that they think we're from Earth, since I made a great show of being delighted to see coffee on sale."

"Well done. I'll get some on to heat while you do breakfast. Now where did I put that special pot for coffee making?"

Over a delicious breakfast of eggs, toasted bread, and cups of hot coffee, we discussed our plan for the day. We agreed that we needed to take some time to orientate ourselves within the city, so we decided to do a tour, aided by the map I downloaded from my ship's computer console. We needed to know the quickest way to get to the port area, where to hide in busy shopping areas if necessary, and how to lose any tails we might pick up by backtracking through alleyways and footpaths. The locations of key buildings would be helpful too, the local Law Enforcement Agency for example, Vidicom theatres, nice and dark for lying low or losing a tail, libraries with research consoles if getting back to the ship is not possible, as well as the usual gathering places for the street bums where we could blend in and disappear if all else should fail.

We needed to know all these things and many more before we felt safe going undercover in a foreign city, especially one as dangerous as anything that involved Gaht. Luckily, both Tinnias and I have the ability to see maps in our mind, to know where we are in that map, and how to get to any location on that map, almost as easily as a native with as little as a day's orientation, so we didn't foresee any problems. One interesting thing the map told us, was the location of several hire-by-the-day locker facilities where we could store gear we might need but didn't want to carry around with us. We could store extra firearms and power cells, along with our Unicoms, our genuine identification documents, data recorders, the stock of miniature cameras and bugs we intended to place within the Gaht compound, and a change of clothes for when we might not need to look like street bums. These locker facilities were popular with the homeless community, for they also provided showers and most have on site hairdressers offering shaves, haircuts, and parasite medication for minimal cost. Many also have laundry facilities for an equally low cost and a few offer creches for children of the homeless who manage to secure a day's work. There are several such places in my home city back on Sigma Prime and they do a wonderful job.

Once the ship was locked down, we set off on my hover bike in our tourist clothes with our holdalls over our shoulders and headed for the main entrance. The attendant smiled as we told him we were taking several days to do a tour and would not be back for a while, and he assured us the bike would be locked up safe and sound until our return. The early morning chill was now almost gone as we made our way to the nearest hover bus stop. Our first call was the locker shop to deposit our gear and change into our street bum clothes. Once suitably attired, we headed out into the rapidly warming morning to acquaint ourselves with the city and discover what secrets, if any, it might hide.

A vast system of alleyways and narrow paths networked the entire city and offered anyone who might be interested, a way of traversing from any given point in the city, to any other point, without ever needing to use the busy main streets. The whole system was horribly complicated and impossible for us to learn in a single day, so we limited ourselves to that portion of it that would enable us to get from the port area to a point nearest to the campsite. Part of this section ran alongside a dried up drainage channel twenty feet deep and forty across, a deep V cut into the ground that ran for miles according to the map and linked the underground drainage pipes to the ocean, a mile north of the Gaht compound at the port. Every few hundred yards, steps were cut into the sides of the channel allowing access to the many homeless who spent much of their time down there, sheltered from cold and wind by the high walls on either side. We saw groups of downtrodden men gathered around fires, their hands held out to the flames, and I acknowledged a twinge of compassion for their plight that sprang to life within my gut.

"I'm hungry," Tinnias said at last. "Let's find a quiet spot where we can eat."

"Good idea," I nodded. We continued until the drainage channel cut off and ran away to the east and we found a stand of trees on some waste ground. The ruin of a small building was almost hidden by years of growth of some kind of creeping plant and after looking around to make sure we were alone, we found a sheltered spot and dug in our pockets for the cold meat and bread we'd packed at breakfast.

"I vote we make sure we never have to dig around in trash bins for food," Tinnias said. "I'm happy to go undercover as a homeless bum but I won't rummage for leftovers in anyone's trash."

I giggled at the thought of my father, a man of high rank with the respect of many back home, rummaging in a trash bin for mouldering remains. Then I remembered that far too many must do just that every day and many of them might well have been men of rank in their past. I was suddenly struck with the desire to do something to help but knew the most I would ever be able to do would be far too little. Tinnias saw me staring into space and nudged me.

"What's up?"

I shrugged. "I guess the sight of all these homeless people has got to me. We have such a nice life and we're just playing at this to get a job done.

They must live this every day and some of them might once have had good jobs like us, had responsibility, men who looked up to them, families. In a way, I suppose it feels like we're making fun of them, acting the part like this."

"I understand," Tinnias said. "I really do. The problem with feeling as you describe is that it's so easy to let the enormity of it overwhelm you. Every single inhabited world will have homeless people just like these and whatever we do, we can't wipe out the problem for them all. All we can do is bring it down to a level where we are able to make a difference and hope that out there, on all those other worlds, there are men who feel as we do, working to make the same small difference. Maybe all of us together will make enough of a difference one day in the future. All we can do is our own little piece of the puzzle."

He was right, as usual, and I thanked him for his wisdom. The chance to spend an extended time with Tinnias allowed me to share his vast wisdom and I was glad of it. I seldom get more than a week or two at a time back home, which doesn't give us a chance to share such deep stuff with each other and now that we did have the time, it drew us closer than I would have thought possible. That day, as we sat in our smelly clothes in a vermin infested ruin on Niruvan Prime, preparing to go undercover on a recklessly dangerous unofficial mission, I knew I loved Tinnias as truly as I could ever have loved my natural parents. At that moment, he stopped being my adopted father and became simply, my father.

When our bellies were satisfied, we set off into the city to familiarise ourselves with the street layout and locations of key buildings. Although large, the city was obviously one of the poorer regions of this world as everywhere had a distinctly dingy quality about it. From the broken windows, bent road signs, fading paintwork, and rubbish piles that all went unrepaired, the faded, dejected nature of the place was obvious. One or two of the stores had music spilling out onto the street but it had a tinny quality that irritated rather than entertained, and only a quarter of the store signage tubes functioned properly. The vehicles that puttered along the streets were dented and dirty and from the smell, we guessed none of them would pass any emission tests back home. After three hours, we felt we knew our way around well enough to be able to blend in, or get away quickly if we needed to, and decided to head for the homeless shelter near the port. We were in the northern end of the city by now and got the shock of our lives as we turned a street and crossed through a small park to see what lay on the opposite side.

It was as if we had somehow teleported to a different planet by the look of the buildings that now surrounded us. Everywhere was clean, the vehicles modern, and the people who wrinkled their noses at us looked like they'd just stepped out of a high end clothes store. Before either of us could say anything to express our amazement, a man dressed in a smart grey uniform came up to us.

"I take it you two are strangers around here then?" he demanded. We nodded. "Well I'm going to have to ask you to turn around and go back the way you came. This area is not for the likes of you."

"Why ever not?" Tinnias asked.

"Because this is where nice folks live, that's why," he hissed. "This is the rich folks' area and they don't like seeing people like you wandering around their neighbourhood. Come on now, on yer way boys." He ushered us unceremoniously back towards the edge of the street and ordered us back across. Not wanting to make an embarrassing scene that might draw attention to ourselves or put us in danger of being detained by any law enforcers, we obeyed. Once back within the now familiar parts of the city, we gaped at each other.

"Well that was something of a surprise," Tinnias said. "I never expected that."

"Me neither," I replied, then started to laugh. Tinnias frowned at me. "I just had this vision of you listening quietly to his telling off and ordering you out of there, then handing him your Agency Identification and arresting him. I'd love to see the look on his face."

Tinnias laughed along with me. "That would be hilarious. I will admit I was momentarily tempted. If it weren't for this job, I might have done, just for the hell of it."


We found the homeless hostel without any trouble and secured the last available room, which was smaller than Tinnias' bathroom back home, unheated, and contained two damp mattresses on the bare wooden floor. The whole place stank of mould and piss and I almost gagged at the thought of sleeping on that disease ridden thing.

"Holy shit, I can't sleep on that, I just can't. Who knows what kind of parasites are lurking in there."

"Yes, you can, Son. I'm doing it too so you won't be suffering alone. We can keep each other's spirits up and there's always the hairdresser at the locker shop if we get infested with anything. Remember all those guys out there who have to sleep like this? Surely we can manage for a few days before we return to our comfortable existence?"

He was using my own compassion against me and I knew it. I glared at him and he grinned. "Okay, smart ass, you got me. Well if I'm forced to sleep here, I intend to do it on a full stomach. The guy on the front desk said they offer a basic meal in thirty minutes down in the basement. Let's make sure we get a seat down there huh?"

"Yes okay," Tinnias nodded. "They don't do any breakfast here so we're going to be very hungry if we don't eat tonight."

The basement room was laid out with several long rows of tables, with wooden stools packed tightly side by side tucked underneath. A serving counter ran the length of one wall, at which there were already at least twenty men queued. A smaller table lay at the end of the room, with places laid for six people.

"I wonder when we get invited to the Captain's table," Tinnias hissed in my ear.

"I wouldn't hold your breath," a voice behind me replied. We turned to face a man of similar height and build to myself and of apparently similar age to Tinnias.

"Just a joke," Tinnias smiled.

"I guess this is your first visit to this fine establishment." Tinnias and I nodded. "What room did you get?"

"Seven eighty three," I said.

The man roared with laughter so hard his face was purple by the time he was composed enough to speak. "Oh, you poor shits. Late were ya?" We nodded again. "Well that won't be happening again I presume."

"I sincerely doubt it," I replied.

"That room is always kept until last. It's a kind of punishment for being late. No one wants to spend the night there, so we try to be in before lock up. My advice is to be here before nine if you want a decent room."

"Thanks," Tinnias said. "We'll make sure to remember."

"What's the work situation like around these parts?" I asked as nonchalantly as I could.

"No better or worse than anywhere else I guess," the man replied. "They do hire at the port each day, but you have to be queuing at the main gate by six in the morning. If you want to be up in time, I'll come and bang on your door."

"Thanks," I smiled. "That would be helpful."

"No problem. I'm Zeno by the way. Ex-military, ex-husband, ex-father, ex-useful member of society. Pleased to meet you both." He extended a hand which Tinnias and I shook warmly.

"Ren," I replied. "Ex-military, ex security, so far escaped marriage."

"Koto," Tinnias added. "Ex-military, old fart extraordinaire."

"How long have you guys been at this end of the social strata?"

"Not long," I replied. "We're still getting to know our way around the life."

"Well you could do worse than stick with me. I fell from grace over twenty years ago so I know plenty about how to survive without drawing attention to yourself."

"Thanks," Tinnias said. "We could sure use a good mentor."

"You're not drinkers or druggies are you? I won't waste my time with those types. They don't want to learn how to survive well, they're too wrapped up in their own self loathing and need to punish themselves."

"We enjoy a social drink if there's the opportunity," I replied, impressed with Zeno's insight into man's nature. "Neither of us touches drugs though, although I will have a cigarette from time to time, if the stress level warrants it."

Zeno nodded, apparently satisfied that we were worthy of his time and attention. "So long as you're both clean, that's fine by me. Ahh, opening time at last. Avoid the fish like the plague, the oceans and rivers here are horribly polluted."

We shuffled our way towards the serving hatch and were each handed a tray which was divided into sections, and a cup. The only choice we were given was meat or fish; the rest of our meal was handed out whether we wanted it or not. There was a meat stew that smelled surprisingly good given the circumstances, two types of vegetables, a starch, a large hunk of very fresh bread, and our cups were filled with a sweetened hot drink. The meat was dark in colour and smothered in brown gravy, so whichever animal it originated from was not obvious. The vegetables were unrecognisable other than their colour, one green and one orange. The green one was a type of leaf as there were visible stringy stems within the green mush. The orange one was just a mush, so your guess is as good as mine. The starch was a grain of some kind, and the bread, still warm and full of seeds. The drink was a disappointingly drab beige. After being handed a spoon and a paper napkin, we made our way to the next three available stools.

The meal was delicious, despite being made by the vat load and being more than a little over cooked. I noticed that everyone around us had cleared their trays with as much enjoyment as we had done, and I couldn't help but comment.

"That was delicious," I said and noticed Tinnias nodding furiously.

Zeno smiled. "That's the main reason why this place never has unoccupied rooms. It's famous amongst the homeless for the food. There should be a gal walking up and down with bowls of fruit in a minute. You're allowed to take two pieces each. If you don't recognise anything, take the largest red ones, with the narrow tops and fat bottoms. They're the nicest ones. Then we listen to the speech."

"The speech?" I asked.

"The guys at the top table," Zeno nodded towards the smaller table at the end of the room at which sat four men and two women. "They're the committee that runs this place. They'll give a speech about the perils of drink and drugs, the importance of not losing your self respect, the need to strive to get yourself back into society and make any announcements that affect us or this place."

I nodded. "I see, okay."

"After that, we have two hour's free time before lock up. If you leave the building, be back on time or you'll be locked out. Smoking is outside only."

The night was chilly as we walked around the block exchanging life stories with Zeno. Both Tinnias and I felt compassion for him as he told us how, after leaving the military at the end of ten years' service with three medals for valour, he married his childhood sweetheart and started his own business repairing and selling hover vehicles. Two children later, he came home one day to find his wife had run off with another man and had taken the children with her. On his home world, to be left like that by a spouse made him a social outcast and he quickly lost his business. With no income and no one willing to employ him, he failed to keep up the payments on his home and found himself homeless, thrown out onto the street with just a holdall of personal possessions on the anniversary of his marriage.

Tinnias and I gave him our rehearsed fake history, which he accepted without question and we shared commiserations as we walked. He brought out a battered pack of cigarettes and offered us both one, which we took

146

despite not wanting to. Call me over sensitive if you want, but it seems to me that when a man who has next to nothing and found himself at the very bottom of society through no fault of his own, offers to share the little he has, to turn down the gift would be an intolerable insult that I was not willing to have a part in. The fact that Tinnias automatically accepted as well, pleased me very much. He has the same insight of which I pride myself, although he hides it more modestly than I. Maybe it's because he's older and wiser that he doesn't feel the need to bang his own drum as fervently, perhaps his life experience has taught him that, ultimately, it's unnecessary. Whatever, I was glad to see him demonstrate it so naturally.

"What sort of work do they offer at the port?" Tinnias asked as he puffed on the cigarette and tried valiantly not to cough.

"All sorts," Zeno replied. "Cleaning the outside areas, loading and unloading trucks, gardening, although just the heavy stuff like digging, nothing that requires any real knowledge of plants, thankfully. Some basic repairs and maintenance of the buildings, repainting, and if anyone has specific skills, they will make use of them. One regular used to be a glazier before he hit rock bottom, so he gets asked to replace broken windows. Another guy we see sometimes worked for a power company a few years back, so he tinkers with the power circuits, fixes any problems they might have with power and stuff like that. They get me to fix their vehicles, since I was a mechanic in my previous life. If you have special skills, tell 'em and you'll get off the boring stuff."

"I don't have any," I shrugged. "The only thing I'm good at is martial arts. I've been in security all my working life. I do know my way around a gun though, but they probably won't be needing me to help them in that capacity."

"I'm pretty good at basic home maintenance and decorating," Tinnias said. "I can fix anything wooden quite acceptably, and I can paint a wall with the best of them."

"Make sure you mention it in the morning then. Now we'd better get back or we'll be walking round the block all night and it's damn cold here at nights."

We lay side by side on the damp mattresses and tried not to wonder what manner of parasite we may have been sharing our humble bed with. We'd said goodnight to Zeno and he'd promised to wake us in order that we all get to the port in good time to be at the front of the usual crowd of eager workers.

"So the plan for tomorrow is to get to know the layout of the place and nothing more," Tinnias said. "We see what we're dealing with before we make any kind of move. Once we feel comfortable we're not out of our depth, we can think about fitting some cameras around the place."

"Agreed," I nodded. "If it becomes obvious we won't be able to fit any listening devices, we'll just have to make sure we get work every day and try to ingratiate ourselves with them."

"And keep our eyes and ears open."

"If they don't search us on entry to the compound, we can take our Agency recorders in. They'll give us something we can use, even if it's not that much."

"Anything is better than nothing," Tinnias said.

I heard him yawn beside me and smiled. "Being homeless is hard work eh?"

"It sure is," he replied. "Let's try and sleep. We might be glad of it tomorrow if they work us hard."

"Goodnight, Dad. Thanks for being with me on this. It's good to be able to spend time together."

"Goodnight, Son. I love you."

"I love you too."

I closed my eyes and was asleep within twenty minutes, despite believing it would be impossible in such dreadful surroundings. In my dream, I saw my natural parents and asked them if they minded that I loved my adopted father. I didn't want them to feel I was betraying them, but they assured me they were happy for me and told me they loved me and were proud of me. I found myself alone in unfamiliar surroundings, so I started to walk down a road that appeared out of nowhere to my left. The road wound its way up hills and down into deep valleys and I was aware of a growing feeling of loneliness within. Just as I was about to panic at my solitude, I saw a derelict building in a field of wild flowers and felt relief flooding through me. Nobody had lived there for years it seemed as the entire structure leaned precariously, held up only by the thick greenery that overwhelmed the whole of one end and a large part of the rear portion. That building meant people had been there and might be close by still, so I quickened my pace, heartened by the promise of civilisation to fill the dark loneliness.

As I drew abreast of the wreck that was once a modest home, an upper storey window flung open and a face peered out, followed by an arm that waved frantically. It was Ren, my law enforcement partner who died on a job we were doing together and the reason for my current alias. As joy flooded through me, I somehow magically transported to the rear garden of the building where Ren waited for me, a huge grin splitting his face in half. We embraced and I asked him where the people were. It was weird, thinking about it in the cold light of waking reality but that's the way of dreams isn't it? Instead of telling him I missed him and asking if he was happy wherever he was, I enquired of the local inhabitants.

"They're there if you want them to be there," he replied in that typical cryptic way that makes perfect sense in the dream but is almost meaningless when awake.

"Okay," I replied. "I guess I don't want them then, since they aren't around yet." Don't ask, it made no sense to me either but I'm telling you everything as it happened to me.

"There are no enemies here, Joss," he said, calling me by the alias I used on the job we did together when he died.

"I'm remembering you," I said. "Just like you told me to, in the good way."

"I know you are and I'm proud of you. Have you seen your parents yet?"

"Yes," I smiled. "In the last village, before the hills."

"Good. Now I want you to promise me something. Can you do that, Joss?"

"Of course," I replied. "Anything for you, just name it."

He smiled. "I want you to remember something important. When you meet the man with the Mokastone, trust him and do as he asks."

"Okay, I'll remember," I promised, failing to ask how I might recognise this friend nor what a Mokastone might be, but then that's the way of dreams isn't it? They only seem weird when we awaken.

"Thanks, Joss. I knew I could rely on you. It's time you were off now, you've a long walk ahead."

After magically transporting myself back to the country road, I began to walk and made no more than a few steps when I was woken by Tinnias shaking my shoulder.

"Wake up, Sam. Zeno just knocked. He's going to wait for us outside."

The morning was chill at that early hour and the thought of washing in icy cold water in the filthy bathroom appealed to neither of us, so we settled for running our hands through our hair and taking a pee before racing down to meet Zeno.

"Do either of you have any money?" Zeno asked after we exchanged greetings.

"I have a few coins I found at a hover bus stop," Tinnias replied.

"And I found a couple by a fast food stall," I added.

"Right, let's pool what we have and see if we can't afford something for breakfast, shall we?"

It turned out that the coins Tinnias and I found were quite high value and we had enough to buy each of us two hot meat pies from a stall around the corner from the shelter. They were delicious, not only because we were very hungry but because they really were very good.

"You did good, boys," Zeno grinned between mouthfuls. "Hover bus stops and fast food stalls are good places to find dropped coins. Vehicle refuelling stops and gambling houses are too. In the warmer months, you can sometimes get casual work gardening for the folks in the better neighbourhoods to the north, and if you fancy getting locked out of the shelter for a night now and again, restaurants and fast food places sometimes hire casuals to clean up and take out the trash bins."

"That's good to know," Tinnias nodded. "If we don't get hired at the port some days, we can do that instead."

"The best way to get a day's work at the port is to be as far towards the front of the queue as possible. Come on, let's go."

# CHAPTER THIRTEEN

We arrived at the port area and found a queue of around a dozen men already waiting outside a padlocked gate. A couple turned and nodded to Zeno and I recognised one or two from the shelter.

"Now we wait," Zeno said. "If no one opens the gate by the time we hear the city clock chiming, we might as well leave."

"They don't hire every day then?" I asked.

"Most days they do, but not every day."

"How long do we have to wait?"

"About a half hour."

I was about to try some casual conversation to while away the time, when singing voices reached our ears, accompanied by the clapping of many hands. We turned and watched as a group of men further down the queue behind us sang, a fast paced song in a language neither of us understood. They accompanied themselves with clapping hands and tapping feet and a couple of them danced, the furious stepping and stamping, clapping, and pained expressions telling us the song told a tale of hardship, adversity, and endurance. It was stirring and I found myself tapping my feet in time without realising. With a series of whooping cries, the song ended to loud applause from the rest of us.

"That was amazing," Tinnias said. "I didn't understand a word but it moved me."

"Me too," I nodded. "They're good, very good."

"They entertain the crowds in the city square on warm summer weekends," Zeno told us. "They were quite famous on their home world some years ago, apparently."

"So how come they ended up here?" I asked.

"There was some kind of political uprising where they come from and they didn't agree with the new system. Anyone who didn't obey the new leaders was regarded as a threat to their national security. They rounded them up and sent them to some hell hole prison digging for some toxic mineral they used in their power stations. Most of them died from the poisonous stuff. These five guys ran for their lives, which meant they emigrated unofficially and have none of the proper paperwork. They can't get good work or buy homes as illegal immigrants, so they ended up here, no money, no home, no possessions other than the clothes they stand up in but they have their freedom."

"I guess there's always a worse way to end up than this," Tinnias said. Zeno and I nodded. I was about to reply when we heard metallic knocks, the sliding of a chain, and the squeaking of the gate as it swung open on hinges that were in dire need of some oil.

"Here we go, boys," Zeno grinned at us. "Remember to tell them all your skills and be keen to work hard. Good luck and I'll probably catch up with you at the mid-day meal."

One by one, we shuffled forwards as the armed guards counted us inside the gate. When Tinnias and I reached the front, the guard stopped us and frowned. After trying a couple of different languages which neither of us understood, Tinnias tried the Common Tongue, a language adopted by all worlds who adhere to the Inter-Galactic Union of Worlds to make communication between races, easier.

"I'm sorry, we don't understand your language," Tinnias said. "Can you speak the Common Tongue?"

The guard nodded. "I've not seen you two here before."

"We just got here a few days ago."

"What are your names and why should I hire you instead of two other guys I know I can rely on?"

"I'm Koto and this is Ren. We're both ex-military and have worked in security for years. I'm handy at household maintenance and am good with plants. I grew all the vegetables for the family, when I had one. Ren here is expert in martial arts and can turn his hand to almost anything."

The guard exchanged a glance with his colleagues before indicating for us to enter. We ran to join our fellows and sighed with relief.

"That was awesome, Dad," I grinned. "You've still got it."

"Never lost it, Son."


I counted twenty three of us as we stood in the small room waiting to be given jobs and made a mental note to make sure we were always within the first fifteen in the queue, just to make sure we stood a good chance of getting hired. Armed guards surrounded us and one stood at the front and addressed us all, a clipboard in his hand. He called out the jobs and selected names from the clipboard for each. He started with the most menial jobs, sweeping, washing vehicles, emptying trash bins and the like, then moved on to slightly more skilled jobs. One guy was given the job of renewing some leaking plumbing, another was set to work rebuilding a section of wall that was in danger of collapse. Zeno was told to tune up a couple of hover vehicles, which then left Tinnias and I alone.

"Okay umm, Koto, you can start by following my colleague here. We have some internal maintenance that the women have been nagging us about. There's some flooring to be laid, a window that won't open, and some decorating. See how you go with that for now."

"Thank you, Sir," Tinnias nodded and followed the guard out of the room.

"Now, Ren. You're into martial arts are you?"

"Yes, Sir," I nodded.

"Are you up for a bit of sparring with some of my guys?"

"Sure thing."

Turning to one of the guards, he motioned towards the door. "Call Spen in would you?"

A bulky man entered and I remembered discovering that three of Belotan's sons train their elite field operatives. Spen must be one of the three, I assumed as I looked him right in the eyes.

"This is Ren," the guard told him. "He says he's into martial arts, so I thought maybe you want to see what he's got and put him to work with your guys. It might be good for them to spar with someone they don't know."

Spen nodded and looked me up and down. "Good idea." He walked towards me. "You look strong, Ren. Not too bulky though. What kind of martial art do you prefer?"

"I've been doing the Damiklonian practice for a while now," I replied.

His eyebrows shot to the top of his head and his bottom jaw dropped open. "You're shitting me."

"No shit, Sir."

"But you're not a Damiklonian, how come you know their martial art? They are highly secretive about it and never teach it to anyone outside their own race."

"Not often, but sometimes they do," I said. "My best friend was Damiklonian and he taught me. We were going to go into business together but he died suddenly."

"How do I know you're not lying to me?"

"I guess you don't," I shrugged as I reached into my clothing and pulled out the necklace I always wore, the long white curving fang carved out of a sacred stone that my friend gave to me as he died in my arms. Spen saw it and I noticed him gulp in awe.

"The Damiklonian Fang," he whispered, more to himself than anyone else. "It could be fake."

"It could be," I replied. "I guess you'll never know until you try me out."

He ran a hand through his hair and stepped back towards the wall. "The floor is yours, Ren. Impress me, man."

I stepped into the middle of the room and closed my eyes as I inhaled several long slow breaths to calm my mind. Five minutes later, I stood, my chest heaving after going through the basic Damiklonian warm up routine, with a couple of extra moves added for visual aesthetics. When I opened my eyes, everyone in the room was open mouthed in awe.

"That was fucking amazing," Spen said.

"Thanks," I replied. "Does that mean I'm hired?"

"It means I'm willing to give you a try. Follow me."


I caught up with Tinnias and Zeno at the mid-day meal provided for us in a large room at the back of the compound. They were already chatting and laughing when I arrived and I was glad to see my father able to relax, even if only for a while. They both looked up when I sat down beside them with my tray of food.

"How was your morning, guys?" I asked.

"I've had it easy," Zeno said. "Tuning up the hover vehicles is child's play."

"I've been laying carpet in the women's quarters," Tinnias said. "It's tough on the knees but I was inside in the warm and the women were friendly and kept me topped up with hot drinks. What have you been doing? You look as if you've been in a fight."

"I have, in a manner of speaking," I grinned. "I was allocated the enviable task of being a punch bag for their field operatives' workout." Seeing them both frown, I sniggered. "They had me sparring with them, to give them some experience with an unknown opponent."

"Did they hurt you?" Tinnias asked, a note of genuine concern in his voice.

"No, but a few of them will be sporting bruises. I think I might've broken one guy's wrist. I hope it doesn't go against me."

"I doubt it," Zeno replied. "They're always boasting about how tough their elite fighters are, then you come along and beat the shit out of them single handed. They'll be embarrassed but probably grateful."

Tinnias nodded. "He's got a point there, Ren. You probably don't have to worry."

"I hope so," I replied as I tucked into the generous meal of meat stew and vegetables, warm bread, followed by a hot fruit pie. We ate in silence, each grateful for the meal and not wishing to waste a moment that could be spent eating. When we pushed our empty plates away and belched, Zeno got up from the table.

"I'm going outside to smoke. You want to join me?"

"No thanks, I'm good," I said.

"I don't think I can move after that meal," Tinnias grinned.

When Zeno left us alone, I leaned forwards. "What's it like inside the place?"

"This is a huge complex," Tinnias said. "Only three of the buildings are used much though. One is where they live, with their women and kids and consists of eight rooms on the ground floor and seventeen on the upper floor. Another seems to be a kind of work cum office base. It has three floors but I only saw the ground floor when I went to get some tools. The third is this building here, which I haven't seen much of, apart from the room we were ushered into when we arrived, and this dining area. I'm guessing other parts down the other end are used as workshops and storage, vehicle maintenance areas and that sort of thing. All the manual labour type stuff is my guess. There is a large area of land at the back where they grow vegetables and keep livestock, and I noticed a small jetty and a boathouse built into the perimeter wall."

"Well done," I grinned. "Great observation skills, I'm seriously impressed."

"Thanks. What did you find out?"

"I spent the morning in a sort of parade ground, like I remember from the military. Part of it is under cover and interestingly, the floor surface has been dug up and replaced by military grade Softcrete, in a delicate shade of vomit. It's surrounded by walls, but only one of them has windows, so I'm guessing there's only one building attached to it. The other three are probably just walls built to keep prying eyes from seeing how their guys are trained. I'm not sure what building looks out onto it, but it's not this one."

"Good job. There are plenty of areas worth putting some listening devices and cameras into," Tinnias said and I nodded. "I can easily put a couple into the workshop when I go to get tools. It might be worth putting a couple in the living quarters too. They might talk about what they're up to over dinner or in bed with their women."

"I agree," I said. "I don't think it's worth putting any in the parade ground itself. All we'll see is men beating the shit out of each other, which will quickly become boring. It wouldn't hurt to put one into the washroom though, the guys might talk while taking a shit."

"They might," Tinnias nodded. "Or we might find ourselves with seventy eight hours of men farting to listen to, which will be equally as boring as watching your guys working out."

My chest hurt from laughing, made all the worse from trying to keep my laughter quiet so as not to arouse suspicion. Tinnias was red faced with the effort and I supposed I was too. Seriously, why the hell are bodily functions so funny?

Our legs ached as we dragged ourselves back along the streets to the shelter, but we had the bones of a plan. Neither of us could face a freezing wash in the filthy sink in our room, so we told Zeno we were going to head to the public bathing house to freshen up and launder our clothes. The men at the compound paid us casual employees by the day, so both Tinnias and I were solvent for the first time in days. After reminding us to be back before lock up, Zeno turned left towards the shelter and left us alone.

"Okay, back to the ship for a shower and change of clothes, then a decent meal," I suggested.

Tinnias nodded. "Even Nutri-Vend is appealing at the moment. Hell, I'd even welcome a Yamelian Pie."

Our laughter echoed off the looming walls of the buildings as we made our way along the quiet streets. "Fuck, you must be seriously hungry," I said between guffaws.

The Nutri-Vend machines all dispense the same menu galaxy wide. No matter if you're feeding a military unit during a war on a Prime world in a major shipping lane, catching a snack during a sporting event on some backwater leisure world, or providing meals for a dozen miners on some un-named rocky moon out in the butt hole of nowhere, everyone knows exactly what will be on offer. One such item is a dessert called Yamelian Pie, a legendary dish whose origins are somewhat shrouded in mystery. The story goes that it is a popular dessert from the Canorly system, right out in galactic sector 83583-3340P. The Canorly system has three large inhabited planets, all of which are the only known location of Mexahedralonium X4. All three Canorly planets produce it in abundance, via the unique mineral make up of their molten cores. With an abundance of volcanoes on all three planets, the bright pink lava flows yield a constant supply, which is sold all over the galaxy at enormous profit for use in the production of a high specification space ship fuel additive. The substance makes Trans Wave Flow Core engines run cleaner and enables them to gain up to twenty-four percent extra speed. Because of the cost of this rare substance, it is used exclusively by the military, where extra speed and agility in the theatre of war can save countless lives.

The Canorly people love Yamelian Pie passionately. As a token of gratitude from the military for providing them with Mexahedralonium X4, they were promised that wherever a Canorly soldier should find himself, no matter what dangers he may be placing himself in for the good of others, he would always have a taste of home to keep up his spirits. Thus, Yamelian Pie will always be on the Nutri-Vend menu. The only problem for everyone else is that no one other than Canorly people like it. Everyone else unanimously agrees that it is one of the most disgusting substances known. Everyone has to taste the stuff once, but no one I knew had ever repeated the experience.

Back at the ship, both of us took long hot showers and sat, wrapped in blankets with steaming mugs of Chaha while our clothes washed and dried. Once dressed and smelling fresh again, we discussed what surveillance equipment we should take with us back to the compound the next day. Once we agreed that we should take at least half a dozen miniature cameras with built-in audio receivers, we packed our backpacks, locked up the ship, and headed back into the city. Our first stop was the bathing house and locker hire facility to retrieve the surveillance equipment we had stored there.

"You're probably going to have to place most of the cameras yourself," I said. "If they decide to keep me on sparring duties, I simply won't have the opportunity, apart from putting one in their washroom."

"That's okay, I should have plenty of opportunities if they keep me on inside duties in the women's quarters. The women talk plenty and we've no idea how much they know. We could glean valuable information just from listening to their chatter."

"That's true," I nodded. "Maybe we should buy some of those meat pies and offer a couple to Zeno. We can't return without having spent some money. We said we were going to the bathing house so we need to at least appear to have spent some."

"Good point, Son. They were nice, let's buy enough for ourselves as well, and cigarettes too. He's offered his own to us several times so we should return the favour."


"Aww thanks, Guys," Zeno grinned as he tucked into the three pies we gave him. "You two smell much nicer by the way."

We sat on the low perimeter wall that marked the boundary of the shelter and smoked, Zeno taking long draws and blowing the smoke into rings that sailed into the clear night sky. Tinnias amazed us both by blowing a smaller ring that travelled right through the centre of Zeno's much larger one, then a third smaller still and finally, a tiny bubble of smoke that shot through the very centre of all three.

"Wherever did you learn that?" I laughed.

"I learned it while trapped in a hole for three days and nights, early in my military career. By the time another company came to help us out and clear the area of snipers, four of us had become experts at it, thanks to the indulgence of the fifth. It gave us something to concentrate our minds on other than the high possibility of dying at any moment. It gives me something to amaze people at parties with," he grinned.

"Did you manage to get a better room?" Zeno asked.

"We're on the third floor this time," Tinnias replied. "Room Thirty Eight."

"Good, you'll have clean sheets each week and your basin and toilet cleaned every other day."

"Wonderful," I replied. "The thought of many more nights in that filthy hole up at the top was not pleasant."

"You'll smell better too," he grinned. "The taps should give you warmish water, warm enough to wash with and rinse out your underwear anyway."

"We should only need to go to the bathing house every couple of days then," Tinnias said. "That'll save a few coins." He looked me right in the eyes and I was glad we'd stopped there on our way back to the shelter for the miniature cameras rather than leave it another day. Without a valid excuse to return there, we might arouse suspicion and Zeno's knowledge was valuable. Besides, we liked him and he was giving up his time and independence to help us survive.

"If we get enough day's work at the port," I said, "we should be able to buy a change of clothes soon. Are there any stores round here that sell used garments, Zeno?"

He nodded. "Several. When you're ready, I'll take you." He yawned long and hard before stamping on his cigarette. "I'm off to bed, I'm not as young as I was and the cold makes my bones ache. I'll see you two in the morning."

We bade him goodnight and watched as he heaved his slight frame up the steps and in through the door of the shelter. Tinnias expressed what I was thinking. "He's not well, Sam."

"No, he's not is he. I wish we could do something to help him."

"When this business is over, we can."

"I wonder if this planet has any medical care for the homeless and poor people."

Tinnias shrugged. "We can ask at the bathing house next time we go."


We waited for Zeno early next morning but he failed to arrive. I was worried but time constraints meant we couldn't take time to go and see him without missing out on a day's work at the port. Reluctantly, we headed out and took our places in the queue. With only five others in front of us, we felt sure we'd get hired. Our plan, such as it was, was for Tinnias to place our devices in each of the rooms he worked in, especially those that looked like they were lived in outside of working hours. I would put one in the field operative's washroom to catch any talk between the men. Anywhere that looked like somewhere people might spend time talking was a potential surveillance zone, so we took plenty of devices and hid them in our underwear and under the linings of our coats. Not until we could return to the ship and listen to the recordings, would we know if we'd wasted our time or not.

Tinnias was again given work decorating the women's quarters and living areas, whilst I was once again out in the cold kicking the shit out of Gaht's field operatives. It was child's play for me to secrete a couple of devices within the washroom, after excusing myself for a pee so I could be in there alone, and I had the whole room covered by three devices within the first two hours. By the time I met Tinnias for our mid-day meal, I was sporting a couple of gashes from the blades my opponents decided to arm themselves with this time. At first annoyed, it turned out to be rather fortuitous as I was taken to the medical facility to have them cleaned up and managed to stick a device beneath the examination bed when the nurse went into the next room for some ointment.

Tinnias' initial horror turned to an appreciative nod when he heard this and happily told me he had managed to place seven devices in five different locations. "Four of the apartments have devices in them, as do both the corridors. I also stuck one in the equipment and supply store where all the labouring staff re supply themselves and take their breaks."

"Awesome. I still have two devices just in case a new location becomes open to us."

"I have four left," Tinnias said. "There are quite a few places I've not been to, both inside the main buildings and outside. There are bound to be places we'll never get to, offices and such like."

I nodded. "We just have to do what we can and hope it's enough."

"How long will your ship's systems record for before it needs backing up?"

"Around a hundred thousand hours," I grinned in reply.

Tinnias gave a snort of laughter. "No need to worry yet then." His laughter then turned to a frown. "That's not law enforcement spec. Who's been fiddling with the ship?"

I blushed. "You're not the only one with useful contacts y'know. Sometimes they find themselves owing me a favour, which I try not to call in unless I have to. I find it's better to have a few outstanding debts owed to me for occasions just such as this one. The person who upgraded my surveillance recording ability felt the service I had provided warranted such repayment."

I could see Tinnias was itching to know more about it, and the difficulty he had limiting himself to an understanding nod and a non committal, "oh, yeah, I understand," was obvious.

"I saved his seven year old daughter from being gang raped by a group of drunken mercs who found his cargo worth far less than they hoped when they planned their raid on his warehouse."

"Shit," Tinnias hissed. "Well done, Son. I'm proud of you."

"If anyone ever finds out, I'll know you ratted me out and I'll tell Mom about the wrinkly you danced ever-so-close with back on Dankera."

"My lips are sealed," he laughed.


We decided to give it a day before going back to my ship to review the recordings, so after our meal was over, we said our goodbyes and headed back to work. As I entered the training yard, I was met by the unsmiling visage of Spen, the training supervisor.

"Where is everyone?" I enquired.

"They'll be away for the rest of the afternoon; a security detail has suddenly become necessary in a neighbouring city."

"Oh, okay. What would you like me to do then?"

I saw him scratch his chin as a grin gradually spread itself across his face. "Well, you could show me some of that martial art of yours."

I guess I knew a request such as this was inevitable, but it still made me feel uncomfortable. The Damiklonian martial art is guarded with great secrecy, and I had promised Ren I would not let him down by showing anyone who asked. Spen would no doubt be upset if I refused outright though, so I made a hasty decision to show him nothing of importance.

"Well I umm," I began, knowing he had some knowledge of Damiklonian culture and would expect me to be reluctant. If I said yes straight away, he would be immediately suspicious.

"What's the problem?" he frowned at me.

"It kind of, goes against Damiklonian culture to give away the martial art to anyone who asks. It would be disrespectful of me to do that. I made a solemn promise to the Damiklonian Lavastra Valkerian, their spiritual leaders, that I would uphold their law."

Long seconds of silence passed between us, his eyes never leaving mine, before he gave a snort of laughter and nodded. "Okay, Ren. Forget I asked."

"Is this going to be a problem between us?" I asked.

"Not at all. I just needed to be sure you're on the level y'know? You wouldn't know that level of detail if you were yanking my balls."

Now it was my turn to snort. "So you were testing me?"

"Yeah. Congratulations, you get to keep your kneecaps."

"Thanks," I replied, unsure how long he intended to let me keep them.

"You can come and help me clean and restock the armoury. How quickly can you strip and clean a Kalarian Laser Pistol?"

"About three minutes, give or take."

He stopped mid stride and looked at me, a frown suddenly creasing his brow. "That's pretty good. How does someone with a standard security background get such skills?"

"I was in the military for ten years before that," I replied. "I like to keep my skills sharp. Call it an obsession if you want but you never know when your life might depend upon it."

"True enough," he agreed and tapped out a seven digit code into the digital lock on the door in front of us, before stepping to the side and beckoning me inside.

I almost gasped aloud as I took in the sight that lay before me and did a full circle of the room as I memorised the seven digit code Spen had used to gain entry. If you're into guns, this was heaven and I would love to have the opportunity to try everything out. I recognised most of it, laser rifles of many different types made up the majority of the hardware, alongside various laser pistols, pulse bombs, smoke bangs, so called because they make a heck of a noise but just give off a thick cloud of choking smoke, a rack of six AB11 Rookies, the sight of which brought a lump to my throat as I remembered the bravery of a man who saved my life with one of these, an act which cost him his own. I couldn't help but walk over to them and run a hand along the barrel of the nearest one as I sniffed away the memory.

"You like the Rookie, Ren," Spen said with a snigger.

I turned and shook away the melancholy. "Someone died saving me, armed only with one of those. I'll always have a measure of affection for them I guess." I marched over to where I saw a rack of Kalarian laser pistols and looked at Spen. "Right then, where's your cleaning kits?"

Six hours later, I stood and stretched my back. Between us, we had cleaned all the laser pistols and two thirds of the rifles, restocked everything with the appropriate ammunition, taken an inventory of the stock, swept and scrubbed the floor. I managed to place one of my remaining recording devices beneath the lip of a rifle rack cradle and was grateful when Spen announced the job finished for the day.

"Well done, Ren," he said as he shut and tested the door behind us. "Go have a hot drink, you've a few minutes before the other workers finish."

## CHAPTER FOURTEEN

The sun was setting across the mouth of the port as I made my way to the dining area and helped myself to a hot drink and snack from the bank of auto vends. Allowing my mind the time to wander as I waited for Tinnias to appear, I was first back in that hell hole prison watching Ronjo die horribly after saving my hide with the almost useless AB11 Rookie. These guns are so called because it's the first firearm given to men who may not have ever used a gun before and may be nervous. Effective at no further than around ten feet, Ronjo had lost his life in the most horrific way. Then I was back in the abandoned railway tunnels watching my best friend, Ren, die after we successfully brought an end to the strange goings on at the mysterious scientific research facility. Lastly, I was back aboard the Drycenian battle cruiser, confused at Vincent's off handedness towards me. I was saddened to discover that it appeared as if he and the Drycenians I had admired for years since we first met, were now working against me. I felt the enormity of the universe around me, dark and cold, and my insignificance became all too clear. For the first time in a long while, I felt afraid and very lonely. I let memories of the delicious kiss I was able to share with Byron before Tinnias and I ran away, lift my heart and hoped he was okay and still loved me.

"I love you," I whispered to the empty room.

Tinnias noticed my melancholic mood as we walked back to the homeless shelter. "What's up, Son?"

"Oh nothing really," I replied. "The guys were out of the port this afternoon so Spen had me help him clean and restock the firearms store. There was a rack of Rookies there, and I couldn't help but think of Ronjo. Then I got to thinking of Ren, which then led me to think of Byron and I guess I allowed myself to wallow a bit."

"I understand. Before rank took me away from the sharp end of things, I had similar experiences in the field. Sometimes this job forces you into short but intense relationships with people, and when you lose them, it hurts. I know it's little compensation, but at least you can be happy Ronjo and Ren died honourably. That way you can be proud of them as well as sad at their loss. You can take comfort from knowing Byron loves you and look forward to reuniting with him."

I nodded. "Yeah. Ronjo and Ren were both good people, the best of men. I'm worried that I'll not get to see Byron again though. I'm sorry to be a wet blanket."

"Son. I'm proud that this job hasn't made you lose compassion. If losing friends and missing those you love didn't hurt you, I'd be worried."

"I hope Zeno is okay," I said.

"He probably just overslept."

"So you're not at all worried about him?" I asked, shooting him a challenging look.

He shrugged and nodded. "Sorry, that was a lame attempt to give you hope. Of course I'm worried. He looked decidedly ill last night."


Our new friend was nowhere to be seen in the basement dining hall of the shelter, and our concern grew. After the meal, we approached a member of the shelter staff and asked about him.

"I'm sorry, he passed away during the night," the desk clerk told us.

Our jaws dropped in horror. "What?" I gasped.

"Oh fuck, no," Tinnias hissed and ran a hand through his hair.

"I'm sorry, was he a friend of yours?"

"Yes," I replied. "How did he die? He looked ill last night."

"His lungs finally gave out it seems. He'd had some sort of illness for years and told us a couple of years ago that he wouldn't be with us for too much longer. He died in his sleep, so the doctor assured us. It was as peaceful as one could wish for."

"What will happen to him?" Tinnias asked. "Will there be a funeral or anything? We'd like to pay our respects."

The clerk grabbed a piece of paper and scribbled an address in untidy handwriting. "This is where all the homeless deceased are taken. If no family come forward within three days, he will be cremated and his ashes scattered amongst the flowers in the public park in the city centre."

I took the slip of paper and put it into my pocket. Tinnias thanked the desk clerk.

"I'm sorry you lost your friend, Gentlemen. We can offer you the services of a counsellor if you wish to talk about your feelings. There's no charge of course. Many of our regulars find it helpful in times such as this. Unfortunately, the life of a homeless person is often neither a long nor trouble free experience. Bad nutrition, lack of protection from extreme weather, and little or no affordable medical care, take their toll. We do what we can here, but it is never adequate."

164

"We appreciate you, please believe us," Tinnias replied. Putting an arm around my shoulder, he steered me towards the door. "Come on, buddy, let's go outside and have a smoke and remember our friend huh?"

We lit cigarettes and between coughing fits, Tinnias and I shared what brief memories we had of Zeno. We laughed at some of them and I was glad of that.

"I suppose it would be facetious of me to remind you that he's now out of pain and in a far better place," Tinnias said.

I nodded. "A little, despite being true. Maybe in a day or two I'll be happy to hear it, just not so soon. Do you think I care too much? Should I be a little more, detached, cold even?"

Tinnias' jaw dropped open. "What the fuck? Hell no. Do you think I'm cold then?"

"No of course not. You just seem more, controlled I guess is the word that fits."

"Well as you get older, the people around you age too. People die. You lose more friends as you get older. I guess you get used to losing folks. It becomes less of a shock but no less upsetting. As the desk clerk said, this life is a harsh one, life shortening to some degree and if you're in less than perfect health anyway, the chances are that the life will take you early."

I nodded and looked at my father. "You're right. I failed to realise that you'll have lost people you care about. Forgive me."

"Always, unconditionally. How about we give the port a miss tomorrow and go check out that address the desk clerk gave us, then go back to the ship and see what our cameras are revealing?"

"Okay, good idea. Let's go inside, I'm getting cold."


Since we had already decided to give the port a miss, we allowed ourselves a lie in and it was nice to let my body wake up naturally, to find weak sunshine shining through the grimy window of our room. After dressing hurriedly, we set out for the locker shop to collect our bags. We were tempted to have a hot shower there too, but the thought of putting on the same dirty clothes made it seem pointless, so we decided to wait until we were back at the ship. Before we left for the bus, I asked the plump woman on the front desk about the address given to me by the shelter desk clerk.

"That's just around the corner from here," she smiled and gave us directions.

"Thank you," I nodded to her and we left.

The building was easy to find and we entered, to find ourselves within a dark and shabby cremation facility. Despite its dishevelled appearance, care had been taken to make it welcoming. Rows of seats filled the main part of the single, large room, a raised dais at the front obviously waited to receive pots and urns of ashes. At the rear of the space, half a dozen chairs sat facing us, and I noticed a long table at one side on which sat a large hot water pot and several packs of disposable cups. Paintings hung on the walls, and from the ceiling towards the rear of the space, hung a wooden banner on which words were painted in a language neither Tinnias nor I understood.

"We give thanks for a life well lived, for struggles bravely borne, for friendship given and received, and offer our souls to the greater universal consciousness."

The voice made us jump and we spun around to see a small, round bellied man smiling at us.

"Beautiful words," I said. "I hope you don't mind us letting ourselves in. We're enquiring about what will happen to our friend who died last night. We were told he was brought here."

"Zeno Mastib?"

I nodded. "Yes, that's him."

"He is here. If no family comes to claim him, he will be cremated three days from today and given a simple service as has become the custom for the homeless community. He was well known amongst the people from the shelters, I expect there to be quite a turnout to say goodbye to him."

"Everyone liked him" Tinnias said. "We only became friends recently but he helped us out and we thought a lot of him."

The man must have seen my distress, as he came forward and laid a hand on my arm. "Would you like to see him? I have to do some filing so you're welcome to spend a few minutes if you wish."

"We would, thank you so much," Tinnias replied.

The man led us through a door in the far left corner and we entered a tiny room containing a basic wooden burial box. He removed the lid and left us alone. Zeno looked calm and serene and I was pleased to see he had been given a good wash, had his long hair brushed, and wore a clean set of clothes. His hands had been placed across his front, and I placed my own on top after leaving a coin in the pocket of the jacket he wore. Back home, it's traditional to put a coin in with the deceased, to pay for the services of a guide to the afterlife.

"Thank you for your friendship, Zeno." I smiled at him, pleased that he was at peace. "No more struggling now, buddy."

"Kalaha mistoy ne badda," Tinnias said quietly in our own Sigma tongue. "Enjoy this new adventure."


Back at the ship, we tossed a coin for first shower and Tinnias won, so I got out some clean clothes for us both and put a pot of coffee on to heat, before switching on the comms so we could watch the feeds from the various cameras we'd placed around the port compound. I discovered quickly that everyone was speaking in the native Niruvan tongue, so I hastily attached a translation module that would allow us to hear everything in Sigman.

Tinnias finally emerged, pink from head to toe from the hot water and I laughed at the sight. "You look like a freshly boiled Tasgil."

"That was the best shower of my entire life," he grinned. "Should we shave do you think? I'd love to get rid of this itchy hair on my face."

"Better not," I replied. "We are supposed to be street bums for a little while longer. It wouldn't hurt to give it a bit of a trim though."

"Okay, good idea I guess. You go and shower and then we can watch the feed while we eat."

As the hot water cascaded down on me, I thought about the case and how it seemed that everyone was against me. I wasn't being paranoid, but I had to acknowledge that all the different threads seemed to conspire to block any attempt to solve the case. There wasn't a single thing about it that could be described as straightforward. Most worrying of all was not knowing how far the Drycenians were involved, and in what way. Of all the races I've met, they are the last ones I would ever expect to get involved in a crime. For them to now appear to be doing just that was not only worrying, but way off the top of the weirdness scale. I could think of no good reason for them to make the decision to get involved with Gaht, possibly even kidnapping Commander Taiko. One thing this whole sorry business was doing, was giving me a far healthier view of these people whom I had almost deified for the past six years. If nothing else, I could take that from this experience. A relationship between myself and Byron seemed impossible to achieve and my heart was heavy with sadness at the love I felt but feared could not be returned. I voiced my concerns with Tinnias and he was as bemused as I was.

"Apart from being weird, it's worrying on another level," he said. "With their technology and medical expertise, the damage they are capable of doing is frightening. Lomas could effectively enslave an entire planet without leaving his swanky quarters on board that ship of his."

"I guess it would be best not to piss them off then," I replied.

Tinnias eyes widened in horror. "Oh fuck, just think what the retribution would be like if they took a dislike to you."

"We wouldn't last a day."

"Promise me, Son, that you'll curb your angry outbursts if we should ever come into contact with them again."

"I promise. I think it unlikely that I'll be able to spend time in their company again. I fear Byron and I are doomed never to be together."

"If he really loves you, he'll find a way. He may even leave them to be with you. I think it might be wise to have a discussion with some Agency top brass when we get home. I might even suggest they take a deeper look into that case they got themselves involved in, the one that got Vincent freed of those murder charges."

"Be careful with that," I said. "If you start rummaging around in anything that could cast a shadow over Vincent, you could find yourself in the cross hairs of their fancy weapons."

Tinnias nodded. "That's true I guess, but the only alternative is to let them get on with whatever they're doing, just because we're scared of their power. That makes my gut twist."

"I know, I understand completely. Oh what the fuck are we to do?"

"Do you want to quit and go home, Son?"

"Hell no. My instinct tells me to pursue this to the end and get justice where it's due. On the other hand, I don't want to put you or the family at risk. I'd never forgive myself if anything happened to any of you. If it was just me involved here, I wouldn't think twice about chasing the truth and the consequences be damned."

"I feel the same. The thing that is uppermost in my mind is how I'll feel when I'm an old fart, sitting on my verandah, peeing my pants and forgetting my own name. To know that I was once in a position to at least try to sort things out properly, but didn't because I feared the fallout, will make me a very grumpy old asshole."

I grinned at the mental image. "Same here. We might never get this close again, there may never be a chance for anyone to get close enough to sort it out. This may be the one and only chance to bring whatever it is they're doing, out into the open. We can't quit now."

"Then we carry on and be extra vigilant."

I nodded. "Agreed."

"The moment it looks like the family are in danger though, I'm quitting probing into anything connected with Drycenians."

"Okay," I reached out my hand and we shook to seal our agreement. "Now what's on those camera feeds?"

For the rest of the day we watched the feeds, interrupted only by the need to pee and eat, and by the time we decided to quit for the day, both our heads throbbed.

"I can't take this for too long," Tinnias said as he stood and rubbed his backside. "My head aches, my ass is numb, and I don't think I'll be able to straighten my knees for days."

I laughed, despite being in a similar predicament. Wincing as I stood and massaged my own knees, I hoped that something would happen soon. "We need an android servant to do this shit for us," I sniggered.

Now it was Tinnias' turn to laugh. "You met one once, didn't you? On a job."

I nodded, remembering the case. "Yeah, he was a nice guy actually, despite lacking an emotional side to his nature."

"A nice guy?" Tinnias asked. "How can an android be a nice guy?"

"You quickly forget they're machines. They're not like the Flarks back home. They talk and behave just like us, apart from the emotions of course, and it feels natural to..." My eyes snapped to the right, the voice from the camera feed demanding my full focus. "Shit, here we go."

"What's up?" Tinnias asked as he scanned the feed.

I pointed to the feed from the camera I'd placed in the armoury and Tinnias read the translation that snaked across the little grey box that covered the bottom portion of the screen.

"I know, I'll mention it, stop worrying."

"Taiko is stronger than we thought, he's making fools of us."

"The boss has called a meeting tomorrow evening, so I guess the situation surrounding our guest and his fucking principles will be assessed."

"I know what I'd like to do with his principles."

"If the Boss is out of patience, you might get your chance. Come on, I'm hungry."

"So he is being held there," Tinnias said as he blew out a breath.

"I wonder where," I replied. "Did you see any rooms that could be used as a holding cell for a valuable prisoner?"

Tinnias shook his head. "No, but there are plenty of areas I didn't go into. He could be in any one of several places. It's like a labyrinth inside those buildings."

"Common sense says he'll be under guard," I said. "We need to look for guys with guns."

"I don't suppose you have any kind of bio scanner amongst your kit, do you?"

I shook my head and laughed. "Sorry. Does the Agency even have such things?"

"Oh yes, you didn't know?"

"No. Why haven't I got one then?"

"I've no idea, but you'll have one as soon as we get home, I promise you."

"Maybe we could rig one up between us. Can you tinker with gadgets at all?"

"I can't even work our laundry machine," Tinnias said. "Sorry. How about you?"

"Well, I'm better than you, but I'm not confident I could invent a bio scanner from a box of spare parts. That's beyond my abilities."

We both sat in silence, each lost in our thoughts and I racked my brain for ideas as to how to make or acquire a bio scanner quickly. With my mind blank, I finally shrugged. "Shit, well I guess we'll just have to do without. I've managed for the past twenty years or so."

"Think logically," Tinnias said. "We approach this like any other kidnapping case. We case the place, find a way in, search, extricate the victim, and get out."

"Some of the searching can be done while we're working there during the daytimes," I replied.

"A map of the compound would be helpful," Tinnias said. "The one we downloaded wasn't comprehensive enough."

My eyes widened as a grin spread across my face. "Of course it would. You're awesome, Dad."

"What?" Tinnias called as I turned and reached for the keypad to log onto the galactic web.

"The place wasn't always used as Gaht's headquarters," I replied. "It must've been something else in the past, before it was a spaceport. A fishing port or industrial unit maybe."

"So we might find details of the place as it used to be, a historical article perhaps."

"Right," I nodded.

Ten minutes later, we were hunched over my console, studying a map of the Niruvan Immigration Reception Centre, as it was called seventy-five years ago. The place had been added to at some point in the intervening years, as there were fewer buildings on the map than we remembered from our visits. One building caught our attention immediately and we both felt hope spring to life within our hearts.

"So that building there used to be a holding cell for those without the proper immigration papers," Tinnias said. "I wonder if it's still a cell now."

"What would you use a cell for, if not for holding a prisoner?" I asked. "An armoury perhaps."

"Which we know it isn't as you've been inside their armoury."

"A store for valuables," Tinnias offered. "Maybe it's where they keep their money stocks."

I nodded. "Could be. Sensitive information could be kept there too. Stuff you don't want getting into the wrong hands."

"Like information gleaned from Agency leaks, banks and stuff like that."

"Yeah. Digital chips, computer drives, even plans for future operations."

"If there are guards on the place, I doubt it's just an information store."

"No, they wouldn't need guards for that," I agreed. "With all manner of ways to encrypt information, there's no need for guards. Without the decryption code, no one could make use of it if they stole it."

"So we ought to make sure we take a good look and see if there are guards on duty."

I nodded. "And if so, the chances are good that Taiko is being held there."

Tinnias stood and stretched. "Good, we have a plan for tomorrow. We're going to have to be up before dawn to make it back to the port in time, so I vote we get our heads down."

The next day saw me back sparring with the men and I was glad as I'd missed my daily workouts since staying at the shelter. I noticed a subtle but distinct change in the way Spen interacted with me and decided to take full advantage of his new friendly demeanour. He was happy to chat in response to gently probing questions, and I was careful not to push too hard. I didn't want to put him on his guard so I started slow and gentle with the questioning.

"So, are you a security force here or something?" I asked.

He grinned. "I guess you could call us that."

"You're part of the local law enforcement then, special ops or something?"

Spen laughed loudly. "No, Ren, we're nothing to do with law enforcement. We're umm, what you might call, an independent security force."

I decided I'd pushed enough, for now, so changed the subject to something lighter. "Well whatever, you have a real slick operation here. I'm impressed, really."

He looked at me and smiled. "Praise indeed, coming from an experienced security agent. Thanks, man, that's good to hear."

I longed to fire more probing questions at him and held myself back with some effort. The last thing I needed was to make him suspicious of me. Not only could it scupper the mission, but it could put Tinnias and I in danger for our lives. I would just have to be patient and take it slow with him. Time was something I'm always happy to invest if it gets the job done, but we had Taiko to think of, and my worry over Tip had not diminished. The longer we took to resolve the situation, the more danger both were in.

During our mid-day meal, Tinnias gave me some news that almost made me spit out my food in shock.

"They had me cleaning one of the unused suites of rooms," he told me as he bit into a delicious meat pie. "A real swanky bedroom and bathroom it is too, seems totally out of place here."

"How do you mean, out of place?" I asked.

"Well this is a port. These buildings were used as warehousing, admin, and everything necessary to deal with the import and export of goods and people. Swanky living accommodations like you get in top hotels just doesn't belong here with these brainless grunts."

"I understand what you mean," I nodded. Maybe it's for the boss, what's his name again?"

"Belotan."

"Yeah, him. Maybe it's his new apartment. Or it could be for important visitors."

Tinnias looked at me in what I've come to recognise as a kind of, I know something you don't, way and I shook my head and laughed. "Okay, Dad, out with it. What do you know?"

"If the conversation I overheard was what I think it was, it's for Ambassador Vazien."

"What the fuck?" I hissed. "Are you sure? You can't speak the language here, maybe you got it wrong."

"I heard them say his name four times. It was clear as day."

"But they may have just been talking about him," I replied. "Maybe he's in the news at the moment."

Tinnias shrugged. "Perhaps, but then why would they hang a wall banner with Vazien's family crest on? There's fancy glassware on the table, and three boxes of those expensive cigarettes, with the picture of the mountain on the lid."

"He always has those cigarettes," I grinned, "and that jug will be filled with purple liquid that he never offers anyone. I wonder what his connection with Gaht is."

"Whatever it is, it has to be on the wrong side of the law. What self respecting politician would associate with a gang as notorious as Gaht? He must be out of his mind."

I blew out a breath and ran both hands through my hair as I tried to come to terms with this shocking twist of events. Tinnias and I thought the presence of both Gaht and the Dankera Collective made the case into something we still weren't sure we could handle alone, but this new information made us both feel tiny, insignificant, and doomed to failure if we dared put a foot wrong. Ambassador Vazien is one of the top ten most powerful men in this sector of the galaxy, with a reach that stretches across many systems, if the rumours are to be believed. I'm not one for gossip, but I'm aware that rumours start somewhere, from some spark of truth.

"Shit," I exclaimed. "How the hell do we move forward now he's involved?"

Tinnias shook his head slowly. "I have no idea, Son. I vote we go back to the ship after work and talk about it."

I was distracted for the rest of the afternoon and Spen asked me what was wrong.

"One of our friends from the shelter died the other night," I replied. "We hadn't known him long but we seemed to hit it off straight away. You probably know him, Zeno, the guy who tunes up your vehicles."

Spen was visibly shocked at the news, his jaw dropped and he stared at me in disbelief. "Shit, no. You're not tugging my chain?"

"I only wish I were."

"What took him?"

"Apparently, he had some lung problem that gradually ate him up inside. At least he passed in his sleep, so he shouldn't have suffered."

"Hell," Spen exclaimed angrily. "I'm genuinely sorry, I liked him.

"Everyone liked him," I nodded. "He didn't have to do anything to make folks like him either, people just did. He was special."

The hours dragged by, and the news of Zeno's passing obviously made its way around the entire port complex, as everyone seemed just a little subdued. I was desperate to get away back to the ship to decompress with Tinnias, talk about Vazien and how it might affect the case and our ability to sort it out effectively. When we finally heard the siren indicating the end of the day's shift, I had to physically stop myself from running to the main gate.

"So Spen was genuinely upset?" Tinnias asked. "You're sure he wasn't acting?"

I thought about it before answering. "No. His reaction was instant, and his body language gave the same message as his words."

"How weird. Gaht is known for many killings and innumerable beatings, so he obviously has no difficulty with meting out death, yet he's upset at the death of an ageing street bum he hardly knows. Incongruous." Tinnias shook his head in confusion. "What do your famous people reading skills tell you about it, Son?"

"They tell me that he's not a lost cause. They tell me that if the opportunity arose, he could turn himself around, like Tip did." Tinnias' frown told me he didn't understand. "He's a thug, yes?" Tinnias nodded. "Sure, he struts around barking orders at the men and seems to flourish under the mantle of power his position gives him but doesn't actually give off a vibe of violence. We know Gaht as a group has done many killings, but I wonder how many Spen has done. I'm willing to bet I could count them on my two hands."

"So it's the power he likes, not the violence," Tinnias said.

I smiled and nodded. "Your people reading skills are building nicely, Dad."

## CHAPTER FIFTEEN

Having decided to sleep in the ship and leave extra early the next morning in order that we get to the port in time, we bought some take away food on our way home and indulged ourselves in a hot shower after eating. Ambassador Vazien was the centre of our attention for the entire evening, dominating our conversation from the start. Our first dilemma was to figure out why he was involved with an outfit like Gaht.

"What possible reason could there be for a public figure, a politician who relies on the admiration and esteem of the public at large, to involve himself with Gaht?" Tinnias said, shaking his head in disbelief. "Gaht is a well known gang network; it's responsible for many killings and thousands of beatings, robberies, and generally menacing behaviour in several systems. If word about his involvement got out, his career is over."

"There has to be a reason that makes it worthwhile him taking the risk," I replied. "He must be getting something out of his association with them, something that he can't get any other way. Find out what that is and we might be on the way to sorting this whole sorry business out."

"The obvious first step is to do some research on Vazien and get our contacts onto it. I have a couple who are suitably placed to look into his background."

"So do I," I nodded, grabbing my Unicom. "I'll make some calls while you get onto the Galactic Web."

I dialled the number and waited. This contact was my best hope for information on Vazien and I crossed my fingers that he would be able to help us out. He answered on the second ring.

"Sam, how are you? It's been ages. I thought you didn't want to do business with me anymore."

"Charik, you're my first choice for anything political. You know how well versed I am in politics."

Laughter came to my ears and I grinned. "So how can I help, Sam?"

"Can you give me some background on Ambassador Vazien?"

I heard a sharp intake of breath. "Vazien? Bless the Gods, why are you digging into him? Sorry, I know you can't tell me. You need to be very careful, Sam."

"Why?"

"You've heard the rumours surely?"

"Yeah, but rumours are hardly ever the truth. I guess there's a spark somewhere at the centre of the gossip, but it's bound to be thoroughly embroidered."

"Don't take that for granted, there's a lot of truth in those rumours. Vazien is a dangerous man. A very rich and powerful, dangerous man. Don't get yourself on his radar for the wrong reasons or you can bend over and kiss your ass goodbye."

"I'll remember your advice. Now what do you know? What is he into that might interest a law enforcer like myself?"

"Would arms dealing be of interest?"

"What the fuck?" I exclaimed. "Surely not. Really? Are you sure? How could I prove that?"

"Let's just say it's more than a rumour. He owns several Razulite mines on Moianal 6."

"Razulite?" I frowned and noticed Tinnias' head snap round and stare at me, wide eyed. "What the heck is Razulite?"

"It's some kind of stone that they add to metal and make a super light, super strong alloy that they use for one single purpose."

"And that would be?"

"Gun barrels."

"So he sells the stuff to gun manufacturers," I asked.

"Apparently so."

"But that's not illegal," I replied. "Immoral perhaps but certainly not illegal."

"The rumour is that he sells most of the stuff to one particular company, that he owns. He then has that company produce guns which he sells to both sides of tribal conflicts, civil wars and the like. By keeping each side armed with gradually bigger and more powerful arms, he keeps up the demand for Razulite gun barrels."

"Holy shit," I hissed. "I wonder how he hides the money trail. Politicians have their bank accounts audited each year. If there was a single credit not accounted for, he'd be in trouble. He obviously has a secret bank account."

"Obviously."

"How the fuck do I go about finding it though? I wonder how many banks there are in this sector of the galaxy."

"Call your financially orientated contacts and get them onto it. You do have such contacts I assume?"

"Are you calling me an amateur, Charik?" I laughed, thanked him and ended the call. "Jeez."

"What's that about Razulite?" Tinnias asked, his research forgotten for the moment. "Is Vazien into gun running or something?" he sniggered.

"Yes," I nodded.

Tinnias gaped in horror. "Shit, I was joking."

"Sorry," I shrugged. "He's mining Razulite, then apparently selling most of it to a company he owns, and using the guns manufactured by that company to arm both sides of tribal conflicts, civil wars, uprisings, that sort of thing."

"Holy shit on a stick," Tinnias exclaimed. "How do we process this information? How does it change the case and our plans?"

"No doubt we'll come up with a plan," I said, "but right at this moment, I'm somewhat floored by this news."

"You and me both, Son. Why the heck has he got himself involved in this shit? He's a politician for fuck's sake, he surely knows he must have a spotless record. He must be crazy."

I nodded. "Ain't that the truth. I must ring another contact and get him onto checking into Vazien's finances. The money from his mines and gun sales must go somewhere."

"His day to day bank account is available for anyone to look at, it's part of the rules for politicians. They get audited every year and their financial records are in the public domain. Any income from his mines could be on there and not get him into trouble. He's allowed to be a business owner on the side. I doubt the gun sales will though, so the likelihood is that he's got another account in a different name."

"How the hell do we find it?" I asked. "Hopefully my contact will be able to help."

"In theory it's simple. You start at the mines and follow the money trail from there." He noticed the frown that cut across my forehead and sighed. "Okay look, the Razulite comes out of the mines and gets sold. You then check into the bank accounts of everyone who buys it. One of them should be the company owned by Vazien that he uses to manufacture the guns. If the other buyers are legit, you can forget them. Still with me?" I nodded.

"You should then know where this other company banks and will be able to check into it."

"It sounds simple when you describe it," I said. "Financial stuff isn't my bag; how come you understand all this shit?"

"I did a few years in the Corporate Crimes Division, back at the beginning of my career."

"Jeez how boring," I remarked.

"Why do you think I left," he grinned.

I rang my best financial contact, the manager of a large bank in a capital city of a Prime world in a major shipping lane. Tens of billions of credits pass through his hands every day and what he doesn't know about finances and banking, isn't worth knowing. He became my contact after his young daughter was abducted by a psycho. He was caught quickly but got off due to three mistakes made on his paperwork. The date of the abduction was wrong, putting him nowhere in the vicinity of the child. The person responsible for questioning the child was accused of interpreting her answers in a manner that was damaging to the accused's defence, and a piece of evidence went missing. I was the law enforcer who made the initial arrest, so I was in constant contact with the family. The father told me that he'd checked out the finances of the defence team and found that a lot of money had been paid to ensure word of the mistakes never got out. The media were simply told that the guy was found innocent.

The child was seriously hurt in the attack, so much that she would never be able to have children. She became terrified of leaving the house and started wetting the bed. The parents begged me for help and I admit that case affected me. That little girl's spirit was broken after the attack and it broke my heart. One night I found myself following the psycho into a dark and lonely alley and, well you can guess the rest. I was unable to hide the damage to my hands, so I had to confess to Tinnias, who told me off, then embraced me as I cried for that little girl. I visited the guy once more, to tell him the psycho had paid for his crime, although not nearly enough, and he was grateful. He gave me his Unicorn number and told me right there and then he would help me out if ever I needed help with the financial aspects of cases.

"Hey Deek, it's Sam."

I heard the smile in his tone as he greeted me. "Sam, hi there, how are you? And how's that boss of yours that you worship like a deity?"

I laughed, Deek always teases me about the way I look up to Tinnias, and I take it in good humour. "He's fine, he says hi." I grinned at Tinnias.

"I'm delighted to hear it. Now how can I help my favourite law man?"

"I hope this isn't too big a job to lay on you, Deek, but you're the only one I know with the knowledge and skills to get it done."

"Come now, Sam, you know I'll do whatever I'm able, and what I can't do, we'll either figure out together or I'll find someone else I trust to help me. Now gimme."

"I need you to look into the finances of Ambassador Vazien."

I heard a sharp intake of breath. "The Keshan guy with the dead eyes? That Vazien?"

"That's the one," I replied. "All Keshan people have those dead grey eyes and damned creepy they are too."

"Right, give me some background. What do you have already?"

"He owns some Razulite mines on Moianal 6. When the stuff is sold, most of it is sold to a company he owns, who then use it to manufacture arms which he sells to both sides in conflict situations, civil wars, tribal uprisings etcetera. We're guessing the income from the mines will appear on his usual bank account, but we reckon any income from the sale of arms won't. He must have a secret account somewhere. We need details of it, plus evidence linking it to Vazien."

"That shouldn't be too difficult," Deek said. "You can see his normal bank account via the galactic web, it's in the public domain as are those of all politicians. I'll start at the mines and follow the money trail from there and see where it takes me."

I turned to Tinnias and grinned. "Okay, thanks Deek, I'm seriously grateful for this."

"Give me a couple of days and I'll call you back."

"Call us at this time of day, for the next three or four hours. We're working undercover and can't have our Unicoms with us during the daytime. We're filthy, bug infested street bums at the moment."

"I'm glad I'm not sharing a jail cell with you then," Deek laughed. "You take care, don't take any stupid risks okay?"

"You're beginning to sound like my dad."

"If he wasn't a contact, I'd be tempted to ask who it was," Tinnias said. "It sounded like you have a really good friendship with him."

"Remember Terramora Prime at night?" I asked, giving him a sideways look.

He nodded. "Ahh, now I understand. He's a nice guy and thinks the world of you, Son."

"How do you know that?" I asked.

"He called me after, y'know, and thanked me for putting you on the case. He spent at least twenty minutes telling me how special you are, how helpful and every other superlative you can think of."

"Did he?"

"Yeah. I'm glad to know you have contacts who are genuinely good people, who care about your wellbeing. It helps me not worry so much when your alone, out there," he pointed to the sky.

"They're not all criminals and bums. Some are nice folks, and the criminals and bums are nice folks too, in their own way."

"I'm delighted to know that. Now I'll make a call and get someone looking into Vazien's personal life. You get his bank account on the console."


Everything seemed to be in order as we checked Vazien's known bank account. As Tinnias had guessed, the income from his mines was there, but one thing was missing.

"It doesn't say they're Razulite mines," I said and Tinnias nodded.

"I'm not totally surprised. Mining Razulite may be legal, even for a politician, but you know how fickle the general public can be."

"But anyone can find out with a few minutes research on any console with access to the galactic web."

"Of course," Tinnias said. "If he tries to cover that up, it then becomes suspicious enough to question his motives. As it stands, this bank account tells us he isn't doing anything wrong."

"I can't wait to see the other one," I said. I noticed Tinnias seemed distracted. "What's up?"

"I hate to admit this, but I think I really am infested," he said as he scratched his head for the hundredth time. "This itching can only mean one thing. Is the public bathing house open at this time of night?"

"Yeah, it's open day and night for the homeless. Come on, let's go and get zapped."

After confirming that we both, in fact, were infested, not only on our heads but I had them in my crotch too, the treatment consisted of the liberal application of icy cold grey goo. Ten minutes cooking time later, we were zapped with a hand held electronic device that acts with particles in the goo, to kill any bugs. We were each given a tube of lotion to calm any soreness caused by our scratching and sent on our way with a smile.

"Promise me you'll never tell the family I had bugs," Tinnias said. "If they find out, I'll have you on traffic duty before you can say howdy pop."

I laughed loudly and looked at him. "I promise."

"Doesn't it bother you, Son? You seem unnaturally okay about having bugs snuggling under your balls."

"I've had them more times than I can count. This job takes its toll you know, in all sorts of unsavoury ways."

"I had them a couple of times when I was working the street," Tinnias said. "I guess we had a better class of criminal in those days. Come on, let's go in this store and buy a couple of beers."


We were up before dawn the next morning for the walk to the port. We wanted to ensure we had a good place in the queue for a day's work and we weren't disappointed. There were only seven men ahead of us and we got in without a problem. Spen nodded to me as I passed him at the gate and I nodded back, eager that he like and trust me. I found my schedule had changed though, as Spen explained.

"Ren, the guys are out on an exercise today, so you'll have to make yourself useful wherever you can. Your skills will no doubt be under utilised, but I'm sure you'd rather have the money than not."

"Oh absolutely," I lied. "I'm happy to pitch in wherever I'm able. Where should I start?"

By the time I joined Tinnias for our mid-day meal, I'd loaded four trucks with crates and boxes, cleaned two large storage rooms, carried a dozen buckets of garden rubbish to the compost area, and taken delivery of seventy five boxes of new supplies, which I then had to haul to the storage rooms and stack in date order so the old stuff got used first. After greeting Tinnias, I tucked into the meat pie with more than my usual gusto.

"You must be starving, Ren, are you missing breakfast?"

"I've spent the entire morning hauling, loading, unloading, scrubbing, and trudging. I'm so hungry and thirsty I could bite your arm off and drink the blood. What have you been up to?"

"I laid a new carpet and built five furniture kits for the kiddies' playroom."

"Oh you poor thing," I teased. "You must be worn out after all that slaving."

"Listen, boy. The carpet was cut on the slant, the room wasn't remotely square, the floor had to first be cleared of nails, all seven hundred and thirty two of them. Then of the five furniture packs, three had bits missing, one had too many bits, and just one had holes that matched up. Fancy swapping jobs for the rest of the day?"

"Ahh, no thanks, think I'll pass. Thanks all the same."

"Lightweight," Tinnias hissed under his breath.

"You know we forgot to check the cameras last night," I whispered.

"We did get a little distracted. Tonight then?"

I nodded. "Okay, but I think we should sleep at the shelter. If we're away for too long, the guys will get suspicious. We're trying to blend in after all."

"Agreed."


Back at the ship, we worked out that we could spend two hours watching the camera feeds before having to leave to get back to the shelter in time to secure a decent room and dinner. The console on my ship can search for certain words and phrases in speech, allowing me to avoid having to sit through every single minute of video. By typing in the words you want to catch, it will speed through and stop when it hears just those words.

"What words do we want?" I asked. "Remember we can run through it as many times as we need to, as we think of other words."

"Well obviously we want Vazien and Taiko. How about Drycenian too, and Lilea? We might be wise to listen for our names, our real names that is. Or both sets, why not?"

I nodded as I typed. "And Lomas, Vincent, Tip Danso."

"Dankera, Belotan, Tyrrin," Tinnias offered. "That'll do for starters. If we think of any more, we can add them next time."

The two hours yielded some unexpected fruit. Vazien was mentioned twice. There was a conversation about the need for newer guns, and how they were to come by what they referred to as a Sleteath, which I took to be some new type of gun.

"It would be great if we could come by a consignment of Sleteaths," a skinny blonde lad I recognised from sparring said.

"It's a bit soon to expect those to come our way," Spen replied. "I'll get the Boss to ask Vazien about them, but they're not even on general sale yet."

The second mention of Vazien's name came when two men discussed the upgrading of the living quarters.

"How's the decorating going?" A man of at least fifty enquired.

"Very well, now we have someone on it regularly, that Koto guy is a hard worker," a young lad who looked like he'd yet to grow pubic hair, replied.

"Good, will Vazien's rooms be finished in time?"

"Yeah, they're all but done, just the swanky soft furnishing and knick knacks to make it all pretty like, as befitting a man of his standing."

Both men burst into laughter and the playback sped on. There was no mention of either the Drycenians or Vincent, and I wasn't sure whether to be pleased or worried. I still had no confirmation that they were either involved or not, so I had no choice but to err on the side of caution and assume they were somehow connected with this whole sorry business.

We walked back to the shelter and used the time to discuss our next course of action.

"Do we carry on as we are and wait to see if anything further happens, or do we do something else and if so, what?" Tinnias asked.

"What else can we do?" I replied. "What are our options? We could go back to Tyrrin 4 and quiz Tip again, but that's unlikely to be successful and could cause problems for us."

Tinnias nodded. "It would tell him we've involved ourselves in his business and know about his connection to Gaht. That could either put us in danger or cause him to bolt. No, that's a bad idea."

"I agree. We could just go home and forget the whole thing," I suggested.

Tinnias laughed. "I can't see you being happy doing that. Besides, we now know there are Gaht spies in law enforcement, and I can't ever hope to work comfortably not knowing who I can trust and who I can't. It would be like the Rime business all over again. There's also Byron to consider. You need some closure on the status of your relationship and going home won't give you that. No, Son, giving up is not an option."

"Well we can't go to Drycenia as we'd never get in and with those teeth, we'd be in serious danger if we pissed them off, which I might just have already done. Going to Lilea is an option I guess, at least we could see what's happening in the Domenico residence, if Tip or the Drycenians are there."

"But that would put us right in the middle of their umm, spiritual friends who might give us away, especially if they see us as a threat."

I nodded. "True. Then we could go back to Tyrrin and investigate Taiko's disappearance. We could ask around his neighbours again at least, if we can't get to his law enforcement buddies."

"Which we won't," Tinnias said. "The local law enforcement will be on the case by now and if we go storming in there, we'll blow our cover."

I shrugged. "Then in the absence of further ideas, I guess we stay here until something exciting happens."

Tinnias sighed loudly. "Okay."

I suddenly felt guilty at dragging him away from the family. Mother and Ambella must be worried sick and will be having to cope with any emergencies alone. I know Ambella's all grown up and working at Law Enforcement now and has all the guys at headquarters to call on for help, but it still felt like I was forcing him to abandon them.

"Listen, Dad," I said before I lost my nerve. "You should maybe go home, Mother and Ambella will be worried about you so far away. If anything happened to you while you're working with me, I'd never forgive myself. I'm so grateful you came when I was panicking, but I feel guilty and don't want you to feel obliged to stick it out. It's okay if you want to go home, I'll be okay."

Tinnias stopped in his tracks and gaped at me. "What the fuck?"

"Please don't be angry," I begged.

"Too late, Son," he glowered. "You're my son and I love you as much as Grellina and Ambella. You need me more than they do right now, so I didn't hesitate. I talked it over with the girls and they practically ordered me to go. Ambella got Arto to move in while I'm gone, and I asked Lowen, Dorny, and Vayna from Headquarters to keep in touch with them regularly too. I call Grellina every other day to check on everyone, and they're all doing just fine without me. How dare you question my love for you and my family priorities."

"I'm sorry, Father," I whispered, choking back tears. "I'd sooner die than hurt your feelings. I was just worried that you might feel you're abandoning Mother and Ambella."

He dragged me into the doorway of a disused fruit and vegetable store and put a hand on my shoulder. "I'm sorry for yelling. Questioning my love for you is guaranteed to raise my wrath."

"Forgive me."

"Always and unconditionally. Don't ever doubt how important you are to me, to the family. I couldn't love you more if you were of my blood. I love the girls, but there's something about the relationship a man has with his son that's special. When you need me, I'll always be by your side. Please try never to doubt that."

I was too choked to speak, so I looked at the floor, embarrassed, and nodded.

"Come on, Son, we want a decent room so we'd better get a move on."

We were lucky enough to secure a room on the first floor, one of the best in the shelter, so we found out later. It looked clean, and the bathroom didn't smell of anything biological. Dinner was the usual meat stew that looked unidentifiable but tasted wonderful, and we ate heartily. Afterwards, we walked up and down the street outside and smoked as we made small talk with some of the other homeless guys. It may sound crazy, but despite everything, I was beginning to like the life we were pretending to live. Granted, we had not experienced severely cold weather, neither had we yet failed to secure a room in which to sleep in relative safety, but so far as my very limited experience went, I felt strangely content.

Tinnias broke into my musings. "You realise we've become smokers. I've been aware of slight cravings for the past few hours. Grellina is going to go mad when we go home with a habit."

"I normally only smoke under extreme stress and have never had any problems stopping when the situation has passed, but I've been craving for over a day now and I have to admit that last night in the ship, I got up during the night for a cigarette."

"We're going to have to visit a medic before we go home," Tinnias said, "for the injections."

I nodded. "Yeah, and the bruises on our asses will be our punishment for being so weak."

"Well if we're going to endure the treatment, we might as well enjoy the habit while we have it. Fancy another?" He handed me the pack and I helped myself.

I had few qualms about sleeping in the bed in our room and couldn't help but compare it with the first one we'd been allocated. Pushing all thoughts of bugs and itchy crotches aside, I stripped and lay down. I awoke to the sound of someone knocking on the door and hauled myself from the bed. The uncarpeted floor was icy beneath my bare feet as I padded to the door, turned the key, and gaped at Ren's smiling face.

"Ren?"

"Hey Sam, it's good to see you again. Can I come in?"

"Of course," I said as I stepped aside. "Sorry, I'm just stunned to see you." Realisation crept into my mind and I frowned. "But this can't be, you're …" I hesitated to say the word that gave me so much sadness. "You died on Deligon 2. How can you be here?"

Ren's over large watery blue grey eyes regarded me as he smiled, then stepped towards me and embraced me. "Just accept that I am here, now, at this moment. I'm here because you're my best friend and I love you."

I struggled to contain the anguished sob that escaped. "I miss you."

"I know you do, and I miss you too. I'm always nearby, remember that okay? I hear you when you think of me, your thoughts reach me with their powerful voice and I'm so proud of you."

"Are you a spirit, like the Lileans talk about?" I asked, curiosity wiping away my emotion.

Ren nodded. "Yes, just like that."

"If you're aware of what's been happening around me," I remarked, "then you must know that we've been stiffed by the Drycenians. It seems they're involved in something terrible, and very illegal. Vincent Domenico too, probably, and Tip is a Gaht leak. We're not sure how to resolve this situation, it's gotten so big suddenly. And to top it all, I'm in love and will probably never see him again."

Ren went to speak, then held himself back and stared over my shoulder, concentrating intensely. Instinctively I turned to look but saw nothing but the dark room. Those lovely eyes again regarded me and the smile returned to his face.

"What's up?" I asked, turning again to look behind but still seeing nothing out of order.

"Nothing, my friend. Don't be too quick to make judgements. There are a myriad reasons why people behave the way they do and not everything said or done is as it may seem at first."

"What are you telling me, Ren?"

"I'm reminding you of your brilliant people reading skills, and how under utilised they've been lately. Don't abandon them, they've served you well and will continue to do so."

"Okay."

"I'm also reminding you of what I told you last time we met in your dreams."

I frowned as I struggled to remember the specifics of the conversation we'd had. "I remember you told me to look out for something, but I can't remember what it is I'm to look for."

"The Mokastone," Ren smiled. "Trust the man who bears the Mokastone. You can safely put your faith in him when you encounter him."

I nodded. "Yes, that was it, the Mokastone. How will I know it when I see it? I've never heard of it before, and who is the man who has it?"

Ren embraced me once more, looked down and smiled at the necklace that still hung around my neck. "You still wear my fang."

"I'll never take it off," I declared. "It's all I have of you."

He shook his head. "Not all. You have me. I'm still with you, just in a different way."

"But I can touch this, hold it in my hand," I said as I clasped the white stone.

"I feel it every time you do," Ren said, "and I know you're thinking of me. It helps draw me close to you while we are so new to communicating in this way. Now I must go, it is almost time for you to awaken." He stepped backwards towards the door. "Don't give up on love, Sam. Promise me."

"I promise. Don't leave me," I whispered, "not again. Ren, please don't go. Ren. Ren." I screamed as he melted away into thin air.

"Sam, Sam, for fuck's sake wake up, Son." Tinnias yelled as I sat up in bed and awoke with a gasp. Seeing me awake, he let go of my shoulders and sighed deeply. "Shit."

"Dad? But where's Ren?"

"You've been calling his name and I couldn't wake you. I was worried sick."

"He was here, we talked like before."

"Before?"

"A little while ago. I was dreaming and saw my parents, then Ren called to me from an old shack and we talked. He said something about a stone that I was to look for. He said the same thing just now."

"You saw him in your dream?" Tinnias asked.

I nodded. "Yes, but it wasn't a dream exactly. I kind of, left my body. I saw it lying here in this bed."

"How weird. What's this about a stone?"

"I forgot what he called it, but its name began with M, and he said to trust the man who has it."

"And did he helpfully give you this man's name?" Tinnias asked.

"Sorry, he was strangely evasive when I asked. I got the distinct impression that he wanted to tell me, but something stopped him."

"That doesn't give us much to go on. I guess we just keep open minds and hope that when he appears, he makes it obvious."

"I guess that's all we can do."

"We might as well get up now, it's only half an hour earlier than usual. We might make the front of the line today."

## CHAPTER SIXTEEN

The atmosphere inside the Gaht compound was different, Tinnias and I felt the tension within minutes of entering. I looked at him and frowned and he gave a slight nod in response.

Spen gave us a speech before allocating the jobs, and the reason for the tense atmosphere, and the larger than normal number of workers became obvious. A visitor was due.

"I want the whole place clean, tidy, and efficient," he boomed. "Every box, crate, and bag is to be in its place, every floor swept and washed, every window gleaming, and every vehicle washed and parked in its allocated space. Okay, so who's good with heights?" Seven hands went up, my own included. "Great, you seven will start with the upper storey windows, the scaffold is already built and in place for you. You'll find buckets and rags in the workshop area, along with the relevant cleaning solution. Do a good job and don't fall, we don't need the paperwork. Go."

With seven of us, it took less than two hours to do all the upper storey windows, and I got a good look at the layout of the place. It was a straight forward design, having been converted from offices to living accommodation when Gaht took over. One side was bedrooms, interspersed with bathrooms. The other side contained a large kitchen and dining room, a room with nothing but stacks of chairs and an outdated holographic viewer and research console, and a large sitting room with comfortable looking chairs and sofas, a Vidicom unit, and several small carved tables. Everything looked comfortable but basic.

Another group were already doing the last of the lower storey windows, so Spen put us on vehicle washing duty. We had this done in less than an hour, after which we were told to sweep and hose down the yard. At one point, I noticed Tinnias walking towards the storage rooms with a can of something in his hands and hoped he was coping with the workload. By the time we went for the mid-day meal, the place looked respectable enough.

"What were you up to?" I asked as we ate.

"Cleaning the living accommodations, some of them at least. The kitchen and dining room, the meeting room, and the sitting room. Then I was scrubbing doors and window frames, and then I went around oiling every door in the place. I even killed that annoying squeak from the main gate. How about you?"

"Washing the upstairs windows, cleaning vehicles, and hosing the yard."

"Not exactly the kind of occupation that taxes the braincells is it?"

"Not really," I grinned. "I wonder who the visitor will turn out to be."

"My guess is Vazien," Tinnias said.

I nodded. "Most likely. Have you ever met him?"

"Once, about three years or so ago, you?"

"I haven't met him in the real sense, but I've been near him at public events while on crowd control and security detail."

"I don't think we need worry about him recognising us. By the way, where are the rest of the men? There were more than this."

"Half got sent home once the bulk of the cleaning up was done. It's just us elite team left now."

"I wonder what we'll be doing for the rest of the day," Tinnias mused as he sat back and belched.


I'd been sparring with the men for over an hour when the sound of a hover vehicle reached my ears. I assumed Vazien had arrived and prayed I wouldn't have to come in too close a contact with him. The last thing we needed was to be recognised after all the work we'd done and the trauma I'd been through. I hoped he would do all his talking and planning in one of the rooms that contained a camera, so we could get a record of anything that might both incriminate him, the Drycenians, or the Lileans, and help us to bring this case to a satisfactory close.

You can imagine my shock therefore, when I turned around upon hearing Spen call my name, and found myself looking into the face of Belotan, the overall leader and founder of Gaht.

"Ren, take a breath. There's someone here to meet you. This is Belotan, our leader." Turning to Belotan, Spen's voice took on a noticeably softer quality than I had become used to. "Sir, this is Ren. He's from the homeless shelter and comes to work here most days. He spars with the men and they're already benefitting from the experience."

"I've heard good things about you, Ren," Belotan said, extending his hand. As I shook it, I noticed the middle finger of his right hand carried a rather ostentatious carved ring, a large brown stone that sparkled with flecks of gold as the sunlight caught it. I couldn't look away, it was beautiful.

"Ren? Are you still with us?" Spen's voice brought me back from … somewhere else.

"Forgive me, Sir," I smiled and shook my head. "Your ring, it's magnificent."

"Thank you, it was given to me by a friend some years ago. It's quite rare so I'm told, it's called Mokastone."

"I believe I've heard it mentioned somewhere," I said.

"Spen tells me you're expert in the Damiklonian martial art."

"Well, I'd hesitate to call myself an expert but I'm a fairly competent practitioner."

"I'd be interested to see a demonstration of that, when Spen can arrange a free hour for you."

"I'd be honoured," I replied.


Tinnias gaped at me, wide eyed in disbelief. "You're shitting me."

"No shit. That ring is the Mokastone Ren told me to look for."

"And we're supposed to trust Belotan, the leader of the biggest gang network in this sector, responsible for numerous murders, beatings, and generally menacing behaviour? This guy is our friend now?"

"Ren said trust the man who bears the Mokastone. I trust Ren without a moment's hesitation and if he says trust Belotan, then I'm inclined to do just that."

Tinnias stopped walking and stared at his feet for long moments. I knew he was weighing up the various threads of the situation in order that the choice he made would be the right one. He looked me right in the eyes.

"And I trust you without a moment's hesitation, so I guess we trust Belotan."

"Let's go back to the ship and discuss how we proceed. I need to check my Unicom as well."

"Yeah, so do I. Shall we get our room booked first?"

"Good idea, it'll give us some extra time to play with."

After securing the same room we had the previous night, we hurried back to the ship. I was happy to notice twenty eight alerts from the camera feed, twenty of them alerting to the name, Vazien, and the other eight, to the name Taiko. My Unicom had one missed call, from Deek, my finance contact, telling me he'd try again in an hour. I was checking the time when it rang and I dropped it in shock.

"Fuck," I hissed as I retrieved it and opened the call.

"Sam?"

"Hi Deek, thanks for calling back."

"No problem. I have quite a lot for you, so you better write this down. Vazien owns eleven mines on Moianal 6, Razulite mines as you said. Seventy five percent of the product brought up from these mines, is sold to a company called Narewa Gun Barrels. Narewa is owned by an outfit called Maghol Berner-Forge, a conglomerate of around fifty or so companies. All of these companies have parent companies, who themselves have parent companies, until eventually we get to a single company, an independently owned bank on Kesh Prime."

"Kesh? So Vazien is behind it after all."

"Yeah, the bank is owned by someone calling themselves Harmun, Child of Actil."

"A distinctly Keshan name," I replied.

"True, but Harmun, Child of Actil, died at the age of eleven months, from Keshan Malady."

"He's taken a dead person's name so he had a birth record and DNA details."

"It's a classic technique used to hide your identity. Now, as for the other twenty five percent of the Razulite, this is sold to legitimate companies, all of whom are legal and legit. The money from this goes into Vazien's normal bank account. The gun barrels manufactured by Narewa Gun Barrels, is sold to an arms manufacturer called Qelmid Lod Arms."

"Also owned by Vazien?" I asked.

"Yes, it's one of the companies owned by Vazien's conglomerate, Maghol Berner-Forge. The arms they produce are sold all over the galaxy, to both sides of tribal conflicts, civil uprisings, and that sort of thing. By arming each side of a conflict in turn, with slightly bigger and more powerful arms each time, he keeps the fight going. This ensures continuing demand for his weaponry and the income this demand brings in. The money is paid into Qelmid Lod Arms' bank account, which is at the bank owned by Vazien, where it is then split into three. One third goes to Narewa Gun Barrels, another third to Maghol Berner-Forge, and the last third stays in the Kesh bank account under the name of Harmun, Child of Actil."

"Shit," I exclaimed. "I don't understand the ins and outs of banking but this sounds like he's in really deep. How does he sleep at night while taking such risks?"

"Search me. Have you got it all written down? I can't send copies of the files as you've not provided a warrant, and I'm guessing you want to be able to use this in court?"

"Yes, I've got it all. Listen, Deek, thank you so much for this, you're awesome and I'm in your debt."

"Oh I think you paid that in advance years ago, don't you? Call me anytime, take care, my friend."


Tinnias was intrigued at the depth of Vazien's involvement, given his status as a politician. Arms dealing itself is not illegal. Arming both sides in a conflict is and both are certainly immoral and could easily end his career. I wondered how he slept at night.

"You'd think the worry of being found out would be too much of a burden," I remarked. "If arms dealing excites him more than politics, and brings in more money, why not resign his position and just be an arms dealer? Why all this secrecy and fumbling in dark alleyways?"

"Because politics gives him the power he enjoys, which is as alluring as money, believe me. There comes a point where you're so powerful that you don't need to worry about being found out or brought to justice. Maybe he's reached that point."

I nodded. "Possibly. Even if he's not, the Drycenians certainly are."

Tinnias ran a hand through his hair. "Son, don't be surprised if we fail to bring this case to the kind of ending we'd like. I'm thinking maybe the players involved are just too powerful and their reach, too long for us to deal with." His Unicom rang and he picked it up. After a conversation that lasted almost an hour, he rang off and turned to face me.

"What's the news?"

"There are two things of interest in his past. First, he's had a long running clash with Taiko. My contact couldn't find out exactly what the cause of this clash was, but it's never been resolved. There are a few theories, the most plausible being that Taiko once poked his nose into some business he was in."

"That was the biggest mistake of his life," I replied.

"Vazien is apparently well known for never letting go of a grudge, and always getting revenge. There's rumours of three killings linked to him, one was a guy of eighty three who was found with his knees blown off a week after being seen arguing with Vazien at a social event."

"Shit," I hissed.

"The most interesting thing though, is talk of the kidnap of his daughter."

"I heard nothing about a kidnap," I frowned.

"No one has, it's not been in the news media. If it really happened, he's kept it out of the public's knowledge. The talk is that he thinks the Dankera Collective have her and allied himself with Gaht with the intention of using them to either get her back, wipe out the Collective, or both."

"I can't see Belotan agreeing to be used as Vazien's personal muscle guy," I said.

"Neither can I. My contact also told me that Vazien and his daughter had a rather volatile relationship since her mother died from River Fever when she was seven years old. She blames him for her death, he got emotionally distant, turned to alcohol to cope, and by the time he snapped out of it she hated him and was in no mood for a reconciliation. You know the sort of thing."

"I see it all too often," I replied. "This job does give you a somewhat distorted view of family life. A lot of my targets have the most awful family histories, some are tragic. I'm so grateful that both of mine have been, and are, wonderful experiences."

Tinnias put a hand on my knee and squeezed. "So how does this change our action plan?"

"It gives us more of a reason to risk returning to Dankera 7."

"What about Belotan and his ring, don't you want to pursue that?"

"Yes I do," I nodded, "so tomorrow, I'll let Spen know we'll be absent for several days due to us having to go hundreds of miles away to attend the funeral of a homeless guy we used to know."

"Because he helped us when we were new to the life, he even saved you from starving to death."

"Okay," I said, "we have a plan. Come on, let's get back to the shelter for dinner."

As we left the port compound at the end of the following day's work, we stopped at the public bathing house to set a recording hub in the locker I'd rented. As we were taking the ship to Dankera, it would be too far away to receive the camera's signals and I didn't want to miss getting something that might help us secure an arrest. Tinnias was all for shaving off our beards and re growing them before returning to Niruvan Prime, but I argued against this. Last time we were on Dankera, we were clean shaven, so our beards would help disguise us. Tinnias very reluctantly agreed.

"The damned thing itches like crazy."

I grinned. "I know, mine does too."

"What do we know about this daughter?"

I tapped a few keys on the console and read from the galactic web. "Olendra, Child of Vazien, is the twenty five year old daughter of Ambassador Vazien, Son of Konmith, from Kesh Prime." Tinnias listened without interruption as I gave him what precious little the web page offered us.

"Well that wasn't exactly helpful," he remarked when I'd finished. "Nothing about their relationship or her personality."

"No," I replied. "Just the basics. There is a photo of her though."

Tinnias craned his neck to look. "Those dead eyes again. They give me the creeps."

"Me too," I nodded. "All Keshans have them. I think it's that shade of grey that does it, makes them look cold and dead. If they were brown or blue it would give their faces a totally different vibe."

"Where is the Collective's base of operations?" Tinnias asked. "Is it that campsite we went to?"

I flipped through web pages until I found what I was looking for. "No, it's in a different city altogether. I'd guess it's probably several hours flying time away from the campsite."

"Does it say anything helpful about the place, size, layout etcetera?"

I laughed and Tinnias shrugged. "You're joking. It doesn't even say where in the city it is, just that it's in a city called Pashlima, which is the capital of that zone."

"The capital?" Tinnias asked. "That means it will probably be quite large. We might find it difficult to track down the Collective at all."

"We need some help here," I said, grabbing my Unicom. Ten minutes later, we had the location, size, and basic layout of the Dankera compound and

Tinnias was already calling the nearest hotel to book us a room with north facing windows, which we hoped would look out over the compound.

"Right, I'll make us a drink," Tinnias said. I flipped the ship into auto pilot and hoped that the three day journey wasn't going to drag.

The time did indeed drag and by the time I switched on the ship's covert module so that our descent would be unseen, we were climbing the walls, desperate to get on with it. We both now had respectable beards and I had to admit, the look suited Tinnias. He laughed when I told him it made him look distinguished.

"That means old with style," he hissed in reply.

Having parked up and locked the ship down in the nearest public parking facility to the hotel, we booked in and were unpacked within a half hour. Having found to our utter delight that our window did look out over the Collective's compound, we went shopping for cold drinks, snacks, and cigarettes, and sat at the window with our scopes. Armed with a photograph of Commander Ranil Taiko, we settled in for the long haul to watch for any signs of him. We weren't expecting to see him wandering around the compound, so you can imagine our utter astonishment when we saw him chatting with a group of men, laughing, and seeming to be having a great time.

"What the fuck?" I muttered.

"He doesn't look like your average kidnap victim, does he?" Tinnias replied.

"Not unless his kidnappers are his best buddies."

This floored us completely; we were at a loss to explain his strange demeanour and I began to wonder if we were being played. The news of Taiko's kidnapping came to us via one of my contacts, so the thought that he might be dicking me around, did cross my mind. I decided to call him up. He answered after the first ring, so he wasn't obviously trying to avoid me.

"Hey, Sam. How can I help?"

"The last time we spoke, you told me Commander Ranil Taiko had been kidnapped."

"Correct. Have you got him yet?"

"Not yet, but are you able to tell me where you got the information from?"

"My cousin's daughter, you know the shy one with the teeth. She recently got a job in law enforcement, as a desk clerk, and has got into the habit of telling us all about her day when she gets home from work. This one time, she told us Commander Taiko had been kidnapped. Then practically the next day, you call me and ask about law enforcement leaks on Tyrrin, so I thought it might be relevant. Did I do something wrong?"

"Hell no, I appreciate your help, always. No, it's just that we've found him and the situation is extremely weird and I wondered who told you he'd been taken. The circumstances we've found him in, made us question the quality of the information given to you and I thought you'd need to know so you can check out your contacts. But since your source is family, I guess the weirdness lives to fight another day."

"What kind of weird?" he asked. "You've got me curious now."

I sniggered. "Well he doesn't look much like a kidnap victim, let's put it that way. I'd say he was visiting old friends and sharing stories of the old days over a lukewarm beer."

"Are you sure you're reading the situation right, Sam? That does seem odd. It might be worth your while calling on the wife to see what she has to say."

"We tried that already and were told by a neighbour that she's taken the children on holiday."

"So your husband gets kidnapped, allegedly, and you piss off on holiday. Wow, cold hearted bitch."

"Indeed," I replied. "Thanks for the clarification, although it doesn't really help us understand this shit."

"You're welcome, anytime."


We kept watch for a couple of days before thinking about how we might proceed. Taiko often left the compound alone to visit a store opposite the main gate, so this was the easiest point at which to confront him. Up to this point, we had seen nothing of Olendra, Vazien's daughter and second alleged kidnap victim.

"So how do we proceed?" Tinnias asked. "We have a couple of options to choose from."

I nodded. "We could simply ask him what's going on," I suggested. "Offer to give him safe harbour with us until we can formulate a plan to get this whole business sorted. Of course, if he should refuse, he could go and screech to his buddies about us, then we'd be dog meat. We'd have to be prepared to make a hasty getaway."

"True," Tinnias nodded. "Or we could take a pro-active stance and kidnap him back, see how he reacts, then keep him in the cell in your cargo hold if necessary."

"We should bear in mind that he might have a tracker fitted by that asshole doctor, if he's in this in the same way they are, they might be working together in this. If he's with us, he could lead them right to us. Again, we'd be dog meat."

Tinnias sighed and ran a hand through his hair. "That's also true. That leaves us with option one, or we could just leave and return to Niruvan, having made a full report of the situation here first."

"Or do both," I said. "We make a full report, we've loads of vidicom of him wandering around in there, laughing and talking with them, visiting the store etcetera. We then pack up, check out of this dump, then go to the store to waylay him. Whether he screeches or not, we leg it back to Niruvan straight away."

"Good plan, Son. Let's do it."

"What about Vazien's daughter?" I asked. "What do we do about her?"

"We've not seen a sign of her so far. We could continue the stake out for a while longer before speaking with Taiko."

I nodded. It made sense to look for her, at least for a little while longer. Our information might be wrong, but we couldn't afford to assume so, not with a life at risk. A high profile life like hers could damage our careers if it were lost. Yeah okay, so I'm practical, sue me.

For another two days we watched and saw nothing to give away the presence of Olendra, so we decided to end the stakeout and waylay Taiko, before leaving with all haste back to Niruvan before the Collective could take our kneecaps as paperweights.

"Hello Commander Taiko," I hissed as he exited the store. Tinnias blocked his escape from behind and together, we carefully steered him into the alley between the store and the bar next door.

"What the fuck?" he exclaimed in shock. "I don't have much money on me but you're welcome to what there is. It's in my back pocket, help yourselves."

"We're not after your money, Commander," I replied. "We just want to know if you're having a good time, visiting with your friends here."

He frowned and peered at me. "Err, yes thanks. Why ever do you ask that?"

"Oh no reason really," I said. "It's just that we heard you'd been brought here against your will, y'know, kidnapped. But you're obviously enjoying yourself, our information must be wrong, don't you agree, Commander? Of course, if you were kidnapped and wanted to get away, we might just be able to help you out."

"I'm fine, thank you anyway. Now if you don't mind." He went to move around Tinnias but failed to squeeze between him and a full trashcan that stank of rotten meat.

"Oh but we do mind," I sneered. "We mind very much, now you mention it."

He sighed, trying to supress his rising anger. I was enjoying myself immensely and was determined to string it out for as long as possible. "Look, I've offered you what money I have, I've assured you I'm here willingly, visiting friends, so if there's nothing else you want, I'd like to leave."

"There's just two more things," I replied. "First, we'd like to know, just to put our minds at rest you understand, why someone would say you've been kidnapped when you haven't. Any idea who might've said that, Commander, and why? After all, we've come a long way thinking you were suffering at the hands of cruel kidnappers, and you being a big noise in law enforcement too, we were naturally worried. It's cost us both time and money, valuable commodities in these expensive time's we're living in. Why, just the fuel costs alone must be, Oh I don't know, maybe…"

"Look I'm sorry you've had a wasted journey," Taiko interrupted angrily. "I didn't ask you to come, nor to spend your time and money on me. All I can suggest is that you use a little more discernment when you listen to gossip in the future."

"The last point, before you head back to your buddies, is this. We were wondering how the girl is getting along."

Taiko faltered before answering and I knew he was about to lie to me. "What girl?" he hedged.

"Oh you know," I teased. "That one with the cold grey eyes. Vazien's daughter. Olendra is her name I believe."

"There's no girl with that name that I've seen. Now if you don't mind." He boldly stepped around Tinnias and strode off.

Tinnias winked at me and laughed. "You're awesome, Son. Now let's get moving and get off this rock before he brings down the whole of the Collective on our heads."

We were both puffing by the time we reached the parking facility, having run all the way from the store where we'd had our strange encounter with Taiko. Within ten minutes, we were heading up into the Dankeran atmosphere and we both sighed with relief.

"That's it, Sam," Tinnias said. "I vow here and now to share a case with you every year from now on. I haven't had so much fun in years."

"You promise?" I asked.

"I promise."

The journey back to Niruvan was uneventful, apart from our need to stop bathing again so we could ensure we smelled like street bums as well as looked like them. Since we arrived back in the small hours of the morning, we locked the ship down and headed to a café for a decent breakfast, before heading to the port to secure a day's work.

We were first in the queue and Spen smiled when he opened the gate and saw us.

"How did the funeral go, guys?"

"It was good, thank you," I replied. "Very dignified."

"Ready to get back to it?"

We both nodded and entered the compound. I spent the morning knocking the shit out of a bunch of field operatives again and was glad of the opportunity to work off some tension. A few minutes before we stopped for our mid-day meal, Belotan appeared and spoke with Spen as they both watched.

"Okay guys," Spen yelled. "Go get your meal and be back here in an hour. Ren, could you stay here for a few minutes?"

Once the guys had left, Belotan strolled over and smiled, the truth of which was verified by the way his eyes crinkled at the corners. He held out his hand, which I shook.

"I'd like to have that demonstration now if you don't mind," he said.

"Sure, no problem," I nodded.

"Okay great, follow me." He led the way across the yard, passed the dining room where men's voices filtered out to us. I suddenly thought of Tinnias worrying at my absence.

"Could I just let my friend know what I'm doing?" I asked. "We always eat together and ever since I was sick, he worries about me."

"Okay," Belotan nodded.

I ran into the dining room and found Tinnias. "I've been asked to give Belotan a demo of the martial art, so I'll be late eating. Don't worry about me okay?"

"Okay, be safe, Son."

Belotan shut the door behind us and I looked around the small office. I knew instantly that he'd brought me there on false pretences, as there was not enough room to do any martial art in there amongst that clutter. I stepped back, glaring at Belotan and wished I had a pistol on me.

"Was she there, Sam?" he asked.

"Excuse me?" I replied. "You said you wanted to see the martial art. Do I do it here, there's not much room."

He smiled and moved a hand across his middle, the light from the bright bulb so recently replaced by Tinnias, making the gold flecks in his ring, shimmer and glint. The ostentatiously large brown stone with gold flecks called Mokastone, the bearer of which Ren had insisted I trust and have faith in. Despite everything I felt telling me I was in danger, I trusted my best friend; that's why I'd taken his name as my alias.

"Apparently so, although we didn't see her ourselves. Someone lied to me very inexpertly when I asked about her."

Belotan frowned. "You have a contact in the Collective?"

"No, we managed to waylay another apparent kidnap victim, one who certainly didn't look kidnapped to us."

"Who?"

I hesitated. Taiko was a Gaht leak, so telling Belotan we knew about him could be awkward. I mentally saw Ren urging me to open up, so I took a deep breath. "Commander Ranil Taiko. One of your law enforcement leaks."

Belotan's eyebrows leapt skyward as his jaw fell in the opposite direction. "Shit. What do you mean when you say he didn't look kidnapped?"

"He was laughing and walking around with them like old buddies," I replied. "He even went to the store every day on his own for cigarettes and beer. That's where we waylaid him. We were all set to rescue him and Vazien's daughter and we were completely floored when we scoped the place out and saw him acting as if he was visiting family on his holidays."

"What did he say when you approached him?"

"He insisted he wasn't kidnapped, that he was visiting family and friends, and that he neither needed nor wanted our help."

Belotan scratched his head and looked at the floor. I could almost hear the questions and thoughts racing around his mind.

"Okay, leave it with me, I need time to think about this. Continue as you've been doing until I have news for you."

"Sure thing," I said. "By the way, can I ask a question?" Belotan nodded. "How come you're not getting Spen to beat the shit out of me?"

"Have you ever heard the expression, the enemy of my enemy is my friend?"

I nodded. "I have, and it's saved my life more than once.

"Well it may be saving mine this time. No one else here knows about you and your father, so keep up your little charade for now. Have the full hour for your meal, I'll let Spen know you'll be late back."

This is where I stop for the day and get some sleep. I'll catch you in the morning. This is Sinclair V-Log Q890/M data log reference point 4136902/621.

## CHAPTER SEVENTEEN

This is Sinclair V-Log Q890/M data log reference point 4136902/622 continuing report.

Good morning all, I hope you slept well. Right, back to the story.

The days followed one after the other in pretty much a predictable fashion. I'd usually be sparring with the field operatives, while Tinnias would be on general maintenance, decorating, and such jobs as became necessary from time to time. My father was shocked when I shared details of my conversation with Belotan, and worried for a time about my safety. It was my turn to be shocked when he shared with me about a conversation he had with the Gaht boss.

"He asked you what?" I screeched in horror.

"He asked me how competent I am with firearms and had me round the back of the compound in the firing range, demonstrating my abilities."

"Did he say why?"

"I did ask him, but all he would say was that if anything should go down, he wanted to know I could handle myself as he didn't want you after his blood if I got killed."

"How can we defend ourselves if we have no firearms with which to do it?" I replied. "They search us at the main gate each morning."

Tinnias shrugged. "I've no idea."

Belotan answered that question the very next day, when he called Tinnias from his mid-day meal, 'to discuss a job that needed doing,' and informed him that two firearms and a supply of ammunition would be secreted in the workers bathroom, in the cistern of a toilet that was roped off as needing fixing. Each morning, we were to visit the bathroom first thing and arm ourselves, then return them before leaving each afternoon.

"They must be expecting a show down soon," I said and Tinnias nodded. "A spat with Dankera perhaps?"

"Vazien and his heavies," Tinnias offered.

"Vincent and the Drycenians," I hissed.

Tinnias looked horror stricken. "Oh perish the thought. Please, if the Gods are real, don't allow that. I wonder if we dare ask Belotan about them, whether they are involved with him or not."

I gaped in horror. "Hell no, I thought about it but didn't have the nerve. I think it might be better not to let him know we suspect their involvement, just in case they are."

Tinnias sniggered. "You're right. Let's keep that to ourselves, for now at least."

Anger welled up inside me unexpectedly. "Why are we so scared of them, Dad? They're just little people with awesome guns. They're not magical, they can't fly or read our minds, and they probably aren't any better than us on a firing range. Good old fashioned marksmanship can bring them down just as effectively as it can a savage with a bow and arrow. And as for Vincent," I sniffed, "he's just a thug with muscles."

"That's true, Son. A little perspective certainly doesn't hurt anyone. I guess it's the mystery with which they surround themselves that causes our fear. We know relatively little about them, they've earned themselves a reputation built on hearsay, myth, and legend, and you know how legends grow out of all proportion to the grain of truth they're built upon."

I nodded. "With Vincent, it's more his sheer size than any legend. We know we're likely to be in terrible pain if we tackle him, so we're naturally cautious. Remember he's a blade man, so he can't be too dangerous from a distance. He doesn't like guns, although he allegedly is competent in their use."

"You're more likely to survive a knife wound than a bullet wound," Tinnias said. "They may look worse but statistically, knives are more survivable than guns."

"Well that makes me feel much better, thanks, Dad," I said and we both burst out laughing.


The next day, Belotan asked us to stay in the compound after the rest of the workers had gone.

"We will feed you, of course, you're not prisoners so you'll be warm and fed and armed."

"Sure thing," I nodded. "Is there a problem coming?"

"Very possibly," he nodded. "Not only will two more competent guns be welcome, but as law enforcers, you'll be able to verify Gaht's adherence to the law in any trouble that takes place. We don't break the law unless we think it necessary and at the moment, we don't. If we do, then you'll be dismissed for the day."

It wasn't an ideal situation but it was better than I could have expected. "Okay, no problem. How do we explain our presence to Spen and the rest of your men?"

"I've already told them I'm checking you out for acceptance into the group, so they won't be too curious. If you get into conversation with anyone here, talk as if you're interested in joining."

"Okay, thanks for the warning. What is the potential problem?"

"A boat with a contingent of twenty very well armed men has moored a little way up the river. We're also expecting Ambassador Vazien to visit this evening and we've reason to believe they might be his hired help."

I frowned. "Why would he start a fight here? I thought he was friends with you?"

"So did we, but after the last conversation you and I had, I checked a bit further and it seems he's also good friends with the Dankera Collective."

"He's playing you off against each other," I said and Belotan nodded. "That's a little unseemly, don't you think? I know I'm a law enforcer, but I know how this shit works, I've been around the block a few times. He's stepped over the line, so unless he has enough power to dominate the situation, he's gonna get a smacking."

Belotan's eyes widened, "Oh he's gonna get a smacking, you can bet your dick on that, my friend."


Once the workers had left for the day, Belotan called us all together for a group meeting to discuss his plan of action.

"Vazien should turn up at eight, but he might want to catch us off guard and be early, so be ready by half seven. Everyone is to wear the light body armour; we don't want him to know that we're prepared too soon. Ren and Koto, we've left the mid-day meal dishes out, so you can be cleaning up there when he arrives. The other groups, you're to be set out as in this plan, look." He unrolled a large sheet of paper, on which was drawn a military style plan of attack and defence. Tactics were discussed for around an hour before everyone was sent for a hot drink before everything started.

Tinnias and I smoked as we drank and discussed where we could hide that would give us cover, as well as a good view of the action. In order that we build a case against Vazien, seeing everything he did or caused to be done, would be advantageous.

"Don't use your firearm unless your life is in peril or the case you're working on will be deemed inadmissible. Law Enforcement Regulation twenty seven, paragraph eight," Tinnias reminded me. "We're not officially on this case, so we'll be treated just like any other citizen. All our law enforcers' privileges will be withheld and we'll be just as accountable as anyone else. We want this guy, so let's do it right, Son."

"Yes, Sir," I nodded.

"Sorry, I didn't mean to lecture you. I just don't want to see you in trouble."

"Hey, you're my Boss as well as my Dad, it's your job to remind me of the regs when necessary."

"I know, but …"

"No buts, Sir," I replied.

"Right then, let's hope for a good outcome, Detective."

The sound of an engine reached us, and one of the field operatives who was polishing a hover truck, nodded at us. We dutifully began to slowly collect the dirty dishes, stack them at the ends of the tables, then carry them to the counter near the sink that was already filled with hot water and detergent. We prepared early as we didn't want the sound of water to obscure any incriminating conversation.

A hover car entered the yard and came to a stop right in front of Tinnias and I, so we both stopped and turned to see who it was, as you would in such a situation. When Vazien exited the vehicle, we turned back to our dishes, keeping our ears pricked for anything interesting. Belotan appeared and greeted Vazien, the two shaking hands and exchanging the usual pleasantries. I was hefting a pile of dishes from the end of a table, when Vazien strode into the dining area and looked around, before settling his gaze upon Tinnias and I.

"Sorry Ambassador," Belotan said. "We had a larger than usual contingent of workers to get the place clean and ready for your visit, and we haven't had time to do the dishes before you arrived. You're a few minutes early."

"No problem at all," Vazien replied, pulling out a chair and sitting down.

Belotan waved to Spen. "Refreshments for our guest at once."

"Yes, Sir," Spen replied and dashed away, returning within five minutes with two women, both of whom carried trays laden with drinks and snacks. Once laid before Vazien, they silently melted away. The two men were still sharing small talk as Vazien raised a cup to his lips and I saw him duck slightly forward and down before the first shots rang out. It was the slightest of movements, just a tiny dip of the head that told me he was expecting the shots that followed and had reacted slightly too early.

Mayhem immediately ensued. Shots seemed to come from every direction, momentarily confusing me and rooting me to the spot. Shaking myself when I felt Tinnias' body brush past me, I ran out of the dining area and looked to my right, to see men climbing over the wall into the compound from the river.

"The boat," I hissed at Tinnias. "They've come at us from the river." Turning to Vazien, I saw him still sitting at the table, drinking and helping himself to a fancy looking cake from a tray of a dozen highly coloured confections. I indicated towards Vazien and Tinnias nodded.

"Ambassador," I yelled above the noise. "We should get you to safety."

"No need for that, Detective," he yelled back, pulling a pistol from inside his smart bespoke suit jacket and pointing it directly at me.

"What the fuck?" I screeched at him.

"You disappoint me, Detective. I would have thought you'd take more care to avoid getting caught on security cameras when poking your nose into business that doesn't concern you."

Shit. He'd obviously seen us on the security camera from the store on Dankera and then came here to see if we were Belotan's men. He had more than enough power to find out who we were, so I wasn't in the least surprised that he knew I was law enforcement.

"Not my business," I replied. "We'd had information that Taiko and your daughter had been kidnapped. You should be thanking us for our diligence, not shooting us."

"You weren't even on the case in any official capacity," he countered, "so it was none of your business. You stepped on my toes and it hurt. Now you'll be paying for that mistake." He took aim at my head just as another shot rang out, this one much nearer than any others so far. This one seemed to be right in the room with us, my ears rang painfully from the sound and it was a few seconds before I saw Vazien on one knee, pain etched across his face. Blood soaked his pant leg and I realised that he'd been shot in the thigh, but he still held his pistol aloft aimed roughly at my head. Tinnias and I hadn't yet drawn our firearms, and we both knew that in the time it would take us to do so, unlock the safety pin, and fire, I'd be dead if he was a half decent shot. It was stalemate for all of three seconds.

The next thing I was aware of was the sensation of falling to the ground, a heavy weight taking the breath from my lungs. As my chest heaved unsuccessfully and began to burn, I fought against the weight that pinned me to the ground as more shots flew around us. As I struggled with the burden, a voice yelled in pain right by my ear. It was a body on top of me, and judging by the way he yelled, he'd just been shot. The chaos of sound around me began to slip into the background as I felt darkness approach. My chest hurt so much but the lack of air was taking its toll, this body was so heavy and I was passing out beneath him, whoever he was. My last thoughts as I saw the last lights wither, were to pray that my father was surviving, then send my love to Byron.

I sprang awake and coughed, then flailed at the face that now loomed, his lips enclosing my own in a kiss that filled my mouth with a vague taste of the warm spice my Mom puts into the cakes she makes. As I coughed, he stood and I found myself looking into the face of Vincent Domenico. The thug with muscles had just saved my life and been shot. Could this case get any stranger?

"Vincent? What the hell are you doing here?"

"Saving you from meeting your maker, idiot."

"Thank you," I said, contrite. "You were shot, I heard you yell."

"Nozzies," he grinned and lifted his shirt to reveal the best body armour in existence. "Vazien got me from ten feet away, so although the armour saved me, it still hurt when it hit."

I coughed and winced at the pain in my chest. "You'll ache for a while," he said. "I had to give you air when you flaked on me."

"You're so heavy, I just couldn't breathe and you wouldn't move."

"Yeah, sorry about that. I work out a lot and it wasn't safe to move with shots flying everywhere."

I suddenly thought of Tinnias and tried to get up. "Dad, where's my Dad. Dad," I yelled.

"I'm here, Son, all in one piece." Tinnias grabbed my hands and smiled. "Let me help you up, come on."

It was only then that I happened to notice everything was quiet. "What's the outcome? Where's Vazien?"

"He's cut and run," the voice of Belotan said. "The moment your friends here made their presence felt, it was all over quickly. The boat crew are down to around half a dozen, and Vazien made a run for it in his hover car when Vincent appeared. He never did say what his problem was, so I guess we're no nearer an understanding."

"He told me he'd seen us in security footage when we approached Taiko on Dankera. When he found out we're law enforcement, he got angry at us poking about in his business and decided to come here to find out if we were connected to Gaht. He must have suspected his disloyalty and double dealing with both gangs was the subject of some debate amongst the leaders."

"Well he won't be doing any more business with us, I can guarantee that," Belotan replied.

"And I can't ask you to testify as the Agency won't accept your testimony. Being the boss of Gaht makes you an unacceptable witness I'm afraid, although you're probably not too bothered by that slur."

"Not in the slightest," he grinned. "It doesn't, however, stop us from giving you everything we know about Vazien, so you can maybe get him in other ways." He turned and waved Spen over, who handed him a data cube. "Here's everything we've found out about him, along with names of people who could be witnesses, people who aren't connected to us or the Collective. I've had some guys onto building a file on him for a few months now, so you're welcome to it. I regret the day he decided to become interested in us, but he's a very powerful man and turning him away would have caused problems we didn't want."

"Thanks for this," I said.

"You're welcome, and I meant what I said by the way. I was impressed with your martial art."

"Thanks." Turning to Tinnias, I smiled. "I guess we go back to the ship and discuss what happens next."

Tinnias opened his mouth to reply, when a voice from the darkness at the back of the room, cut in.

"You could, or you could let us fly your ship back to the battle cruiser while you and your father go in the shuttle with the troopers." I peered into the gloom and Toma stepped out of the shadows. He shouldered his weapon and smiled.

Commander Byron stepped out and stood beside him, gun still dangling from his hand. "Sam," he said, tears springing from his eyes as he took another step forward, dropping the gun to the floor. We closed the gap between us in a rush and I flung myself into his open arms. I was vaguely aware of people slinking discreetly away but I didn't care, my love was in my arms again and still loved me.

"I'm so sorry," I whispered. "Please don't hate me."

"I love you," he replied. "Your letter broke my heart. I was calling you a hundred times a day but you never answered your Unicom. Please don't ever do that to me again"

"I promise. It's been agony, missing you. I was sure you'd hate me. I'm so happy to see you again."

He took my face in his hands and kissed me, neither of us caring who could see or what they might think. I had my love back in my arms and that was all that mattered at that moment.


The journey to the battle cruiser was more comfortable now that I didn't have to pilot the shuttle. I still ached and knew I would be in some pain for a day or two. The familiar shuttle bay stretched out before us and as always, I marvelled at the cleanliness and efficiency of everything. Lomas and Grund were waiting. Lomas swept towards me once the siren blared to let us know the air had equalised.

"My dear friend, I'm so sorry for your suffering, and for our subterfuge. I hope that once you know why it was necessary, you'll forgive us," he said as he embraced me. "Tinnias, how glad I am that Sam had you with him while his mind was in turmoil at what had transpired here the last time you were aboard."

"We're confused but willing to listen to everyone," he replied for us both.

I shook hands with Grund. "Hello, Sam. I'm so glad you're both unharmed. Welcome back. If you decide to remain and work further with us, I'll be picking that data cube apart and seeing what we can gain from it."

I nodded. "I'm glad to hear that, I can use a console but beyond that, I'm out of my depth. I'd probably end up wiping it clean by mistake." I remembered doing just that to a case board once, a few years ago on a case back at Sigma headquarters. That moment still brought a stab of guilt whenever I remembered it.

I looked at Tinnias and saw him grin. "Yes, Son, best leave that to the experts."

"Come then, friends. Let us go to the Observation Room and have some refreshments as we talk."

Over the next three hours, everything was brought out, explained in full. Angry thoughts were expressed, apologies were offered and accepted, shame was felt despite assurances that it wasn't necessary, and tears were shed.

"You see, Sam," Lomas explained, "Arshad told Doctor Jam that we needed to meet with you urgently, which we did. What we didn't tell you was the reason he gave for the need. Doctor?" Lomas looked toward the far corner, where Jam was sitting so quietly that I hadn't realised he was there.

"He told me that you had just embarked upon a case that would ultimately cost you your life and allow a dangerous criminal to continue to cost lives on many worlds. He said it was now time to bring this man's crimes to a halt, and that you must not be lost in the process as you have so much still to do before it is your time to journey to the land of the dead to be with your lost loved ones."

I looked at Tinnias, who gaped back at me.

"He also told me that we would have trouble convincing you to keep away from this case, that you'd charge ahead anyway despite our warnings, so he advised us to allow you to proceed, but to be close by, in a position of unseen control. That's why I placed the tracker inside you, just in case we needed to get to you quickly. He also told me you'd had it removed and were very angry with me. I apologise for what you feel was a violation, but your life depended upon it. As it was, we lost you for weeks and were panic stricken by the time we found you right where we never wanted you to be, in the Gaht compound."

"Can I ask a question?" I said and Jam nodded. "The illness you said I had, was that made up?"

His head shot up and he met my gaze for the first time, his mesmerising yellow eyes shining with both immense sadness and intense purpose. "No, that was the truth. I swear as I sit here, that was the truth."

I nodded as I wondered at the strange mix of emotions I saw in those eyes. "Okay, thanks."

"He said we must secure the help of Vincent and Kyle, so I made sure to suggest we go to Lilea before you could suggest otherwise," Lomas said.

"We needed to discuss what we were to do to ensure your safety and help you in whatever situation you might get yourself," Vincent said. "That's why it was felt necessary that I give you the cold shoulder, to stop you from asking questions of me and wanting to take part in discussions. We had to put you off to keep you safe, but I guess I put you off too much as you took off the moment we left for the surface of Lilea. I'm so sorry for causing you such anguish. You helped Farra and me so much when Gabriel was missing and I'll always be your friend. Please know this, no matter what else you forget, remember that."

He was genuinely distressed and I remembered someone once telling me that he hated lies and deceit more than anything else in life, although I couldn't remember why. I saw his black eyes moisten and realised the lies he was forced to tell must've caused him as much pain as they did for me.

"Thank you for explaining," I said.

"Jam's, Vincent's, and Kyle's guides kept us informed of your progress, albeit in that annoyingly cryptic manner they insist upon," Lomas said, "so as we fought to find you again, we had a little idea of how you were doing. We tried calling you every day but you never answered our calls. We despaired for you."

"We knew you'd probably be able to trace us through my Unicom or spin us some more lies to get us back, so I blocked your numbers."

Lomas nodded. "We guessed that was the most likely reason."

"How is Tip involved in this?" I asked. "I was told he was a Gaht leak, is that true or was he in league with you guys?"

"He was in league with us from the beginning, but he is a Gaht leak, although an officially recognised one. He's working with the full knowledge of the Tyrrin Law Enforcement Agency, and he reports anything of interest to them as they try to build a case against the other leaks they think they might have."

"Oh they definitely have," I nodded, "Several."

"It was Tip that first alerted us to you having got yourself interested in the case. We knew your friendship with him would ensure you poke around and get yourself into danger, so we put our heads together and worked out a plan, together with the guides' help of course. And your friend Ren's spirit then came to help us."

The mention of Ren had me struggling, and failing, to control the stab of emotion that pricked at my eyes. "He came to me in dreams," I said. "He helped me, told me to trust Belotan."

"No wonder he was so accommodating when I cornered him in the compound," Vincent remarked. "It was he who let us know of Vazien's expected visit, and arranged for Kyle and me, Toma, Byron, and a few Troopers to be there to keep you safe."

"He did? Does anyone know if he's okay?"

"He was shot in the arm but he'll survive," Jam replied.

"I'm glad to know that," I said. "For an inter galactic criminal with an epic reputation for violence and many deaths to his name, he's actually a nice guy."

"It would be nice to think he'd use this experience to clean himself up a bit, but I somehow doubt it," Tinnias said.

An awkward silence hung in the air now that the explanations were done. I knew apologies were needed, so I leapt into the aching void.

"I'm sorry for my angry words on our last visit," I said, looking at Lomas. "I had no idea and thought the worst. I guess this job erodes your faith in people's good nature. I also need to apologise for the disrespectful comments I voiced and which your spirit friends will no doubt have informed you in glorious technicolour. I want to say, if only I'd known the truth but you're right, I would've got myself involved anyway. I would no doubt have viewed your pleas for me to stay out of it as suspicious and accepted it as proof that I should get involved." Looking at Vincent, I blushed as I remembered all the things I'd thought about him. "I'm sorry for being rude to you, Vincent."

"I forgive you, absolutely," he replied immediately. "I may be a thug with muscles, but I'm a forgiving one." He looked at me and grinned as I blushed to the roots of my hair.

"Oh shit," I hissed as everyone laughed.

"Now you understand how your father felt when I reminded him of our exchange when I called him on the Unicom. What was it you called me, Tinnias?"

"Oh Your Majesty, please don't, I couldn't bear it."

Now that the mood had lightened a little, Lomas smiled. "Now we have the painful part done, we can approach the question of how you wish to proceed, Sam. If you wish to allow us to work with you on this, we are at your disposal in whatever manner you might need. We have the fastest ship in the galaxy and the best technology you can use. If you'd rather not trust us further, we hold no grudges and you'll go with our love and promise to be at your side if ever you should need us in the future."

"There's no other people I know of I'd rather trust than you," I replied, "and I don't hate you either. I was angry and expressed myself a little too freely. I'm used to being alone, the only people I meet every day are criminals and crazies and people I'd have no business trusting. It'll take time for me to not keep leaping back into solo mode when I feel got at. Ask my Dad here, he's been through it since asking me to join his family." Tinnias nodded. "If you feel happy to start over, I'll try harder to keep my mouth shut and my thoughts to myself. Your help would be great."

"I agree, Son," Tinnias said, putting a hand on my shoulder and giving a squeeze.

"Does anyone have a problem working with our two friends here?" Lomas asked. The room remained silent for long seconds and I mentally sighed with relief. "Right then, you can have the same room you had before. Do you want to umm, freshen up before dinner?" The guffaws echoed in the lofty room and both Tinnias and I blushed and laughed along with them.

Byron had taken hold of my hand in the Gaht compound as we entered the shuttle and still held on to it tightly. "I'm so relieved you're staying with us," he said. "I was imagining all sorts of horrors and was worried sick about whether I'd see you again."

"So was he," Tinnias said. "He never stopped thinking about you and worrying, remember that okay?"

"I will, thank you, Tinnias, I'm happy to know that. Come on guys, I'll help you carry your bags."

"I'm looking forward to using your wonderful shower," Tinnias grinned, "and not having to share it with a smelly street bum." Seeing my frown, he laughed. "Surely you don't want to share a room with your Father when you have your Vishlam back beside you, do you?"

"What's Vishlam?" Byron asked.

"It's our word for girlfriend, boyfriend, chosen special lover," Tinnias explained. "It works for all levels of commitment and all genders."

"Ahh. We have a similar word, Bactish."


The hot water was wonderful and I stood for many minutes just letting it cascade down over my body, warming its way through to my bones before scrubbing myself three times to get the street off me. When I finally stepped out, I wrapped a towel around myself and fiddled with my razor but found its battery dead.

"Shit," I hissed.

"What's up?" Byron called from his balcony.

"My bloody razor is dead."

"Use mine, it's in the second drawer down."

I rummaged and took out what I thought looked most likely to be a razor and turned it over in my hands. I'd never seen something so obviously modern, it looked positively space age and I sniggered.

"How?" I called.

Byron appeared in the mirror beside me and took the gizmo from me. "Like this, watch." He showed me how to switch it on and I frowned.

"Where's the blade?"

"There isn't one, it uses P A L light."

"You're shitting me," I said as I held it up to my face and pressed the switch. "Whoa, you're not shitting me, Bro." Five minutes later, I rubbed my face after the closest shave of my life. "That's fucking awesome."

Byron laughed at my incredulity, and I turned to face him. "I'm so happy to see that smile again," I said quietly. He didn't reply, he was too busy kissing me.


Tinnias and I were both delighted to be rid of our itchy beards and have a thorough shower and change of clothes. I felt years younger now I was clean and fresh. Byron and I decided to call on him on our way to dinner and I hardly recognised him. We were about to go to the Obs Room when there was a knock at the door. Tinnias opened it and we saw Vincent standing there.

"Wow you two look years younger," he grinned. "Jam wants to check you out, Sam, to make sure the doctor at the refuelling station did a good job."

"Okay," I nodded. "As soon as he's less busy, I'll go and find him."

"He's gone back to the medical bay already."

"Okay, I'll go now. Thank you, Vincent, for saving my ass back there. I owe ya one."

"I'll write that in my little book of favours owed," he grinned as he embraced me. I forgot he was a touchy feely type of guy. I'd have to get used to that, although having been kissed on the lips and now hugged, we should be the best of friends by now.

Jam looked up as I entered the medical bay and I smiled. "Reporting as ordered, Doc."

"Ahh good, I just want to make sure that the surgeon on the refuelling station did a good job. He probably did, but I'm a picky sort of person when it comes to medical matters."

"No problem."

"Remove your clothes and stand on the pad so the scanner can do its thing."

A few minutes later, Jam peered at the holographic display and scratched his chin. "Hmm, he's done an okay job but he's left the power wire in. It looks like he capped it off though so it should be fine if you want to leave it. Or I can remove it if you wish. It's not needed now you're back with us, so if you want it out, it's a five minute job."

I hesitated as a rash thought burst into the forefront of my mind. "I umm," I faltered.

"Take all the time you need to think about it, there's no hurry. It's not causing any problems that I can see. If you'd rather, I can ask Doctor Lear to do it for you."

"What? Hell no, that's not why I'm hesitating. It's just … Well, can you put it back in?" I asked gingerly, afraid of his reaction.

He looked up from his medical console and gazed into my eyes, surprise obvious in his expression. "Back in? Why? I thought you felt …" he faltered.

"I did, but that was before I understood. I have a problem with lies and deceit and it got to me. I'm sorry I was so offensive, please believe me. You must hate me after the things I said."

"No," Jam replied quietly. "I hate what you said, but not you, the person. I admire you, if I were to be totally honest. To do the job you do and still function as a normal, well balanced person takes strength I'm not sure I possess."

"I guess your guide, Arshad, will have told you what I said. You must have felt bad hearing that. I can't take it back and not say it. All I can do is explain and apologise."

"I felt pretty awful, I admit," he nodded. "In my defence, I did express concern to the others when it was suggested, but I was out voted and at the end of the day, your safety was paramount. I hate losing any friendships. As you are aware, there are too few genuine ones."

I nodded. "You have insight, Doc. Can we start over? I'm sorry, unreservedly."

"And I accept, without hesitation. Let's start over. Now, about that tracker. Rather than put it back in, I was planning to offer you both a BioMed implant as soon as we get a new supply." He indicated the small, kidney shaped metal plate all the Drycenians have on their forearms. Vincent and Kyle have them too and I had wondered what they were.

"I was wondering what those were," I admitted.

"Without getting too scientific, they not only contain a tracker, but there is a probe that goes into the main artery that runs up your arm. It monitors the blood for any contaminants, infections, anything that shouldn't be there, removes them, then treats them in such a way as to render them inert and harmless. You'll notice a small grey pellet appear every so often, which you can discard and forget. I get a six hourly update on your health and location, the implant's health too, and if I feel something needs my attention, we know where you are and can get to you without wasting time hunting you down. There is also a one way emergency call feature, should you need to call us for help in an emergency. If you'd prefer just the tracker, that's fine. We should have some BioMeds in a week or so. It's your choice."

"Whoa," I exclaimed, staring at him in awe. "That would be awesome. I'd love one of those. To know you're keeping watch will give me considerable comfort, despite my angry words recently."

He smiled. "Okay then. As soon as the supplies arrive, I'll get you back here, it's a half hour job and an overnight stay. I'll remove that bit of wire at the same time, to save slicing you up too many times."

I grinned. "Thank you very much."

"Remember, Sam, you'll be in contact with Byron now, so you've no need to feel isolated anymore. If you need us, just ask him and we'll do the rest."

"I will, and I'll try not to be a nuisance, I promise."

## CHAPTER EIGHTEEN

I spent a wonderful night with Byron in the most comfortable bed I'd ever slept in. It was my first experience of love with my own gender and Byron was a gentle and patient teacher with me and I, an eager student. It was a very much revived law enforcer that strolled into breakfast with Byron, Tinnias, and Jam the next morning. Vincent waved at us to sit with him and Kyle, so we loaded our plates and strolled over.

"Morning guys, did you all sleep okay?"

"Yes thank you," I replied. "I slept like a baby."

"I stayed up far too late enjoying the balcony in my room," Tinnias grinned. "That's the most amazing technology I've ever seen."

"I was awake for a few hours," Jam added. "One of my nurses is off sick so I took her shift when Elka finished hers. The four hours I got was actually more refreshing than sleeping for ten hours at a stretch."

"I slept for the first time in what seems like months," Byron said. "Not having to worry at last is wonderful."

"Kyle and I talked well into the small hours, as is usual when we get together. We're both a bit bleary eyed this morning."

"It's fatal getting us to share a room," Kyle said. "We never get any sleep because we spend all night talking."

"You can have a room each if you'd prefer," Jam said. "There's plenty spare."

"That would just mean one of us would have further to walk each night for our chats," Kyle said and we all laughed.

I thought about Kyle as we ate and chattered. I'd met him once before, when working the Domenico case when Gabriel went missing, but it was a brief encounter that didn't allow me to get to know him at all well. His dual heritage of half Lilean and half Drycenian made him more of a mystery to me than each of those races do when taken separately. He's built like Vincent, big and muscular, with the typical tanned complexion and star shaped birthmark on his chest that they all have. He has the Drycenian yellow eyes and fangs and I must admit, the mix of the two races as it manifested in him, was a good look. He wasn't loud and confident like Vincent and in many ways, he reminded me of Doc Jam. The quiet demeanour, sensitive and thoughtful nature, and apparent introversion told me that he probably needed Vincent more than Vincent needed him.

Tinnias told me that Kyle had saved him in a similar manner to that which Vincent had saved me, by lying on top of him while bullets flew around our heads. It was a miracle that neither he nor Vincent were seriously hurt, and I owed Kyle a debt of gratitude for saving my father. I knew Tinnias would have already given his own thanks, but I was grateful too and wanted him to know.

"Kyle," I began. Everyone stopped and looked at me and I blushed. It occurred to me that it was as if everyone was waiting for me to explode with anger and disrespect. Maybe I'm over sensitive, but the way everyone stopped talking and the electricity in the air told me I was not wrong. I sighed, realising that regaining their affections would be a long journey. I decided it would probably be best if I didn't talk much from that moment on, at least while in the company of the Drycenians and Lileans.

"Yes, Sam?" he regarded me with intense direct eye contact which I learned later was a typical Lilean thing they do as part of their unspoken communication etiquette.

"I haven't thanked you for saving my Dad down there. I'm in your debt for that."

"You're both welcome, anytime," he smiled, the gesture crinkling the corners of his eyes.


Once breakfast was done, Lomas suggested we reconvene in a couple of hours to begin the process of looking through the contents of the data cube Belotan gave me. Doc Jam said that since my chest was still a little tender, I should refrain from my martial art practice for a week, although a not too strenuous warm up routine wouldn't hurt. Gentle jogging was allowed, but lifting weights was forbidden. I changed my clothes and made my way to the cargo hold where I remembered it being nearly always quiet and deserted and went through my full warm up routine five times, before spending an hour jogging around the perimeter of the huge space. It also meant I got to see Byron as he worked, which was lovely. Back in the room we shared, I showered and changed clothes, then got myself a cold drink and relaxed before going to find Tinnias.

"There you are, I've been looking for you," he smiled.

"I've been working out in the cargo hold, or what passes for working out anyway. The Doc has forbidden anything too strenuous, so it was a warm up routine and some jogging."

"How is your chest feeling today?"

"Still a bit painful. Coughing is a no no and sneezing is totally out of the question. It's a good job I don't have allergies. I'm glad he banned me from working out; it makes me feel less guilty at not feeling able to."

"How do you feel about everything that's happened over the past day? I must say I'm relieved that they're on the right side of the law after all, and although I agree with you about feeling violated, I kind of understand why they felt it all right to put the tracker in."

I nodded. "I'm relieved too, and very grateful they turned up when they did and saved our dicks. I feel a bit like a naughty child though, which isn't a great feeling when you're a grown man with a responsible job you're good at."

"In what way do you feel like a naughty kid?" Tinnias asked.

"Like I'm being punished for saying the things I did. I know they seemed to accept my apologies, but there's just something about everyone's manner towards me that tells me they don't trust me not to start yelling and being rude. I may be over sensitive but it's like everyone has lost the mystery I was so enamoured by for all those years, the people I hero worshipped have disappeared and these very nice but untrusting and inflexible facsimiles have been put in their place. The only one I feel totally comfortable with is Byron. Does that make any sense?"

"Totally," Tinnias replied. "And I did notice the sudden change of atmosphere at breakfast when you addressed Kyle. When you then thanked him, I could almost hear the collective sigh of relief. I feel bad for you, Son. How can I help you feel better?"

"By doing what you do so naturally, being here and being you. I'm so glad you're here with me on this, who knows what trouble I'd be in with these people if I was alone."

"Remember I'm always on your side, even if you should ever be wrong or misguided, foolish or reckless. I love you and don't you forget it."

"I won't, thanks, Dad. Now I guess we'd better get back."


Grund was busy fiddling with the holographic streamer when we entered the Obs Room, so we sat down and waited. Tinnias chatted with Byron, who came and sat with me, while I kept my mouth firmly shut. I reached for his hand and felt his squeeze it in response. When everyone was seated and the streamer was ready, Grund nodded at Lomas, who stood and addressed the room.

"Okay everyone, it's time to see what the data cube can tell us. Grund, the floor is yours."

"Thank you, Your Majesty. Okay, so after having a brief scan through, I can tell you that there is much that might turn out to be very useful information. There are several things that point to scandal and cover ups, a possible murder by Vazien himself, many unhappy employees, details of arms sales, companies owned by Vazien, bank details of those companies and every employee, recordings of conversations wherein Vazien talks about problems with his daughter and his regret at her birth having occurred, and more conversations in which he gives some details about a plan he's hatching to secure total control over the entire Law Enforcement Agency network, galaxy wide."

"Shit," Tinnias exclaimed and gaped at me. I gaped back and nodded.

"There is quite a bit we don't need to examine in great detail here and now," Grund continued. "Bank and employee details, company details etcetera, I can collate all the information into a more user friendly document that will be not only easier for everyone to understand, but will be acceptable as evidence in court, should a trial ever be forthcoming." He looked at me and I nodded. "There is a journal written by Vazien's late wife, Kandil, Child of Barlot. She died when Olendra, the daughter, was seven, apparently from River Fever while on holiday. In the journal, she talks about Vazien's temper, his violence towards her and Olendra, and the fanatical way he pursued wealth and power."

I leaned in to Tinnias, "we could get the paper and handwriting verified by our forensic team. If we prove it genuine to the time period and the wife herself, it casts a cloud over Vazien that we can hopefully build upon with other stuff."

Tinnias nodded, before addressing Grund. "Can we perhaps begin a list of those things we feel will be useful in building a case, and add this journal to it?"

"Absolutely," Grund nodded, taking up a clipboard and writing hurriedly.

"We could go so far as to exhume the wife's body," Jam said. "I can tell you within a few minutes if she contracted River Fever by the usual method, ingestion of tainted water, or if the pathogen was injected. That would tell us whether she was murdered or not." Grund wrote everything down, word for word as Jam spoke. "We'd need all the usual official permissions first of course, but there would be no official need for Vazien to know about it."

"There is also a letter written by a junior doctor by the name of Orlan, Child of Fars who attended her when her death was reported. In the letter, which he lodged with his family lawyer in case of his own death being deemed suspicious, he talks of being persuaded by Vazien into providing the Ambassador with a phial of the River Fever pathogen for what he was told was, private research. He says he felt sure Vazien had used it to kill his wife but couldn't prove it and worried for his own safety if he were to report it. If we could get to this man, he might testify."

"We could certainly ask," Tinnias replied.

"There are also documents detailing Vazien's ownership of one hundred and seventeen mines on twenty seven different planets, many in the name Harmun, Child of Actil."

"The same name he uses for his secret bank account," Tinnias said.

"And which he uses on documentation detailing his ownership of many of the companies under the conglomerate, Maghol Berner-Forge. There are other names for some of the companies and many of the mines are in different names. There are eleven different aliases I can trace back to Vazien so far, another five I can't quite prove the paper trail for, and a dozen or so that are just hearsay."

"This is getting scarily big," I whispered to Tinnias, who nodded wide eyed at me in response.

"Yet more documents prove his ownership of twenty-three patents, all of which pertain to the mining of Razulite and the manufacture of arms. He also owns his own moon, which no one can visit and about which he is not open to questions. A fleet of private security ships are on constant patrol, so getting there unseen is all but impossible, even for us."

"Shit," I hissed in astonishment. Tinnias gaped at me and shook his head in disbelief.

"The other documents contain company and employee addresses, together with details of employees families, their social standing, and anything that might be used against them as leverage, sexual affairs, violent behaviour, crimes as teenagers, suspect friends etcetera. The rest of the cube contains the recorded conversations. Do we trudge right on or shall we break for a drink, snacks, smoke, pee, etcetera?"

"Let's take a half hour break," Lomas said. "Is everyone okay with that? Sam and Tinnias, are you smoking these days?" Tinnias nodded. "Okay, there are designated smoking rooms on each deck, you'll find the nearest next door, or you may use the balcony in your room."

"Want to smoke, Son?" I nodded and followed him out, tugging Byron along with me, and into a nice but basically furnished smoking room in which four Troopers sat, long cigarettes in their hands. They smiled as we entered.

"Wow, now that's a cigarette," I grinned at the delicate object that must have been easily the length of my hand. I'm willing to bet I won't find them in any corner store I frequent."

"You might, actually," one of the Troopers replied. "They're from Halmex 3. We buy a huge crate of them once a year to keep the smokers aboard, happy. Would you like a few packs?"

"Oh yes, we would," I replied, taking a long draw on the one he offered and lit for me. It was mellow but flavourful, without a hint of bite that might cause you to cough. I blew out the smoke and smiled as I watched Tinnias, eyes closed and gently exhaling a thin plume of blue smoke.

"That's lovely," he said once he'd opened his eyes to find me grinning at him. "It's worth continuing to smoke for these."

Byron laughed. "If you wish to, you can get the Doctor to put an implant into you that prevents your body taking up the harmful shit from cigarettes. You get all the enjoyment with none of the risk. It's just an injection to put it under the skin. Two minutes and you're protected for life."

"The only thing you'll notice is that your pee will change colour slightly," one of the troopers added.

"I guess we're persuaded," I grinned at Tinnias, who nodded.

"Awesome," the first Trooper exclaimed. "Social misfits of the galaxy, unite."

"Hooahh," Tinnias and I chorused, pumping our fists into the air.


Of the phone calls, which totalled two hours and thirty eight minutes, most were of no real use in building a case. Seven contained direct evidence of Vazien's deteriorating relationship with his daughter, with clear statements of his regret at her having been born.

"If he hated her so much, it would explain why he didn't report her apparent kidnap," Tinnias said.

"If she was kidnapped at all," I whispered into his ear when everyone had finished agreeing with him.

"You've reason to doubt it?" he asked.

"Just a hunch," I replied. "I'll bet you fifty she ran away."

"You're on."

Eighteen conversations contained direct references to Vazien wishing to increase his hold on the Law Enforcement Agency and to branch out into gaining control of the system that governs the setting up and handling of trials and sentencing of prisoners. He spoke of wanting to increase the number of inside leaks he could call upon, especially those amongst the higher ranks who had more power than detectives or chase, catch, and deliver guys like myself. In one particularly astonishing conversation, he laid out plans for the placing of judges and jury foremen in strategic court establishments, men who would be directly under his control. He went into incredible detail about the training of these people, how he expected to exercise the control he wanted, and how they would be punished if they let him down.

"I wonder why he wants to control trials and sentencing," Tinnias said. "That wouldn't benefit him, surely?"

I shrugged. "Search me, I'm lost for words at this point," I replied.

"He's drunk on power," Byron offered. "When you get to a certain level of power, it seems to take hold of some people and they get a bit power crazy."

I grinned. "A bit?"

Three conversations were obviously with the Dankera Collective and contained statements that proved he was trying to set up Gaht. I came to realise while listening, that although he was allied to Gaht and apparently working with them to their mutual benefit, he was also doing the same to the Collective. The statements he made in these conversations proved he was trying to initiate a fight between the two gangs, with everything staged to ensure as far as possible, that the Collective would emerge as victors.

"It's almost as if he's seeking revenge after being slighted, like a kid in the schoolyard," I said to Tinnias."

"How do you work that one out?"

"The statements he makes, the inflection of his voice, it's subtle but obvious, to me anyway. We should give Belotan a call and ask him about his association with Vazien, whether there's ever been any cross words between them. Maybe Vazien wanted power within Gaht but Belotan refused, so now he's gone to the Collective in a huff, in a childlike attempt to 'get them back.' It seems that way to me as I listen to him."

"You could have a valid point there, Son. Mention it to the group."

I shook my head. "It's just a hunch. We don't want to waste anyone's time chasing a vague hunch we can't prove, especially with so much other potential evidence to plough through and disseminate."

He looked at me hard for several seconds before nodding. "Okay."

I felt Byron squeeze my hand and looked at his beautiful face. I smiled and squeezed back and he seemed relieved.

At the end of the recordings was another single document which detailed names and contact details of apparently unhappy employees. It was titled, Unproven Rumours and I was immediately interested. Experience told me that disgruntled employees were often happy to talk, especially if they had been thoroughly punished for complaining.

Tinnias and I looked at each other and grinned. Finally, we had something we knew would bear fruit.

"We should make some calls while we're waiting for the exhumation order," Tinnias suggested.

"I couldn't agree more," I replied.

The intercom boomed, bringing the room to silence. "Detective Samelan Sinclair-Vaylo to Comms please, there is a personal call for you."

"Top Deck, Sam," Byron said as I stood. In a moment of rash bravery, I leaned down and kissed him and left the room.

"Detective Sinclair-Vaylo here," I said once I was alone.

"Hi Sam, how are you both?"

"Tip?"

"Yeah." A silence hung between us as I struggled to choose a response I felt comfortable with. Tip broke the atmosphere by talking first. "Have I lost your friendship?"

"Umm, no. No of course not. I guess I'm surprised to hear from you."

"I'm sorry, Sam. For the lies. By now you'll know why we felt it necessary."

I felt emotion prick at my eyes and I didn't want another emotional struggle just yet. Tip's dismissal of me seemed so genuine that it was only now I knew why it happened that I realised just how much his angry words hurt me. I guess it was a result of the time I'd put into him when he was new to the job, I had a vested interest in him being a good law enforcer and enjoyed our regular chats and get togethers. To be rebuked so firmly and so well by this man with whom I felt a deeper connection than most, hurt. The part I had taken in the great changes he made to his life made his quick and immediate ostracism of me both shocking and deeply hurtful. I was not yet ready to handle this.

"I umm …" I faltered. "I can't do this right now. Give me some time. I'm trapped in a corner here so I can't deal with this just yet. I'm sorry." I hung up and fought with my emotions before leaving the room and decided to stop at the next smoking room before rejoining the group.

Everyone looked up as I entered the Observation Lounge. "Everything okay, Sam?" Lomas asked.

"Yes, fine, thank you, Your Majesty. No problem."

Tinnias looked at me questioningly as I sat beside him. He raised his eyebrows as if to say, 'well?'

"Tip," I whispered as silently as I could.

"He nodded, mouthing 'okay' as he turned his attention back to the group.

Byron leaned towards me. "How did it go?"

I turned to look at him, fighting with my emotions. "Not good."

"I'm sorry, my love."

"That's everything on the cube," Grund said as he switched off the streamer and sat down. "Anything you want collated, listed in a different form, expanded or simplified, whatever, you have only to ask," he said, looking directly at me.

"Thank you, we'll most likely be taking you up on that offer. You've done an excellent job today, well done."

"I agree," Lomas said. "I'm so glad you came to work with us, Grund. Now shall we break for lunch and start the discussion and post mortems with a refreshed outlook and relaxed mind?" Everyone nodded, so I stood.

"I'm going for a smoke," I said to Tinnias.

"Good idea," he replied.

Once I felt my mind relaxing under the influence of the cigarette, I sighed aloud.

"How did it go with Tip?"

"It was umm, awkward."

"Oh? I'm surprised to hear that. Out of everyone involved here, I'd lay money on your friendship with him being the one you feel easiest repairing."

"I was surprised too," I admitted. "When I heard his voice, I found I was more hurt than I had realised."

"So how did it go?"

"I told him to give me time. I said I wasn't able to handle it right now, what with everything that's happened over the past weeks."

"Was he all right about it?"

"I've no idea, I hung up on him."

"Oh, Son, I'm sorry."

"Now you know why I always defend my slightly distant social manner. This job costs friendships, it doesn't breed them. Everyone I've loved has either died or left me."

"Hey," Byron said sharply. "Your job bred our friendship, and now our relationship. We'd both still be lonely if it weren't for your job, and I've no intention of either leaving you or dying just yet."

I hugged him tightly. "I hope this isn't awkward for you. I'm kind of ... at odds with your people at the moment and I hope you don't find me disrespectful. You must tell me if you find yourself with problems because of us."

"I don't care what anyone says or feels about us," he replied. "If they don't like it, tough shit. My heart is with you, always, and they can either accept it or accept my resignation. This, us, is too important to let anyone interfere with."

"Byron," Tinnias said as he squeezed his shoulder. "Where have you been all our lives?"

"Waiting for him," he replied, pointing at me. "I've been patient and I'm not in the mood to let anyone pull us apart."

I sniggered. "I'll try anyone's patience."

"Ain't that the truth," Tinnias replied and we laughed. "I understand how high a price this job demands, so never believe you're struggling alone with this. I may be an ageing deskbound busybody who gets in the way of real detectives, but I was one myself once."

I grinned. "You're never in the way, Dad. During that Rime business, your help and leadership kept me going."

"Do you want to eat lunch?"

"No, I had plenty for breakfast and that will do me until dinner."

"Me too, I've never been able to handle the three meals a day thing. Two is just right for me."

I nodded. "It's like your body is constantly battling with an overload of food all the time, there's no let up. It can't be healthy."

"Shall we walk and talk, remain here and smoke, or go back to one of our rooms?"

"Let's go to a room," I said. "Lomas said we can smoke there on the balcony, and there's the drinks dispenser, or we could get some beers from the ship. I think there's a dozen left."

"Do you need to be left alone to discuss cop stuff?" Byron asked. "I can find gainful employment in the cargo bay until you're done."

"No," Tinnias and I chorused. "Come with us."

"Okay, sounds like a fine idea, come on."


"Hello there, how can we help?" the guy smiled as he rummaged in the huge toolkit. A shuttle sat on a pad nearby, missing several panels. Like a medical specimen, its open body showing the internal organs for everyone to see. Although my knowledge of mechanics is basic, and my interest in such male orientated matters, limited, I was fascinated to see the guts of such an advanced piece of technology. As I stood looking, another Trooper fitted the panels back on, looking at me over his shoulder several times. They didn't at first see Byron with me but smiled when they did. "Hi, Boss."

"Hey, guys. We're just getting something from Sam's ship. We won't be in the way for long."

I was more than a little annoyed but rather than get angry, I resorted to sarcasm. "It's okay, Bud, I know nothing about mechanics so your secrets are safe with me."

"Thanks," I heard Tinnias say to the first Trooper that had said hello to us. He strode towards my ship, which nestled in a corner at the far end. I jogged to catch him up and within five minutes, we were heading back down the corridor with my last dozen beers.

"Did I hear you talking to one of the mechanics?" Tinnias asked as we entered Byron's quarters and put the beers into the cooling unit.

I switched the cooler to maximum so the beers would be cold within twenty minutes. "Yes, did you see what he did?"

"No."

"One of the shuttles had some panels off the side, I guess they were servicing it or something, and when another guy saw me looking, he quickly put the panels back, and kept looking over his shoulder at me."

"Really?" Tinnias asked. "Are you sure? That seems a little brazen, don't you think?"

"I'm sure," I nodded. "And I had something to say, I'll warn you now in case I get another ass whooping."

Tinnias laughed aloud. "What did you say this time, Son?"

"I told him I know zero about mechanics, so any secrets would be perfectly safe."

He bent down, hands on his knees as his guffaws filled the room. "How did he react?"

"I've no idea, you started walking towards my ship just then, so I forgot him and followed you."

"Oh, Son, you make me laugh every single day, I love you."

"You're reading more into it than was there," Byron grinned. "I've worked with that guy for nearly thirty years and I happen to know that he thinks you're a really good person, he's told me so more than once.

"I'm sorry. I guess I'm feeling cornered and defensive." I kissed him and opened the door to the balcony. "I wonder if someone could leap over the railing and kill themselves," I mused aloud as I peered over the stylish railing, "or would the force field keep them in?"

Tinnias grinned. "It's funny, I was wondering that same thing the first time I saw it."

"Imagine if you could end it all that way, what a way to go huh?"

"Horrific," Tinnias replied and shuddered.

"That's impossible," Byron said. "Why does everyone always ask that?" he sniggered. "The forcefield keeps us inside as well as the void of space, out."

We got ourselves a beer apiece and sat on the balcony. It was lovely there, surrounded by the silent void, hypnotic even. Byron slipped his hand into mine and without even realising it, I dozed off. When I came to, I found myself walking along what could only be a corridor within a ship. It wasn't the battle cruiser though, there was none of the little stylish flourishes that cover even the most utilitarian item in the Drycenian world. And it was silent, I could have been alone aboard, if it weren't for Ren's presence beside me.

For many minutes it seemed, we didn't speak. Words weren't always necessary between Ren and I, his presence was enough, his habit of walking just close enough for our shoulders to touch was enough to let me know he was there, sharing my emotions and thoughts in the way that only empaths can. The empathic bond that he built between us was so natural it was both subtle and immensely strong and allowed me to truly love him without it seeming in any way inappropriate. His appearance within my dream world gave me huge comfort, and I found myself hoping that it would continue after this case was finished.

"I'll be here as long as you want me to be," he said softly.

"Thank you," I replied. "I saw the Mokastone guy by the way. He helped us. I trusted him as you told me to."

"I know, and I'm proud of you for your faith in me."

"This case is getting worryingly big and complicated. Vazien is a very powerful and vengeful man. I'm not sure we can conclude this the way we want to."

"Sometimes, people cause complications where there were none. It's difficult to believe that the line the evolution of a given situation takes over time, could be simple, so they create complications in order to make things seem more real."

"What are you telling me?" I asked. "That it's not complicated after all and I just think it is?"

"Because things usually are." Ren smiled. "I remember you once telling me, not long after we first met, that the oldest sin in the book is also the most widespread. You told me that no matter how far across the galaxy you could travel, no matter what manner of person you were to encounter, they would all share one trait."

"Greed," I nodded.

"Greed," Ren smiled. "It seems such a simple truth but it affected me greatly. It helped me see things in perspective and suddenly, I didn't feel quite so far from home, nor so afraid of my position in a universe where I was the different one, the true alien amongst aliens. You might think of it as a throw away comment of little consequence, but for me it was, and still is, a deeply profound wisdom. Remember it now, as you struggle with your growing fear of this powerful new enemy, and he will regain more realistic proportions in your mind. This will help you make the right choices, unencumbered by the fear that often prevents forward momentum."

"I must admit, I'm finding it hard to know how to proceed," I said.

"I've noticed. Sometimes you find yourself rooted to the spot and unable to move, even to hide away, because he seems mystically powerful and that just makes you feel useless." I nodded. "This fear is not only preventing you from advancing this case, but it's changing you, for the worse. You doubt yourself now, feel unworthy, insecure. The Sam I knew was so confident in himself and his abilities, he bordered on the arrogant."

I stared at Ren and grinned. "Really? You never told me that. I'm sorry, it wasn't intentional. I had no idea I was being arrogant."

"See, you're doing it again."

"Doing what?"

"Doubting yourself, apologising for yourself. You never used to do that when I was still alive in your physical world. The problems you're having with your relationship with the Drycenians, the Lileans, Tip, it's all caused by your suffering the worst ailment of man, fear. Fear is the greatest mind killer, Sam and you're suffering. You fear being less than your neighbour, being unworthy of acceptance, being left out and left behind, and you sense a plan to unseat your confidence in yourself. You've begun to withdraw, to attack before being attacked. You sense a conspiracy that isn't there."

"I guess you're right, thinking about it now. I do feel less than I felt before this case, and I'm feeling attacked here, amongst these people. The only one I truly trust is Byron, but then I worry our relationship will cause problems for him, that his people will judge him harshly for loving me."

"He is a grown man, Sam, and well able to make decisions for himself. Don't assume he will choose his own people above you. His love is immensely powerful, as is yours. This love was meant to be, it was decided a very long time ago. Don't make problems where there are none, and don't lose yourself, Sam, please. Now I'm no longer in your physical world, my ability to help you is limited, but I'm here beside you, just as I always was. I hear you when you think of me, I feel your pain when you grieve for me, and my soul sings with joy when you remember me in the way I told you about, the Damiklonian way."

"I try to do as you said."

"I'm proud of you, Sam."

Tinnias shook me awake. "Time to get back to the discussion, Sam. Are you okay? You were calling out in your sleep."

## CHAPTER NINETEEN

We talked for hours and by the time we stopped for another half hour break, we had the bones of a plan. While the Drycenians went through the red tape of getting an exhumation order for the body of Vazien's wife, Tinnias and I would work our way through the list of possible witnesses to get as many to testify as possible. Once we had some willing testifiers, we could work out the most efficient route to visit them all for a chat. We wouldn't be able to do formal interviews of the type I do every day in my job as a chase, catch, and deliver guy, but that doesn't mean our chats couldn't be conducted properly and recorded as evidence.

As we smoked, I thought about what Ren said. As I allowed my mind to dwell on his wisdom and think about all that happened in this case so far, the mystery and fear melted away as Vazien revealed himself to me in his true form, a greedy politician with too much power for his own good. Greed is the most fundamental of humanoid traits and is at the very core of every race created. I've dealt with countless greedy cons and crazies over the years and I knew without a doubt that sooner or later, that greed causes mistakes.

"You still with me, Sam?"

I blinked and looked at Tinnias. "Huh? Sorry, I was miles away."

"What's up?"

"Nothing, I was thinking about something Ren said."

"Oh?"

"He said I'm allowing fear to cloud my ability to see Vazien for what he truly is and reminded me of what is at the core of most people like him."

"And what is that?"

"Greed. Putting the fear aside, he's just another rich and greedy con with domination issues. The mystique with which he surrounds himself hides this somewhat, makes him appear frighteningly powerful, which renders us unable to act in an effective manner to stop him."

"That's true. I like Ren, he was very wise. I'm glad he was your friend."

"Is."

"Huh?" Tinnias frowned.

"Is, not was. He's still there, just in a different way."

"You're getting all spiritual on me now, Son." He scratched his head and Byron sniggered.

"I have little choice," I replied. "He's there, we talk, he tells me things that then happen, speaks about stuff that I hadn't even admitted to myself. And the quality of the experience is different than a dream, more solidly vivid, more alive. I can't explain well enough, you'd have to experience it for yourself. I never sought to become a believer in this stuff. I was happy enough being slightly sceptical but now, how can I not believe?"

"I'm glad you believe," Tinnias said. "Now you can't call me a fairy for being a believer myself."

We laughed as the door opened and Jam entered. "Ahh there you are. I heard on the chatter line that you're both after the smoking implant."

"Yes please, that would be awesome," Tinnias replied.

Jam put down the small packet he was carrying, opened the lid and fiddled with what looked like a gun. "It goes just under the skin, lift up your shirt would you." In less than two minutes, Jam was putting the little gun away and smiling at us. "There you are, Gentlemen. Give it a day and then you'll be fully protected from all the harmful substances within cigarettes."

"Thank you very much," I said as I tucked my shirt in. "We appreciate it."

"No problem, could I be so bold as to cadge one off you, I left my pack in my quarters."

"I would never have pegged you for a smoker, Doc," I laughed.

"Well why not, since I can do so in complete safety. A man really ought to have one vice, don't you agree?"

"Totally," I replied. "Why not indeed. I have and enjoy it immensely."

Toma grinned as he entered the smoking room. "Me too. It's time to get back to it next door."


"That would be the most efficient route to get to all six," Byron said as he studied our list. Is there an order of priority to them, are some more likely to testify or have more useful information?"

"We wrote them down in the order we think is best," I replied. "This one at the top, Preataq Jormla is my possible choice for first visit as his experience is the most dramatic, and pretty tragic. He used to own a haulage company, and Vazien sometimes used the company to ship ore from some of his mines to processing plants elsewhere. This was all done by the book but the vessels were always significantly overweight. From this it was assumed that something else was being carried that had not found its way on to the manifest and since Vazien was always shipping cargo at these times, he was the obvious cause. The shipping company went out of business quite suddenly, after the headquarters building was bombed, killing thirty seven employees. The official record said terrorists were the cause of the blast, but no one was ever charged with the crime and no known terrorist organisations ever claimed responsibility. Preataq Jormla of Q'endlash, is still alive and living on his home world, Terramora Prime."

"Shit. And he's happy to testify?"

"His first words to me when I called were, 'so you've finally got around to doing something about Vazien huh?' so I'd say yeah, he'll testify."

The tribesmen from Zibandin are worth a visit next," Tinnias said. "These two tribes, Lakshwel and Viralong, were the two largest tribes on Zibandin 8. Eleven years ago, Vazien approached the leader of the Lakshwel and offered them cheap arms in return for permission to dig for Razulite on their land. His company had discovered a large deposit right underneath the middle of Lakshwel territory. They agreed and allowed him to place two mines. Official records say he paid them for the right to mine, but there are several tribesmen who say differently. Once the mines were bringing up the Razulite, Vazien began dealing them short. At the same time, he approached the leader of the Viralong tribe, who by this time had been reduced considerably by the Lakshwel's superior fire power and offered them a similar deal. They readily agreed and he sank a mine into their territory after finding another, smaller deposit beneath their land. As before, once the mines had brought up the best of the product, he began dealing them short. By the time he abandoned the mines, the Viralong had all but been wiped out and just a few Lakshwel survived."

"Holy shit," Byron exclaimed. "He wiped out two whole races of people just to sink a couple of mines?"

"Not only that," Tinnias continued, "but due to the mining, the surrounding land, which contained both tribes' most sacred sites, fell into several giant sinkholes. The few tribes that are left on the planet no longer welcome any outsiders and anyone who ventures there is met with extreme violence."

"If we can't go there to talk with them, how can we verify this story?" Byron asked.

"Vazien employed several tribesmen to run the mines and when he left, they went with him. Having worked alongside the one viewed as the bringer of death to their world, they were outcasted by their tribes. There were forty three of them at the time they left Zibandin, but only eighteen are still alive today."

"How did the other twenty five die?" I asked.

"Accidents mostly, according to the man I spoke to. Two died from diseases contracted from the inhabitants of planets they were working on, one died from injuries sustained during a fight, and another was gored to death by a Tigadema, which is a sort of huge cat with long fangs and poisonous spines down its back."

"So twenty one of the Zibandin people died from various accidents?" I asked and Tinnias nodded. "I'm guessing these were mining accidents."

"Correct."

"How fucking convenient."

"Indeed. All might not be lost however. Of the eighteen still employed, four have spoken out about Vazien. They sent a message by courier to the other tribespeople back on Zibandin, telling them everything and asking for prayers of forgiveness."

"Are they still alive?" I asked.

"As far as I can tell, yes. They're on Glarian 4, working a Tachanium mine."

"Awesome," I grinned. "We can go and get 'em. It sounds like they'd be willing to talk. Then we can go and see a man named Captain Listler. When I saw his name on that document, I was shocked as I've heard of him. He was a high ranking military officer from Solar 3, or Earth as its inhabitants call it. He found his way into the media after being dishonourably discharged due to causing the death of his entire unit. It was claimed he was a coward and while helping to supress a civil war on Jarlash 3, he gave up the whereabouts of his unit to save his own skin. One hundred and seventy five soldiers were executed, it was claimed, while Listler ran away in an army shuttlecraft. At first, I couldn't understand why Listler's name was on the list."

"What's his connection to Vazien?" Byron asked.

"Jarlash 3 was one of the places Vazien was mining Razulite," I replied. "We can't be sure but he was probably arming all sides in the conflict to ensure he could remain there with his mine. He's still mining there today, and the conflict is still going on."

"So that was the civil war Listler was sent to quell?"

"Yes."

"So where is he now?"

"He runs a dirty bar and cafe in a beach resort on Qaigon 7."

"If we can get to all these people and persuade them to testify, we'll have the beginnings of a case."

I nodded. "With these statements, and the three others on this list, we have the beginnings of a file against him that will stand up in court."

"Shall we stop for the evening now?" Lomas asked. "Dinner will be in two hours."

"Okay," I nodded. Since Tinnias and I had Unicom calls to make, we decided to use the Comms room. It gave me the perfect excuse to not sit with any of the others. "It would make sense for us to go to another room so you folks don't have to worry about being quiet while we're on calls." Everyone thought it was the most sensible thing, so we were able to avoid everyone for two hours by having the Comms room to ourselves. We took it in turns to nip twenty yards down the corridor to the nearest smoking room, and I felt more comfortable not having to worry about offending anyone with a throwaway comment or have them worry about me seeing their secret technology. Of course, Tinnias, like Ren and Byron had done, thought I was over reacting and I knew they were all probably right.

"Relax about it, Sam," Tinnias soothed. "You don't need the stress. Even if you find it hard to believe, at least accept it as a distant possibility that you might be over reacting."

"Okay," I agreed. "I know you're both undoubtedly right, and I am trying to get over it. I've been alone and self sufficient for so many years, it will take more than a few hours to change my ways. Cut me a little slack huh?"

"Of course. I just don't want you to suffer when it's not necessary."


We stopped in the smoking room after our calls were done and Byron kissed me as if we'd been apart for a year. It was wonderful. Five minutes later, we entered the Obs Room and sat down. Lomas stood and addressed everyone. "Okay, my friends, let's have an update so we each know what everyone else has achieved. I've ordered that dinner be delayed for an hour so no need to rush. Sam, Tinnias, perhaps you'd begin."

"Okay," I said. "So far we've secured agreements from seven individuals on the list from the data cube. We think our first call should be to Terramora Prime, the home of Preataq Jormla. Next, Glarian 4 to chat with the four tribesmen from Zibandin, two from the Lakshwel tribe and two from the Viralong. Third, Qaigon 7 to interview Captain Listler from Solar 3"

"Knowing how he likes to arm both sides in a conflict, we think the uprising was probably his doing and he no doubt didn't approve of this military upstart interfering," Tinnias added. "We also have the man who was the young medic at the time Vazien's wife died. His name is ..." he fumbled through our notes.

"Orlan, Child of Fars," Jam said.

"That's the one, thanks, Doc. He has apparently expressed deep regret at having supplied Vazien with the phial of River Fever pathogen all those years ago. It's not guaranteed that he'll talk to us, but we feel he's worth a try. Then we have Umboi Trel d'livliel, a man who used to own a gun manufacturing firm on Maltak 9. He invented a gun that used sound instead of bullets or lasers. Vazien approached him to make a deal to supply the weapons but ended up stealing the blueprints and got it patented in his own name. When Umboi complained to Vazien, he was beaten so badly he lost the use of his left arm. All people from his world are left handed, so the injury rendered him unable to write, feed himself, or do much of anything that needed a steady dominant hand. He learned to do some things with his right hand, but Maltak folks apparently regard right handers as being marked by a demon from their folklore, so they tend not to want to learn to use them. He's had to move to another planet, due to being ostracised by his home world. His safety became at risk after his home was repeatedly vandalised, death threats being painted on his front door, fire bombs thrown through windows etcetera. He now lives on a planet with the designation T43725 Alpha Gammatron Delta. It doesn't have a name, which means it's still in the process of being colonised."

"Oh that poor man," Jam said, shaking his head sadly. "We have to stop Vazien. So many have suffered so much at his hands."

"Now we come to a man named Klackan Sthleit Liteil Crion Hamlusq," I said. "I hope I got it right. Moianal names are a real headache to pronounce. His case is extremely tragic, but by its nature, means if we include a visit to him, we must move quickly. There isn't much time to waste with this guy."

"Why not?" Vincent asked.

"Because he has just a few months to live, due to Ambassador Vazien. He is supervisor at one of Vazien's Moianal based Razulite mines. Some years ago, he began to suspect that Vazien was taking money and not accounting for it properly. There were gaps in the accounts that caught his attention. When he asked about it, Vazien assured him he would investigate it. A couple of months later, Klackan drove over a land mine on his hover bike, which exploded and covered him in Ring Coolant, which is illegal now because of the Loigot it contains. The device had been placed in the entrance to his driveway, so it was definitely meant for him. There was some trouble with a local environmental activist group at the time, and they got the blame. Klackan was fine for years, until a few months ago when a doctor found the Loigot had become active within his cells. He could be cured if he travelled to Qelashmid Prime where there is the only known cure, but travel firms demand such high insurance costs that he can't afford to get there. I would suggest that if we decide to talk with him, we do so without delay."

The room fell silent and I sat down. For long seconds, no one spoke and I saw a few hands wipe at moist eyes, Vincent's and Jams included. Kyle was the first to speak, and when I looked at him, he was making no effort to hide his tears. My admiration for the man increased ten-fold in that single moment.

"Your Majesty," he implored.

"Yes, of course we will. Arrange it, Jam."

The doctor nodded, sniffed, wiped his eyes. "I'll do it now," he replied and left the room.

"Thank you," I said quietly.

Jam returned ten minutes later and informed us that the medical bay was fully prepared to deal with a case of Loigot poisoning and that a team of troopers were ready with a medi-pod, a self contained air tight pod in which the sick can be placed for transportation in the field. Pumps allow air borne medicaments to be administered in a constant flow, and keep any air borne contaminants out.

"That's good, I'm pleased we can help him," Lomas said. "Now how about the exhumation order?"

"I've set in motion all the necessary official requests etcetera for an exhumation order for Vazien's wife," Jam reported. "I've called in a favour and through a series of favours from one to the other, we'll have the relevant documents soon. I don't predict any problems and I'm able to confirm that Vazien won't find out. We should have the right permission within three days. We could begin our journey there now, Commander Byron says it will take five days and eight hours at the battle cruiser's top speed, and it takes us past the first port of call for Sam and Tinnias, so we can get their first interview on the way."

Lomas and Toma exchanged a look and I saw the King nod to his son, who got up and went to the intercom.

"Bridge," a voice declared.

"Set course for Kesh Prime, top speed please."

"At once, Sir."

"And we'll be calling into Moianal 6 on the way."

"Right, setting the detour now. We're on our way, Sir."

Kyle asked to sit with Byron, Tinnias and I for dinner, and I took the opportunity to try and get to know him a little better. I had met him briefly during the Domenico case but he seemed to spend every moment with Vincent and hardly spoke to me. The man who sat opposite me now was confident and self assured, and I guessed we had Vincent's influence to thank for the transformation.

"You seem different than when we last met," I said, "during the Domenico case."

"In what way?" he asked

"You just seem more, oh I can't explain really, it's a subtle thing. Sort of, more here with us. I remember you as seeming to be on the fringes of everything. Maybe my memory is wrong."

He smiled. "No, you're right. I may look largely Lilean but my personality was naturally very Drycenian, which meant I was, as you say, on the fringes all the time. I grew up a bit of a loner, due to my dual heritage and never really got much of the usual practice in social matters. As you're no doubt aware, Lilean males tend to be extrovert, confident, and show their emotions passionately. I couldn't be more different if I'd wanted, but thanks to Vincent's friendship and love, I've been able to, catch up, so to speak."

"I hope you don't mind me mentioning it," I said. "The difference is so marked I felt compelled to say something. I'm sorry if I'm being forward, I've had no one explain anything about social etiquette around Lileans and I seem to remember someone saying you have some strict rules. I'm not really a social type, as you must have realised by now."

The four of us sniggered and Kyle nodded. "There are a few rules of communication but don't worry, we can't take offence at anyone not of our race who doesn't understand them. We'll know if any offence is meant, believe me."

"Oh yes," I replied, "your spirit friends will no doubt blab on me."

"Sometimes they blab, but surprisingly infrequently. They have annoyingly strict rules about what they can tell us and what they can't. Rarely do they let us in on someone's private conversations, only if it directly affects our destiny or the fulfilment of a life mission. You might be surprised how little we were told of your conversations and verbal planning while you were lost to us."

"Oh," I said. "We assumed you'd all be getting a blow by blow account of everything we said and thought."

"Not at all," Kyle laughed. "We knew when you had the tracker removed, and we were given some insight into your fears as you began to think maybe we were the bad guys."

"That did worry us," Tinnias said. "We lost sleep over that, I admit. We've taken it for granted that two very powerful races are well intentioned, and when we began to entertain the idea that you both could possibly be on the other side of the law, the possibilities for chaos were frightening."

"I'm sorry we caused you such anguish," Kyle said, concern etched across his face. "Not for a moment did we wish to do so."

I shrugged. "We know now, that's the main thing I guess."

Kyle leaned forward until his face was just inches from my own. "Bullshit," he whispered.

"What?" I laughed.

"Waste your time brushing it off as nothing if you want, but I can see right through that no problem at all." I averted my eyes and blushed as I sniggered with embarrassment. "There you are," he said, pointing at me, "those red cheeks give you away."

Tinnias and Byron burst out laughing and I glared at them.

"Seriously," Kyle continued, "you should talk it out and let it go. It won't just disappear on its own by burying it inside. You'll just get an ulcer and still be fucked up in the head."

"You sound just like Ren," I replied. "That's exactly what he would say."

"He's a nice guy," Kyle nodded. "I've met him a couple of times, in the hinterland."

"The what?" I asked.

"The hinterland. It's a place we go to meet with our guides, our spirit friends as you call them. It's a place between sleep and wakefulness, between the living world and the land of the dead. It's safe there and we can talk with them, work through problems, and learn how to communicate with them. It's a step further down the road from where you've met with Ren in your dreaming time. Once you get more adept at finding him and hearing him, knowing the signs of his presence and how to reach him at will, he will take you to the hinterland for your times together."

"I'm beginning to realise when he's trying to tell me something. I get this dark heavy feeling inside when something is wrong or I need to be careful. I've always assumed it was just my law enforcer's hunch, and maybe it was, before Ren. Someone said you Lileans have a similar reaction."

Kyle nodded. "Yes, I have that same dark heaviness you describe. Vincent will talk about his radar blipping. Everyone experiences it differently. It's good that you're recognising it so soon, you're a natural. I know Ren has been anxious to start communicating since his passing, but he had some stuff to work through first, to balance his own soul. The empathic bond the two of you share meant he felt your grief as strongly as you did, and it slowed his progress just a little. He is a strong soul though and managed to step aside from it, but it hurt him to do that as he knew you were feeling that he was nowhere nearby, when you'd expected him to be."

"I do remember being disappointed that there was no sense of him at all. It upset me, but at the same time I knew it shouldn't have done. When we die, we go somewhere else, we're done with this world and this life and I knew he had no reason to be hanging around me. I sort of got used to it but I was amazed and delighted the first time I saw him, when this case began."

"You'll find your progress at communicating with him will move forward tremendously once you get into the swing of it. It's a knack, a sort of, mental step sideways. Once you get it, you'll be flying."

"Did you know your guide when they were alive?" Tinnias asked. "Are they always friends or family members or can they be strangers?"

"They are never family members. The bond is so strong that they might find it difficult at such time as your destiny necessitates you suffering, to stand back and let it happen. Family would naturally want to protect you from such experiences but often, it is those times when we progress the most. My guide was unknown to me until I met Vincent. One of the downsides of my dual heritage meant I was unable to hear or know about my guide and I was convinced I didn't have one. Doctor Jam put an implant into my brain to overcome it. She was a total stranger to me, and she lived physically several hundred years ago. She's been a guide to seven Lileans before me. Vincent's guide is also a stranger to him, as is Tip Danso's. Farra has Vincent's father as her guide, so you see it can get a bit complicated."

"It's fascinating," Tinnias said and I nodded. "And you tell it so that it's easy to understand."

"Thank you. Any time you have questions or worries, about anything connected with us, you can ask me. Don't be shy."

"I'll probably take up that offer," I said. "I hope I don't become annoying, again."

"You won't. It's a pleasure to help someone be able to deepen their friendship with us. That's a privilege, not a burden."

"See, that's what impresses me," Tinnias said, pointing to Kyle. "It's what I call, working wisdom. It's the sort of wisdom that's just there all the time. It comes out in normal conversation and makes a difference to everyone. Anyone can memorise inspirational quotes and stand on a platform to speak the words that came from another's lips, but when you have working wisdom, everything you say means something profound. You can't learn working wisdom, you either have it or you don't, and you Lileans have it by the bucket load. I love it, I could listen to you people all day long and not be bored."

"That's high praise indeed," Kyle said. "Thank you so much."

A shadow fell across the table and I looked up to see Vincent smiling at us. "Hey guys, I'm going to work out soon. Sam, I hear you practice the Damiklonian martial art. You want to spar with Kyle and me?"

I nodded, "Sure, I'd love to."

"Okay, give dinner an hour to go down and we'll meet in the cargo hold."


I was somewhat taken aback when I arrived in the cargo hold an hour later. The sight of two huge Lilean males in their prime, stripped to the waist and waiting for me, stopped me in my tracks. When I remembered that I had agreed to this, the humour of the situation had me bent over, shrieking with laughter, the lofty room taking the noise and sending it bouncing around the walls.

Vincent and Kyle looked at each other, then frowned. "Was it something I said?" Vincent asked.

"I've no idea," Kyle replied.

I looked up once I'd regained control of myself. "I'm sorry, no offence. I've just realised I'm gonna die in horrible agony," I replied, fresh guffaws again bouncing around the room. "And I agreed to it in advance," I continued, red faced from laughing.

"Oh come now, Sam," Kyle grinned. "Don't worry, kiddo, we'll be easy on ya."

"Will you?" Vincent remarked, grinning at Kyle. "I won't."

"Is this you two against me?" I asked. "If so, I'll just go and shoot myself now if you like. That'll save you working up a sweat."

Vincent laughed. "How about every man for himself?"

Kyle nodded. "Suits me."

"That's fine," I added, and started with a few stretches.

Over the course of the next 2 hours, the two Lileans gave me the toughest workout I'd experienced since Ren passed. They were big and heavy, and their fighting relied upon their single greatest asset, their brute strength, which was formidable. Until I got used to them, I spent more time on my back or my ass on the floor, than on my feet, but gradually, I learned to use the speed and agility my slighter frame afforded me. I realised that huge size is not always your friend and while extra muscle power is useful, the ability to move quickly often gives an advantage.

The martial art I practice, taught to me by Ren, is a stylized representation of the type of fighting his distant ancestors used in battle. This means that I don't have any real fighting skills but I can act them out with great style and flourish. It is more effective when used defensively, as it relies upon blades of many types if being used for attack. I had inherited Ren's collection of Damiklonian War Daggers, as they're called, but I hadn't bothered to bring any with me to spar with the Lileans. I successfully blocked and dodged their every attempt to grab at me and many times, I caught them off guard with a kick or punch. It didn't all go my way though, both men had me on my back a few times, but I held my own, even if, as I suspected, they were holding back so as not to kill me with their bare hands.

By the time we finished for the evening, Vincent had a split lip and Kyle, a black eye and sprained wrist. I knew I would have a black eye and maybe a swollen lip too, but I'd enjoyed it very much and grinned from ear to ear.

"That was awesome, thank you both," I said.

"You have great skill, Sam," Kyle remarked and Vincent nodded. "I'm hurting, truly."

"And I'm bleeding," Vincent replied. "It's been a long time since anyone's been able to draw blood from me. I'm seriously impressed, I mean it."

"Aww shucks, I know you were holding back so I'd survive. Thanks for not breaking my back with your bare hands or something."

We all laughed as we puffed our way through a couple of laps jogging around the perimeter of the huge room to cool down slowly. They swore they hadn't held back but I didn't believe them, those two man mountains could easily kill me, they must've done. I didn't mind though, I had enjoyed it very much and although the Damiklonian Martial Art is maybe not designed for fighting Lileans unless armed with a couple of War Daggers, it was very useful experience for me. Vincent, being a blade man himself, was very interested to know about the daggers, and I promised I would show him the collection when we had some time. We jogged back along the corridors and up the staircases to our rooms, said our goodnights, and I felt we had bonded some.

## CHAPTER TWENTY

The journey to Moianal 6 was largely uneventful. Tinnias and I spent our days on the Unicom and managed to set up a list of several more willing interviewees. Various people from Vazien's past, from neighbours, childhood friends, even a past mistress, all went onto our list. We thought it best to have too much information we could then cherry pick the best from, rather than not enough.

I still kept a distance between myself and the Drycenians, apart from Byron of course but I tried to be civil and made sure I showered them with gratitude every time they so much as smiled at me. There were two or three occasions when it seemed Lomas was trying to pry his way into a chat about my emotions, but I successfully steered the brief conversation away and made it abundantly clear, albeit in a very subtle way, that he was not welcome going there with me ever again. I thought I was doing marvellously, retaining my self sufficient mind set whilst doing the social thing and not pissing off the Drycenians again. How wrong can a man be?

Every evening was spent sparring with Kyle and Vincent, and one evening, before our clash, they asked if I would show them the War Daggers.

"Sorry to keep asking," Vincent said, "But you know me and blades. They turn me on."

I grinned. "Yeah, I know. Come on then, they're stored in my ship."

The expression on his face when I lifted the lid on the Damiklonian storage box in which they were housed, was priceless, and I couldn't help but laugh.

"Holy fucking shit, they're gorgeous. Can I touch? Oh please let me touch. I'm gonna touch, I have to touch." He reached in and Kyle and I laughed aloud.

"I know you're a blade guy," I said, "and there's probably no need, but I'd be remiss if I didn't warn you that although they're strictly ceremonial now, they're deadly sharp. Please be careful."

He took out and examined each one in turn, asked about their use, history, and names. Each war dagger has a name, usually descriptive of its use in battle, and Ren had taught me well as the knowledge all came back to me as I passed it on to the Lileans. He was particularly taken with one named the Breaker of Hearts, a short tubular weapon with sharpened vertical ridges down its length.

"Tell me about this one," he begged.

"The Breaker of Hearts," I said. "It's designed to slip between the ribs and into the heart. If your aim is slightly off and the blade hits a rib, the design is strong enough not to break as a flat blade might. It does maximum damage to the heart, tearing it to pieces from the inside as you rotate the tubular blade in both directions." I demonstrated by thrusting it forwards, then rotated my hand at the wrist, back and forth, making the blade spin as I gripped it. "This is the last weapon you would call upon in a real situation, when all the others have failed you, or what is more likely, when you have failed them. You can only use the Breaker of Hearts at very close range, no more than arm distance, so it is your last resort. At such close quarters, you will usually lose your own life while taking that of your opponent, but if used correctly, the Breaker of Hearts will ensure you die with honour."

"That's awesome," he replied, blowing a long breath and shaking his head as he gazed lovingly at the blade. I knew he wanted it, but I was not about to give it to him. On the one hand, I didn't want to break up Ren's collection and on the other, I didn't feel worthy enough to choose who to allow into the very private world of the Damiklonians. If Ren wanted me to give it, he would let me know.

"Let's get a drink before we hit the cargo hold," Kyle suggested so we stopped at the next smoking room we came across, got a drink from the dispenser, and I smoked one of the new brand the Troopers had given Tinnias and I. The talk was mostly about my blades, and I was glad to have something that encouraged Vincent to see me as an equal, rather than an insect of little value, as I felt whenever I was around him. When the talk settled onto the usual topics, he sat forward and looked at me, his eyes holding my own with an intensity that I found a little unsettling. It was like he was looking right into my soul and allowing me to see into his at the same time. For the first time, he hid nothing of himself, offered me full access to the deepest regions of his inner self.

"I had a call from Tip this morning."

"You did?"

He nodded, still holding my gaze. "I did. He mentioned your conversation."

"Ahh, and now you're going to tell me off."

His head snapped back in shock, the open door slamming shut in surprise. "What the fuck? No of course not. I'm just letting you know that he was very upset about your last conversation. He was crying, and I spent nearly an hour talking to him, trying to reassure him that you didn't mean it, that you were still getting your head around things, and that you'll call him soon enough to explain things. Was I wrong to do that?"

"No," I replied quietly. "I'm getting used to my position here. It's a situation I've not been in before, so it'll take time for me to get used to the rules and feel comfortable."

"Your position?" Kyle frowned. "How do you mean?"

"As the recalcitrant child, the naughty teenager who needs a firm hand."

"Is that truly what you feel?"

I nodded. "Well, yeah. I have a problem with lies and deceit, I always have. Not just because I'm a law enforcer, because of shit that's happened. I've always been alone, partially from choice as this job has cost me too many friends and loved ones. And when I react to the lies and be rightfully angry about being dicked around by people with a superiority complex they probably don't deserve, I'm still the bad guy. I get the silences, the sideways looks that say, 'is he going to shout and yell again?' but when I say, 'okay I'll take a step back and leave you alone,' that's wrong too. I can't do right for doing wrong. So yeah, I feel like a naughty child that can't ever please anyone."

"Am I part of the problem?" Vincent asked.

"It's not a problem," I replied. "I'm just keeping my head down and my mouth shut. That way I can't offend anyone again. Hopefully it won't be long until we can get Vazien put away and you'll all be rid of me."

"You know that stuff before was lies. None of it was true. It was necessary to save your life, but then you went and got involved anyway and we nearly lost you. You would've died in that compound if we'd not got there in time. We knew your death was coming up for weeks in advance and we worried and fretted about it like you wouldn't believe. It kept us awake at nights, I tell you now. When you took off and got the tracker removed, we despaired. Jam got a tank ready so that we might revive you if we could find you within seventy two hours. We planned the quickest route back to Sigma so we could take care of your mother and sister while they grieved for you, and we were too busy to deal with our own feelings because too many others would need our help if you were lost. Byron was beside himself with worry for you. Kyle and I were truly scared of what he might do if you were lost. Then we found you, saved you in time and you're back here and we're trying to deal with our feelings too. We want to be relieved and welcome you back, hug you and tell you we love you. We want to be angry and yell at you for running away and not trusting us. We also know we lied to you. We know it was necessary because you would never have agreed to just leave things

248

alone if we'd been honest about everything. We can't take those lies back and we feel you're punishing us for lying to you."

"We're all pushing against each other," Kyle said, putting a hand on Vincent's shoulder. "And none of us are making any forward progress."

"I know how it feels to be persecuted by liars. I was sent to cryo stasis for permanent incarceration because of someone lying and paying others to lie as well. I was on the run for years because of lies and thought I'd always be running. I had no parents and no friends and I almost ended it so many times, so don't you dare think you have a monopoly on being lied to." He sighed deeply, ran a hand over his bald head and looked up at me. "I'm sorry for yelling, Sam, but you're so fucking closed off sometimes I want to punch you. Your father must have the patience of a saint and I hope that Byron does too."

I sniggered at that remark and nodded. "Tinnias and I have known each other for over twenty years, he's got used to me I guess."

"We're all struggling here, Sam," Kyle said, "but we're failing to work together to get through it. Everyone is so fixated on how they themselves are hurting that we're all just pushing against each other. It's not just you, it's all of us. We end up doing what people always do in such situations."

"Closing off for self protection," I said and they both nodded.

"Come on," Vincent said, getting up, "let's go and work out." We headed down the corridor and he suddenly stopped and turned to me. "By the way, I'm sorry for calling you a Merc back when Gabriel was missing. I know you were offended."

"Thanks," I replied. "I guess most folks don't know the difference, but it's still something I find insulting."

After having cleared the air between us, I found Vincent easy to get along with and began to genuinely enjoy the company of both men. We were bonding so well that Vincent shared with me some of his experiences leading up to the thing that made him so famous, his killing of the Transmortal Army, the most feared race in the galaxy and killers of millions. His suffering was beyond my imagining, all because of the lies of his step brother, Wesley, and yet he'd emerged with his sanity intact and a compassion for people that surprised me. I realised he'd more than earned his right to a slightly over confident and extrovert nature, and I felt soul crushing guilt at my own difficulty in handling being lied to. How could I compete with his achievements? It was impossible, so I tried to accept the guilt as the cost of my personal growth, tucked it away down deep inside, and decided I would just get on with the case and pour my heart into loving Byron.

"What was it that happened, Sam?" Kyle asked on the morning we were due to arrive at Moianal 6.

"Huh?"

"The other night, you said you have a problem with lies because of shit that happened."

"Oh, that," I replied.

"Will you talk about it with us?"

Once again, I found myself comparing Kyle to Ren and remembered the time when he got me to tell him about it, after I'd already said I wasn't ready to bring it up.

"Twenty years ago, there was a girl I was close to. I'd just asked her to marry me and got her acceptance when a con I was building a case against, hired someone to pay me back for rattling his cage too hard. She was kidnapped, taken to an abandoned warehouse, raped, and shot seven times. He recorded himself doing it, then called me up and played the tape. After telling me where she was, he rang off. I went around to the place and found her body. It was a mess; he'd done one hell of a job on her, believe me. The con lied about his crimes, lied about hiring the killer, lied about having any involvement in her murder and eventually, his lies got him off without a stain on his character. He's still a free man today and he's still alive, despite several people begging me to tell them his location so they can make him pay, because I'm a law keeper not a law breaker. I can't even get justice for Merellia because I hate lying. Even her father blames me and got Ren killed by blowing our cover to the wrong side so he could, as he put it, 'be the cause of me losing someone I love,' like I caused him to lose his daughter."

"Shit," Kyle hissed quietly. "I'm so sorry. I can't begin to imagine how you must've coped, going through that."

"By not feeling," I replied. "It may not be healthy for my soul but it works for me. Call me anti-social if you want, it keeps me sane."

"How are you coping with having to feel now you and Byron are together?"

I smiled as his gorgeous face and lovely eyes filled my mind. "It's not something I feel I have to cope with. I don't feel I want to hold feelings back where he's concerned, I don't feel the need or desire."

Vincent grinned and looked at Kyle, who sniggered. "Awwwww," they chorused and we laughed.

"How come you're not a crazed killer by now?" Vincent said. "Shit like that would've sent me right over the edge."

"I don't know," I replied. "I've wondered myself. Maybe being a law enforcer helped, I've no idea. Thanks to Ren, her memory is now something that brings a smile rather than pain, so I've moved a step or two forward, even if there's one planetary system I won't go to, for fear of meeting the con responsible."

"Which one is that?" Vincent asked.

I hesitated before answering, torn between whether to tell or not. "I can't."

"Why not?"

"Because we're going there to interview one of the potential testifiers, and I'm dreading it. I've successfully avoided the place all these years and now, with all this shit that's going on, with the lies and feeling paranoid, this place turns up on the list. How much more fucking worse can things get for me?"

"Oh much worse, believe me," Vincent said and Kyle nodded furiously. "You wouldn't believe how much worse there's potential for. Even if you never trust me again, trust me on this."


The heat on Moianal 6 was furious. I felt my shirt getting wetter by the second, it stuck to my back horribly. The shuttle landed a little way off from the Razulite mine, where it would be hidden from prying eyes that would be shocked at seeing the strange yellow eyed people with fangs inside it. Tinnias and I trudged across the dry sandy ground, stopping several times to drink from the bottles provided by the Drycenians. When we finally reached the boundary fence and made our way around to the gate, we were exhausted. A man came to meet us.

"Hi there."

"Hello, we have an appointment with Supervisor Klackan," I said. "Is he around?"

"Sure, come on in. He mentioned something about expecting visitors. Through that door and to your left." He pointed behind us, so we thanked him and entered. The cool air hit us right away and we both sighed with pleasure.

"Ahh, the off worlders have arrived," a voice from our left said. We went through a gap in the wall to find the thinnest man we'd ever seen, standing and smiling in our direction. "That sigh is only heard from those not used to our temperatures."

I grinned. "How do you cope in this heat," I said.

"I was born and raised here; you get used to it. You must be the man who called me, I recognise that accent. Sit, I'll get you both a drink." With the use of a stick, he staggered into the next room, emerging a few minutes later with a tray, expertly balanced in his one free hand. I took it from him and put it on his desk. "Help yourselves, it's non alcoholic and delicious."

I switched on my data recorder. "Are you still happy to talk with us?" Tinnias asked. Klackan nodded. "Right, well the circumstances of this case are such that it is not yet prudent for us to announce our presence as investigating the many complicated threads of what is proving to be one of the most awkward and dangerous cases we've come across. Because of this, we cannot take a formal statement from you at this point. What we can do, is record your story in your own words, and should you agree, get you to sign a declaration of intent to testify. This means that should we get to a point where we know we have enough evidence to instigate an arrest warrant, you will then be formally interviewed. Since we'll already have the recording from today, that formal interview will be quick. Now I have to ask you if you wish to continue."

"I do," Klackan said.

"Okay." "Please begin by giving your full name, age, occupation, and addresses of your residence and place of work."

"My name is Klackan Sthleit Liteil Crion Hamlusq, I'm fifty years old, Supervisor at Razulite Mine number V 217, sub zone 8, region 12, Harrapsin, Moianal 6. I live at building 38, Harrapsin Village, Moianal 6."

"Are you giving us your story willingly, without coercion or bribery?"

"I am."

"Have you had it explained that this is not a formal interview, and that you may be required to provide one at a later date?"

"Yes."

"How do you know Ambassador Vazien?"

"He owns this mine, and ten others here."

"Please tell us, in your own words, of what happened to you eight years ago."

"Okay. Well despite being the boss around here, often there's not much actual work for me to do, so I decided years ago to take a course of study that would give me the knowledge of accounting I lacked. I seemed to excel at figure work and it became a habit to keep a regular weekly check on the books here. It gave me something to do in the quiet times and I thought Vazien would be pleased. I already knew that he had access to the mine's funds, via the bank account into which all monies are paid. As owner, he has the right to access the funds. He is also expected to provide adequate accounting to explain why he might take funds, and what he used them for. It quickly became apparent to me that money was going missing without any accounting for those funds being evident anywhere. I don't have access to the bank account, just the books here so I had no idea who was taking the money."

"What did you do with this discovery?"

"I told Vazien what I'd found. I felt that, as the owner, he should know about it and I suppose I presumed he would have the power, and desire, to sort it out."

"How did he react?"

"He promised to look into it. Nothing changed though, money kept being taken and no accounting for it ever appeared. I mentioned it a couple of times and each time, he said he was looking into it, urged me to be patient, that he was busy but to trust him to get it sorted eventually. He said he could always put more money into the account if things got really dire, but he didn't foresee the problem going that far."

"Did you ever find out who was taking the money?"

"No, but after it became clear that Vazien seemed to be dragging his heels and giving me excuses, it did cross my mind that it could be him, but I had no actual proof of that."

"Okay, thank you for that clarification. Please continue."

"I've always been keen on hover bikes and finally decided to treat myself to my dream machine, right around the time this money business was going on. It was a D'harcha Double Pipe 3000 in the darkest blue you ever saw. Like the sky at midnight it was, oh she was beautiful, took my breath away when I saw her in the shop. One day, I was going home from work, and as I turned into my driveway, there was a huge explosion. I remember flying through the air, then a crushing sensation as the bike parts landed on top of me. I broke both my legs, went deaf for a month, and got covered in eight litres of Ring Coolant, which is illegal now because of the chemicals it's made from. I'd driven over an S82 flat head land mine that had been buried in my driveway. During the next six months or so, I recovered well and then got on with my life. Eventually, the bombing was attributed to an environmental activist type group that had been doing the rounds, setting fires, sending a few letter bombs, that sort of thing. Five months ago, during my annual health check up, the Doctor found that the Loigot from the Coolant, which had lain dormant within my cells all these years, had decided to wake up. I've less than a year to live and by the time I die, I will be bed ridden, comatose, doubly incontinent, and fed through a tube. The only ones with a cure are on Qelashmid Prime, but travel firms demand such high insurance to convey me, that I cannot afford it. I will go to my grave believing Vazien is responsible and I pray with everything I have that you manage to bring him down."

"Do you have anything more to add?"

"No, that's everything."

"Are you willing to sign a declaration of intent to testify?"

"Absolutely."

Klackan signed the declaration, I switched off my data recorder, and thanked him for his candour.

"Now, Sir," I said. "Gather your belongings would you."

"Why?" he frowned.

"Because we're taking you to get cured, for free. We're not confident that Vazien will ever be made to pay for his crimes, he's a very powerful man, and I want you at least to have some recompense. Come on, the medical bay is ready for you."

"I umm, I don't know what to say," he faltered.

"No need," I smiled. "Now we have a bit of a slog, so you tell us when you need to stop and rest and if you can't go on at any time, our friends will come and get us."

Klackan gathered his few personal belongings and told his second in command he was feeling ill and would be off for a few days. I put on the comms headset given to me by Byron and we set off.

"We're on our way guys, have some cold drinks ready would you."

"Sam, It's Doc Jam here. He won't have much stamina, so he'll need plenty of rest stops. I'd say every hundred yards or so. Let us know the moment he gets into difficulty breathing or has chest pain or numbness in the legs and we'll come and get him."

Halfway back to the shuttle, Klackan sagged in our arms and I noticed him put a hand to his chest and wince slightly. I stopped walking and called Jam. "Doc, we have chest pain here, help."

"We're on our way."

Two minutes later, a rather surprised Klackan was being introduced to the Drycenians.

"Hello there Klackan. I'm the Doctor around here and my name is Jam. Don't be afraid, we're harmless, ask Sam. I'll have you feeling well again in no time." He waved the troopers over. "Medi pod please guys."

Once Klackan was installed within the medi pod, we jogged back to the shuttle and shot up into the Moianal sky. A medical crew were waiting and whisked the pod away the moment the shuttle bay doors closed. Lomas came up and smiled.

"I'm so glad we're at least able to help one of Vazien's victims. Did you get his story?"

I nodded. "Yes, we got it all. Thank you very much for helping him. He's extremely frail, he can't have long left. I've never seen a man so thin."

"We're happy to help whenever we can. Now what's our next stop?"

"Kesh Prime, for the exhumation," Tinnias replied. "There are a couple of Vazien's old neighbours who agreed to talk to us too."

Lomas nodded, "oh yes, that's correct." He stabbed at the nearest intercom.

"Yes, Your Majesty."

"Kesh Prime with all haste please."

"Right away, Sir. Is our new passenger aboard safely?"

"Jam is attending to him now."

"Oh that's wonderful news."

During the afternoon, when Jam could safely take a few minutes off from the medical bay, everyone gathered in the Observation Room to hear my recording of our chat with Klackan.

"Will we be able to verify the accounting discrepancies?" Byron asked.

"Yes," Jam replied. He gave me this when I was helping him undress." He handed me a data cube. "He asked me to get this to you, Sam. It contains copies of the mine's accounts showing every financial discrepancy."

I took the cube, "thanks, this is great. It's a bit old fashioned but we should be able to find a machine that'll accept it."

"Let's have a look," Byron said, leaning over and taking it from me. "Ahh yes, I can deal with this, no problem."

"We have four days and two hours to fill until we reach our next stop," Lomas said, "so it gives us plenty of time to plan the exhumation and visits to the medic and neighbours. I suggest we take the evening off and do other things. Give our minds a rest for a few hours. Does anyone disagree?" No one spoke. "Right then, do any of our guests have anything they'd like to do that they can't do anywhere else?"

"I wouldn't mind a few lessons towards my level three pilot's licence," Kyle said. "If Byron has the time."

"I'd love to have some more lessons on one of those, oh what are they called again?" Tinnias asked.

"Battle boards?" everyone chorused.

"That's them, yes."

Lomas went to the intercom. "This is Lomas, could a couple of troopers volunteer to give one of our guests a battle board lesson please. In the cargo bay in twenty minutes?"

Tinnias grinned at me like a kid with a new toy. "Awesome. This is just awesome."

I laughed. "They are fun, huge fun."

"What about you, Sam. Any bucket list items? It doesn't matter how silly, if we can achieve it, you will have it."

"Well there is one thing I've always wanted to do, more than anything else I've fancied having a go at. I don't know if you'll be okay with it though, I guess it goes against every safety regulation in existence."

"Then I want to do it too," Toma said and came and sat next to me.

"And what is it?" Lomas asked.

"Tether flying."

I heard a gasp from Vincent as he leapt to his feet and joined Toma and I. "Oh hell yes, me too."

Lomas went to the intercom again.

"Shuttle bay. How can we help, Your Majesty?"

"Open the Bay doors please, and then prepare four suits for tether flying. Make sure one of them is Vincent's."

"Yes, Sir, at once."

Lomas tapped a button and waited. "Bridge, Your Majesty."

"Bring the battle cruiser down to half cruising speed until further notice please."

"Immediately, Sir."

"Who's the fourth person?" I asked.

"If you think you're going tether flying without me, you've another think coming young man. Shall we?" He strode towards the door and I grinned at Toma and Vincent, then leaned over and kissed Byron.

"Enjoy yourself, my love," he whispered.

"See you at Dinner?" I asked and he nodded.

"Absolutely."

"This is the fulfilment of a lifetime ambition," I admitted.

"For me too," Vincent grinned. "Wait till Farra hears about this, she's gonna be pissed."

"I've done it once before," Toma added.

Lomas stopped and turned to gape at his son and heir. "Oh have you indeed?"

"Don't worry, Father, I was very well looked after. I do actually want to be King after you, you know."

"I'm delighted to hear it."


The shuttle bay crew helped us into the suits, checked and re checked everything three times before giving us the go ahead to move towards the open bay doors. The aching void spread out before us and a ripple of terror flooded through me.

Once Toma and Lomas were out enjoying themselves, the shuttle bay supervisor addressed me and Vincent. "Now then, Sam and Vincent, your tethers are five hundred metres long and have an electrical charge that makes them repel each other. This helps prevent you both getting tangled up with each other and having to be rescued. It also means you'll feel a bit of a sting if you touch the tether. It's not life threatening but you will feel it. Don't worry if you do inadvertently feel a sting, there's nothing wrong and you're not about to float off into space."

"That's a relief," Vincent remarked and I nodded.

"If you should get tangled, don't panic and try to sort it out yourselves. We'll be watching you all the time you're out and if that should happen, we'll be there to untangle you."

"Okay," we said together.

"The tether is not nearly long enough to allow you to get anywhere near any part of the ship that is dangerous, so feel free to go wherever you wish as far as the tether will allow. At no time must you unhook your tether, no matter how tempted you may be, and you will be tempted, believe me. You can float too far away very quickly. Do I have your word, Gentlemen?"

"Absolutely," Vincent said.

"Totally," I added.

"You must obey any and all commands from myself or Lomas, immediately and without question. And when we tell you to return, you return."

"Okay, no problem," I grinned.

"We'll be good boys," Vincent said.

"Right, we just have to wait for Lomas and Toma to finish and then you can go."

What seemed like hours later, but was less than half an hour, the supervisor addressed us again. "Gentlemen, hold onto the safety bar while we get you tethered." I felt someone fiddling at my back, then hands took hold of my arms.

"Come with me, Sam, to the other side of the bay doors. Lift your heels, wait a second for the boot to disengage, then step forward, that's it, now the other foot. Well done. Okay now hold the safety bar with your right hand and lift both heels at once. I've got hold of you, don't panic. That's it, both boots are now disengaged. Are you ready to go?" I gave him a thumbs up and he gave me a little push.

Emptiness on an epic scale enveloped me and I shrieked as I flew from the shuttle bay, Vincent to my left, whooping with excitement. A voice came through to us from the Supervisor.

"Look down at your hands. In your palms you'll see a keypad. Two buttons on each hand, each with an arrow on it. Up and down on your left palms, left, and right on your right palms. They control your thrusters, give them a try."

We soared, slalomed, turned loops and flew like angels, arms outstretched and we laughed and howled like little boys. All at once, I stopped and looked into the great expanse, trying to analyse how I felt. Vincent came up and stopped ten metres to my left.

"What's up, Sam?"

"Just look at it, Vincent," I said, sweeping my arm across. "I've never felt so alone yet so free, both at the same time. This could almost make me believe in God."

"So alone yet so free, I like that, that's wisdom, Sam."

"Isn't this just the most awesome thing you've ever done in your whole life?" I asked and he nodded.

"By a million miles," he replied. "Come on, slalom bumps."

We zig zagged, coming together in the middle just close enough to bump fists, it was great fun.

"Two more minutes guys," the Supervisor's voice said through our headsets.

On our next bump, Vincent grabbed my wrist and we flew, hand in hand and he used his up and down thrusters to send us into huge waves, then I added my left and right to add a sideways motion to the waves. To the right and up, then to the left and down.

"I feel like Star Flyer," I laughed. "Crime fighting Lord of the Great Expanse."

Vincent leaned back so he was in a standing position and put both fists on his hips. "Fighting evil from one edge of the galaxy to the other," he boomed in as deep a voice as he could.

I roared with laughter and launched into the theme song of this popular children's Vidicom serial. Vincent joined me and we could hear the shuttle bay guys laughing through our earpieces. We yeehawed and whoopee'd ourselves almost hoarse and it was with some reluctance that we obeyed the Supervisor when he called us in.

"Time to come back now guys."

# CHAPTER TWENTY ONE

The next part of our journey was a seven day haul to Kesh Prime, so we tried to think of ways to occupy ourselves so the time wouldn't drag. We made a list of ideas.

"Battle board lessons," Tinnias grinned. "They're amazing."

"We could always have a game of murder mystery," Lomas offered.

Vincent roared with laughter, "Oh yes, let's do that. Last time we did it, I almost peed myself laughing. It's the best laugh ever."

I grinned. "I haven't done that since I was a kid. Okay then, who wants to be the Administrator?"

"I'll do it this time," Lomas said, "but someone else does it next time so I get to play. I'll plan everything and we can start after lunch, is that okay with everyone?"

The rules are simple. One person takes the role of administrator and decides who is going to be the victim or victims, who is the murderer, how it was done, why it was done, and any clues that are to be deliberately left, and the false leads too. He then takes each player aside and tells them their role. Once everyone is clear on their role, the game begins. Whoever successfully guesses the murderer and the reason for the killing, wins.

Lomas had little information for me. "Sam, your business partnership with your long term friend, Vincent, has just broken up, due to his alcoholism and stealing from your brother and other business partner, Kyle. Kyle is also a passionate collector of farm animal nipples, which he dries, mounts, and displays at local art and craft shows. This hobby necessitates him being expert in the use of all manner of sharp tools, which causes him to quickly become a suspect. You are worried when you hear of Kyle being questioned about the murder of a local milk curdler, Byron. You know he's innocent of the crime as you and he were at a movie theatre together at the time. Vincent doesn't yet know that you're already in talks with a new prospective business partner, Grund, and you are scared to tell him. There will be further instructions as time goes on."

The game began and Vincent had to find me and Kyle in a business meeting with a prospective new business partner, have a screaming row, and storm off in tears. I almost wet myself, he was such a good actor. Later, I found myself in a bar, the bartender, who looked suspiciously like my father, telling us about a local milk curdler, Byron, who had been found with his neck broken in an animal stall, next to the body of a huge beast bred for meat. The animal had two of its eight nipples removed. Jam played a cop who arrested Kyle and played bad cop, alongside Toma's superb acting as good cop and quickly brought Kyle to tears, with Vincent causing mayhem in the reception of the 'police station.'

After being told I had to instigate a talk with Vincent, to sort out our unfinished business, I happened to notice he had a cut on his right hand, which seemed to be getting infected. It was as I was drinking in the 'bar' and discussing the murder with the bartender, that he introduced me to Doctor Elka, from the local hospital. This caused me to remember the cut on Vincent's hand and I asked the doctor about the dead beast found alongside the milk curdler. It turned out that this beast often passed on an infectious but ultimately harmless rash to anyone who has too much contact with its blood. Everything fell into place and I went to find Lomas.

"Vincent is the murderer," I said. "He did it to frame Kyle because he blames him for getting him kicked out of our business partnership. During the screaming row we had while interviewing Grund, he told us he found a letter Kyle signed, inviting him for an interview, before the murder happened. He has an infected cut on his right hand, probably gained through too much contact with the blood of the animal he killed to make it look like Kyle did it, to further make him look like a suspect."

Lomas grinned and went to the intercom. "All actors to the Obs Room please, the murder has been solved and the wicked murderer, found."

We celebrated with a bottle of alcoholic spirit brewed by the Drycenians and spent many hours laughing and reliving the heinous murder.

"You're quiet, Sam." Byron said with a yawn as we lay in bed. "You okay?"

"Yeah, I'm fine," I grinned at him. "The game was fun, wasn't it?"

He laughed. "Yeah. I shall make sure to let everyone know how you found the killer of a poor milk curdler and saved the reputation of an innocent nipple collector."

"It's the highlight of my career," I replied and we both laughed as we relived the game.

It seemed like immediately following my conversation and laughter with Byron, I found myself walking the same corridor, Ren at my side. I delighted in the feeling of his presence and spent long seconds allowing his essence to flow into me before I spoke.

"It's good to see you again, Ren."

"I'm joyful how much you laughed and allowed yourself to have so much fun today, Sam. Your soul really needed it. It was long overdue and I urge you not to leave it so long in future. Schedule in regular down times, please, my friend. For your own mental wellbeing. Promise me."

"I promise. Can I ask you something?"

"Of course."

"Are you happy, in whatever state of being you're in? Is being here for me holding you back in any way?"

He smiled and shook his head. "You do not hold me back, my friend. You're remembering your conversation with Kyle, aren't you? He told you we'd met and explained about me having to step away for a time just after I passed." I nodded. "Fear not, Sam. The bond we enjoy was making me anxious to be at your side, which distracted me from spending the necessary time adjusting to the way things are here. I struggled for a time, which meant I could not be effective in guiding you and could not evolve myself either. Once I listened to those advising me, things improved quickly and I was able to come back to you. I'm sorry you felt I had deserted you when I passed. I felt your heart hurting and heard your calls for me. I knew your mind searched for me and I'm sorry I caused you pain. Please forgive me."

I stopped and gaped at him. "You've done nothing that needs forgiveness, Ren. Don't ever think that, not ever."

"I know, with my mind, but the bond we share makes me need to hear your words, despite feeling it from you."

"I forgive you, absolutely." He smiled and we walked on in silence for almost a minute, during which I felt the reassuring touch of his shoulder against my own, that always brought me so much comfort.

"At some point, not too far ahead, you will find yourself needing information that only Belotan can give you. Do not be afraid to ask, for he is still trustworthy."

"Okay, thank you, I'll remember. Can I ask another question? It's very personal and I feel a bit embarrassed asking, but it's playing on my mind."

"Of course. Don't ever be too embarrassed to ask me anything. I am here to help and assist you, no matter how delicate the subject matter might be."

"Thank you. It's just that … well you've had more experience with men than I have. I'm nervous about how to please Byron."

"You've no need to be," he smiled. "Does he know you're nervous and worried about it?"

"No," I admitted. "I'm too nervous to mention it," I sniggered and Ren laughed.

"So you're too nervous to tell him you're too nervous?"

"Yes," I laughed.

"Oh, Sam, you're something else, you know that? You've no need to be nervous, about talking to him or pleasing him. This is just the kind of thing you should be talking about with him. Let him reassure you, guide you, and show you how to let your body lead the way so you can follow. In asking for his advice and help, you're allowing him to know that you trust him with your deepest fears. This is something he needs right now in order that the wound caused by your sudden separation be healed."

"Did I hurt him very much?"

"Yes, he was so shocked and upset that he tried to steal a shuttle and run after you. It took Vincent and Kyle hours to calm him and reassure him that they wouldn't rest until you were safely back in his arms."

I gaped at him. "What? Oh no. Oh I'm so sorry. He never said, neither did anyone else. Oh fuck, how do I repair this? Please help me, Ren."

"By telling him everything, all the time, and letting him know that you need him just as much as he needs you. He will have separation anxiety for a while and will need you to keep in touch regularly and not get annoyed with his constant requests for promises to return to him. He will be a bit clingy and not like to leave you alone for long, other than when his work demands his time. Even then, a visit every now and then will do wonders. He will not thrive by being yelled at or told off, and when you find yourself infuriated by his behaviour at any time, as people often do, you will need the strength to quell your instinct to berate him. Drycenians do not thrive in relationships where there is any verbal violence at all."

"I feel awful causing him so much pain. Can I share this conversation with him?"

"Yes, if and when you feel it appropriate and when there is time for the emotions such a conversation will bring forth. As for pleasing him, do not fret so, my friend. Your love for him will lead the way. Follow and enjoy it."

"Thanks for being so open and honest about it," I replied.

"I give you my word, I will always be honest with you, even when I know you won't like it. There will be times when you will have angry feelings towards me due to the way circumstances play out for you. Always remember I'm here with you, no matter what passes between us, angry words or love, I'm here beside you always. Never fear looking for me after angry words, promise me."

"I promise."

"Now you must return and wake up, a new day is beginning. Oh, you can give the Breaker of Hearts to Vincent if you wish to. I'd be happy for him to have it if you want to give it. The collection is yours now, not mine. I trust you completely."

After breakfast the next morning, I walked Byron to Engineering to begin his shift and kissed him.

"Don't work too hard, my love," I smiled.

"Is that an order?" he grinned.

"Most definitely."

"What's on your agenda today?"

"I'm going to give one of the Damiklonian Daggers to Vincent, he's been hinting for days and Ren said he can have it. As far as the case goes, we can't do much until we have all the visits completed, so I'll be twiddling my thumbs until I can hold you again."

"That won't be long," he grinned and kissed me.

"You promise?" I asked.

"I promise."


I entered the smoking room and lit a cigarette. Normally I would be bored as hell during these trips between systems, but now I had Byron in my life, I enjoyed having time off to spend with him.

"You're looking happy Bro," Vincent said. "It's nice to see. Do I know who the cause of this new Sam is?" I grinned and heard Kyle snigger.

"Possibly," I admitted. "I just hope he is too."

"He is," Kyle replied. "Now you're back with us."

I knew he was referring to what Ren told me, but I was not prepared to discuss it until I was able to speak to Byron about it first. It would be disrespectful and although everyone knew what happened while I was gone, they didn't know I knew about it. I was not ready to be told off by them until Byron and I had worked things out.

I put out my cigarette. "Hey guys, are you doing anything for a few minutes?"

After exchanging a glance, they both shook their heads. "No, what's up?"

"Could I have a few minutes of your time?"

They followed me along corridors, down to the lowest deck, and into the shuttle bay. I waved to a mechanic. "Just getting something from the ship."

He nodded and gave me a thumbs up, so I jogged over and lowered the hatch. Once the knife box was open, I reached in and brought out the Breaker of Hearts. "I want you to have this," I said, offering it to Vincent. "I can't think of anyone more trustworthy with a valuable blade, and Ren is very happy for you to have it too."

Vincent gaped in shock as he took the knife from me. "Oh, Sam. I don't know what to say."

"How about umm, thanks, man," I suggested and Kyle laughed.

"Oh, thank you so much. This is awesome. I will keep it safe, I promise. Wow," he grinned and examined it closely.

"Well he'll be in a good mood for the rest of the day," I grinned at Kyle. "If you want something off him, today's the best day to ask, I'd say."

He laughed. "You're on his dinner invitation list for life now, Bro."

I was about to reply when the intercom boomed. "Sam, Vincent, and Kyle to the Obs Room please."

"Looks like we have an update," I said as we jumped down from the hatch. "Let's hope it's a good one."


We entered the Observation Lounge just as Byron stood and addressed everyone.

"We will arrive at Kesh Prime in the early hours of the morning, so if we leave in the late afternoon, we will be sure to find Doctor Orlan at home. Darkness falls early this time of year on Kesh."

Lomas nodded. "Yes, we don't want to do an exhumation in broad daylight do we? Even though we have the right documentation, we need time to get things done before Vazien finds out. Where is he, does anyone know."

"He's aboard the Galactic Council liner heading for Laminaqua 3 for a Galactic Summit." Byron replied. "Don't worry, he's far away but in case any of his eyes and ears should see us and inform him, darkness would be preferable."

"Jam, can you assure us that we can have the body reburied in such a fashion as to avoid any suspicion of interference?"

"Absolutely. I know where I need to take samples from in order to ascertain how the River Fever got into her system. It won't take more than a few minutes, even with photographs and all the proper evidence Sam needs as well. No one will know we were ever there until they have to."

"All I need is to prove it is her," I said. "A DNA sample won't take more than a minute. I won't be able to get a retinal scan after this length of time; she's been dead for years. Even prints will most likely not be viable. She's no doubt just bones by now."

"Prints won't be a problem," Jam said. "I can inject her fingers with a plumping solution that will fill out where the flesh has withered. So long as the flesh and skin still exists, you will have prints."

"Awesome."

"What are the potential problems?" Lomas asked.

"The main one is if the doctor doesn't want to talk," Byron said.

"Or if he rats us out to Vazien," I added.

"Or if the body isn't there," Jam said. That silenced us and we all stared at him open mouthed. No one knew how to respond. Lomas finally broke the silence.

"Jam. Are you telling us something we need to know or offering a possibility?"

"Oh, I'm just offering a possibility. If someone has already ratted us out, she could've been moved. It's not beyond the realms of possibility."

Lomas sighed with obvious relief. "Thank the heavens for that. I thought you were about to tell us Arshad had told you something."

Jam looked shocked, then laughed. "Oh, sorry. No, nothing like that."

I grinned at Jam. "It's the way you said it, Doc."

Lomas and Byron both nodded. "He does this sometimes," Lomas said. "He has a knack of leaving just enough of a profound silence before saying something that totally floors us."

Jam blushed. "I apologise, gentlemen."

"No need, my friend," Lomas replied. "You've saved our necks many times with this gift, and the lives of those we love. We are blessed to have this gift to aid us when we need it most."

"Yes indeed," Byron added.

We gathered at dusk in the shuttle bay for the trip down to the surface of Kesh Prime and our meeting with Orlan and the exhumation of Olendra's mother, Kandil. King Lomas, refusing to be a mere figurehead to his people, would lead the party as usual with his son, Prince Toma at his side. Commander Byron was in charge of the party of a dozen Troopers who would be our armed security if necessary, and Jam was there to take charge of the exhumation and get his samples. For the first time in ages, I felt like a passenger and despite being grateful for their presence, it knocked my ego a little.

"We're going to land in a quiet corner of the burial facility," Byron said. "It's a ten minute walk to Orlan's dwelling, Sam. How do you want to do this?" He looked at me as if reading my mind and I was grateful for the reminder that I wasn't superfluous after all.

"I have to be present while the exhumation is happening," I replied. "Any samples taken and the resulting evidence has to be done according to Agency procedures. That may not be what you'd describe as the best, or most efficient way, but it's the only way any evidence will be admissible in court."

"Do we actually need Orlan to be present before we can exhume the body?" Lomas asked.

"No," I said. "Jam has provided all the documentation we need. We need him to testify against Vazien."

"Would it be prudent therefore, to find out if Kandil was murdered before you risk yourself by approaching Orlan?" Jam asked.

"It would," I agreed. "Let's do the exhumation first. Get your samples and find out if she was murdered or not. How long will that take?"

"A few minutes."

I nodded in satisfaction. "Okay then, once we know either way, we can go and find Orlan or not, depending upon the results of Jam's tests. Once we're through with Orlan, we can go and visit the two neighbours. They're not far from him, thankfully. Is everyone okay with that?"

Everyone nodded and we boarded the shuttle. The trip was short and we were on the ground in under twenty minutes. The evening was rapidly darkening and I was glad to notice the burial facility was not overlooked by buildings or busy highways. Situated just outside the city on a slight incline, we could see the city spread out before us, the noise of vehicles and faint music just reaching our ears. After making sure the shuttle was well hidden, Byron took the lead, following the quiet beeping of his locator.

"This way," he pointed ahead. "It's not far." He set off and we followed, picking our way through the burial plots. Simple stones a foot high and six inches wide, covered in foreign writing and symbols I did not recognise.

"I hope someone amongst us reads the language," I hissed as I looked at each stone in turn. "They all look identical to me."

"I have a translation unit," Byron grinned. "It would be unfortunate to dig up the wrong one, wouldn't it?"

I nodded. "Especially if we found they had indeed been murdered."

Byron stopped, pointing to a stone to his right. "It's this one. Okay guys, come on, dig her up." He indicated to four Troopers who stepped forward with a small box. A hose entered one end and exited the opposite end. Once switched on, the unit made the faintest hum as they poked one end of the hose at the ground covering the burial. By means of suction, the soil covering the burial entered the hose and was discarded out the other end, thus avoiding the need for digging. In less than five minutes, the unit came upon a large stone and the Troopers switched it off.

"Damn," Byron said as he looked at the stone. "We didn't bring our Casmets. Okay everyone, come on." He bent down and dug his fingers under the lip of the stone, indicating for everyone else to do the same. I took off my backpack and rummaged.

"Hold up there a minute. I have something in here." I laid the small box on the ground and opened the lid. Inside were six small cubes a centimetre square and an oblong control box. Lomas' eyes lit up at the sight.

"Oh my word, Sam. You've been talking to Vaylon Rabramas, haven't you?"

I grinned. "Yeah, a while ago. He gave me this as a parting gift. For services rendered you might say." I quickly fixed each of the small cubes to the edges of the stone and with the control box in hand, the stone lifted effortlessly from its resting place. I set it down to one side and peered into the hole.

"You met the Nahdan's?" Byron asked.

"Yeah, I did a job that took me there a little while ago."

Inside the hole was a body wrapped in a cloth shroud and I frowned. "That's a body," I said.

Toma sniggered. "Well isn't that what we came for?"

"But she's been dead for years," Byron replied. "She should have little flesh left by now."

"Oh yes of course," Toma said. "How stupid of me. How odd."

"Odd, yes," Jam nodded as he reached down into the hole. "But helpful."

"How?" I asked.

"It tells me that her body was completely taken over by the River Fever bacteria when she died. That particular bacteria acts as a sort of preservative to the host it invades." Taking a small cutting tool, he looked up at us. "When I cut the shroud, there's going to be one heck of a smell, so be prepared. Anyone with a weak stomach, move away. We don't want the evidence contaminated."

I looked at Tinnias. "Dad, take a step or two back, you know what you're like. By the way," I said as I reached into my backpack for my can of sterifilm. "Here, Doc. Spray this over your hands first if you don't mind. It seals your skin like an impermeable glove and avoids you contaminating the scene while allowing you free use of your hands." Jam dutifully held out his hands to me and I sprayed them, back and front. Once happy he would not contaminate any evidence, I nodded and he cut the shroud. Five of us were sick, myself, Byron and Tinnias included and I stood back with two of the Troopers and heaved deep breaths to try to calm my stomach.

"Hell fire," gasped the Trooper to my left. "That's awful."

"I don't think I'll be wanting much dinner tonight," said the other.

"Bodies don't usually smell that bad," I exclaimed as I wiped my mouth. "Even at their most smelly, it's never that bad. Remind me never to become a forensic doctor on Kesh Prime, nor to date the women here."

My two companions laughed and before long, the three of us had tears streaming down our cheeks and the humour was as black as it gets.

"You're incorrigible, Sam," Byron grinned. "Okay, Jam's done and about to reseal the shroud. You can get your prints and whatever else you need, then put the stone back."

Once the stone was in place, I put away the six cubes and controller and stowed them carefully in my backpack. This unit was one of my most precious possessions, given to me as a gift at the end of a particularly trying case and had earned their keep many times by helping me lift heavy objects when necessary. They saved my life once when I found myself entombed by a rock fall on Siberian 7 after a fire fight with some pirates. By the time they were safely stowed away, the Troopers had refilled the hole effortlessly with their suction machine. Jam was crouched down at his mobile lab unit and we waited silently as he dipped little sticks into test tubes, poked the sticks into a machine and tapped at a display screen. After five minutes, he looked up at us.

"She was definitely murdered."

"You're sure?" I asked.

"No question," he replied. "Her stomach and digestive tract contained none of the tell tale traces I would expect to find from having ingested contaminated water, which is the usual way one contracts the disease. Her blood vessels however, are riddled with the unique black spotting where the bacteria takes hold in order to digest the cells around it. I have nano cam footage to prove it."

"How does that indicate murder?" Lomas asked.

"The bacteria only remain viable for around fifteen minutes once inside a living host. It's just long enough for it to find somewhere nearby to lodge itself, digest the cells around it, and divide into three, the original cell and two brand new ones. The original bacterial cell then dies while the new ones move on and repeat the procedure. In this way, the disease spreads out from the point of entry, killing the cells of its host as it goes. Therefore, the pattern of black spotting shows the journey taken from point of entry, to the point where the damage was so great as to cause the death of the host. She was injected in the upper left bicep. The bacteria travelled up to the shoulder by way of a brachial vein, then split into two groups. Half went down to the heart and half went up the neck towards the brain. The brain stem was damaged enough to cause death, but so was the heart. I cannot say whether she died of a heart attack induced by the bacterial damage, or whether brain stem death occurred first, but that's of little consequence really. She died as a result of River Fever induced cell damage to the heart and brain stem, the bacteria having been administered by person or persons unknown, into her upper left bicep by means of injection."

"You'd swear to this in court?" I asked.

"Any court in the galaxy," he replied, holding my gaze with those mesmerising yellow eyes.

"Okay, thank you very much. Let's get all the evidence bagged and tagged properly, then go and find Orlan."


Byron led the way with his locator softly beeping and we found the small house occupied by Orlan and his wife. A small wooden door flanked by two windows on either side from which light glowed. On the upper story was a balcony and two more windows. After listening carefully at the windows, we heard soft music from within.

"He's listening to music," Lomas hissed.

"There are no voices," Byron said. "He's alone."

I nodded and approached the door, Tinnias at my side. Indicating for our friends to keep to the shadows until we needed them, I knocked. A tall man opened the door and I recognised him immediately from the photograph Byron showed me from his hours of research.

"Orlan, Child of Fars?"

"I am he," the man nodded. "Who are you and what is the purpose of this visit? You are not Keshan."

"Detective Sinclair-Vaylo of the Inter-Galactic Law Enforcement Agency," I said as I held out my identification. "This is Commander Vaylo, I indicated Tinnias, who offered his own ID. "I am here to ask you about the murder of Kandil, child of Barlot."

His eyes widened at the name and he glanced over his shoulder. "That was years ago. Why is it being investigated now?"

"Because we want you to help us convict Vazien. It was you who gave him the phial of River Fever bacteria wasn't it?"

"Well I err …?" he began.

"Good evening Orlan. My name is King Lomas VII of the Drycenian Nation," Lomas said as he stepped into view, swiftly followed by the others. "We are helping the detectives in their quest to bring Vazien to justice, not only for the murder of his wife but for many other crimes as well. We know that Kandil was indeed murdered by an injection of the River Fever bacteria, but we need your testimony to help us pin it on Vazien."

"Drycenians?" Orlan exclaimed in surprise. "The Drycenians are at my door?"

"We are," Lomas nodded. "And we'd very much appreciate not to have to stand here in the cold much longer. May we come in? I'm very old and would welcome the chance to sit down."

Orlan stepped aside and we entered a large room that appeared much smaller than it was due to the abundance of furniture it contained.

"Thanks," I smiled as he shut the door and turned to face us. I switched on my data recorder and placed it on the table. "We won't take up much of your time. Are you willing for me to record your story? It's not an official interview, that may come later if you agree."

"Sure, why not," he sighed.

After going through the initial questions required by the regulations, I smiled.

"Thank you very much. Could you start by telling us your name, age, occupation, and addresses of your residence and place of work?"

I am Orlan, Child of Fars. My age is forty nine and I'm a Doctor of Medicine, grade five. I work at Hamamet Medical Centre, City nine eight three, Kesh Prime. I live at building seven, street seventeen north, City Nine Eight Three, Kesh Prime."

"You once expressed a belief that Vazien was the cause of Kandil's death."

Orlan nodded. "I did. I was a junior medic in those days. I wanted to become a research chemist and worked in a privately funded laboratory owned by one of Vazien's companies. He approached me one day and asked me for a phial of River Fever bacteria without it going through the usual documentation procedure. When I asked why, he said he was helping a friend who wanted to do some research that would help his career and that our lab would be getting a substantial financial bonus in return for overlooking the usual procedures. I didn't want to, but he said that without the money, the lab would have to be scaled down and I would lose my job, so I agreed and gave him the phial. A month later, the lab was expanded and filled with new equipment and we all got a large bonus. Two months after that, Kandil died, apparently from River Fever. Vazien said she caught it during a holiday they had taken that summer, which was right after I had given him the phial. I knew at once what had really happened but what could I do? Vazien was a powerful man even back then and I was just a junior medic with big dreams."

"Are you willing to sign a declaration of intent to testify?" I asked. "We can offer you and your family protection until this case is over. When the time comes, I can arrange for you to be taken to a safe place where Vazien will never find you."

Orlan turned away and paced the room, wringing his hands as he fought an internal battle. Three times he paced back and forth across the room before turning to me.

"Yes, I will testify. It will probably do no good and Vazien is sure to kill me for this, but at least there is hope that the galaxy will finally know what that man is. The more people who know, the less power he will have over them."

"Thank you," I said. "His Majesty will talk to you now about taking you to safety."

The neighbours were happy to talk to us, and we learned that when they lived next door to Vazien, many screaming rows were heard by several of the neighbouring families. From what they gleaned by eavesdropping, it seems Kandil accused Vazien of having affairs and he made little attempt to deny it. The husband, Arlat, told us they distinctly heard Vazien say that he would kill her one day if she didn't shut her mouth and stop yelling.

"There was no mistake," Arlat explained. "A month later he was telling us how she died from some infection she got on their holiday. We always wondered if he did actually murder her, and we were so happy when he moved into a fancy mansion in the capital."

"He asked you to work for him, didn't he?" the wife, Basita said and the man nodded. "Well I told him straight, if you go and work for that man, I'm going back to live with my parents and taking our son with me. Gave me the creeps he did, honestly."

"He asked me to be his PR man. Keep the media at bay by spinning them some vague nonsense and that sort of thing. I took it to mean he wanted me to cover up for him by lying to the media. I wasn't comfortable with the idea so I said no. I told him I was taking early retirement as we were considering emigrating and starting over somewhere warm and sunny."

"He kept on asking," Basita added. "Three times after that he asked. Offered the most outrageous salary but lying isn't worth any amount of money to us. We're honest people just trying to have a nice life and raise our son to be a good man like his dad."

"How did Vazien take your refusals?" I asked.

"He told me what a shame it would be if our son got sick and we couldn't afford good doctors," Arlat replied. "Maybe I'm being over dramatic but we took that as a threat."

"That was enough for us," Basita said. "After that, we sold up and moved here without telling a soul. We changed our names and took our son out of school. I even dyed my hair and persuaded him to shave his off. He looked so funny." They both giggled at the memory.

"Was the threat ever carried out?" I asked.

"The night we moved out," Arlat explained, "our old house burned down, with all our furniture and belongings inside. We spent the night in a hotel as I was too nervous to spend another moment there. We'd arranged for our stuff to be moved a couple of days later. We lost everything but the clothes we stood up in."

"We've no proof it was Vazien," Basita continued, "but we'd not told him we were going and because all our stuff was still inside, it looked lived in from outside. I even left a couple of lamps on to make it look occupied to deter burglars. We know it was him. Even without proof we know it was him. You'll never convince me otherwise."

"Thank you very much for sharing that with us," I said after they signed the declaration. "His Majesty will now tell you about what will happen if and when we are able to charge him."

I must break off for a couple of hours. I'm due to testify this afternoon and need to get myself looking smart. I'll carry on this evening. This is Sinclair V-Log Q890/M data log reference point 4136902/623.

## CHAPTER TWENTY TWO

This is Sinclair V-Log Q890/M data log reference point 4136902/624 continuing report.

Hello again. I'm happy to report the psycho got a long stretch at Latterways. I'm glad I wore my lucky shirt. Okay, where was I? Oh yes, we'd just finished on Kesh, hadn't we?

Back aboard the battle cruiser, Tinnias and I got everything bagged, tagged, and stored as Lomas ordered the ship to rush to Terramora Prime to have a chat with Preataq Jormla of Q'endlash about the bombing of his haulage firm.

I heard Tinnias sigh deeply. "What's up, Dad?"

"I've been thinking about how we approach things when, and if, we feel it's time to make this an official case. We're going to have to hand everything over to the Agency guys and just hope they're not leaks. I admit I'm worried."

"So that's what Ren meant," I said.

"What?"

"The other night, Ren said there would come a time when we would need information only Belotan has and assured me that we can still trust him. He'll know who his leaks are and who aren't, and if we explain that we don't want to cause him any direct harm, he might be happy to tell us. My contact can do some digging to find out who is leaking to the Dankera Collective."

"Oh, good, that's cool."

"I'll make a couple of calls," I said, fishing for my Unicom.

"I'll get us some snacks and a drink. I'll see you in the smoking room."

I handed Tinnias the list of twenty seven names. "This is everyone Belotan has in law enforcement. There's only one back home so that's a relief. My contact will get back to me either today or tomorrow, with the Dankera list and any he knows for sure are Vazien's leaks." I puffed on the cigarette and smiled.

"That's a relief," Tinnias said. "We can safely do the official stuff via Headquarters back home. Now we can relax. How long till we get to Terramora Prime?"

"Two days four hours."

"Okay, I've arranged some more Battle Board lessons in a half hour."

I grinned. "Are you enjoying it?"

"It's great fun," he nodded. "but my ass is a bit bruised."

"You should've seen mine when I learned," Vincent said, having just entered with Kyle and Byron and heard Tinnias' remark. "It was painful to sit down for almost a week."

We all laughed and I realised that for the past couple of days at least, I'd really started to feel relaxed and confident in everyone's friendship.

"What are you going to do to fill your time, Son?"

"He's going to join Kyle, Byron, and me in a laser battle in the cargo hold," Vincent announced.

"Am I?" I asked. "What's a laser battle?"

"You've done the warrior games," Tinnias said and I nodded. "Well it's a bit like that only with real people instead of holograms. You really don't know what laser battles are?"

I shook my head. "I guess I've lived a sheltered life."

"Well today you're getting an education," Kyle said. "You'll love it, trust me."

Tinnias nodded. "You will love it, Sam. It's just your kind of thing."

"It's the best fun ever," Byron grinned.

Vincent explained as we made our way to the cargo hold. "You have armour on, much like the warrior games, but you have a team of guys. There will be four teams and you work your way from one end of the cargo hold to the other, around the obstacles, and avoiding getting killed by the other teams. Like the warrior games, each hit they score loses you a percentage of your life. When it runs out, you die for an allotted time agreed beforehand. Then you must catch up to your team as they can't win and get home until you've rejoined them. Two teams go at a time, the winning teams then play each other to get the final winning team."

"Sounds straight forward enough," I said, assuming that I'd find this a total breeze, seeing as how I'm used to firearms and have had to fight for my life on so many occasions I've lost count. What I failed to realise, is that I've never fought either the Drycenians or the Lileans before, and they're both top quality marksmen. I downed a few troopers and got a few shots into both Lileans, but I died myself four times before my team came a disappointing third place overall.

We took a break before another game. "I never realised what an awful shot I am," I said. "I need to spend some time in a firing range. I'm ashamed of that performance."

"We can help you if you like, Sam," one of the troopers offered. "If the boss is okay with it. We can take you through some of the training we're given. It'll give you a different way of approaching it than just a firing range. It might help, you never know."

"Sure," Byron nodded. "I'll oversee the training myself."

"That would be great, thank you very much," I said.

"Can I join in?" Vincent asked.

"Me too," Kyle added.

"Sure, the more the merrier."

After a further two more games, we stopped for some lunch and as the exercise had made me hungry, I decided to eat this time. We all chose not to shower, as we intended to work out and spar after lunch. I was certainly going to get fit on this job, if nothing else. Having sparred with them several times by now, they had started to use more of their strength on me, and I felt more comfortable using more of my own speed and agility against their brute strength. Despite the difference in our dimensions, we were well matched and they had little advantage over me. The difference in our approach and fighting styles, complimented each other. The only way they had an advantage over me was in the effortless way they were able to inflict pain.

At one point, I ended up flat on my back, having avoided Kyle landing on top of me and squashing me flat, and Vincent crossways across me, his right leg intertwined with both of mine in such a way that with the slightest of movements, I felt my kneecaps being pulled apart. I screamed in agony.

"Okay, I'll tell you all the secrets, anything, just stop," I begged and we all laughed. With one more twitch of his leg, which brought a fresh volley of screams from me, he jumped up and grinned as I hugged my knees to myself and groaned.


Tinnias and I prepared ourselves for the trip down to the surface of Terramora Prime.

"You ready, Son?"

"Totally. You?"

"Yeah. Let's hope we manage to secure another testimony."

Two huge six legged creatures came rushing towards the shuttle as we landed in front of the house. The noise they made was half wail, half a sort of gulping yelp and sounded distinctly unfriendly. Their sandy brown hair matched the colour of the earth and bore no distinguishing markings, save for darker brown tufts upon the tips of their large forward pointing ears. Their eyes were large, featureless, and forward facing, giving them excellent binocular vision and depth of field ability. I realised right away that there could be no hiding from these creatures with such highly tuned hearing and sight. Running would not be advisable either, the huge muscles upon their rear ends indicated a power and endurance beyond the reach of my own. The six legs were arranged with the extra pair at the front and they appeared to work in tandem with the other front pair. The front legs on each side moved together, not opposite like four legged animal's legs usually do. Because of this, their movement appeared the same as any other four legged animals. You might assume that an extra pair of legs on such a creature would make their movement awkward, insect-like perhaps but this was not the case at all. I found them fascinating to watch and didn't notice a man approaching the shuttle until I heard him yell at the creatures in Terramoran. They quietened immediately and lay down on their stomachs. The man spoke to me as I cowered in the open hatchway.

"Hi there, do you speak the common tongue?" I asked.

"Who are you and what do you want? Are you from Agricultural Affairs? I haven't exceeded any quotas. I have all the documentation to prove it."

"Don't worry," I smiled as reassuringly as I could. "I'm not here to study your books. I'm Detective Samelan Sinclair-Vaylo from the Inter-Galactic Law Enforcement Agency. I called you a few days ago. Can we talk to you about your haulage company?"

He looked down at the ground and ran a hand through his hair, the merest hint of a smile lifting one corner of his mouth. Placing both hands upon his hips, he looked up at me.

"So, you've finally got around to investigating Vazien. About time too. Come on in."

The house was comfortably large inside and as Tinnias and I sat on the proffered leather chairs, the place felt welcoming. The two fearsome animals that greeted our arrival now lay panting at our feet, one of them sniffing at my boot with interest. Preataq entered the room carrying a wooden tray on which were three tall glasses of cloudy liquid. He set the tray down on a small table, shooing away an inquisitive nose that sniffed towards the nearest glass.

"It's home made, from the orchard in the south pasture," he informed us. "Non alcoholic I'm afraid. I have an allergy and have to abstain."

"It's delicious," Tinnias said after taking a long draw on his glass. "We appreciate your time, umm, what do you prefer to be called?"

"Preataq is fine."

"You guessed why we're here."

"As soon as you mentioned law enforcement and my haulage company in the same breath, I guessed the day had finally come when someone was on to the truth."

After going through the necessary preliminaries, our talk could begin. "Can I ask you for some background about your company first?" I said.

"Sure, what do you want to know?"

"The basics."

"Okay, well I took over the company twenty six years ago when my father died. I was the fifth generation son to take over. It started out with a single ship, one pilot, a navigator, a mechanic, and two warehousemen. They lived and worked the company from a tumbledown shack and none of them got paid for nearly a year. Everything they made went back into the business and when the company became profitable, each was given a ten percent share in lieu of back payment of wages. They had the option of selling their share back to my ancestor or any of the others if they wanted actual money, with the promise that they would get the current market value for it. None of them took up the offer though. He'd picked good men to work with and all of them stayed with the company until the day they retired."

"It's hard to find reliable partners in business nowadays," I said.

"He'd known them all for years. They grew up together, went to school together, dated girls together, and got drunk together so it made sense to go into business together when the opportunity presented itself I suppose."

"So he started out with just a single ship."

"Yeah."

"How long was it before the company grew?"

"Within five years they had seventeen ships, each with a crew of thirty. By the time I took over, our headquarters was the tallest building in the city and our annual turnover was in the tens of millions. We were one of the most well known and well respected haulage firms out there. Until Vazien arrived that is."

"How did you meet him?" I asked.

His face clouded as he remembered. "We hauled for several mining firms in those days and one day, the Managing Director of one of them asked me if I'd be interested in hauling for another mine owner. I said sure, I'm always interested in more business, so told him to give the guy my number. About a month later, I get a call asking me to go and meet this guy who was looking for reliable haulage for his product. I went to meet him and found myself having a drink with Vazien."

"What did he want from you?"

"He told me he was looking for haulage for the Razulite he mined and that he was prepared to pay extra for good security. Razulite is valuable and always attracts pirates, so he told me he was prepared to pay for one of our ships to be made extra secure in return for our promising him exclusive use of it. we were expected to promise that we would refuse to haul Razulite for anyone else, no matter what payment was offered. If we reneged on the deal at any time, the ship would become his property, seeing as how much money he would be spending on it."

"And you agreed?"

"When he offered us three times what we asked, yes we did. He paid for a complete overhaul of one of our largest ships; new triple thickness Splendite outer hull, full sensor relay update, the latest security systems, multi-bandwidth communication system complete with military grade encryption and decryption, you name it, he had it fitted and paid for it out of his own pocket. He even paid for security personnel on board. All we had to do was pay for the usual crew and turn down any other enquiries from Razulite miners. That wasn't exactly difficult either, there aren't too many Razulite miners looking for haulage. I talked it over with the other guys who co-owned the company and although we all thought it was a bit odd, we decided the money was too good to turn down."

"So what went wrong?"

"Nothing, for almost a year. Everything was great until we ran into a random stop and search in the Oberlauer Shipping Lanes in sector eight hundred and seven."

"That's one of the busiest shipping lane systems," I remarked. "They often have stop and searches there. I've been stopped a few times there myself."

"Right," Preataq nodded. "So had we, often. We never had a problem before though, but this time we got a notice of infringement of galactic weight limits."

"How much was the infringement?"

"Fourteen tons."

My eyes almost popped. "Fourteen tons? Did someone miscalculate or something?"

"That was my first thought. I went through all the documentation several times but there was no mistake. Everything tallied with the weight we thought we were hauling. We even weighed the product, barrel by barrel and crate by crate but we couldn't find the extra fourteen tons. I got onto Vazien about it and he said he'd investigate it from his end. Four days later I got a notification that there had been a mistake by the stop and search crew and that our infringement notice was now invalid and could be forgotten."

"Did you believe that explanation?"

"I had no choice. The fine we escaped could have bankrupted us, so we decided to be grateful and carry on. Between ourselves, we thought Vazien was probably bribing someone to turn a blind eye."

"Or several someones," Tinnias remarked and I nodded.

"Yeah," Preataq replied. "There was much talk between us about what Vazien could be into, but no one dared ask him about it. At least not until the third time it happened."

"So that was not an isolated incident?" Tinnias said.

He shook his head. "No, it happened five times in all. Each time we were over by several tons. We'd get an infringement notice, I'd inform Vazien, and several days later everything would just go away. After the third time, a couple of my crew reported that the company was the subject of rumour and gossip among other haulage firms. They'd met some other haulage employees on their days off and found out that Jormla no longer enjoyed the spotless reputation we were used to. The gossip was that we would haul anything, however illegal it might be, if the money was right. When it started to affect the rest of the business, I became worried. We noticed our turnover falling, slowly at first, but then we lost four long term customers in one month and none of them would explain why they no longer wanted to deal with us. Even after I offered to lower the price, they refused to do business with us. It was after that loss I decided to speak with Vazien about it."

"How did that conversation go?" I asked.

"Not particularly well, as you can imagine if you know much about him. It started out civil enough, but when I tried to demand an explanation, he became threatening. He told me if it weren't for him, Jormla would still be a local outfit and that we should be grateful to him. Before he got two men to escort me off his property, he hinted that he could break the company as easily as he'd made it. He was right too, he had made us, financially anyway and without the money he paid us, I would have been forced to downsize the company considerably. We would have lost many staff, some real estate, and several ships. Add to this the fact that many employees enjoyed a certain lifestyle thanks to Vazien and I didn't want to be responsible for people losing their homes and being forced into poverty. I was in a horrible position and didn't know how to get out of it. I was the one who was keenest to get into the situation in the first place and now I was forced to watch my company name being dragged through shit and if I tried to do anything about it, a lot of people would suffer hardship."

"What happened in the end?" I asked. "I mean, I know your headquarters was bombed, but how and why did the end come?"

Preataq shrugged. "I had an emergency meeting with the other co-owners and discussed it. We had just had our fifth infringement notice, which again had been magically and mysteriously dealt with by Vazien, and we were all worried sick as to where this was leading the company. We talked for hours, argued the pros and cons of breaking with Vazien, the inevitable cut backs that would ensue and how we might recompense those staff affected. The result was a unanimous decision to tell Vazien that we were no longer prepared to do business with him. I called him and told him we needed his attendance at an emergency meeting and we told him together, all six of us."

"How did he react?"

"Surprisingly calmly actually. He reminded us that the ship he used would be taken by him as financial compensation and we agreed. Another run had already been scheduled for a week ahead, so we agreed to do this last run, after which we no longer wanted his business. He asked us to reconsider but we told him our decision was final. During the run, my engineering staff encountered a wiring problem that necessitated them removing some panelling from the cargo hold in order to access the appropriate electrical conduits for repair."

I grinned. "I can imagine."

He looked at me sideways. "Indeed. Anyway, during their efforts to make repairs, they discovered several hidden compartments built between the new outer hull Vazien had ordered be fitted, and the old outer hull that was still in place. The compartments were full of crates of weapons and ammunition."

"So the rumours are true after all," I said.

"That he's into illegal arms dealing? I'd say so, yeah."

"I don't suppose there's any chance of you proving these claims is there?" I said hopefully.

"Would Vidicom footage do?" He asked, smiling at my astonishment.

"It would do nicely. How did you get it?"

"I could never let go of the problem of how and why we had been so heavily overweight. It bugged me from the first time it happened and I wanted an explanation. We took the chief engineer into our confidence and asked him to do some digging. We had discussed the problem many times and the only thing we ever came up with as a possible explanation was hidden spaces behind panelling. Crazy as it sounded, it was the only thing we had a hope of investigating and as it was going to be our last chance, we took it. Turns out we hit the jackpot too. It was easy for the mechanics to produce a problem and as Vazien had never employed his own flight crew or engineers, it was down to us to fix it. Once they got the panels off it was simple to have a look around when the security guards weren't looking. By using a multi phase engineering camera that can look right through most metals, they saw the crates behind the inner panelling. When the security guards went to take their meal break, they got the panels off and had a good look around. It took no more than a minute or so to open the crates, take a look, reseal them, and put the panels back. By the time the next security team took over, the guys were busily changing a wiring connector."

"And you have it all on vidicom?"

"Yes. Dated, timed, the works. I'll fetch the data chip. Help yourself to some cake, my neighbour makes it for me." He got up and left the room, leaving us gaping at each other.

Tinnias helped himself to a large slice of cake. "You realise that helping us will put him in considerable danger. Vazien is a powerful man, his reach is long."

"We'll offer him safety with us, as we will with anyone prepared to testify," I said. "Lomas already said he can commandeer another battle cruiser for the sole purpose of harbouring our witnesses for as long as necessary. They will have full access to all on board facilities for the duration."

"That's great" he said. "I doubt we could hope to win this case without their help. I'm so glad we were wrong about them."

I nodded, "I'm with you on that, totally."

Once Preataq returned I bagged and tagged the data chip before asking him about the bombing. "How did the bombing come about?"

He smiled before answering. "He came to see me out of the blue about a month or so after that last run was over. We were in the process of downsizing, deciding which staff should go and which should stay etcetera, when he just turned up at headquarters one day and asked to see me. He asked me again to reconsider but I refused and told him I knew about the hidden compartments and the crates of arms. I was angry and told him I still hadn't decided whether or not to go to law enforcement about it."

"That wasn't the wisest decision you've ever made, my friend," Tinnias said.

Preataq nodded. "I know but it was the only way I could hit back. I didn't tell him about the vidicom though, I didn't want to put my engineering staff in danger."

"How did he respond?" I asked.

"He laughed it off at first, but then said he had so many friends everywhere that no one would believe me. He said if I knew how powerful he was, I would be more respectful and that if anything happened to my company or its staff as a result of trying to smear his name, it would be on my conscience."

"He directly threatened you with physical violence?"

"Yes. The vidicom footage of that conversation is on that chip I gave you, after the on-board footage."

"You filmed it?"

"After what was found on board the ship, we decided that every encounter with Vazien should be recorded."

"You should become a law enforcer," I said.

He grinned. "Anyway, eight days later, our headquarters was broken into one night. Nothing much was taken though, just a couple of digital consoles and some personal belongings. The next day was the first day of our annual audit, so everyone was on site. No one is allowed to take time off during the audit, so we had our complete staff compliment on site, apart from those who were in flight. Mid way through the morning, a bomb went off in one of the reception area offices. Thirty five died and twenty two more were injured. It blew up vertically and left a pear shaped hole right up through the centre of the first four floors of the building. That was the end of Jormla Inter-Galactic Haulage. With compensation claims by the families of the dead and injured, as well as claims by those companies who had business with us, we went under quickly. I split up what was left between the other co-owners and officially went out of business."

"You took nothing for yourself?" Tinnias asked.

"No. It didn't feel right. I felt responsible for the whole thing and to take any money seemed wrong when so many others had paid such a terrible price. I tried to do as much as I could for the families of the dead and injured but it wasn't much. I managed to pay for the funerals and got several families rehomed when the banks threatened to repossess, but that was all I could do. I had no money left; I even sold my own home to help pay some medical bills but when the money ran out, I was unable to do any more for them. My relatives let me live in this place as it's only used as a holiday home during part of the year and stands empty most of the time. I've been able to make it something of a going concern over the years too. I grow fruit and vegetables and sell them locally at markets and small produce stores. I supply a few restaurants with vegetables during the season as well. It's a complete change of pace and I like it. There is little stress now, and I have my two friends here for company."

"Are you willing to testify against Vazien?" I asked. "Knowing all that would entail for you, the risks and the real possibility of his getting away with everything no matter what we do?"

"Yes. I'll do whatever is necessary. Even if we lose at the end of it, I feel I owe it to my former staff members."

Everyone was delighted to know we had another definite testifier, and Lomas personally assured Preataq that when the time came, he would be welcomed aboard a Drycenian Battle Cruiser for safety. At first, he didn't want this, his concern for the two pets whose company he took such comfort in, his greatest priority, but with Lomas' promise that he would not be expected to be parted from them, he agreed. We watched the vidicom of the hidden cache of arms and gaped at the quantity of them.

"Hey, Dad, look." I hissed in amazement. "Those are Amberlight Canons. You can decapitate a man at a mile with one of those."

Tinnias shook his head. "He's no business giving such weapons to guerrilla fighters and primitive tribesmen. I won't even let my chase, catch, and deliver guys have them. Do you remember how you bent my ear begging for one when they first came out?"

I grinned. "I do. We could've done with one on Dracunya Prime eh Vincent?"

The big guy smiled as he remembered our adventure there, the trip that almost cost me my life, twice. "Yes it would've come in handy, but you had that awesome seven leaguer though. Do you still have that thing?"

Tinnias looked at me sideways. "You have a seven leaguer? Where ever did you come by that?"

I grinned at Vincent. "I do still have it. It's an antique and worth a fortune so I won't be getting rid of it anytime soon. I got it from a contact in the arms trade," I said, looking at Tinnias."

"Can I have his number, Son?"

"Where are we headed next, Sam?" Lomas asked, his finger poised over the button on the intercom.

## CHAPTER TWENTY THREE

Having wished Tinnias luck as he set off for another lesson in controlling the Drycenian Battle Board, I went for a smoke. I thought about the case and was pleased that we were able to gather promises of testimony and some good evidence at last. If everything progressed like this, we had a real chance of bringing Vazien to justice. I was so deep in my thoughts, of the case and my relationship with Byron, that I didn't at first hear my Unicom beeping. When I did, I shook myself out of my musing and answered it.

"Detective Sinclair-Vaylo."

Hi, Sam. Can you talk?" It was my contact, hopefully with the names of at least some law enforcement leaks working for the Dankera Collective. Maybe even some of Vazien's insiders too.

"Hey there, yeah. Do you have anything for me?"

"I do. You wanna write these names down?"

I grabbed my old fashioned notebook from my pocket. "Okay, shoot."

By the time I thanked him and ended the call, I had a list of ten names, together with their location. Two were Vazien's insiders. Seeing the two lists together and realizing that law enforcement had even that many leaks, dismayed me, but I was pleased that Sigma seemed to get off lightly. We had only one Gaht leak and no Dankera Collective or Vazien ones and I felt lucky. Tinnias would be pleased, I thought as my Unicom rang again.

"Sam, it's Kyle."

"Hey, what's up?"

"Are you busy?"

"No."

"Any chance you could come by our room as soon as possible. You weren't in your room and your Unicom was busy just now. We've been trying to get in touch."

I was immediately worried. "Is anything wrong?"

"No, don't worry," I heard the lightness in his tone and my anxiety lifted a little.

"I'm on my way."

The door to the room the Lileans shared was open, but I still knocked before I went in, shutting it behind me. I didn't want to offend them yet again. Vincent was speaking to someone on his Unicom. Kyle smiled at me and indicated for me to sit. I looked at him and frowned.

"What's wrong?" I whispered.

He grinned widely. "Nothing. How many more times are you going to ask me that?"

"Why all this cloak and dagger then?"

"How better to get the attention of a law man?"

I punched his shoulder and grinned.

"Yeah I know," Vincent was saying. "Try not to worry, everything will be fine, I promise. Listen, have I ever let you down? I'm passing over the Unicom now." He held out the unit to me. I gaped at it, then at him, then back at the proffered Unicom. Kyle nudged me, so I took it.

"Detective Sinclair-Vaylo," I said a little hesitantly.

"Hey, Sam, how are you feeling now?"

I sighed and closed my eyes. "Tip, hi. I'm err, fine I guess." I balled a fist and shook it dramatically at Vincent, who grinned shamelessly.

"Can we talk?" Tip asked quietly. "Please don't hang up on me again. I'm sorry for everything. When my guide told me you were heading for a tragedy, I couldn't let it pass. Our time together gave me some insight into you, and I knew you'd never agree to leave this case alone if we just asked you. Unfortunately, your stubborn nature made the lies our only option. Believe me when I tell you that I fought the decision hard, ask Vincent. I knew it would hurt you after everything you've experienced. I know it may sound weird, but even if you never stop hating me, at least I know you're alive and still able to change so many lives for the better like you do every day. You're safe and that's the main thing, even if you never forgive me."

"I forgive you, absolutely," I said quickly. "I went off the rails but I'm getting back on track now, and no doubt in the future I'll look back and realise how much this taught me and it will probably change me for the better. I had no idea how much of a wreck I was, so this has at least taught me that." Out of the corner of my eye, I saw Vincent shake his head.

I heard Tip sniff and realised he was struggling with his emotions. "I'm so glad to hear that, Sam. Without your friendship, I'd still be someone evil, hurting innocent folks. You put everything on the line for me so I could change my life, I can't lose your friendship, I just can't."

"Hey, you did the work back then, not me. There was a time when I was in a situation that made it seem as if everything I'd come to believe about my life was broken before my eyes. I was given the chance to change my life, but even though I knew it would have made things easier, I didn't have the courage to take the opportunity. You were the strong one, Tip, not me. At the end of the day, all I did was hang around and get in the way."

"I would argue with you on that point, Sam, but thank you, for everything. I'm so relieved we're still friends. When I was first warned about your imminent involvement, I hoped maybe it would turn out to be wrong, that something else would turn up to distract you, but when you turned up here on Tyrrin, my heart sank. I've been hunting Vazien and his Gaht connection for quite a while and now the danger is passed, I'm glad you're on board and helping."

"You know you've several leaks at the Tyrrin Headquarters, I presume? Both for Gaht and the Dankera Collective. Do you want a list of names?"

"Yes please. I know of one other Gaht leak. I'm supposed to liaise with him sometimes, to get information passed to the Gaht top brass. I'm not party to information about who else may be on their payroll though."

I fished in my pocket for the list and read him the four names relevant to the Tyrrin Headquarters. "Be careful, Tip, don't get them suspicious or you could be in danger. We're too far away to be of much help at the moment."

"I will, thanks for this, Sam. I'm sorry for getting Vincent and Kyle to gang up on you like this, but I was so worried and you wouldn't talk to me. Your silence was painful for me, Lileans do things differently."

"I'll get them both to educate me," I promised. "I'm sorry I hurt you."

"I forgive you. Let's start over huh?"

"Yeah, great idea."

"I have to go now, I'm on duty in a half hour. Good luck with your side of things. I love you, Bro."

"I love you too, be safe, Tip." I ended the call and handed the Unicom back to Vincent. "Thank you."

"You're not angry at us?" Kyle asked.

"No, the longer things went without contact, the harder it was to make contact to fix things. You know me, when life fucks you around, run away."

"He was suffering too," Vincent said, "but he's far away and on his own. I was worried for him."

"Yeah I know, I was a selfish asshole," I nodded.

"No you weren't, you were feeling trapped and reacted to defend yourself," Kyle said.

"His turnaround was all down to his own hard work, I did nothing, but I'm flattered he thinks so."

"Don't say you did nothing," Vincent said. "You understood, you still understand. Never underestimate that. It's a huge deal."

"I never thought of it that way," I replied.

"Then promise me you'll try. Shall we go and see if the troopers are free to give us some firearms training?"

"Oh yeah, great idea," Kyle said.

"I really need it," I grinned. "Judging by my performance during the laser battle. How emasculating that was."


"Remember to breathe, guys," Byron reminded us. "Don't over think it, the gun is an extension of yourself, a part of you. You know instinctively how to aim, you can do it instantly, just lift your arm and fire. Know you'll find your target, don't for a moment question it. It should just be like pointing at the target, the firearm should feel such a natural part of you."

He drilled us for hours and we soaked up the training like hungry children. I knew right away it was making a positive difference and would make my job that much safer. The troopers set up a system of holographic emitters and with piles of crates and all manner of other stuff, had a course set up for the three of us to make our way through. We were in our element and would have happily remained there until well into the night. It was with some reluctance that we thanked them and helped clear the cargo hold before deciding to go for a sauna before dinner.

Tinnias and several troopers were already in there when we entered. I grinned at my father's bright red face as he wiped the sweat that dripped from the end of his nose.

"You look well cooked, Dad," I said.

"I feel it, Son. This better be good for me or I'm going to be mighty annoyed."

"How's the battle board going?" Vincent asked. "You still enjoying it?"

"I love it," he replied with a grin. "I want one, I so want one."

The troopers laughed. "Everyone says that," one of them said.

"All three of us said it too," I admitted.

"Dream on, Pop," Kyle replied with a snigger.

"How's the ass?" Vincent asked. "You want me to get you a cushion?"

"I've only fallen twice today."

"That's awesome," I laughed. "I'm proud of you."

During dinner, we discussed the rest of our visiting schedule.

"We arrive at the Glarian system tomorrow evening," I said. The two groups of tribesmen are working different mines. Byron found out earlier today while researching their exact location."

"How far apart are they?" Kyle asked.

"Several hours shuttle flight," Byron replied.

"Shit," Tinnias said. "So we stay here for longer or split up."

"Yeah," I nodded.

"What's it like down there?" Vincent asked.

"It's pretty primitive," Grund said. "There's no military, no Law Enforcement Agency outpost, no space travel apart from that brought in by off worlders like us. The people live simply but they're a little reserved. Not unfriendly exactly, they just keep themselves to themselves until directly approached by off worlders. Don't offend them though, they hold grudges."

"Would you say Sam would need armed escorts down there?" Tinnias asked. "We're going to have to split up to get both visits done in good time."

"Well I'd feel happier if he wasn't alone, let's put it that way," Byron replied, "but he can probably do fine without a group of heavily armed troopers. I'll get a couple of volunteers and we'll go with him. You'll take a couple with you too. The three of you would be fine. Just keep to yourselves and be polite when forced to interact. Always keep in mind that you're visitors down there and don't touch anyone. They're not touchy feely like we are."

"Okay, that's fine," Tinnias nodded. "So which one should we do? The Lakshwel are in a built up area, the Viralong are out in the wilds."

"We'll take the rural route," I replied and Tinnias nodded.

"Fine. Here's a note of their names and work duties. You'll have to use your initiative when working out how to get to them, but you can keep in touch with us for help if need be. If things go to shit, get back here, okay?"

"Okay," I nodded. "Now I'm going for a smoke."

Byron and I sat in the smoking room and discussed possible scenarios for the next couple of days. We didn't foresee any real problems but we knew it would be sensible to be prepared for anything. Tinnias entered and puffed gently on his cigarette.

"How's it going, Boys?"

"Fine," Byron said. "We don't foresee any problems, but you never know, things can get fucked up very quickly."

"Especially when I'm involved," I said.

Tinnias laughed loudly and was about to reply when the intercom buzzed. "Samelan, come to the medical bay please."

"Jam," I said. "I wonder what's up." I pondered as I kissed Byron and ran from the room.

"Hello, Sam, come on in."

"Anything wrong, Doc?" I said.

"No, I thought you'd like to meet your friend, Klackan."

"He's okay now?" I asked.

"He is," Jam nodded. "He's through here, follow me." He led the way through a door and I hardly recognised the man who looked back at me. The lifeless grey skin and sunken eyes were gone, replaced by a new and vibrant energy. Life raced around his veins and arteries, his strength now obvious, where once he was as weak as a child as he stared death in the face. I was amazed.

"Wow, Doc, you're a miracle worker. How are you feeling now, Klackan?" I asked as I reached for his hand.

We talked for several minutes, which he spent mostly thanking everyone for giving him his health back. When I saw him yawn, I left him to sleep and stole quietly away.

"Doc," I said, taking his hand. "You amaze me more every day. You're one special guy, thank you."

Tinnias was delighted when I reported back. "You should see him, I hardly recognised him."

"That's great news," he grinned. "I'll go and say hello later."

We said our goodbyes and promised to keep in touch via Unicom. Once the shuttle bay doors were open, I lifted off the pad and headed out into the void, three volunteer troopers in another shuttle behind us. Once we were clear of the battle cruiser, I arced down towards the planet below. Although confident that without having space travel themselves, the chances of them having any sort of sophisticated trackers and scanners was slim, I engaged the covert module anyway, just to be sure. After traveling at high altitude for over an hour, I lowered the nose and headed down.

"The nearest and safest place to land is about a mile from the mine," I said. "There's some abandoned buildings and lots of trees, so we can disguise the ships quite easily."

"There, that large building to the left," Byron pointed. "There's enough room for us both in there?"

It was a bit of a squeeze but we managed to park up, side by side, under cover and hidden from view.

"Nicely done, Sam. You're an expert pilot."

"I've been doing it a long time, and I know my girl well," I smiled, patting the flight console tenderly. "Now let's find some brush to fill the doorway."

Once we were satisfied the ship was well hidden, I got out the information on the two Viralong men we were here to talk to and looked at the photographs. Their faces were slim, almost to the point of being bony, the lack of fat making their noses and chins seem abnormally long. The eyes were small, round, and gave them a squinting appearance. They made me feel uncomfortable for some reason, and I wasn't sure it was merely their appearance. For several minutes I gazed at the photos, but the feeling refused to go away. Eventually I shook my head, sighed deeply, and got up.

"What's up?" Byron asked as I paced.

"It's just…" I began, then shook my head and continued pacing. "Maybe it's only…"

"Come on," he encouraged, "spit it out, Bro."

"My gut is twitching like hell, which means something's wrong here. I was fine until I saw their photographs," I said. "Then it all went to shit and now I'm anxious. Ren told me this is when he's trying to tell me to be careful."

"Let's sit tight and see how we feel in the morning," Byron said. I agreed, so we decided to relax for the evening.

"I wonder if the hunting is any good around here," I said when I saw Byron fishing through my stash of military ration packs. "I couldn't face curried

Boghorn for anything. Let's see if there's any hunting first, then if we strike out, I'll have the Boghorn."

"Okay," Byron nodded.

An hour later, our bellies grumbled as the smell of roasting meat teased our nostrils. We found to our delight that there seemed to be an abundance of a good sized creature with long ears and sandy coloured fur, and a lake nearby offered us impressive fish. I was all for catching a fish to compliment the meat, and Byron nodded his agreement.

"We don't have any fishing equipment though," he said.

I kissed him and grinned. "Watch this and be amazed, my love." I lay down by the side of the lake and slowly lowered my hands into the water amongst a clump of leafy plants that swayed in the gentle current. Twenty minutes of jokes and taunts later, I made Byron and the troopers jump when I suddenly turned on my back and held my hands above me, the large fish flailing in my grasp.

"Holy fucking shit," a trooper exclaimed.

"That's incredible," said another.

"You never cease to amaze me, Bro," Byron laughed.

"You have to teach us how to do that," the third trooper begged.

The meat and fish were delicious and our hunt was successful enough that we had plenty for all of us to fill our bellies, and some left over for the next day. When it got dark, we put out the fire and Byron set the troopers onto a watch rota, each taking a four hour watch and sleeping in the spare shuttle. Glad to be alone at last, Byron and I went back to the ship, locking ourselves securely inside. I checked my armoury, wondering whether to take anything, and if so, what. I decided laser pistols would be the best choice and locked the cabinet.

I noticed Byron had been quiet and a bit introverted for most of the evening. "You okay, Bro?" I asked, sitting down beside him. "You seem quiet, anything wrong?" I heard him sigh and knew it was time to address the events surrounding my sudden disappearance. I put an arm around his shoulder, drew him towards me and kissed his cheek. "I'm so sorry I made you suffer so much. Ren told me what happened. Please talk to me about it."

"Hold me, Sam, Just hold me." I held onto him tightly without saying a word.

When he was able to talk, he looked at me with his lovely yellow eyes. "I don't know how to make it better," I said.

"I got your letter, and although I understood what you were trying to say, I was shocked that you could leave so easily and without talking to me about how you were feeling. It was like you didn't trust me to understand your feelings. I felt like I was in the way and that you'd be fine whether we stayed together or not. I did understand you were struggling because of the lies, and I hated every moment of having to be a part of that. I felt like I'd pushed you away and wanted to come after you and make you understand the truth so you would give me another chance."

"Shit," I hissed. "What I wanted to say came out all wrong. I was trying to let you know that if you decided you didn't want me, that I wouldn't make trouble for you or stalk you like a psycho or anything. I wanted to tell you that I would try to understand and accept it if you hated me, although I'd be an emotional wreck for the rest of my life. I worry that you're torn between being loyal to your people, and being loyal to me, that you'd resent me for putting a wedge between you and them. I do admit that I'm still learning to let my feelings out freely. After a lifetime of protecting myself and losing family and friends to this damned job, I became expert at not allowing my feelings their full voice or expression. I'm still learning that bit and it will take a bit of time to learn to do it right and express things properly."

"I do understand that, Sam. It's not just you now though, there are two of us in this relationship."

"I'm so sorry. How do I make it hurt less for you?"

"By talking to me rather than just leaving when my back is turned. Tell me how you feel, don't just act without speaking. You don't have to let our relationship get in the way of your job, just as I'll never let my people get in the way either, they never have to, but we need to maintain this together. Please don't do that ever again, it nearly killed me and I'll never be able to forget those feelings."

"And don't let me forget either," I said. "Never forgive me, ever. I made a mistake and hurt you and that hurts me."

"How can I not forgive you? I love you."

"When Ren told me, I suddenly understood the chilly atmosphere when we returned. I knew everyone had lost faith in me, but now I understand why. They all love you very much, never forget that. Even if I give you cause for doubt, they won't. Don't ever think no one cares."

He nodded. "I know I'm very lucky to have such a nice family feeling with the people I work with. I never take that for granted."

I was aware of guilt coming up behind me, wrapping its arms around me like the familiar friend that it's always been, and mentally sighed with despair. I was at a total loss as to what to say, so I held Byron close and we clung to each other without speaking. I was not going to complain about the guilt this time, I knew I deserved it. After almost half an hour, I took hold of his hand and led him to my modest bedroom. We deserved an early night, I decided.


A cold breeze woke me and I shivered, looked around and found myself in an icy landscape. I was naked and wrapped my arms around myself as my teeth began to chatter, my breath clouds quickly turning to fine icy dust and falling to my feet.

"Shit, where am I?" I stammered, unable to speak properly as my jaws rattled against each other.

"You are inside your heart," the voice answered, making me jump almost out of my skin. I didn't recognise the voice; it certainly wasn't Ren's. It was female for one thing.

"Who's there?" I called.

"I am here to admonish you, Samelan Sinclair," she said, appearing before me at last. She was a mature woman with an elegant and upright beauty. Her silver hair was piled atop her head and the red velvet coat that brushed her ankles looked startling against the white landscape around us.

"Who are you? Where is Ren?" I was immediately suspicious.

"I am here because the bond he shares with you prevents him from saying those things I am about to say."

"He's never been shy of telling me his honest feelings before," I replied.

"Well he is now. You made a grave mistake Samelan and hurt your lover more than he would ever deserve. He suffered when there was no need. You caused him pain so soon after bringing him the joy of new, deep love, and the tears he shed were painful."

"I know," I whispered quietly. "I know and I'm deeply sorry. I can't take it back and make it better and I don't know how to fix it."

"You could try understanding his pain."

My head snapped up, anger flashing through me unbidden. "What? You think I don't know pain? You really believe my life has been one long party? My parents died when I was nine years old and I had no one to look after me, to explain, or care about my wellbeing. No one cared that I'd been hurt more than I deserved. My girlfriend was murdered in the most awful way and I found her body, after being forced to listen to her being raped and shot, to hear her screaming for me. There was no one to care for me as I grieved. My only friend was murdered in my arms and once again it was me who was left to grieve alone with no one to hold me as I cried. Don't you dare lecture me about pain and suffering. I know how Byron felt because I've felt the same so many times and that makes it even worse for me because I should know better. Even then, I still made the mistake anyway and now I have the guilt and the worry that he'll leave me because of it. You know what then? There'll I'll be, alone again with no one to give a flying fuck."

"And what would have made things easier for you to bare, Samelan Sinclair? In all those circumstances, how would you have coped better?"

"By having someone with me, even though they couldn't go back and change things. Just to be there with me, to listen to my ramblings and self pity, to hold me and let me know they cared even though they were powerless to change things. To lend me their strength when I had none. There's nothing more that could've been done except to let me know I didn't have to be lonely as well as alone."

"Don't you think Byron deserves those things?"

"Of course I do, and I'm trying to do all of that and more. I guess I didn't realise how badly he'd cope. I thought he would be able to be more objective and understand without so much emotion. I never knew he was such an emotional man; the Drycenians always seem so calm and understanding. I was wrong, completely wrong and I hate myself for it, and I know it doesn't matter a fuck to anyone but I suffered too. Every day we were apart I worried for him, missed him, fretted about how he would be feeling. I felt lost without him, like part of me was missing. Remember this, lady, I was the one who was lied to here and he was a part of those lies too. The way the Drycenians and Lileans were behaving made it clear to us that they were involved in the crimes and we knew what that meant for the galaxy. Believe me, bitch, those two races are probably the most powerful and able out there and if they decide to work against the law for a change, we're fucking screwed. No one thought I deserved the truth, that maybe I would be able to understand if they'd just been honest. Oh no, Samelan can't handle the truth, let's lie to him and give him the run around just to be complete dicks so he goes around in circles and disappears up his own asshole. Yes, I hurt my lover, I hate myself for it, I'll never be able to make it right or make up for it and I might very well lose him over it, but I was lied to and not trusted with the truth. Despite that, I'm still trying to hold onto his love and fix it any way I can because I won't be able to function without his love. How dare you tell me off like a five year old? You know fuck all." I turned my back and walked away, not knowing or caring where I was going.

"Bro? please don't leave me." Ren's voice came to me loud and clear."

"Not now." I yelled and walked on.

I leapt awake and cried out into the darkness and it was several seconds before I realised where I was. I was in my bunk on my ship, Byron beside me, his face riven with concern, having been woken by the commotion.

"Whatever's the matter, my love?" he asked, running his hands through my hair and holding me. "You were crying out and flailing around like you were having the fight of your life. I was so worried."

"I'm sorry for the fuss," I replied as I fought to control my breathing. "Just a nightmare. I have them sometimes, from the stress. Thank you for being here," I kissed him and we held each other.

"What was it about?" he asked.

"Everything was ice, like the polar ice caps and I was naked and freezing. Some woman appeared and started telling me off like a little kid. I gave her a few home truths and then I woke up."

"Telling you off?"

"Yeah, like I was a naughty school kid or something. Fucking bitch. I was so angry; how dare she talk to me like that?"

"Who was she? Did you recognise her?"

I shook my head. "Nope. She looked like a stuffed up school teacher who hadn't been laid for a decade."

There was a long moment of silence then as one, we both burst out laughing.


I awoke first and reached for the two photographs of the Viralong men we were supposed to be meeting and found to my delight that I no longer felt any danger as I gazed at them. The faces stared back at me and I felt no darkness within, no heaviness in my gut. Suddenly, the photographs were ripped out of my hands as Byron flung them to the floor and reached for my groin. Later, once showered and dressed and preparing breakfast, I told him of the photographs.

"I wonder what was wrong last night then," he said.

"I've no idea but it's fine now, whatever it was."

After breakfast, we armed ourselves and locked the ship down before setting off towards the mine. It didn't take us long to make the journey, within half an hour we saw the tower looming ahead and stopped to scope the place out for a few minutes.

"There's a guard on the gate," I said, handing the scope to Byron, who looked, then passed it to the troopers.

"He's not armed though," Byron said. "Not that I can see, anyway."

"That's good," I replied.

"So we just turn up at the gate, smile sweetly and ask for…what's his name?"

I nodded. "Carlmond Zibrathnil Deya de-Symblont Heilemil Wolmla."

"Excuse me?" Byron said. The troopers and I burst out laughing.

"Mind you," one trooper continued, "with that nose he can probably smell us from here so he'll most likely be waiting for us."

Once I'd managed to control myself and wiped the tears of laughter from my face, I scowled. "Stop it, I have to interview him and keep a straight face."

"Sorry," he giggled. "I couldn't help myself. That's one heck of an organ though isn't it?"

"Oh please," I begged, almost choking with the effort of trying not to laugh.

"It's almost as big as my cock," Byron hissed and we all laughed until our stomachs ached and not until we were spent did I dare venture further towards the mine. The man on the gate came towards us as we approached and I smiled.

"What name?" he demanded. "Why you here?"

"I'm here to speak with this man." I held out a piece of paper on which was written the impossibly difficult name of one of the men I was to interview."

"You are Sam?" he asked and I nodded.

"Yes, I am Sam."

"He waits for you, come, I show you."

## CHAPTER TWENTY FOUR

I rang Tinnias and told him of our progress. "We've got one interview done but the second guy is on holiday and won't be back at work until tomorrow. He's told us to return tomorrow mid morning, so we're here for another night."

"Okay, thanks for letting me know. How did the interview go, anything new?"

"He said he saw Vazien with at least three different mistresses. The same three faces kept appearing at the mine, one of them he recognised as the daughter of a tribal leader from another Zibandin tribe. He said he knew her because he always wanted her himself. He also showed far too great a working knowledge of firearms for a relatively primitive tribesman. I showed him photographs of various guns and he knew their make and model, capacity, firing rate, everything. He took us out the back of the mine office and showed us a firing range he'd set up with metal cans. He used his own fully automatic laser pistol with extra capacity magazine, extended barrel, and triple strength laser power pack, which sported the name, 'Qelmid Lod Arms' on the grip. He confirmed Vazien gave it to him."

"Holy shit," Tinnias said. "He surely can't know about Vazien's companies, so that is good evidence, if we can prove it."

"The guy can neither read nor write, so he's certainly not read about it on any company memos."

"Awesome, Sam."

"How did you do with the Lakshwel guys?"

"One of them kept a list of everything Vazien gave to them, along with the date it was given. There are seven large shipments of arms in all, each one more powerful than the last. He confirmed that Vazien abandoned Zibandin when the mines ran dry, and offered them no further help with the fighting, nor any recompense when their sacred sites were destroyed. He just ran away and left them to get on with it. When they begged him for help, he told them they could go and work for him at other mines, for no pay. He told them their payment would be somewhere to live and a meal each day. They turned him down and when they were banished by the other tribal leaders, they hitched rides on military ships, worked their passage, and found work where they could."

"Shit. People are just another commodity to him, to be used and thrown away. I really hate assholes like that. No compassion for anyone, not even family. I'll bet his daughter wasn't kidnapped at all. I bet you she ran away. That wager is still on by the way. Fifty says she legged it."

I heard him laugh at the other end and it lightened the mood a little. "Keep in touch, Son. Have you had any cause for concern so far?"

"None so far," I lied, winking at Byron, who grinned and shook a finger at me.

"Okay, thank you guys. I appreciate you."

"We'll keep in touch, I promise," I said.

"Yes, please do. Be safe, all of you."

I ended the call and smiled. "Thanks for not ratting me out, he worries too much."

"How did your natural parents die?" he asked.

"There was a bomb on the Puntileno Bridge and they were halfway across when it went off. Their car plunged two hundred feet into the sea below and was buried beneath several other cars caught up in the blast. I was one week from my ninth birthday."

"Shit, I'm sorry for your loss, Bro. Have you met them, since you've had Ren with you?"

"Not yet."

"You will. Ren will know when it's the right time and arrange it for you."

"I'll probably be a wreck that day," I grinned and we laughed.

"I was, when I saw mine for the first time. It's a good emotion though, despite being so strong. The healing is amazing, you wait and see."

"What happened to your parents," I asked. "If you don't mind telling me."

""There was a shuttle crash. It was landing and there was something wrong. It crashed into the crowd that was waiting for it. My parents were going up to the battle cruiser for a party, so they were amongst them. They weren't the only ones to die, thirteen died and twenty were injured, five lost limbs. I wasn't the only orphan that day."

"I'm sorry, my love." I hugged him close and kissed the tear that ran down his cheek. "I guess you didn't really understand much about it, being so young."

"No. All I knew was that they never came back. I'd been sent round to Lomas and Siska's for the evening. The royal nanny was babysitting Toma and as we were friends with the royal family, I often went there to play or to be babysat, and Toma often came to us for the same reasons. All I knew was that I was taken there to be looked after while they went to the party, but I never left. Lomas decided to take over guardianship of me and I grew up with his children."

"Where you happy in his family?"

"Yes and no. It wasn't that I was unhappy with his family. They loved me and gave me a lovely life and I loved them, but my real parents had left me and not come back and I didn't know why. It was a few years before I was old enough to be given the details. Up until then, they just said they were living in Rashnorgian, which is our word for the afterlife. I couldn't understand the concept of the afterlife and them being invisible, and they kept saying they still loved me. I would always ask them why they left me if they loved me, and of course, they couldn't answer in a way a five year old would understand and accept. Once I was old enough to be given the details, I understood why they never returned and was able to come to terms with it."

"Did anyone help you as you dealt with it?" I asked, holding his hand.

"Oh yes, it's the rules. When I joined flight school, I was required to see a counsellor to make sure I was in a settled place emotionally. I'd never have got off the ground if I'd refused and I really wanted to be aboard a battle cruiser, Lomas' one in particular. I thought it would be a waste of time and I did it to get into flight school, but as it turned out, it helped enormously."

"That's good. You don't call Lomas, Dad though."

"No, it's not our way. Although an adoptive parent does the job the real parent did, we never call them father and mother. Our belief is that in doing so, we'd be disrespecting our real parents who gave us our life. Things were a lot stricter in the time when those kinds of rules were brought in and although times have changed, some of them stuck. Have you noticed that he always says I'm like a son but he never says I am his son?"

"Yes, he's said it a couple of times since I came aboard."

"That's because of the same rule. I can't claim royal status, nor any privileges royal status gives, unless he decrees it officially. I couldn't be his heir either, not that I would want to be. Can you imagine the furore with a king who was in a same gender relationship? Man, that would be embarrassing."

"Is that not allowed then?" I asked.

"No. It's the only rule about gender and sexual preference we have. The King must take a wife and produce children to continue the line. He could have a male lover but he would have to be extremely discreet. He wouldn't be allowed to take part in any official events or benefit in any way from his relationship with the King. He would be required to disappear, effectively. Having been part of the royal household, I know how intrusive and controlling royal protocol can be. It would put an enormous strain on a relationship having to be almost totally invisible, like a ghost."

"What a nightmare situation?"

"Indeed. Now who's turn is it to cook?"

"Yours actually," I grinned, "but I'm happy to help."

"Thank you. By the way, I dreamed of Ren last night, after your nightmare."

I was immediately on my guard. "Really? What happened?"

He told me we have to find Vazien's daughter because she has information that will help us."

"That's helpful. I don't suppose he told you where she can be found, did he?" I asked.

He shook his head. "Sorry, he just said her past will lead us to her."

"They're always so damned cryptic," I said and he grinned.

"I guess we do some research tomorrow then," he said as he cut slices off the remainder of the meat we stored from the day before.


Our second interview provided us with some very interesting and helpful information. This man decided early in Zibandin's relationship with Vazien, to make detailed records of everything. He gave us a complete timeline of the Ambassador's entire history in connection with the planet and its inhabitants. He even secretly met with a few other tribal leaders and got information from them. During the interview, the first man we'd seen the day before was present, so we were able to discuss with them both about what would happen when it came to court. Both agreed to testify and expressed interest in spending time aboard a space ship without having to work for their bed and board. I told them not to tell a living soul about our conversation and to wait for a further call.

"This has been a productive visit, don't you think?" I remarked as we unlocked the ship and began clearing the brush from the open side of the building under which we'd sheltered.

"Yes, very. I'm quite enjoying being a temporary law enforcer's side kick," he grinned.

I kissed him. "There's nothing temporary about you, Bro, remember that."


"What's our next destination?" he asked as I gently manoeuvred the ship from the cover of the building and lifted her up into the sky.

"Qaigon 7," I replied. "Captain Listler from Solar 3 lives there."

"That's Earth isn't it?"

"Yeah."

"Be careful with him, Sam. I'm sure you already know, having been there yourself, but they are a reserved and mistrusting people."

I nodded. "I learned the truth of that the hard way."

"How does this man fit in with the case," he asked. "I'm beginning to lose track of all these connections. How do you manage, Sam?"

I grinned. "You get used to it. I've been doing this a long time and I learned years ago to use my mind like a filing system when it comes to work stuff. That way, I know every bit of information and can call upon it when I need it. It's hard to explain but it works for me. Plus I keep detailed records of course, the legal system requires it. As for Listler, he was accused of cowardice and court martialled."

"Oh yes, I remember you mentioning it."

"Then we have an ex-mistress and some … oh fuck, I totally forgot. How stupid of me."

"What's up?"

"Huh? Oh, it's just that I forgot about the neighbours. I've spent hell knows how many days with the Lileans around and I forgot about the neighbours."

"What neighbours?" Byron frowned.

"When Tinnias and I went back to Tyrrin after leaving you last time, we found out about Taiko and decided to check out his wife and see what she could tell us."

"So?"

"We got there and there was no answer, but a neighbour called to us and told us the wife and kids had gone on holiday."

"Why is that important?"

"Because she said they were holidaying on Lilea. She can't have been mistaken as she made a comment about the whispering trees, how beautiful they are. Tinnias and I assumed they were with you and that accounted for your unfriendliness towards us."

"Oh. How totally odd."

"I meant to ask Vincent and Kyle but completely forgot until now. I was going to say we have another neighbour of Vazien's to interview too. That reminded me."

"Maybe they are there," Byron said and shrugged. "They're not the only Lileans in existence. Maybe they truly do have friends there."

"But Taiko isn't there," I said. "I know that because we talked to him on Dankera 7. I don't know where his wife and kids are though, they could be there. It just struck us as an odd coincidence, especially after we'd just had such a hostile encounter with Vincent."

"And you took it as further evidence that they were involved in totally the wrong way."

"Well, yeah. You can't be angry with me. At that point, I'd only met you all once before, and Vincent spent the entire time calling me a Merc and making me feel like I was in the way of his search."

"I'm not angry," he said. "Did he really make you feel that way?"

"Yes, it pissed me right off too."

"It's no excuse for rudeness but he was so consumed with worry about Gabriel."

"Of course it's a valid reason," I replied. "They don't have to apologise."

"Maybe it was a way of saying Tip was involved."

"But why would a neighbour know about Tip, and then go to such lengths to be cryptic?"

"But maybe the wife said it to the neighbour, meaning Tip."

"But why be cryptic like that to just a neighbour?" I replied. "It makes no sense whichever way we try to explain it. No, the only way it makes sense is if it's true and they did go to Lilea on holiday."

Tinnias came running up to the hatch as soon as the shuttle was safe. "Hey there guys, are you all still in one piece?"

"We're fine, Dad," I replied and we man hugged. "I have some great information for everyone."

"And a weird conundrum," Byron added.

"Oh?" Tinnias frowned. "Let's get to the Obs Room and debrief. Or would you rather take a while to relax first?"

"Let's get right into it while it's still fresh," I said and followed Tinnias out of the shuttle bay.

Once the reintroductions were done, Lomas called the room to order. "Okay everyone, what do we have from Glarian to add to the file?"

"My first interview was straightforward," Tinnias replied. "He confirmed Vazien sold them arms, each load being more powerful than the last, and then he suddenly stopped giving them anymore and disappeared from Zibandin. The second interview was more productive. He had been keeping a list of all the shipments of arms given by Vazien, with the dates they were given and what type and model of weapons they were. I have the list here," he held up a sheet of paper he'd bagged and tagged for evidence. "Each shipment is quite a bit more powerful than the previous one, but the number of items in each shipment went down each time. There were seven shipments in all. He confirmed that after Vazien left, several of their sacred sites fell into a large sinkhole that appeared one night. He told me he had stayed up late discussing the problem with some friends when they heard a loud bang that shook the ground, after which the sinkhole appeared."

"A loud bang?" I said. "That sounds more like a bomb to me."

"Me too," Tinnias said. "He gave me a soil sample from around the hole. Their religion says they must always pray on their ancestral soil, so they took a bag of it when they were banished." He held up six small pots of soil he'd bagged and tagged. "There's another pot I didn't bag and tag. Byron, you can have that one to analyse."

"Sure, no problem," Byron replied.

"Awesome, Dad," I nodded. "You'd make a fine law enforcer."

He grinned. "That's praise indeed O Great One."

"Well my interviews were productive too," I said. "The first one was a man who confirmed that he saw Vazien with at least three different mistresses, one of whom he recognised especially because for a long time he'd wanted her for himself. He also seemed to have far too great a working knowledge of firearms for a relatively primitive tribesman. He showed us a small firing range he'd set up behind his office building, with a few metal cans as targets and demonstrated great skill, in our opinion. I showed him pictures of various firearms and he was able to identify them all, along with the capacity, firing rate, range etcetera. His own weapon was a very modern and fully automatic laser pistol with extra capacity magazine, extended barrel, and triple strength laser power pack. Along the back of the grip, was the inscription, Qelmid Lod Arms, and he confirmed Vazien gave it to him."

"But couldn't he have found out Vazien owns Qelmid Lod Arms and just said he gave it to him," Toma asked. "I don't believe that by the way, but we have to prove it beyond doubt or the case could fall apart."

I grinned. "He can neither read nor write," I said. "He couldn't sign the declaration of intent to testify with anything other than a thumb print."

"That's awesome evidence," Byron smiled.

"Our second interview was just as informative," I continued. "This guy gave us a complete timeline of Vazien's entire history in connection with the planet and its inhabitants." I held up a bundle of papers with scrawled handwriting on them, which I'd carefully bagged and tagged. "He even secretly met with a few other tribal leaders and got information from them. During the interview, the first man we'd seen the day before was present, so we were able to discuss with them both about what would happen when it came time to testify. Both agreed to testify and expressed interest in spending time aboard a space ship without having to work for their bed and board. I told them not to tell a living soul about our conversation and to wait for a further call. I hope I didn't say the wrong thing, Your Majesty."

"You did exactly the right thing, Sam. I'll call later today to confirm everything you told them and let them know I'll call when it's time for a trial."

"We're on course for Qaigon 7," Byron said, "and I have Listler's address in my locator unit. He lives right in the middle of a busy city, so you and Tinnias will have to go alone I'm afraid. There's just no way for us to be there without being noticed."

"No problem," Tinnias replied. "A large city offers us the kind of cover that open countryside doesn't."

"How do you mean?"

"Anonymity," I said and Tinnias nodded. "Two men are instantly lost within a large crowd, especially when they dress and behave normally. You'd be surprised how little notice people take of each other."

"I never thought of that," Lomas said.

"How long until we get there?" I asked.

"Well … "Lomas began, then shared a look with Byron, who grinned.

"What's wrong?" I said. "Come on, spit it out."

"Under normal circumstances, the journey would take us eighteen days and several hours, but if we were to umm, well if we …"

"Not a tube system," I hissed in horror. "Oh shit, I'm gonna drown in a sea of puke." Tube systems are very new technology, invented by three of the most technologically advanced races known, one of which is the Drycenians. They make the journey between two places in space, shorter by bending space somehow, the science of it is way beyond me. It dramatically shortens travel time, but the side effect is extreme nausea and vomiting when you come out of the tube at the other end.

"Now, Sam, don't panic, please." Jam said, having entered with Klackan, who was now able to be up and around. "First of all, I'd like everyone to welcome Klackan, who is now feeling much better so I've let him out of bed for a while."

"Lomas went over to Klackan and shook his hand. "Hello, my friend. I'm King Lomas VII and you're most welcome. Make yourself completely at home, I assure you that Jam is the best doctor this side of blue hypergiant S378B."

"You're all so kind," Klackan said meekly. "I'd forgotten how it felt to be well. Thank you for giving me my life back."

"Sit, help yourself to refreshments," Lomas said. "No need to wait to be invited, just leap right in before it's all gone."

"Next," Jam continued. "I can reassure you, Sam, that you won't suffer as you probably have done before. We are working on this technology all the time and things have moved forward sufficiently for us to be able to prevent the nausea, or at least eighty percent of it or so. If you really can't face it, we can always go via the shipping lanes, but it is a long trip. The choice is yours."

"I'll hold your hair back, Bro," Byron said and everyone laughed.

"Oh all right then," I said. "If I suffer, it's you I'm coming after, Doc."

"Wonderful," Lomas grinned. "So in two days and a couple of hours we'll be at the tube system entryway. Being co-inventors means we won't have to pay, so that's a further bonus. Travelling time in the tube is umm, how long Byron?"

"Nine hours, Sir."

"Right. So we have two days in which to relax."

Tinnias decided to ask to do some tether flying, so Lomas accompanied him, while Vincent, Kyle, Byron, and I, had another laser battle followed by some Drycenian firearms training. I was pleased with my performance this time; the training having helped re-sharpen my skills as a marksman.


The tube system entryway lay four kilometres ahead of us, its open maw hung in the void, the churning blues and purples of its event horizon inviting yet dreadful. We'd arrived three hours ago and had some red tape to go through before being allowed to take up position. Now we were waiting while the stabilisers got to full strength and as the time went on, my nervousness grew. Jam had issued everyone with sick bags, in case bathrooms were full when the need arose, but he swore blind few of us would be affected. I tried to be calm but I have a fear of puking and I paced the Obs Room, trying to control my nerves.

"Come and sit down," Byron said. "You know if you're going to be affected, it will be at the end of the trip, not the beginning."

"Yeah, I guess I'd forgotten that," I nodded and sat down. "It's just that once we're in, there's no backing out and I have a phobia about puking."

"We're with you, Son," Tinnias said. "And you know me, I'm the worst puker in Law Enforcement. If anyone should be worried, it's me."

"Are you?" Kyle asked. "With what you see every day, you're a puker? Doesn't a strong stomach kind of, go with the job?"

"Don't you believe it," Tinnias replied. "During that Rime business, I puked more in those few weeks than during the previous five entire years. Remember that, Sam?"

I grinned, "all those expensive shirts I had to throw out," I said. "But yes, he is notorious for his weak stomach."

"We're people, not robots," Tinnias replied. "We have the same flaws and failings as everyone else. We just learn to step aside from them."

"How can you not get emotionally involved?" Vincent asked. "With murders for instance or when kids are hurt. How do you cope?"

"It does affect you sometimes," Tinnias replied, "but we have a good team and we help each other through it. Cop humour is black for a very good reason. We need the outlet for what can be dark and painful emotions brought on by the most terrible sights, things people shouldn't have to see. And of course when you've got family in danger, that adds to the stress." He winked at me and I smiled back. "We've nearly lost you a few times, haven't we, Sam?"

I nodded, "There have been times when I truly began to believe I wasn't going to make it through the next hours. Thankfully not often, but it's happened a few times. We all have scars from this job, most of them the non-physical kind, the ones that do the most damage."

"No wonder your walls are so strong," Byron remarked, taking hold of my hand. "Whoa, here we go folks." The ship gave a lurch and leapt into the gaping jaws of the tube entryway, the blues and purples of the event horizon swallowing us like something out of a science fiction movie.

"Oh jeez," I hissed and squeezed Byron's hand. He squeezed back reassuringly.

Lights streamed past us at incredible speed, creating illuminated rods of neon, all colours of the rainbow lining the tunnel as we sped through, a rollercoaster in the cosmic void. The intercom boomed.

"We have now entered the tube system to Qaigon 7. Viewing windows will be closed and locked for your comfort, and balconies have been disabled. If anyone feels nausea or dizziness, report to the medical bay where a medical team is waiting." I watched as a black screen swept across the viewing window, blocking our view of the beautiful neon light show outside.

"Why block the windows?" Kyle asked.

Tinnias nodded. "Yes, I thought it was beautiful."

"We've found that watching the tunnel as we speed through, enhances the unpleasant side effects, Lomas explained. "It messes with your brain chemicals and it has some effect on your ear bones too. I forget the finer details. We discovered that the personnel who didn't have access to any windows, never got the nausea, so we experimented and discovered that by covering the windows and blocking out the view, fewer people suffered."

"Oh, well that's good to know," I grinned. "I feel better already." Everyone laughed and it lightened the tension considerably. As the end of the journey approached, we felt it prudent to return to our rooms where we knew the bathrooms were not filled with anxious troopers. Tinnias commandeered the one in his room, while I sat with Byron in ours. He was supremely confident that he would be fine while I sat in silence and hoped.

The lurch told us we'd successfully exited the tube system and we waited to see how we would react. I'd used tubes a few times and each time I've been violently sick afterwards, so much so that I actively avoided them after the third occasion. This time though, we both sat looking at each other and wondering who would be sick first. Eventually, we burst out laughing.

"Looks like we're both going to be okay," I said.

Byron handed me a hot drink and I inhaled deeply. "Coffee," I said with a smile.

"I saw your supply on your ship, so I got some for you," he said, sipping at his own cup.

"Thank you, my love, that was very thoughtful. I'm always going to be here for you," I said after a pause. "Even when I'm at work and we must be apart, I shall call you every day and I'll still want to know how you're feeling and coping. I'm never going to hurt you like that again."

"Thank you," he smiled.


Qaigon 7 was a beautiful pink planet and we all commented on how pretty it was. Byron told us the colour is due to minerals leeching into its ocean. "It also makes the water very warm, even in the dead of winter," he informed us. "Now here's Listler's address and a map. The nearest parking facility is here, where I've put a red circle. His residential building is this red X, and the bar he works is the red square. The bar is open in the evenings and long into the night, so I'd suggest planning your visit for no earlier than mid-day as he probably sleeps in."

"Thanks for this," I said. "We have a couple of hours to get our bearings and check out the locale, so if you're ready, Dad."

"Sir yes Sir," he grinned. "I can do this on my own if you'd rather stay here and chill."

I noticed Vincent's head snap around and his eyes find my own. I pretended not to notice. "No, I want to do it."

He nodded. "Okay, come on then."


The city was modern and eclectic but had an overcrowded feel. The buildings were built right on the roadside, with narrow walkways that forced everyone into single file, one in each direction. The stores offered the usual multi-cultural fare, given the fact that Qaigon is situated near to a major shipping lane and is a natural stopping off point for long haul travellers. My attention was caught by one store selling shoes and I noticed a particularly nice pair that would add some class to my wardrobe.

"Remind me to purchase those after the interview," I said and Tinnias grinned.

We found a small café and used what time was left to discuss tactics. Tinnias was all for the direct approach but I urged caution. "Earth people are reserved and naturally suspicious. They aren't exactly unfriendly, but earning their trust takes time and is easily lost. They're a bit fickle like that and will drop you the moment you offend them. True loyalty doesn't come easily to them. If we push too hard, he will clam up and we'll get nothing."

"Okay, we'll take it slow. I'll defer to your experience of his people as I've never met them. He's ex-military though, so he should have something of an honest streak, especially as his own honesty was questioned. We might find he has a hang up about deceit which will work for us."

"That's true," I nodded. "I didn't think of that. I'm so glad you're here with me, Dad. I hope you meant it when you said you'll share a case with me each year."

"Oh I meant it, Son. I haven't had so much fun in ages. It's knocked years off me. I also meant it when I said I'm happy about your relationship with Byron. He's such a nice guy and so obviously adores you, it's plain to see. Everyone has commented about it."

"I hope you don't think I was keeping it from you by not telling you right off," I said. "This is so new to me, I had to get my own head around it before I could worry how you'd react."

"Hey, I was a young guy searching for an identity once you know." He gave me a grave stare and I gaped in astonishment.

"Really?"

"Really. Now that's a secret I never thought you'd be finding out."

"Wow, I'm stunned. Can I ask umm ..."

"A military colleague in my unit when I did my ten years. It lasted a few months until he left Sigma to take a job elsewhere. It had never been truly serious or anything, we were both just experimenting and finding ourselves, so I didn't mourn the loss. I don't regret it, but I don't shout about it. Not because I'm ashamed, but because it was so long ago. It served its purpose in my life back then. Telling you now is helpful to you, so I've brought it up to share it. I told Grellina the moment our relationship became serious and she was fine about it, quite curious actually, she made me blush, I tell you now."

I laughed at the thought of my parents discussing the finer points of sexual union between two males. I was learning things about them I'd never have guessed in a hundred years.

"Come on, it's time we were going." I paid for our drinks and we left. Listler's apartment was on the eighth floor of a modern tower block. I was grateful to find the elevator working and noticed just one or two spatterings of graffiti. The area was obviously not the most up market in the city, but neither was it the worst. We found the apartment and I knocked.

## CHAPTER TWENTY FIVE

A bearded man in underwear and a vest opened the door. "Yes, what are you selling?"

"Captain Listler?" I asked.

"For my sins, which are many in the eyes of mine enemies," he replied, hand on his heart and gave a slight bow.

"You are Captain Listler?" I repeated, having not understood the meaning of the obvious colloquialism.

He scratched his head. "I was, yes, alas, no longer. I was trying to sound clever, but failed, it would seem."

"Ahh, my apologies for the misunderstanding. I'm not too well read on Earth colloquialisms. My name is Detective Samelan Sinclair-Vaylo of the Inter-Galactic Law Enforcement Agency. This is my superior officer, Commander Vaylo. We'd like a few minutes of your time to discuss Ambassador Vazien."

"Take a seat," Listler said after inviting us in. "Forgive the mess. I've not got around to hiring a cleaning woman. I'll make some tea."

"What's tea? Tinnias asked.

"It's the Earth version of Stronk," I replied. "It's very nice."

"Stronk?" Listler smiled. "You must be from Sigma Prime."

"Correct," I nodded.

"I had a good friend from there when I was in the military. His parents used to send him bags of Stronk powder and I got to quite like it. He was from somewhere he called, oh what was it? Tulip, or something like that. He said it was right next door to Hells Gate."

Tinnias and I gaped at each other. "Tunipz," I said.

"That's the place. You know it?"

"It's a district in my home city. Hellgate is the park at the centre of Tunipz. It used to be a dangerous place but the locals have cleaned it up now and it's a nice area."

"Small world eh?" Listler smiled. "Now what's this about Vazien and how can I help put the bastard away?"

"Bastard?" Tinnias asked.

"Lomash," I grinned.

"Oh, forgive me my ignorance. We understand from records that you and your unit were sent to Jarlash 3 to help quell an uprising. Is that correct?"

"It is."

"And would we be right in assuming that you fell foul of Vazien when you found out what he was doing there?"

"You would."

"Would you be prepared to give us a recorded statement, and then at a later date, testify when we have enough to make an official case?"

"I'd be happy to. Happier than a pig in shit. Just lead me to it and gimme the stick, I'll stir it myself."

I got out my data recorder, placed it between us, and went through the preliminaries before asking for his story.

"Can you tell me how you came into contact with Ambassador Vazien?"

"I was sent, with my unit of one hundred and seventy five of the best soldiers in the IGMF, to Jarlash 3 to investigate and quell an uprising that had come to the attention of the IGMF top brass. We got there and set up camp and found that there were four tribal groups fighting each other for land rights and access to a water source, a sacred river. We befriended and had discussions with the four tribal leaders, who told us there was a man from the sky who gave them guns so they could win over their enemies and have the land and water for themselves. We noticed their weapons seemed far too modern for tribesmen, and their knowledge of firearms was shockingly extreme. They had obviously had some training and been given these weapons. They were military grade; tribesmen would not have access to them legitimately. Shit, even myself and my men didn't have them. We asked about this man from the sky and they told us he lived under the ground near the mouth of the sacred river. We went there and found a Razulite mine, which was owned and being run by Ambassador Vazien."

"Did you approach him?"

"I did. I informed him that supplying those weapons was against the law, as they were military grade and never meant for the open market, and that such a crime was punishable by jail time."

"How did he react?"

"He laughed at me and dared me to try and make something of it."

"And did you?"

"I never got the chance. Within two days the four tribes came at us and slaughtered every one of my men. The next day an IGMF police ship turned up and arrested me for cowardice. Vazien made a statement that said I'd asked him to get me out of there and offered him a shipment of guns as payment."

"Can you prove any of this with hard evidence?"

"Would a witness do?"

"It would do nicely."

"What he didn't know, and never found out, was that my best friend and sergeant witnessed all the conversations, but he'd been ill when the fighting happened, so he survived in the underground bunker we'd dug for ourselves. When the fighting stopped, I told him to hide and let everyone think he'd died too, so he could witness everything. I made a few phone calls and got him picked up within a week and taken away to safety. We're in touch regularly and he still remembers everything and says if ever it comes down to it, he'll gladly testify."

"What is his name and location?"

"His name is Kewendri Lallion. He's eight years old."

I gaped at Listler, who grinned. "Huh?"

"Everyone makes that same face. He's from Ohla. Their orbit is huge which makes their years worth four Earth years. So in Earth terms, he's thirty two. He's currently working quietly in a shipping warehouse on the moon of Corroptima 8. He's using the name Uri Lukin."

"Just one more thing Captain," I said. "Are you prepared to sign a declaration of intent to testify? This case isn't official yet, that's why I haven't read you your rights or given you the official lecture. It's just a chat we're having here but we might as well do it so the records are legally acceptable as evidence."

"Absolutely. Where do I sign?"

We shook hands with Listler as he showed us out. "Tell no one, Captain, as much for your safety as anything else. Someone will call you later today to confirm everything we've told you, and to let you know how he'll be in touch when the time comes to get you into witness safety."

"Thank you, Detectives. I've lived with the shame of this false accusation for years and it never gets easier. I served the IGMF faultlessly and to be accused of being a coward is worse than anything. I'd rather be called a murderer than a coward."

We stopped on the way back to the ship and I purchased the shoes, while Tinnias splashed out on a new shirt. Further down the same street, he called me over to a window of a store selling various knick knacks. "Hey, Sam, you have to buy this for Vincent." I went over to look and saw the battered second hand vidicom movie sleeve adorned with a painting of a bald man with huge muscles. The title, 'The Transmortal Terror – a tale of prophecy,' adorned the top in faded black type.

"Oh wow, he'll love it, I have to have it," I laughed out loud and went inside.

"Don't tell him," I said. "I'll get Byron to check it and make sure it's working properly, then tonight he can announce a movie night over the intercom and when we all sit down, this plays. It'll be hysterical."

We made our way back to the ship and I noticed Tinnias looking at me quizzically.

"Are you okay, Son, being here I mean?"

I nodded. "Yeah. It's weird. I thought it would be traumatic coming here, but I just feel tired of all that anxiety. Carrying it is a burden and I'm no longer strong enough. That man no longer has any power over my emotions. Merellia has gone and I reached a place of peace with it. Now my life is different and I no longer live in the same head space as back then. Is that bad of me? Does that make me a bad person?"

Tinnias gaped. "What? Hell no, I'm amazed and delighted at your courage and proud of how you've grown."

I smiled and was about to thank him when a heavy ball of darkness burst into life in the pit of my gut. I gasped, my eyes widening with shock as adrenaline sent fear racing through my spirit and into my consciousness. I knew with every fibre of my being that terrible danger stalked us, was creeping up behind us so close it could grab us at any second. The smile froze on my lips as the world around me faded into mist and I might have remained there indefinitely had Tinnias not shaken my shoulder. I was not at first aware of his attempts to communicate with me, and it was not until he shook me so hard I stumbled to one side that I turned and looked into his face and saw concern.

"Son? What's the matter? Talk to me."

"Run," I managed to whisper as my eyes focussed at last on his own. Wasting no more than a couple of seconds, he roughly grabbed me and we ran towards the exit and the bright sunny street outside. A figure stepped out from the cover of an aging shuttle in a decidedly unflattering shade of vomit, and another appeared from behind a magnificent ex racing craft sporting a paintjob I fully intend to copy when I have money to burn. More clicks from behind told me we had six well armed heavies surrounding us. We stopped running and raised our hands like good boys.

The tallest of them sauntered towards us with a grin on his face. "That's the spirit, Detectives. Now let's get the preliminaries out of the way shall we? My friends here are Mallis, Dillish, Choppy, Lenk, and Po. We're the ones with the upper hand here, so that means you do as I say."

"What do we call you?" Tinnias demanded.

The guy glared back. "Sir," he sneered.

"Look," I sighed. "We all know how this goes so let's cut the crap. "Just tell us what you want and fuck off so we can all get on with our lives."

"Now then, Detective, no need to be rude when we've only just become acquainted. The first thing I want is a sit down and a hot drink, so come on, open her up and invite us in."

I turned and walked back to my ship, opened the hatch and went to the Nutri-Vend. There was no way I was wasting my precious coffee powder on this bunch, so I indicated for them to help themselves.

"Cups are on the shelf above, help yourselves."

"Okay, Sam, here's what's going to happen," he said when they were all sat down with drinks. "You and your father here are going to fly us all back to that Drycenian hulk up there, just like you normally would. At no time will you tell them or in any other way indicate to them that you have passengers aboard. When you enter their shuttle bay, you land just inside the door so they can't shut the bay door behind you. You got all that?"

My heart sank at the growing realisation that these thugs intended to harm my friends, and my mind raced as I sought a solution. I tried a bluff, knowing I was wasting my time.

"They're not waiting for us, they've gone to attend to other business. We only spent a few days with them while they changed a valve on my port engine flow sequencer. My ship is good, but she's not good enough to catch them up."

"Come on, Sam, don't fuck me around or I'll lose my temper and you really don't want that to happen." He stabbed at his Unicom. "Is that Drycenian hulk still in orbit?" he asked, then smiled. "Wonderful, thanks." He put away his Unicom, cocked his head to one side, and raised his eyebrows at me.

"Well I had to try, didn't I?" I said, shrugging my shoulders as I climbed into the pilot's seat. "You would've done the same thing."

"I guess so, I'll let you have that one. Let's go, I'm looking forward to some genuine Drycenian cooking. Is their food nice, Sam?"

"It's wonderful," I nodded as I lifted the ship and headed out of the parking facility and into the sky.

"They don't eat live worms or anything like on those science fiction movies do they?" a voice behind me asked. All six of our captors laughed.

"Nothing like that," I assured them. "Although I doubt you'll be alive long enough to sit down to dinner with them."

"Especially with the bay doors open," Tinnias added. "Why do you want them left open anyway?"

"They'll be unable to creep up on us with the doors open," the guy replied. "It'll allow me the personal space I'm used to while we work on our relationship."

"They do have space suits y'know," I remarked.

"Have you ever had a firefight while wearing a suit with an opponent who isn't hampered by one himself?"

I hadn't, but the contradiction of his statement was obvious. "Without a suit, you'll be a sitting target in here. They can take all the time they need, knowing you can't escape."

"If you shoot the windows out, you die," Tinnias added. "If you try to run and hide among the other shuttles, you die. You might as well put a sign around your neck that says, 'shoot me,' because however you look at it, you give them that upper hand you're so proud of."

"I'm pretty sure they'll be keen to ensure your safety, Sam, don't you?"

"I doubt that," I replied. "I'm nothing special to them. When your back is against the wall, you have to make choices and they'll more than likely choose their own before outsiders."

"I'm willing to bet you a hundred there's one good looking engineer who might disagree with you. Are you man enough for that wager, Detective?"

He had me there and I blushed. Fuck this blushing, someone has to be able to cure this shit somehow. I had no reply to that truth and he sniggered behind my back. Another thing that occurred to me was the need to ensure

Byron didn't come rushing into danger himself, not knowing we had thugs aboard. I wasn't prepared to risk him like that. If only I had a way of letting him know what was going on. It was then that I glanced at Tinnias and saw him making a subtle gesture with a finger. It was almost like a come here gesture, and I looked at his reflection in the cockpit window and frowned. He pushed his hand forward no more than an inch, pointed forwards, then moved the finger up and down sharply. All the time his eyes darted from me, to the console before us, then back again. He was indicating something on the console, wanting me to press something, but what?

"It's a good job they couldn't hear you asking about eating live worms," Tinnias said. "They would probably have been offended if they heard that, don't you agree, Sam?"

Realisation hit me like a rock and I cursed myself for being so dense. Tinnias had put in the emergency communicator for me to use in just this kind of situation. I'd never had need to use it so forgot it was there. Byron had tweaked it so it would automatically call the Drycenians, as he trusted his own people more than he trusted the Agency, which was probably wise. When our captors were looking in another direction, I tapped the button and Tinnias winked at me.

"You still haven't told us why you've captured us at gunpoint," I remarked nonchalantly. "I'd be interested to know, since it's my neck you're after."

"We're presuming of course that Vazien is behind it," Tinnias said.

"I must say I'm flattered he regards me worthy of six armed thugs," I sniggered, determined to give Byron as much information as I could, without it seeming obvious.

Tinnias dutifully laughed along with me. "It's been years since I was held at gunpoint, Son. I guess I've still got it after all."

"You'll never lose it, Dad."

"You mean to tell me you still don't get it?" our head captor replied. "You surely realise by now how the Ambassador hates being disrespected."

"So this is vengeance for his failure to kill me on Niruvan Prime," I said.

"No, you dumb cock sucker, it's vengeance for interfering in his business, for asking questions about him, for trying to get false charges stuck on him."

I gaped at that remark. "What the fuck? False charges? You do know he murdered his own wife, wiped out two whole races of people, maimed and killed countless others who objected to their livelihoods being ruined by his greed? You are aware of that, aren't you?"

"Vicious rumours, all of it. You've been listening to gossip, detective. You should know better."

"Vicious rumours?" I roared with laughter. "You're either a bad liar or an idiot."

"Careful, detective. When you no longer have to manoeuvre this bucket of bolts, it'll be safe for me to smack that stupid smirk off your face for good."

He was right and I had a mental image of Byron, his face purple with anger, yelling at me to shut the fuck up and stop provoking him. I shut my mouth, contrite. I pulled up to a halt several hundred metres short of the bay doors.

"What the fuck are you doing, Sam?" our captor demanded. "Don't make a mistake or you won't live to regret it."

"Relax for fuck's sake," I said. "There's all sorts of protocols involved in getting aboard. I can't just walk in the door like I own the place. I have to seek permission no matter how much they like me, and I have to do it the right way."

"So get on with it so we can get that King of theirs and his son, kill you all, and get out of here in this crate."

So that was his plan. "Why do you want to kill them? They've done nothing to Vazien. They're not involved in this business."

"Oh really? And just when did this spirit of non involvement start huh? Was it before or after Niruvan Prime?"

We glared at each other until I, as the unarmed one, graciously backed down.

"Okay okay, take a breath here and let me concentrate or I'll forget the language." I reached for the comms headset.

"The language?" he asked. "You mean you gotta speak in Drycenian?" I nodded. "Wow."

"Hey, Boss?" a voice from behind called. "How are we going to know what he's telling them?"

"There's nothing he can say that they won't know themselves soon enough."

"They could shoot us down," another voice remarked.

"Not with him taking it up the ass with their engineer, they won't."

"How can you be sure?"

"Cos they're in love, ain't ya, Sweety?" he leered, his face inches from my own. How the hell did Vazien and his crew know about Byron and me?

"If you've finished your schoolboy taunting, can I hail them now or what?" I asked. He sniggered and waved his hand towards the headset.

I was taking a chance speaking in my own Sigma tongue, but it was the only way to speak with the Drycenians openly and ask for their help. "Drycenian ship, this is Sam. We're being held prisoner by six armed thugs, care of our politician friend it seems. I'm to set down just inside the shuttle bay so you can't shut the doors behind us. They want Lomas and Toma as additional prisoners and they say they're going to kill all four of us. I've told them I have to seek permission to board in your language and I'm hoping that none of them speak Sigman. Tell me what you want me to do guys. Oh, and no heroics. I refuse to be the cause of the two of you being murdered."

"What the hell was all that about?" our captor asked.

"You have to say the proper things, the appropriate greetings, give the right level of respect, ask for permission to board in the right and proper manner. It all has to be done using loads of respectful terminology and self prostrating to show the royals the respect they are used to receiving. Even their own people have to do it, although with not quite as much bowing and scraping."

The comms crackled and Lomas' voice made me feel at once, safe and secure. In fluent Sigman, he told me of their hastily arranged plan. "Sam, Lomas here. Don't worry, we're not going to let any harm come to you. Byron has a group of troopers and is suiting up as we speak. They are hiding themselves amongst the ducting and pipework on the roof of the shuttle bay and intend to gain entry via your emergency docking hatch above your bedroom cubicle. Can you please assure us that your bedroom door is closed, or get it closed under some pretext? Byron told me to remind you not to provoke them, although he used slightly different terminology, if you get my meaning. Set the ship down as far inside as you can, we can always pretend we can't shut the doors. It would also help if you can think of anything to delay them. Offer them some food or something and I'll make sure any negotiating takes an inordinately long time. We're with you both, and we're coming to get you."

"The bedroom door is closed," I replied and switched off the comms. "Okay, here we go, just got to wait for the doors to open and we're in."

"Nicely done, Sam. What was all that you were saying anyway?"

"I haven't the faintest idea," I replied. "They taught me what to say and I learned it by repeating it over and over. I've no need to understand it, I just know they want to hear it before they'll let me in."

"Who was that talking, was it the King?" he asked.

I forced a laugh. "Don't be daft. The King doesn't bother himself with such mundane tasks. No, that was his advisor."

"He sounded like an old fart to me. What's the King like?"

"He's around my father's age, maybe a few years older."

"And the son?"

"He's around my age."

"That doesn't tell me much."

"Well I'm sorry but I don't hobnob with the royal family much. They're far too busy to sit and be buddies with cops, and you don't just ask them about their lives like with regular folks. Ahh, here we go, the doors are opening."

I steered the ship inside the shuttle bay and inched forward until the captor boss snapped at me.

"That's far enough, Sam. Set her down and switch off. Let's not spoil this new friendship we've got going here."

I did as I was told, then allowed myself to be led at gunpoint down to my cargo hold where Tinnias and I were restrained. Once alone, I let myself out of the cuffs and checked the corridor outside.

"We should be okay if we keep our voices down," I hissed as Tinnias massaged his wrists.

"Well done for that language trick, Sam. I'm proud of you. I'd never have thought of that."

"Lomas wants a delay, so what do you suggest?"

"We could ask for something to eat if we're going to be here for long."

"Someone should be down here soon asking me to work the comms for them. It won't work for anyone but me. Byron fixed it with a voice recognition thing."

"Better get back into the cuffs then. I don't suppose you have any arms stashed away down here, do you?"

"No, but I'm damn well going to," I replied and we both sniggered. "If there were less of them, I'd have them disarmed and restrained in minutes. I can't take six on though, not with guns."

"We could always use that boss guy as a hostage to make the others behave themselves."

"So long as they like him, yeah. If they don't like him, they'll probably be happy for us to kill him."

"Then we'd be back where we started," Tinnias sighed.

I nodded. "With a body on our conscience. If he's dead, we can't prove he captured us."

"Someone's coming," Tinnias hissed.

The door opened and three of the thugs entered. "The boss wants you up top. The comms won't work without your magic touch it seems."

Back in the cockpit, I went to put on the headset but the head captor took it from me.

"I'll do the talking this time. You make it work and stay working. If I have to keep carting you up and down every time I want to talk to them, I'm going to quickly become annoyed."

I spoke into the microphone and used my code that told the comms to work for anyone who wanted to use it, then looked at him and smiled. "It's all yours."

"Good boy."

"Are we going to be here long?" I asked. "If so, can we have some sandwiches sent in or something. Dad and I haven't eaten all day."

"Neither have we, Boss," one of the other thugs said and I noticed a couple more heads nodding in agreement.

"Can I get my cigarettes before I go back down?"

"Okay, go with him, Po and Mallis."

I went into the rear hatch area, noticing that the bedroom door was firmly shut, retrieved a new pack of cigarettes, and returned to the cargo hold.

"Could I have one hand free so I can smoke?"

"No, but we're happy to wait while you have one, especially if you offer them around to your guests."

"Help yourselves," I said, handing the pack over. I offered one to Tinnias and we gratefully inhaled and felt our anxiety calming immediately. "I suppose I'd be wasting my time offering you safety from Vazien if you help us," I said.

"You would," the one called Po, remarked.

"We guessed as much," Tinnias replied. "We had to try though. I'm sure if the Drycenians do let you survive long enough to escape back to Vazien, the Ambassador will happily protect you and your families despite this cock up."

"After all, that stuff about his violence is all just vicious rumour, isn't it?" I added. He held my gaze for a few seconds longer than normal and I knew my comment had hit home. Hopefully it would sit inside his mind and begin to rot it from the inside out and encourage him to consider changing his stance.

"I bet you've even dealt with the families of other crew members like yourself who've fucked up or just not got Vazien what he wanted," Tinnias said. "I wonder who'll get the job of doing yours."

I heard the crack, followed by Tinnias' yell as the butt end of Po's gun found his jaw, and I lost it.

"You fucking asshole," I screamed. "I'm gonna fucking kill you for that. I hope Vazien kills your whole family, I hope he rapes your women and kills your kids you piece of shit." I struggled against the restraints, forgetting in my anger that I knew how to uncuff myself. It was a good thing I forgot as I would've killed him right at that moment. The two of them backed out and shut the door and I continued screaming obscenities at them, as much to let the Drycenians know something was wrong as to vent my anger.

Tinnias groaned beside me, tears of pain streaming down his face. His jaw was broken, that much was obvious and having suffered a similar injury myself more than once, I knew the pain he would be suffering right then. The door burst open and the captor boss entered, his face like thunder.

"What the fuck happened? Po said you attacked him. Make sure you tell me the truth or so help me I'll finish you both myself right here and now. I don't need this shit with Vazien holding a hammer over my head. Speak, damn you."

"Attacked him?" I yelled. "Oh yeah, fully restrained, cuffed hand and feet but somehow we attacked him. I'm going to twist his ugly head right off his fucking body, you bunch of half wits."

He approached me and I guessed he was about to punch me but I was still so angry I didn't care. To my surprise, he crouched down so he was eye to eye with me and sighed.

"Detective, Sam, please try to control yourself just long enough to tell me what happened. You can insult us all you want afterwards, but I need to know who to kill. I don't want to off the wrong guy now, do I?"

"He broke my father's jaw with the butt of his pistol, just because he said Vazien is likely to kill all your families if you fuck this up, which is guaranteed, believe me on that. There is no way the Drycenians are going to let you survive this. I'm expendable, we have an agreement on that. It's too important to get Vazien taken down to let personal stuff get in the way. We need a doctor here, please."

"Do you have a med kit aboard?"

"Of course, what kind of idiot do you take me for?"

"An angry one, sure. Tell me where it is."

"Behind you, on the wall above the poster with the landscape."

He fetched it down and ripped open the lid, shaking his head as he examined the contents. "You need to update this med kit, Sam. This is pitiful. Shame on you."

"It's on the list," I growled.

"Is it a long list?" he asked as he ripped open an injector and examined the label for the fourth time.

"Yeah."

"Well I hope your med kits are near the top. If not, they should be. I'm shocked, truly." He went over to Tinnias. "This is a pain killer, according to the label. It'll help some. Okay?" Tinnias nodded and grunted, then sighed as the injection took effect.

"Thank you," I hissed.

"I've spoken with that advisor you talked with and asked for the King and his son to come aboard. They refused, obviously, so I've asked for some refreshments while discussions are ongoing. I'll make sure you get your share. How do I get those cell bars out and fixed? I'll be able to uncuff you so you can be a bit more comfortable."

"The mechanism is over there in the corner. Lift the switch and unhook the catch while pulling for all you're worth. It's a bit stiff and clanky but it works." I watched as he struggled with my cell bars, breathing heavily when he finally got them fixed in place.

"Fucking hell, Sam. Your housekeeping is shockingly bad. Is there anything aboard that works properly?"

"It all works properly," I bristled. "She's the finest example of modern engineering and I'll thank you to be more respectful to her. She's not a crate, nor a bucket of bolts as you put it so eloquently."

He laughed loud and long. "Pilots and their ships. I'm more of a bike man myself so I kind of understand. Well now you're both safe and secure, you can let yourself out of the cuffs and be more comfortable. I'm assuming you can let yourself out, most detectives learn how."

We uncuffed ourselves. "What do you take us for, amateurs?"

"I apologise for the behaviour of my colleague by the way. Unsavoury as our business often is, there's no excuse for rudeness or thuggish behaviour. He will pay for his error, believe me."

I thanked him and he left us alone. I went to Tinnias. "Is that injection working? How's the pain now? Tell me how to help."

"Okay," he mumbled slowly. He sounded drunk and I winced at the memory of my own experience of a broken jaw. "Painful. Will live."

"I'm so sorry I got you into this," I hissed emotionally. He reached for my hand and grasped it tightly, looking into my eyes with love. He shook his head carefully.

"Big mouth," he pointed to himself.

I nodded. "That comment was a little over the line I guess. I'm proud of you for taking the risk."

The door burst open and a trooper walked in with a large box. He was suited up and turned to look at the captors.

"You can take off the suit now," the captor's boss said. The trooper put down his box and began taking off his suit. I recognised him as one of the regular shuttle crew and remembered his astonishment at my fishing skills on Glarian 4. With the suit off, I saw he wore a waiter's uniform.

"You asked for some food?" he said to the captors as he opened the box to reveal two trays of sandwiches, a bag of snacks, and several packs of cigarettes. He pushed the box over to the captor boss who raised his eyebrows in appreciation.

"Wow, lovely spread. Thanks, man."

"You're welcome. I've been told that I can expect to be refused permission to leave. Should I enter the cell with the detectives?"

The captor boss scratched his chin, then grinned. "Well you have two choices as I see it. You can either join the detectives as another hostage, or you can earn your freedom by doing your friends here a favour."

"A favour? What kind of favour?"

"One of my guys overstepped the mark and injured Sam's father, who is now in needless pain because of my man's inability to control himself. I don't like that, it's the kind of thuggish behaviour that really gets me angry. Despite the type of work I get involved in, I do have some standards. I reckon my man deserves to pay for his misdemeanour and if you were willing to collect that debt, I'll let you go back to your people."

"You mean you want me to kill him?"

"Yeah. Sam here told me all about your principles and how you don't let personal attachments get in the way of what is important to your people's safety, etcetera etcetera. I like that in people, but I find so few are truly able to be that principled, don't you agree? You'd earn my respect if you proved Sam correct and the respect of another is worth more than gold, I firmly believe."

"And if I refuse?"

"Then you join the detectives in the cell and I get to understand my position in our negotiations." He looked at the trooper and grinned, then indicated for two of his men to hold Po down. Po struggled and quickly begged for his life. "Well? That is a gun on your hip, is it not? What's it to be, man?"

Without batting an eyelid, the trooper took aim and fired into Po's chest. The captors all jumped in shock and watched as Po began to convulse, then went limp. I couldn't believe what I'd just witnessed, but my experience with the Drycenians told me all was probably not what it seemed.

"Holy fucking shit, he did it, Boss. He shot him, as cold as you please. Jeez, Boss, we should cut and run, I don't want to mess with this crowd. They're dangerous, man."

"Do I get to leave now?" the trooper asked, reaching for his suit. The captor boss nodded, the expression on his face one of shock and disbelief. In any other circumstance I would've laughed aloud but I was worried as to how this situation was developing. Confined and unarmed, I was useless and despite my martial art skills being good, I knew I wouldn't be able to take on five armed men. I felt so impotent I could've cried.

The trooper got into the suit and reached for his helmet. "Enjoy the sandwiches, gentlemen. If you require any more, you have only to ask." At that moment all hell broke loose. The door opened a crack and something came flying into the cargo hold as he turned to me and yelled. "Hold your breath you two." Tinnias and I obeyed as the room quickly filled with some yellow smoke. The smoke was so thick I couldn't see my hand in front of my face and as my lungs began to struggle, I heard my name called softly.

"Sam, come here." I followed the voice and felt a hand. "Here's breathers for you both." I grabbed them, crawled back to Tinnias and we both heaved deep breaths. No shots were fired and within five minutes, all five remaining captors were restrained and the foul smoke, dispersed by my powerful air scrubbing system. Jam ran to Tinnias and with the help of two troopers, led him away to the medical bay for treatment. The five restrained captors were led away by the security guys and Byron, Vincent, and Kyle ran to me. After assuring themselves that I was okay, Vincent and Kyle went to help escort the struggling captors and Byron hugged me.

"Thank you for rescuing me, again," I said and kissed him. "You're my hero."

"I'm so relieved you're all right. You need to curb that tongue though, you were being very provocative. They could've shot you."

"Yeah, I know. Lomas gave me your message. I take it this guy is just asleep and not dead?"

Byron nodded. "Yeah, he'll be dreaming for a few hours yet and when he wakes, he'll have a headache like no other. Shame."

I leaned down to kiss him but frowned when I heard him scream. That scream was filled with fear and desperation and I couldn't work out why my love would suddenly make such a noise. My mind began to struggle as I tried to work out what had happened to him, but the pain was making concentrating difficult. The last thing I was aware of before darkness embraced me, was to wonder why my body felt so stiff all of a sudden.

## CHAPTER TWENTY SIX

I drifted into darkness and recognised the comforting warmth from my previous visits to this peaceful haven. My mind emptied and as my consciousness lost its awareness of having been a physical being, alive and able to think independently, I became just energy. Memories slipped across my awareness but I felt no need to hold on to them. They slid past and were gone, and I felt nothing at their having disappeared. Freed from physical encumbrances, my being expanded until I felt as if I filled the entire universe, then all at once I was tiny, a single atom of minute energy within the warm embrace of this safe dark womb. Down and down I went, to where I did not know and had no ability to care. I was at peace for the first time and I gratefully succumbed to its depths.

Noise came to me and my descent slowed although not from my own volition. Somehow, that noise had the power to prevent me from going deeper and I fought with it. Wresting myself from its hold proved impossible however, and as it became louder, it forced me to listen. The energy of those sounds was weirdly familiar but I was unable to understand how or why, I just knew I had to listen despite not wanting to. The energy of those sounds resonated with my own energy, it felt almost as if that energy was my own energy, so well did it fit with me. That energy was me somehow, represented me, defined me in some way. I concentrated on it, needing to understand how and why it connected with me so completely.

"Sam. Listen to me, Sam. Reach for my voice. I'm here for you."

What are those sounds, what is this hold they have over me and why do I feel such a connection with them? These and other questions raced throughout my energy but I had no answers to any of them.

"Understand me, Sam. Listen and understand. Come to me now, be with me, I need you."

One of the sounds began to form a coherence with my energy and slowly, understanding grew. Sam, what does that sound mean and why does it feel so familiar? Needing to know, I reached for that sound with my energy and for a split second, nothing changed. Then all at once, memories flooded back but this time, emotion swept over me in painful waves as each memory reconnected with me, slipped into its rightful place and filled my empty mind. I lived each one anew, the emotions as fresh as the day the memory was made and when at last I'd relived my whole life moment by moment, I saw my best friend Ren, standing before me. He smiled, tears streaming down his cheeks as he opened his arms to embrace me.

"Ren?" I gasped as I went willingly into his arms. "What's happening? Please help me understand."

"What's your last memory, Sam?"

I forced my mind back. "Byron told me off for being provocative to our captors. Then I heard him screaming, or I thought I did. I remember wondering why he would make such a noise when he was so happy I was safe again. I tried to kiss him but my body wouldn't obey. It felt all stiff and I couldn't move it."

Ren nodded. "Think back further, to the split second before you heard Byron screaming. Listen for any other sounds that seemed out of place or odd."

I pushed my mind back further and relived the scene. The foul smelling smoke, being given the breathers by a trooper, Vincent and Kyle wanting to know if I was all right, before going to help with the prisoners, Byron and I alone in my cargo hold with the body of Po and then I heard it and cried out in shock.

"Oh fuck no, he shot me in the back. No, please tell me it's not true. I don't want to be dead. Please help me, Ren. I promised Byron I'd never leave him alone again. I can't die yet, I've only just found love. Tell me what to do, please, I'm begging you."

Ren held me as I screamed in anger and cried in desperation. When I had some control, he looked into my eyes. "Don't worry, Bro, I have no intention of letting you die. That's why we wanted to involved the Drycenians. We knew you were destined to die if you took on this case, and we know only the Drycenians have the ability to bring you back from that place. We told them you must not be lost in the fight to end Vazien's evil, and thanks to their knowledge and skill, you won't be."

I gaped. "But we all assumed Niruvan was where I was to die."

"I know you did."

"So why didn't you tell us the truth?"

"Because it's destiny we're messing with here. That's serious business, Sam, believe me, Vincent and Farra know only too well how easy it is to fuck up the destiny of others when you mess with this shit. You were destined to die and you did so. All I did was bring you back, I didn't stop you going there."

"So I was dead, properly dead?"

"As a door handle."

"But now I'm alive again, my body I mean?"

"Totally. It was necessary to allow you to look into that place for just a moment, and I don't mean simply to lessen the ripples of destiny for others. Remember years ago when you were doing your ten years military service?" I nodded. "You had an altercation with the Transmortals, didn't you?" I nodded again. "When Jam asks you about that encounter, be open and honest with him and he will explain. It will take time and everyone is desperate for you to wake up. You've been here for over a week, Sam. I almost despaired at ever finding you and then you fought valiantly to remain."

"Thank you for bringing me back. It seems inadequate just saying thank you but it's all I have."

"You can do much more than thank me. You can live, be positive, trust more, love yourself deeper, give yourself permission to be happy. Those things are worth more than gratitude."

"I will, I promise. Remind me about it if I begin to falter."

"Oh you can count on that. Now it's time for you to return to your body. Jam has been by your side the whole time, he even slept in a chair beside your tank and hasn't dared sleep for the past seventy hours. Byron has slept on the floor beside your bed every night and sat beside you every day. Tinnias has been distraught; Vincent and Kyle haven't dare leave him alone for a second. Never again doubt the depth of love every one of your friends has for you."

"I won't doubt ever again."

Ren sniggered. "Yes you will, Bro, just stamp it out quickly and in time, you'll lose that self doubt. Now go on, get out of here and back to the land of the living where you belong before I kick your ass for fighting me so hard."


My first physical sensation was one of floating and it was a few seconds before I remembered that my body was inside one of those tank things. I allowed my consciousness to coalesce with my body before opening my eyes and looking around. As my hearing returned, beeps and buzzes came to me, and voices, their words seeming urgent and excited. I turned my head and stared into Byron's large yellow eyes, smiled, and delighted at the grin I saw split his gorgeous face in half.

"Welcome back, my love. I've missed you so much."

Knowing I was unable to speak, I put a finger to my lips, then placed it to the side of the tank. He returned the gesture and I smiled as Jam's voice reached me.

"Hello Sam, welcome back, Bro. Can you hear me okay?" I nodded. "Good. Do you see those two buttons down to your left, one red and one blue?" I nodded again. "Red for no, blue for yes, see the screen above your head? Press them and see what happens." I pressed one then the other and saw the words Yes and then No appear on the screen and nodded. "Wonderful. Now I'm going to ask you some questions to make sure you've come back to us intact, then I can decide when I'll be able to let you out of there. Firstly, are you warm enough?"

By this slow but effective method, I was pleased when he told me I had all my senses and faculties in the proper order and could come out of the tank in twenty four hours if nothing untoward happened. When I saw Jam try to hide a yawn, I wrote the words Sleep and Bed, on the side of the tank, then pointed to him. He nodded.

"I'll get my head down for a couple of hours when Doctor Lear comes on duty."

I wrote the word Bed, again, then pointed to the chair and shook my head.

"You know about that?" I nodded. "Wow, who blabbed on me?"

I grinned and wrote Ren on the side of the tank. They both laughed and it was lovely to hear such a positive emotion again. At that moment, Tinnias rushed in, tears streaming down his cheeks and a broad grin on his face.

"Son. You're back. Oh thank all the gods in existence. I'm so sorry, it was my fault this happened. If I hadn't made that smart comment, this wouldn't have happened."

I wagged a finger and shook my head, then gestured for him to come nearer to the tank. He came right up to the side and peered in, whereupon I poked out my tongue and gave him a single finger. Everyone burst out laughing, including Tinnias and he nodded.

"I understand, Sam."


A day later I vomited the last of the fluid from my lungs and gasped in fresh air at last. Byron helped me into the special shower that helped get the silver garment from my body, and within two hours I was dressed and eating a small but delicious meal.

"Sorry it's not much but you've been gone for over a week and if we overload your stomach you'll just throw it back at me," Jam explained. He'd slept for eighteen hours straight and was a little annoyed not to be woken earlier but conceded that his skills needed him sharp and focussed.

"I understand, Doc. This is delicious."

"How does your neck feel?"

"Heavy with this thing on all the time but I guess I'll soon forget it's there."

He nodded. "Within a few days you won't notice it. Once your neck muscles readjust to the extra weight, it'll be just a part of your body like all the others."

"Do I have to do anything to it? What should I avoid doing. How do I take care of it?"

"All you have to do is leave it alone and forget it's there. You can live your life completely normally. You can swim, sunbathe, take a mud bath on Alibaloma 8, work out, get sweaty, all the things you usually do in a normal life. The only thing you need to remember is if you're taken to a medical facility other than a Drycenian one, you must tell them not to interfere with it as it's keeping you alive and any fiddling by curious medics will kill you. I've got a medical alert notice for you to keep with your papers as well."

"Okay, forget it and leave it alone, I can achieve that."

"I'm discharging you but I want you to report to me each day for tests, at least for a while until I'm happy you're completely back to normal. I want you to promise me you'll tell me the moment you feel anything weird or out of the ordinary, no matter how insignificant it may seem at the time. Byron, you must promise to rat him out to me, even if he tells you not to."

Byron grinned. "I will, Jam, don't worry."

"I'll be a good boy, I promise," I laughed.

"You'd better, now go on, get out of here and enjoy being alive again."

I took Jam's hand. "You're the best of men, Doc. I said it before and it'll always be true. How can I say thank you in a way that's appropriate for what you've done for me, for us? All I have is my love and respect and I give it to you with my gratitude."

"They are worth more than gold," Jam said, squeezing my hand.


We went to find Tinnias and he spent an hour bringing me up to date on what I had missed, which wasn't much as far as the case went. He cried some more, apologised too much, and I told him not to be a twit each time. Byron hugged him and told him we both loved him, and I was overjoyed to see them bonding so deeply.

"Let's get the team together in the Obs Room and discuss what's next, shall we?" I suggested and they both nodded. We met Vincent and Kyle on the way and I thanked them both for taking care of Tinnias while I was hovering between life and death. Lomas had been a regular visitor while I was in the tank and he embraced me as we entered the Obs Room.

"It's wonderful to have you back, Sam. We were all so worried; you took so long to return."

"Ren told me it's connected to an altercation I once had during my years in the military. Something to do with the Transmortals I encountered."

"I didn't know you'd had dealings with them, Sam," Byron said.

"Neither did I," Vincent agreed.

"Nor me," Kyle added.

"I did," Tinnias said, "but how is that relevant now? That must be over thirty years ago."

"I've no idea. He said Jam will explain at some point."

"I'll ask Arshad next time I see him," Jam said, "although from what I know, I can probably work it out for myself." I noticed Vincent, Kyle, and Byron were all nodding. "Am I right in thinking you were somehow connected, mind to mind, with a Transmortal at some point?"

"Yeah. He stepped out from behind a tree and grabbed my face. I tried to look away but he forced my mind to pay attention. I just heard him tell me not to worry, that he would be with me always, when my military buddy shot him right between the eyes."

"No wonder you took so long to come back," Vincent remarked. "Ren had to allow you to die before bringing you back, to break that Transmortal connection."

"Isn't that how they did their shit on people?" I asked. "They took them to the edge of death for a while before bringing them back changed. Didn't they?"

"Yes," Byron nodded. "I'm guessing that when your buddy shot him, his mind was still connected to yours. That means part of his mind survived inside yours. It's probably been working its shit all these years inside your head without you even knowing it was there."

"Arshad will confirm things," Jam said. "I'll tell you the moment he tells me anything about it."

"Okay, so what's next in the case?" Lomas asked. "Are we still on the case in fact?"

"We damn well better be," I remarked. "After what I went through, I fully intend for Vazien to look me in the eyes and know he failed to bring me down. I'll chase him till I'm old and grey. By the way, how are the prisoners?"

"Oh they're fine," Byron remarked. "They're languishing in unbridled luxury in our lock up."

"Do they know I'm alive?"

"Not yet. Funny thing was, their leader, Brakely his name is, he was quite angry when he found out Po shot you in the back. It seems that Po killed his wife and son just a few weeks ago after they voiced concern about Vazien and his motives. His loyalty to the Ambassador is weirdly extreme and when you, Tinnias, made that comment about Vazien killing his family, he was angry at not being given the acknowledgement for having already done it himself."

"Whoa," I hissed. "I'm going to enjoy visiting him then."

"Grund and I have good news and bad, which do you want first?" Byron announced and Grund sniggered.

"The bad," I replied.

"The other set of neighbours you planned to interview have emigrated. They're no longer on Vilalishk. Six months ago they came into some money via a large inheritance, changed their identities, and emigrated to Kylanlil Oberna 2."

"Shit," I hissed. "That's weeks out of our way."

"If it helps, I did get in touch and they're happy to talk about Vazien now they feel safe. I hope I didn't overstep the mark."

"Of course not," I said, reaching out to caress his cheek. "Thank you for doing that. We'll add them to the list as additional testifiers and if we do get to a trial, we can think about making the journey then. Now what's the good news?"

"I found the son with the broken fingers and toes, and the prostitute wife of the other son," Grund announced. "They're both still on Niruvan Prime. The guy is one of the homeless community, and the wife still works in a whorehouse. She has a long standing drug habit that cost her custody of her children, who are now in an orphanage."

"Do we have a ship nearby Niruvan?" Lomas asked.

Byron went over to the computer console and tapped. "Yes, Sir. Captains Shirat and Poslek are both within a day's journey."

"Thank you, I'll go and make a few calls." Lomas left the room, followed by Toma.

I hugged Byron. "Thank you for doing that, both of you." I smiled at Grund.

"There's more good news yet," Grund continued. "I've found Vazien's mistress."

"You have? That's wonderful. Where is she?"

"She's changed her name and is working in a whorehouse on Deep Space refuelling station Omega 8, under the name Jalima Wentslone."

"Awesome, and it's right on our way too."

"Omega 8 is right nearby the other end of the tube system, so we can be there in a day."

"Is everyone who was sick, okay with doing the tube again?" Lomas asked when he returned to the Obs Room. "Be honest now, don't suffer if you can't face it."

"I don't mind," Tinnias said. "It was less traumatic than it used to be and over very quickly."

"Yeah, let's do it," Vincent added. "No one enjoys puking but it's forgotten quickly."


"Can you help me with something?" I asked after wandering around engineering for several minutes and getting thoroughly lost before finding Byron.

"Of course, Bro," Byron said. "What's the problem?"

"Remember the thing about the neighbours I told you about?"

"Yeah."

"Can we maybe bash some ideas, exchange views or something. It's too weird not to give it some thought."

"Sure. I mentioned it to Vincent and Kyle and they're going to get their brains onto it too."

"Awesome. Now why in the hell would a woman go on holiday the moment her husband is kidnapped? Doesn't that seem oddly cold to you?"

"Because he beats her," Vincent said as he and Kyle entered.

"Well yeah, that would explain it, but we've no proof," I said. "How did you come to that conclusion anyway?"

"I didn't, she did," he replied and handed me his Unicom.

I took it and held it to my ear. "Hello, Detective Sinclair-Vaylo here."

"Hi, Sam, it's Farra."

"Oh hi, Farra. How's the family? Is Gabriel okay?"

"He's great, thank you. Vincent told me about this wife and kids thing, and asked me if he was kidnapped, what would make me take the kids on holiday instead of staying at home and worrying."

"Okay, and what is your take on it?"

"The only thing that would make me go on holiday and not worry about my kidnapped husband, would be if I had no reason or desire to worry. If our relationship had soured, say if he beat me or was having it away with other women every night. I'd probably give up caring pretty quickly."

"Of course, that has to be it. Thank you so much, you're wonderful. Listen, I umm, don't suppose …"

"I'm already on it. I'll call Vincent the moment I have any news."

"Fantastic, I owe you one. Remember that." I handed back the Unicom to Vincent and fist pumped the air.

Byron grinned. "What did she say?"

"She said she wouldn't bother staying at home worrying about her kidnapped husband if their relationship had soured. Say, if he beat her or was screwing someone else, or some other domestic misdemeanour. I'm willing to bet she's only stayed with him because of the kids, and probably his money too if truth be told, and might be only too willing to talk."

"So she probably does genuinely have friends on Lilea," Byron replied.

"Looks like it," I nodded. "Farra is going to do a bit of discreet digging."

"Awesome."

"We're approaching the tube entryway," the intercom boomed. "All viewing windows are now closed for the duration and all balconies are switched off for safety. The medical bay is open and ready to receive anyone who feels they need assistance."

"Here we go again," Vincent said, rubbing his stomach."

"I'd better sort through all of our evidence in my ship, what little there is of it anyway. These statements are the bulk of it so far." We chatted as I rummaged in my secret evidence hideaway and I reckoned I was as happy as I deserved, given my life and behaviour thus far. I had my health back, my father with me, and a brand new and passionate love. My heart tried desperately to dwell on everything I'd done to fuck it all up, but I fought it valiantly and concentrated on the new happiness I was experiencing.

"We don't need these anymore," I said removing the tracking equipment Tinnias and I had found throughout our ship, and the tracker that had been inside me.

"There's a lot of data chips there, Sam," Byron said. "Have you been through them all?"

"Most of them are mine and contain recordings of the Gaht compound. Tinnias and I placed a few cameras early on, before we knew what your stance was. We haven't been through all of them though, there's hours and hours of it and the thought of sitting on our asses for days on end isn't pleasant. A console screen can become a very helpful sleep aid, believe me. I had thought we'd go through them while travelling between locations, but something else came up to distract me," I grinned.

He sniggered. "Hand them around, that way we'll get through them all in a few hours. You never know what could be on there."

"We got some good information from Tip's files," I said. "He'd obviously been tailing someone as there were photographs of people meeting, a couple having sex, people passing packages over, that sort of thing. There was some vidicom clips with similar content to the photographs, except for one clip of me walking around the apartment and another of me disabling all the cameras. There was a secret file that gave us lists and lists of names, two hundred in all. Law enforcers, celebrities, bankers, politicians, even some company owners, along with details of all their bank accounts, addresses, and all information about every one of their close family and friends. Another file listed a load of banks, with details of all staff and their families. Eighty five banks from five different systems."

"Shit," he said and I nodded.

"Indeed," I replied. "Tip was nothing if not thorough. He also had two secret Unicoms. One had made calls but not received any, and the third had received calls but not made any."

"So he was really covering his tracks."

"I'm not surprised. Both Belotan and Yanit are very powerful and dangerous men. They have a huge gang network at their beck and call. If they want you dead, you're dead."

"Yanit? Who's that?"

"The Dankera Collective boss. He personally threw us out of Dankera 7, but he did give us this bottle though, as a gift." I handed over the small bottle. "He said it's one of only fifty bottles."

Byron looked at it. "Nice, we'll try it when this case is over, shall we? Now let's get to it with these data chips."

"Kiss me first," I said.

Twenty minutes before we were due to exit the tube system, the last of the vidicom recordings was handed back to us. Tinnias and I checked over the notes from each of the viewers.

"We have several conversations that mention Vazien," Tinnias remarked.

"We had one that showed Belotan receiving a Unicom call, in which he says the words, 'law enforcers huh?' and then says your real names," a pair of troopers told us.

"So someone called him up and sold us out," I said. "I'd love to know who."

"I've no idea, but it was probably Taiko."

"How do you know that?" Tinnias asked.

"Because when he answered the call, he said, 'hello Commander,' when he greeted him."

"So how did Taiko know it was us?" I asked and looked at Tinnias, who shrugged.

"Fuck knows. I guess it's someone in the Dankera Collective, but I've no idea who. Only Yanit knew who we really are."

"Or it could be one of the Dankera women," Byron offered.

"Wrinkly," Tinnias grinned. "Or that bit of skirt who tried to have her wicked way with you up against that tree."

"Dad, for pity's sake," I blushed as everyone roared with laughter.

"I take it wrinkly was too old and feeble to stand against a tree?" Lomas asked and the laughter was even louder. I nearly peed my pants at that.

"Or it could be Vazien's daughter," I said when I had control enough to speak.

"How do you work that out?" Byron asked. "You said you never saw any sign of her on Dankera?"

"We didn't, but I reckon she's not kidnapped at all. Listen, we know they don't get along, her and Vazien I mean. Supposing she wants revenge on her father and tried to set him up for murdering a couple of law enforcers. Cop killers are not treated well in prison."

"It certainly sounds like a valid theory," Vincent said.

"I agree," Tinnias nodded. "So we have to find her, don't we?"

"She shouldn't be too hard to track down, being famous and easily recognizable. I'll do some research," Byron said and left the room.

"We're going to be out of the tube in a few minutes, if anybody wants to secure themselves a bathroom," Lomas said.

"Oh shit," Vincent said and ran down the corridor with Kyle. Tinnias hurried into his own while I strolled to the smoking room and lit a cigarette.

Fifteen minutes later, the intercom boomed. "We have now exited the tube system and the viewing windows and balconies are once again available for your use. We shall be arriving at Deep Space Refuelling Station Omega 8 in three hours and eleven minutes."

"Now we've got all the evidence we have fully recorded, bagged, and tagged," I said once everyone was back in the Obs Room. "I'll take it all back to the ship and lock it away. We have a list of everything in here, for reference."

Tinnias nodded. "Okay, I'm going to pay Jam a visit. He said he'd help me out with a tan."

"Okay, I'll see you back in here when we get to the Refuelling station to discuss what we're going to do." Tinnias nodded and we parted company. I went back to my ship and stowed away all the evidence in my secret safe place.


I'm going to take a break for a few hours to prepare for some visitors. This is Sinclair V-Log Q890/M data log reference point 4136902/625.

## CHAPTER TWENTY SEVEN

This is Sinclair V-Log Q890/M data log reference point 4136902/626 continuing report.

They stood me up. Can you believe it? I slaved for hours getting the house clean and they wait until they're half an hour late before calling to say they're not coming. No wonder I'm anti social.

"Okay, Son, how shall we handle this? We've no idea if she knows anything or if she'll be happy to talk. She could still be in touch with Vazien and could tell him we've been sniffing around."

"I don't think they're still involved," I said. "For a start she wouldn't be at the whorehouse if she were still his mistress. Second, why change her name and disappear, what would she be running from if not him?"

"Us."

"You have a point," I agreed. "Maybe Vazien decided he wanted a bit more discretion and ordered her to change her name."

"But would he still want her, with her being a working prostitute now?"

"Ahh, we don't know that she is," I said. "Just because she's at the whorehouse doesn't mean she's working. She could be running the joint or just renting a room to hide out. The girls take care of each other"

"Well I think we should take things gently until we know how she stands," Tinnias suggested.

"Agreed," I nodded. "Let's go, shall we?"

Vincent and Kyle came with us. They had a long list of items to purchase for several members of the crew, so we agreed to meet in the bar in two hours. We queued to have our papers checked then walked along the corridor to the main shopping area. The whorehouse was easy to find, the neon sign flashed gaudily and we strolled over and knocked. A dumpy redhead opened the door and smiled.

"Hello gentlemen, looking for some relaxation are you? Do you want separates or are you looking to share?"

Tinnias was about to answer when I cut in. "We'd like to share, please. I believe you have Jalima Wentslone working here. She comes highly recommended so we'd like her if possible. We're happy to wait if she's busy."

She regarded us for several seconds before the smile reappeared and she stepped aside. "Come on in, I believe she's just become available."

The surprisingly nice looking blonde swayed up to us and said hello, before ushering us into the next room. "This way my lovelies."

Once inside and alone, I introduced myself. "Hello Jalima, or should I say Cassalia?"

The smile fell from her lips and she made for the door. I stepped in the way. "Relax, we're friends, please just hear us out before you run away."

"Who are you and what do you want?" she said, fear written clearly in her expression.

"Please don't be scared, Cassalia," Tinnias soothed. "We're from the Inter Galactic Law Enforcement Agency and we're hoping you'll talk to us about Vazien."

"Why?" she demanded. "What would I know about him?"

"Much, I would guess," I said. "You clearly know who he is as you didn't say, 'who is he'. And seeing as how you were his mistress for years on Zibandin, I'd say you probably know quite a bit. We're hoping you'll share it with us so we can put the asshole away."

This seemed to placate her somewhat. "I'll say anything you like for the right price."

"We just want the truth, and the payment is a galaxy without him in. Isn't that good enough?"

She took hold of her blouse and ripped it open, revealing a deep scar that ran across both breasts. "It's a bit late to soothe me with promises of a safer universe. I still have this to remember him by."

"He did that to you?" Tinnias asked. "Don't you want him to pay for that in jail time?"

"I want him dead, is what I want," she snapped. "I'm afraid you've had a wasted journey. I'm not running the risk of angering him again by talking to cops and judges."

"I'm really sorry he did that to you," I said, handing her my card. "Call me if you change your mind. We have powerful friends helping us. I give you my word you'll be safe."

We left and went to the bar. I wasn't surprised by her reaction; prostitutes often react that way even when they've been badly mistreated and many refuse to report their aggressors for fear of further reprisals. Their job gives them a victim mentality, it becomes ingrained and difficult to bypass. Also, the court system still sees them as unreliable witnesses, so it probably wasn't too much of a loss.

"I'm not surprised, Sam," Tinnias said and sighed.

"Neither am I," I agreed. "It's a shame that he has so much hold over people even from so far away." We got drinks and sat down.

"I reckon that the only things we've left to do is interview the guy who invented the sound gun, then find the daughter and see if she'll talk," I said.

"We need to be very careful with her. If she did sell us out, even to get Vazien in trouble, it makes her dangerous to the whole case. If she doesn't feel what we're doing will give her enough satisfaction, she could sell us out again and that would fuck everything up."

"I'll make a couple of calls and get people onto checking her out properly before we make contact," I said. "The moment Byron and Grund find out where she is, I'll know who to call."

"Once she's been dealt with either way, we'll have to talk about how we proceed from there. Whether we have enough evidence to make a case, who to give it to, the usual stuff."

"One thing is obvious," I said. "We give the case to Sigma Headquarters as we have only one leak we know about."

Tinnias nodded. "At least that question is easy to answer. Here's the guys."

I looked up and saw Vincent and Kyle approaching and forced a smile. "Got everything you wanted?" I asked.

"Apart from one of the trooper's Admalian loaf mix, which was sold out, yes," Vincent replied.

"How did it go with the woman?" Kyle asked.

"It didn't," I said.

"Oh? Why not?"

"She's scared of Vazien and won't talk to us or testify for fear of more reprisals."

"More reprisals?" Vincent asked. "So she's had some already?"

I nodded. "A huge scar right across both breasts."

"Shit," Kyle exclaimed. "No wonder she's scared then."

"Quite."

"What's next in the case?" Vincent asked.

"We have one more interview, then we check out Vazien's daughter and see where the land lies with her."

"What do you boys want to drink?" Tinnias asked, getting up.

"Lammish beer if they have it," Vincent replied. "If not, Kambino will be fine."

"I'll have the same," Kyle added.

We chatted about the case until we finished our beers. "Another beer apiece or do you want to go back to the ship?" Tinnias asked.

"Let's have another …" Vincent began but trailed off as his eyes glazed over. I was going to ask him what was wrong but I noticed a heavy weight in my gut that lay inside me like a rock. I looked at Kyle, who was holding a hand to his middle as he squeezed his eyes shut.

"Oh no," Vincent hissed.

"Something's wrong," I added.

"We've been here too long," Kyle said. "We need to get back to the ship really fast."

"What's wrong, guys," Tinnias asked. "Son, what's the matter?"

"I don't know, but something awful is happening. We need to leave right now."

The four of us leapt up and headed towards the exit, to find ourselves face to face with half a dozen mountainous men who blocked our exit.

"Now then, Gentlemen, not running out on us I hope."

"Who the fuck are you and what do you want?" Vincent snapped.

"Who we are is none of your concern right now, and it seems like we have what we want, doesn't it? This way, friends." He indicated down the corridor. "And I wouldn't try anything, we are more than adequately armed."

"They don't allow any weapons on refuelling stations," I said, "everyone knows that."

"The man leaned forward until his face was inches from my own, "I think you'll find everything has its price, my boy.""

"And Vazien is rich enough to pay," Tinnias replied.

We were led through a door marked, 'Station Personnel Only,' and found ourselves at the top of a spiral staircase. Seeing as there was only one direction in which we could go, I started down. Down and down we went to what must have been the very lowest level of the station. Along a corridor and through another door and we were in what looked like a typical security headquarters of the type you find in most large companies and public buildings. Once we'd been secured into a cell containing four beds, four jugs of water, and a toilet in the far back corner, the men left us alone.

"I knew everything was going too well," I said. "I just knew it. Fuck. Shit and fuck."

"Relax, Bro, if you can," Vincent said, putting a hand on my shoulder. "Don't waste energy getting angry just yet. Let's see how things pan out. Come on, we've all been in this type of situation before, so let's not panic yet. We don't want to lose you again, Byron would never forgive us."

"I don't even have a dart pistol," I moaned.

"I have a blade in my boot," Kyle whispered.

"You do?" I gaped.

He nodded. "I never go anywhere without it."

"How come the station scanners didn't pick it up?"

"It's wrapped in a cloak," he said, using the colloquial term for this highly sophisticated piece of technology that prevents anything inside it from showing up on scanners.

"Where the fuck did you get one of those, and where can I get one?" I said."

Vincent grinned. "The Drycenians gave them to us."

"Oh well we can forget that then, Son," Tinnias said and I nodded.

"I'll make a few calls around my contacts," I said. "It'll be costly but they should be able to find one. I've thought about it a few times and meant to ask but never got around to it."

After what seemed like a half hour, the man who had done all the talking returned with two of his heavies and returned our bags of belongings. He came up and stared at me, looked me up and down, and sneered. "So, you like to fuck guys eh?"

"Don't worry, you're not my type," I replied quickly. "I like them with a brain."

"That put's you out of the running then, buddy," Vincent snapped.

A flicker of anger flashed across the man's mouth and he approached the cell and bashed his rifle on the bars, inches from Vincent's face. Vincent however, never flinched. I was deeply impressed. I looked at Kyle and saw him on the verge of laughter, so I quickly looked away. He'd already had his ego bruised by Vincent, one of the best looking guys in existence, to have the rest of us laughing would be asking for painful retribution.

"Which one of you wants to tell us why two cops were visiting our whorehouse, and why you left so quickly? You both got hair triggers or something?"

"So just because we're cops, we're not allowed to fuck?" Tinnias said. "And we would've too if there'd been anything worth having in there. They were a right dirty bunch. We have standards you know. If there was a committee, I'd be reporting you to it."

That last statement almost made me laugh out loud. Holding it in was becoming painful now and I couldn't help but grin.

The guy was incensed. "Maybe you need persuading to tell me," he said, indicating one of his colleagues, who rolled his shoulders around and tried to look menacing but only succeeded in looking fat and slow. I'd have him down easily, even without the Lileans' help.

"Then you'll lose whatever leverage you think having us here gives you." I replied. I'd done this so many times it was almost boring. "Look, guys, you want to know what we're doing, and we don't want to tell you. Vazien obviously has you by the balls, so we'll do you a favour and not tell him you fucked up. So come on, let's be grown-ups huh?"

He indicated for his two heavies to leave. Once he was alone, he approached me and stared at me through the cell bars. "Maybe he doesn't care about leverage," he said. "Maybe he just wants you out of the way."

"Again? Then how's he going to react when he finds out what a fuck up you are?" I said, holding up the magazine from his now empty rifle and smiling. Before he was able to recover from the shock, I reached through the cell bars, grabbed his fingers that held the trigger guard, and pulled his little finger back the wrong way, hard. He yelled in pain and dropped the rifle, which I had reloaded and pointed at him in under six seconds, a record for me.

"Unlock the cell, there's a good boy," I said. He did as he was told and I led us out of the cell. Indicating to Tinnias, I let the guy see me aiming at his face while he was searched.

"Baklon Jeeta-Farlo," Tinnias said into my data recorder. Once he added the guy's thumb print, retinal scan, and blood sample, he cuffed him to the cell bars.

"Right, if we hurry, we'll make it back in time for dinner," I said.

Vincent and Kyle were awestruck. "You're amazing, Sam," Vincent grinned.

"That was fucking awesome," Kyle added.

"Well done, Son, I'm proud of you," Tinnias swelled with pride.


Back in the Obs Room, Byron gave us an update. "Grund and I have discovered several rumours concerning Olendra's location, but nothing concrete yet. We know where she was up until a month ago. After that, it's rumour and speculation."

"When Ren told you to find her," I said, remembering our conversation, "he said her past will lead us to her location, didn't he?"

Byron nodded. "Yes, let me think on that. If we research her life story, we might get a clue. Give us a couple of hours before you ring your contacts." I grinned and winked at him and he smiled at me.

"I think it might be prudent," Tinnias said, "to remain here near the refuelling station just in case Vazien decides to pay us a visit and cause trouble. At least here we've got armed back up and powerful people to witness what happens."

"Oh we can defend ourselves," Toma said. "Don't you worry about that."

"I know," Tinnias replied, "but if we fight back, even in defence, we lose the moral advantage. No one can say we provoked them or caused the trouble, if we keep our hands clean."

"Very true, Tinnias," Lomas said. "Good thinking. I agree, we'll remain within the boundary of the station until we know where to go to find Olendra."

"You should've seen the way Sam here disarmed that guy," Kyle said as he relayed the story to everyone. "It was the most awesome thing ever, even we didn't notice what he was doing until he held up the magazine."

I laughed. I'd been taught how to do that by one of the best thieves in the business, who happened to be one of my most reliable contacts. He said it would benefit me far more than money ever could, and he was right. It had saved my ass on many occasions.

"It's been a useful skill over the years," I admitted, with an embarrassed smile.

"It was amazing, Sam," Vincent grinned, "I'm seriously impressed."

Tinnias laughed. "It always gives me goose bumps seeing you do that, Son."

The chatter continued for several minutes until I remembered something that had me running back to my ship to rummage in the evidence stash. Finding what I wanted, I headed back to the Obs Room. I found Lomas making himself a drink. He didn't appear engaged in conversation with anyone so I strolled over.

"Sir?" I asked.

"Sam, how can I help?"

"What's this?" I held up the carved metal box Tinnias and I had got from Tip's safe.

He took it from me and examined it from all angles closely before replying. "Wherever did you get this?"

"I got it from someone's safe," I replied.

"Yes but who's safe?"

"If I tell you, I want to know what it is? Deal?"

"Deal," Lomas smiled. "It's a bomb."

"What the fuck?" I hissed. "Are you shitting me?"

"Unfortunately not. Now who's safe was this in?" He asked, handing it to Byron, who ran towards the door with it.

"Tip's."

"Oh fuck," Byron said. "Does he know what it is do you think, Sam?"

"I haven't the faintest idea, sorry. He hasn't even asked me if I took it, so he's either not been into his safe lately, or he doesn't want to bring it up, for whatever reason."

"Ring him, right now please," Lomas said. "Ask him about it, where he got it, everything he knows about it. Oh and don't tell him what it is until I give you the nod."

"Detective Danso here," the familiar voice said.

"Hey, Tip, it's Sam. How are you?"

"Hi, Sam. I'm fine. Is everything okay? How's the boys?"

"Hey, Tip," Kyle said. "We're great, thanks."

"Listen, Bro," I said. "After Dad and I did a moonlight dash from the Drycenians, we went back to Tyrrin briefly and turned over your place."

"I know. Malea told me you'd been in for a rummage."

"I'm sorry, I didn't know the truth about which side you were on and I was so worried you'd been got at by a blackmailer."

"It's okay, really. Thanks for caring."

"The thing is, inside your safe was a Drycenian metal box. Very pretty it is, all carved and decorated. You know it?"

"So that's where it went. I've been wondering."

"What is it, by the way?"

"It's an ancient puzzle box apparently. I was told they give it to their kids to stimulate their brains, so they start being clever right from day one. I was going to give it to Kyle's daughter when she's born."

"Where did you get it?"

"From a trooper on Captain Bax's battle cruiser. He gave me a ride home a few months ago and this trooper gave me the box as a gift."

"What was this trooper's name, if you can remember?" Lomas cut in.

"Hello, Your Majesty. Umm, his name was, let me think, Shob, Shab, something like that. Sorry I can't remember exactly; I only met the guy once."

"No matter, that will do nicely," Lomas replied. "Thank you, Tip."

"Is there a problem?" Tip asked. "Have I got the guy into trouble or something. Should he not have given it to me?"

"Tip," Lomas said. "I'm ashamed to tell you that even the Drycenians are not immune from greed and evil. It seems we have a rotten piece of fruit in the bowl, as they say."

"How do you mean?"

"That's no puzzle box. The item you speak of is quite different, and I'll be happy to gift you one myself when we next meet. This box is, I'm sorry to tell you, a bomb."

"What the fuck?" Tip hissed. "And Sam has it? Get it the fuck away from him and quickly."

"Fear not," Lomas assured him. "We have the situation under control now. Thankfully, Sam had the presence of mind to come and ask me what it was. I'm so glad all our friends are still safe. Most relieved."

"The guy must be on Vazien's payroll, or maybe one of the gangs. He gave it to me not long after I got accepted as a law enforcement leak for Gaht."

"Oh we'll find out the truth, don't worry about that. I'm sorry this happened to you, most ashamed that our friends have been put in danger by one of our own. He will pay for his misdemeanour, I assure you."

"Thank you, Sir. Are you okay, Sam?"

"Shocked, like we all are. I had that thing in my ship since Tyrrin. The frozen scream is the one thing I truly dread. You take care now okay? Keep in touch."

I rang off and Tinnias grabbed me and just held my face in his hands. No words were spoken, his eyes said it all. He hugged me close and I heard him sigh deeply. "Oh shit," he exclaimed in both shock and relief. "Shit, shit, shit."

"What's up?" Vincent said, having just entered the room after delivering the various items from the station to their purchasers. We told him the story and he went white. I looked at him and saw his eyes moisten.

Tinnias put a hand to his shoulder and squeezed. "It's okay, Byron has it and is making it safe right now."

The intercom boomed. It was Byron. "You're Majesty, everything is safe now, Sir. Everyone can relax."

"I need to call Captain Bax," Lomas said and left the room.


The atmosphere, somewhat subdued due to the appearance of the bomb and the knowledge that a Drycenian had done something with intent to cause suffering, lasted well into the evening by the time I noticed the energy lightening. After taking an hour to allow our dinner to go down, Vincent, Kyle and I made our way to the cargo hold to spar. A group of Troopers were there and approached us meekly.

"Hi guys," I smiled, determined not to treat them all with suspicion like I had before.

"We want to say we're sorry for what one of our people did. It shames us all when one tries to cause harm. Causing suffering is no longer our way, we left that behind thousands of years ago. We hope it doesn't prevent you from continuing to trust us with your friendship."

"I refuse to let anyone, wherever they're from, harm the friendship we enjoy with the Drycenians," I said. "There's good and bad in every race, whatever your size, colour, belief system, how many legs you have, or whatever name you give to your deity. No people are perfect, I'd be out of a job if they were. You're our friends and nothing will change that."

"We've been through difficulties," Vincent said. "Remember the Zaltoid? If our friendship can survive that painful time, it'll survive this, no problem."

"We'll always be proud to be your friends," Kyle said. "Don't ever doubt that."

"Thank you, guys," the troopers smiled, their relief obvious.


Byron and I fell asleep, still locked in our embrace and I allowed his smell to fill my soul. His body odour was intoxicating, I'd never been aware of anyone's body smell unless it was unpleasant but this one was beautiful and I drank it in greedily. Suddenly, a noise outside caught my attention and I sat up. I turned to see if Byron had woken but he was no longer beside me and I frowned. Silence answered my calls, so I got up and checked the bathroom and balcony but found myself alone. Where could he have gone and how the fuck did I not notice him get out of my arms, out of the bed, open the door, and disappear so expertly? The corridor in both directions was empty, so I wandered down towards the cargo bay and engineering, the two first choices when looking for Byron.

Engineering was deserted, which I found odd. Surely a ship the size of the battle cruiser would have engineers on duty day and night? I shook my head and wandered to the cargo bay, flung open the door and looked down the huge space to the far side but saw no one. I turned to leave, then heard a groan from my right, between two stacks of storage crates, so I crept over and peered around the side. The sight that met my eyes sent me cold to the bone. Vincent, Kyle, and Byron were there and all three were as naked as the day they were born and from their movements, I gathered that they were soon to enjoy a shattering climax.

My throat constricted painfully each time I tried to scream and no matter what I tried, I could only make a rather disappointing strangled gasp. I ran from the cargo bay, hurtled along corridors without caring where I was going, eventually finding myself in the deserted ship's bridge. I just had time to register how odd it was that the bridge was deserted before flinging my full body weight against the huge viewing window, which shattered. There was a moment of panic, then an icy stillness before I felt myself pulled violently out through the broken window, followed by all sorts of things left lying around the various bridge work stations. The battle cruiser shuddered to a halt as I continued on my trajectory into the stygian void and as it became a dot in the far distance, I sent my love to Byron one last time.

I leapt awake with such force I fell from the bed onto the floor, gasping in terror and hugging my knees as I tried to cry silently so as not to wake Byron. My stomach gave a lurch and I struggled to my feet and staggered to the bathroom, just making it in time to avoid puking all over the floor. Once my stomach settled, I swilled my mouth and gargled with some mouthwash before heading back to bed. Byron was awake and sitting up.

"Sorry to wake you, my love," I said and kissed him. "Had to pee."

We snuggled together and were asleep quickly, but a noise from outside caught my attention. By the time I awoke for breakfast, I'd been through the same nightmare five times and decided that there was no way I was enduring that every night, especially while working on this damn Vazien case. I knew I had something on my ship that would help me out and dragged myself into breakfast with Byron. He was obviously worried for me and kept asking if I was okay.

"Just a nightmare, nothing to worry about," I smiled reassuringly. "Thank you for caring about me, I love you."

"Was it the same as the one the other night?"

"No. This one was the classic, running along corridors then finding yourself at a dead end with nowhere to go, type."

"Maybe you should have a word with Jam."

"The less we dwell on it, the less power it has. That's what Mom and Dad always said to Ambella when she was a kid. I've always been prone to nightmares, usually when I'm stressed, as we all are with this case. I once had the exact same one twice a week for three months, I thought I would never be free of it but it eventually stopped."

"Okay, I'll try not to nag, but the moment I think you're struggling, I'll be on you so hard you'll wish you'd listened to me earlier."

I grinned. "Never stop nagging. It shows you care. Come on, let's eat."

During breakfast, Byron told us he and Grund had found Olendra's location.

## CHAPTER TWENTY EIGHT

I sat in the cockpit of my ship and waited for someone to answer my call.

"Hello?"

"Haven't you washed those ears yet?" I said.

"Raucous laughter made me smile and we spent a couple of minutes just saying hello and laughing.

"How can I help, Sam."

"I need to find out about someone, quietly, obviously."

"What's her name?"

"Olendra, Child of Vazien."

"You mean Ambassador Vazien's daughter?"

"Yeah."

"Shit, no wonder you want it kept quiet."

"Why do you say that?" I asked, turning at the sound of footsteps approaching. Vincent winked and Kyle waved a cup at me. I nodded and he went to make coffee.

"You probably know already, but you need to be careful with him. He's one dangerous fuck."

"How?"

"Come on, Sam, don't play me, Son. I've been at this way longer than you."

I laughed. "Sorry, I'm just interested in your take on it."

"He has long arms. Piss him off and you might find those arms around your neck. Be careful."

"Yeah, that's just about the same as what I've found. I'm not being paranoid then."

"Hell no. Why are you after his daughter? Has she finally had enough of him?"

This was interesting. "Ahh so I was right, there is bad blood between them."

"Oh yeah, it's quite well known. The rumour is that he tried to seal a business deal by selling her hand in marriage to some company owner in return for a merger or majority share in his company, it depends which rumour you're hearing. She objected and ran away. He sent his heavies after her and brought her back for the wedding but the husband to be died the day before the happy event. He either fell down some stairs or crashed his car, again it depends which rumour you're listening to. The guy's eldest son takes over the company and the daughter happily marries him, but they refuse the merger, or share sale or whatever it is and send Vazien packing. He was angry of course and vowed revenge. Fast forward a year and the girl's husband goes to jail for embezzlement of company funds. The daughter then vows revenge on Vazien. That's about where we are now. Next instalment, same time next week, turn on and tune in, be there or be square."

I laughed. "How do you know all that?"

"The guy she married is a distant cousin of my neighbour, who happens to work for me and couldn't keep a secret if his life depended on it. He's a great source of information about the Vazien saga."

"This is awesome, I knew you'd be able to help me out. I'm in your debt."

"Could I redeem that favour right away? Sorry to be rude but I have a ticket."

"Give me the details and I'll make it go away."

I wrote down the details of his parking misdemeanour and he promised to be back in touch with Olendra's location. I thanked him profusely and hung up, then dialled another number.

"Hi Kia, how are you hunny?"

"That sounds like Sam. It's been ages, when are you coming home?"

"When I can, you know this job. I have a favour to ask of you."

"Will this earn me dinner and dessert?"

"Dinner certainly."

"No dessert? You haven't gone and met someone have you?"

"Yeah."

"That's awesome. Is it serious?"

"Very."

"Who is she?" I didn't answer. "He?"

"Yeah."

"Wow, Sam, I never knew."

"Well you know me, always like to be different."

"I'm pleased for you, I mean it."

"Thanks hunny."

"Okay, so whose ticket needs dealing with this time?"


I put away my Unicom and turned to face Vincent. "Wow, that's incredible. I rang this contact to ask him to tell me about Olendra, and he proceeds to tell me all about why her and Vazien hate each other, the whole story. It turns out, one of the people concerned is a distant cousin of his neighbour, who works for him and has a loose tongue."

"That's great. What's the story?" He asked.

"He tried to sell her hand in marriage for a business deal. She ran but he got her back. Then the husband to be died, which was probably her doing, and his son takes over the company. Soon after, she happily marries him. They both turn down Vazien's business deal and send him packing. A year later, her husband goes to jail for embezzlement and she vows revenge on Vazien."

"That would give her plenty of reason to set you up," Kyle said, handing steaming cups of coffee around. "To get yours and Tinnias' murders pinned on her father would be the right sort of revenge for getting her husband sent to jail."

"Definitely," Vincent nodded.

"I reckon so," I added. "Once we know where she is, I can get a couple of contacts onto digging a bit deeper, then we'll be able to figure out whose side she's on and whether we can risk talking to her or not."

"I've been thinking," Vincent said. "About when the time comes to make this official. We've found out that Vazien has leaks and many people on his payroll are in law enforcement and I think we can safely assume there are many we'll never know about. There could be judges, jury members, all sorts working for him. We really don't want him to get off, do we?"

"No we don't," I agreed.

"I was wondering if it might not be worth at least thinking about giving the case to Donaldson of the ANA. They're supposed to be unbribable, and he got me cleared of those false murder charges. Everyone trusts the ANA, knows they're open and honest, that's why they are who they are. They are a neutral and trustworthy arbitration body, who oversee trials and sentencing when honesty and transparency is paramount. They take control of all the most major and news worthy trials. I'm preaching to the converted, Sam. You know all this already, but it occurred to me that it's worth considering."

"It's definitely worth thinking about. I'll mention it to Tinnias. Thank you."

"I didn't want to interfere but it seemed like a good idea, since we have problems knowing who we can trust at the moment."

"Help is never interference and I always welcome help. Without the help of my contacts, I'd never get anyone behind bars. Sharing ideas and discussing options often brings in stuff I'd never have thought of on my own. Everyone has their own unique view, and even if it doesn't solve anything, it's worth hearing."

My Unicom rang. "Detective Sinclair-Vaylo."

"Hi, Sam, it's Farra."

"Hi Farra, how's everything? Are you okay?" Vincent looked up.

"Yes, I'm fine, thanks. I'm calling about the Taiko wife and kids."

"Oh, yes. You've found something?"

"It seems her brother married a Lilean woman, and she's come here to visit with them rather than be on her own while her husband is kidnapped. I met her in a café and got talking; us being non Lileans gave me something to use as a conversation starter. She felt vulnerable when her husband didn't come home, and then she got a call saying he had been kidnapped but so long as she didn't make a fuss, he wouldn't be harmed. She said she's scared; she was crying as she told me but it was fake. I don't think she misses him at all and, get this, she had fourteen bags of shopping from expensive stores; clothes, shoes, perfume, the lot. She said she doesn't know who did it, but with her husband being an important person, she knew it was a risk. She says law enforcement haven't been that good to her, but when I said did they know where she is, she admitted she'd told no one. If you ask me, I'd say she only stays with him for the money."

"That's wonderful, you've validated what I thought, thank you so much," I said. "You're awesome. Listen, Vincent's right here, I'll hand you over."

"It's a pleasure, Sam. It took me back a bit, getting involved in something again."

"Well that was interesting," I grinned at Kyle.

"Oh?"

"Farra found her, staying with her brother and his Lilean wife for company while her husband is gone. She was faking being scared but had been on an expensive shopping spree."

"Wow. How does that affect the case? Do you think she's involved?" he asked.

"No, I don't think her domestic issue is connected at all. She's a gold digger, why cut off the hand that feeds you by having him kidnapped? That explains Taiko's attitude when Tinnias and I waylaid him. He must know she doesn't love him."

Vincent handed back my Unicom. "Jeez, what a bitch."


At Byron's suggestion, I spent a couple of hours in the shuttle bay with the mechanics, who took me through the basics of engine maintenance, so I was more up to date with my skills and could fix some problems myself, should they occur while I'm alone in the void.

"I want you to do this every day, for a couple of hours," he said. "It's good for you. I'll feel happier knowing you have a chance to fix a problem and get to help, rather than be alone and scared."

"I agree," I replied. "I did make the effort to learn a few things, which went a long way to lessening the burden of fear, but with some training from you guys, I'll probably be building my own ship within a week."

We laughed as we headed to the cargo bay for some firearms practice with the troopers, after which I spent a couple of hours sparring with Vincent and Kyle. By the time they went to sit and boil in the sauna, I felt as though I was in with a chance of reaching an excellent level of general fitness for the first time. I used the opportunity to race back to my ship and rummage in my secret personal hiding place for the pills I'd been given a couple of years previously. These are highly illegal and came my way by pure chance when a contact of mine asked me for a favour. He was being investigated for some burglaries and didn't want the pills found if his place was searched, so I took them off his hands. They're tiny and bright blue, each one guaranteed to keep you awake for two to three days. The three bottles I had would help ensure no sleep for nightmares to intrude upon for a couple of years, if it were safe to take them all the time. You can take three in a row, then you need at least four hours of sleep before taking another. After three days of no sleep, you tend to go very deep during those four hours, so if any nightmares should happen, I'm unlikely to remember them.

I took one, then replaced the bottle in my hiding place and returned to the room I shared with Byron, to shower before dinner. Halfway through the third verse of one of my four favourite shower songs, Byron joined me.

"Just to save water you understand," he grinned.

"Hell yeah," I nodded. "We must take care of the environment."

"I've found her, Vazien's daughter."

"You've found her? That's great."

"She's on Kopechli 8, in a mansion owned by her husband's family. It's in Ranmash City, the Lorland Mansion."

"So she's keeping her head down."

"It would seem so, yeah."

"I'm very grateful for this, thank you, my love.

"You're welcome, anytime."

I kissed him and we laughed. "You're amazing," I grinned.


When we were out of the shower, I called another contact. "Hi, Kami, it's Sam."

"Hi, Sam, how are you?"

"I'm very well, thank you. How's the family?"

"Growing up and growing old. How can I help you?"

"I need someone tailed for a while. Can you spare a couple of guys?"

"Sure, who is it?"

"Her name is Olendra, Child of Vazien. She's on Kopechli 8, in a mansion in Ranmash City, the Lorland Mansion."

"That wouldn't be Ambassador Vazien's daughter would it?"

"Yeah."

"So you just want to know where she goes?"

"Actually no, I'm not too interested in where she goes. I need to know what she's up to and why, who she's talking to, what she may be planning. Is she up to no good, basically?"

"Okay, give me a week or so and I'll report back, sooner if there's anything really juicy."

"Yes please, especially if it concerns the Ambassador in any way."

"Right. Speak soon, Sam."

"Okay," I said as I put away my Unicom. "Now, we wait." It was then that I remembered about the Vidicom I'd bought on Qaigon 7, which had been forgotten due to the appearance of Brakely and his crew. "Oh shit, I totally forgot. Bro, we found something awesome in a second hand store on Qaigon and just had to buy it. I thought you could help us with a little subterfuge." I showed him the vidicom and he grinned.

"My god, this is going to be hilarious," he said.

"That's what we thought," I said. "We thought if you check to make sure it works first, then tonight, announce a movie night for everyone. Then when this plays, everyone will bust a gut."

Byron laughed. "Oh I hope it works, I so hope it works. This will be the best laugh we've had in ages."


Lomas' voice came through the intercom and the three of us stopped our sparring to listen. "This is a general announcement. Tonight we have decided to have a movie night, and everyone is required to attend. This is a new entertainment feature for us Drycenians, so we will be relying on all our guests to help us enjoy it. The cargo bay vidicom theatre will be open from ten."

"Movie night? Kyle said. "That's unlike the Drycenians."

"Maybe we're passing on our bad habits," I offered.

He shrugged, then had me bent over in agony, my arm up my back and begging for mercy. He let me go and I grabbed the nearest of his legs, twisted it around and sent him sprawling. With a fairly graceful leaping twist, I landed in a seated position in the small of his back, his leg pinned beneath my own. Kyle grabbed me around the neck with one arm and hooked his other under my right armpit, the flat of his hand pushing my head from the rear, his other arm choking my throat from the front. With a twist and duck, I was free, grabbed his arms and brought him over my head and onto his ass in a graceless heap. Vincent then pushed me forward, sending me flat on my face on top of Kyle. He then sat on top of me and sighed.

"Two at once, I win."

"If I hadn't held myself back," I grinned as I got up, "you'd have a broken leg."

"And if I hadn't held myself back," Kyle added, looking at me and grinning, "you'd have a broken neck."

"So we all win," Vincent said, helping us up. "You're really competent, Sam, and you're making me work. Your speed and agility are more than a match for my strength. It means you can run away faster."

Kyle burst out laughing and I admit, it was funny. I couldn't be offended. After a brief stop for a drink, we continued for another hour before heading back to our rooms for a shower.

The cargo bay lights dimmed, the large screen the only illumination. All around me I saw heads and had some considerable difficulty controlling the urge to laugh. Tinnias was a couple of rows in front of us and slightly to our left. I saw him turn and look at me, a broad grin on his face. Everyone waited for what seemed like several minutes for the screen to come to life, when it did, a roar of laughter exploded.

The Transmortal Terror – a tale of prophecy filled the screen with the obligatory spooky music and Vincent covered his face with his hands.

"Oh God, where did this come from. Who found this?"

"That would be me," I admitted. "In fact, Dad saw it and dared me to buy it for you. I had to, I just had to."

He looked at me and burst out laughing. "I had no idea shit like this was out there. How embarrassing."

We watched, laughed our way through most of it, jeered at some parts, and by the time it finished, everyone declared it the most hilarious thing they could remember in months.

Byron was grinning from ear to ear. "That was awesome, Sam. Well done for buying it, however much it cost it was worth every hilarious credit."

"That was the funniest shit I've seen in ages," Tinnias said, coming up to us with a grin.

"I believe this was your doing," Vincent said.

"Guilty as charged. To be honest, I just saw it and brought it to Sam's attention. He bought it, so technically …"

"Hey," I hissed, "whose side are you on?"

"Err, mine, actually," he laughed.

"That was the best thing I've seen in ages," Kyle laughed.

"It was," Vincent agreed. "I haven't laughed so much, about myself, in a long time."

"So we need to go to Kopechli 8," Byron asked and I nodded. "I'll call Lomas and tell him." He punched the intercom and spoke to Lomas, who immediately ordered the ship to Kopechli 8.

"Thank you. That's helpful actually. T43725 Alpha Gammatron Delta is on the way there, so we can call in and get our last interview while we wait for news of Olendra."

Byron frowned. "T43725 Alpha Gammatron Delta? What is that again?"

"It's as yet unnamed, which tells us it's in the process of being colonised. The guy who invented the sound gun lives there, Umboi Trel d'Livliel."

"Is that the gun or the guy?" he asked and we laughed.

"The guy," I sniggered. "Don't do that again," I wagged a finger at him and grinned. "You're a bad man, my love."

That night, I pretended to go to sleep until Byron's breathing told me he was asleep, then I lay awake and used the quiet hours to go through the case in my mind, allowing it to form itself into a coherent pattern of evidence so that it all made as much sense as was possible. I got up to pee and smoke a couple of times and Byron didn't wake up. I was glad of that, there was no need yet to let him know I was having nightmares of his infidelity.

We went to breakfast and I gave Tinnias the updates. "That's helpful. We can get our last interview done without going out of our way, especially as it's a long trip to Kopechli 8."

"Vincent told me something interesting too," I said. "He suggested the ANA oversee the trial."

"Oh that's a wonderful idea," Lomas said. "Donaldson is beyond reproach and everyone knows the ANA are transparent and trustworthy."

Tinnias nodded. "I agree it's a good idea, but there is one small problem."

"Now why am I not surprised," I said and Tinnias sniggered.

"In the normal course of events, the Law Enforcement Agency would first examine the case and then decide to invite the ANA to oversee things. It's a sort of, professional courtesy thing."

"So we can't just go to the ANA ourselves and hand over the case notes and evidence and say, here you are guys, it's all yours?"

"Well technically we can, but it would be akin to saying we've no faith in the very agency we work for. It would be not just stepping on their toes but slapping them on the ass too."

"Who in the agency has the right to make the decision to invite the ANA?" Vincent asked.

"The Trials and Sentencing Liaison Department headed by a Liaison Superintendent and his or her two assistants. Only that one person can invite the ANA. There is one in each headquarters, and ours is Superintendent Shirabli."

"And he's our single leak," I said.

Tinnias nodded. "Yes, or at least the single one we know of. Vazien probably has more we'll never know about."

"What about the one on Tyrrin 4?" Kyle asked. "That's the only other planet we could begin the case from, seeing as how Taiko vanished from there."

"That would be Superintendent Aglin. He wasn't on the list but one of his advisors was, and Tyrrin has four leaks we know of."

"Well I don't know about anyone else but those few facts alone give me reason not to trust the Agency," Vincent remarked. "I'd say you have just cause to go straight to the ANA yourselves."

I noticed several heads nodding, and I had to admit, I agreed. "I have to agree," I said. "It's not an ideal situation and we might get our hands rapped for it, but at the end of the day, getting Vazien off the street is the priority here. If you'd rather step back and avoid trouble, I'll not give you grief about it," I said to Tinnias, who looked at me aghast.

"What the fuck? You seriously think I'd go against you on something like a job? Don't forget you asked me to work with you on this case, not take the case over. You asked me here and that means for this case, I'm not your boss. Didn't you realise that?"

"Well no," I replied. "That kind of thing goes above my head. I'm just a chase, catch, and deliver guy."

"I have no hesitation in trusting your opinions on anything, Son. Remember, you do this every day. I've been a desk bound paper pusher for years so I will always defer to your experience and knowledge. Don't be afraid to remind me of that anytime you feel it necessary. If I hesitate with an answer, it's not automatically because I disagree. Not having done this in a while means I may be unsure, out of my depth even and at such times I need the assistance of your experience and knowledge."

I nodded. "Okay, thank you. Well I agree we have reason enough to go to the ANA directly, even if it's just to get Donaldson's advice. He may have a different solution we've not thought of or don't have authority to access."

"That's true," Kyle nodded. "You never know what obscure rules and loopholes there may be lurking in the dark corners of the regulations."

"And if anyone knows them, Donaldson does," Vincent added.

"I must say I wouldn't hesitate to trust him myself," Lomas said.

"So are we all agreed and happy with that?" I asked and everyone nodded.

"Good. So let's head for Kopechli 8 and stop off at T43725 Alpha Gammatron Delta on the way."

"Right," Lomas nodded and headed for the intercom. "Byron?"

"Nine days and fourteen hours, Sir.

"Okay everyone, we have plenty of time in which to relax. Who's for murder mystery?"

We enjoyed another round of murder mystery, with Tinnias as murderer. I was playing a musician with a drug habit who fell foul of my dealer, Klackan. The following day, Byron announced he'd invented a treasure hunt game. He'd hidden clues around the ship, in the form of riddles that we had to solve in order to know where to go for the next clue. Some of the riddles told us to get certain items to help us, keys, crowbars, water bottles, all manner of stuff, which later clues would require us to use in certain ways in order to progress through the hunt. At one point, I saw Tinnias and Grund, clad in suits, making their way carefully along the outside of the battle cruiser's shuttle bay in order to find a clue they were convinced was there. Another time, Byron's Assistant Chief Engineer, Lish, Klackan, and I had several floor panels up in main engineering and proudly displayed the clue we'd found buried there.

When we found a clue, we had to place our team name in place of the clue, so the next team to get there would know who had found it and could come and look for us to share the clue. Points were awarded based on who found clues, who had to share from other finders, and who never found any. Every hour, the team with the current lowest score was disqualified for an hour. Once all the clues were in, the top three teams were allowed one hour to make up their minds where the treasure was hidden. They then told the adjudicator, who announced the winner, if there was one. The finder of the treasure got a certain block of points, and the ultimate winner was the team with the most accumulated points at the end.

Everyone congratulated Jam and his team for winning the bottle of Tolompka. Every day, I would spend a couple of hours with the mechanics in the shuttle bay, and I learned more and more about my ship's engines and how to care for her better. Vincent and Kyle joined me for firearms practice with Byron and the troopers, we had laser battles, sparred daily, and I spent my nights awake as Byron slept in my arms.

On the third day of our journey, Lomas called Kyle for a private chat in his quarters. Vincent and I looked at each other and frowned.

"Does he do this a lot," I asked. "Call you aside like that? Kyle hasn't done anything wrong, so I wonder what's going on."

"I've not known him do that," Vincent replied. "He's usually very open and honest and does everything without worrying who can hear. I hope Kyle's okay."

Just over an hour later, Vincent was called to Lomas' quarters and rushed over, worried sick about Kyle now. Two hours later, they both returned and told us that the Trooper from Captain Bax's ship had admitted handing the bomb to Tip when he found out he planned to gift it to Kyle's daughter when she was born. The intent was to kill Kyle and the baby, as the Trooper didn't like Drycenian blood being mixed with that of other races.

"I'm sorry that happened to you," I said.

"Thank you," he said. "It's not the bomb itself that's upsetting. Laine would warn me way before there was danger, her stern approach would ensure I took notice of such a warning. No, it's the knowledge that such a degree of hate exists that I find difficult. How can anyone hate so passionately? I'll never understand that."

Something he said caught my attention. He said his spirit friend, Laine, has a stern approach. That made me immediately think of the woman I'd seen in the first nightmare, the ice world.

"By the way, Kyle. Your spirit friend, Laine. What's she like?"

"She's authoritative but kind. She can come across as cold but she cares deeply. Her authoritative nature helps give me the push I need sometimes."

"What does she look like?" I continued.

"Well, she's as tall as me, mature but not old, and she has silver hair that she wears all up on top of her head in some elaborately weaved creation. Oh, and she always appears to me wearing a floor length red coat with a fur collar. Why?"

"Ahh, I think I've seen her, that's all. When you said something about her stern approach, I felt some familiarity inside my mind."

"You saw her? Wow. Did she speak to you? What did she say?"

"I can't remember," I lied. "I just have this image, nothing more, sorry. She's beautiful, in a mature woman sort of way. Elegant."


T43725 Alpha Gammatron Delta was still almost pristine, having just begun to be colonised by settlers. The military had been there for years, helping to set up a working administration system, security force, and proper law and order procedures. It was a small planet, so the initial plan was for it to become a refuelling planet. These are much like the refuelling stations but on a much bigger scale. There are hotels, facilities for ship maintenance and upgrade, a military base, manufacturing and industry sectors, and of course, a refuelling port. It was to be run under the guidelines and regulations of the Inter Galactic Military Force, having become the latest signee of the Inter Galactic Union of Worlds. It is not a place one goes to live, it is a place of work, where the workers also live.

The man Tinnias and I came to see, Umboi Trel d'Livliel, was once the owner of a gun manufacturing company on his home world, Maltak 9. He was working in one of the new hotels on the planet and smiled at us as we approached his reception desk.

"Good morning to you, Gentlemen. Welcome to Gammatron. Will it be two singles or will you be sharing?"

"Actually, it's you we've come to see," I said. "I called you a couple of days ago?"

He nodded. "Ahh yes, the law enforcement guys. Vaylo and Sinclair-Vaylo, yes?"

"That's correct, I'm Sinclair-Vaylo."

"Would you two be related or is the name pure coincidence?"

"Father and son," Tinnias smiled.

He nodded, seemingly satisfied with our answers to his interrogation. "Okay, through that door there, get yourselves a hot drink and relax. I'm off duty in forty five. I'll come and get you."

## CHAPTER TWENTY NINE

Umboi led us to his staff accommodation. The room was small but had a nice view from the tiny window. A long valley stretched to the horizon, virgin forest as far as the eye could see. It was beautiful, untamed, and fresh.

"Please sit," Umboi said, indicating a couple of folding chairs. "My facilities are basic I'm afraid but they work for me. The less one has the more one can focus one's mind on work, don't you agree?"

"I do indeed," I nodded. "I've lived by that very same principle for the last twenty years."

He sat on the end of his bed, supporting his useless left arm with his right, placing the wrist comfortably on the left knee so it wouldn't dangle and be damaged further.

"What do you wish to know about Vazien, and why?"

"You are one of many people harmed by Vazien. His crimes have come to our attention and the scale of them is such that we believe it is time we worked with those willing to help, to deal with him officially."

"But he's been a bully and a crook for years," Umboi said. "You've only just noticed? Come on, I'm many things but stupid isn't one of them."

"Of course we know," I said. "We've known for ages but as you no doubt know, he is a very powerful man with a long reach and it is only now that hard evidence and willing testifiers are making themselves apparent. Without both of these, we are doomed to failure and he has a certain reputation for revenge."

"Okay, I understand. So what do you need to know?"

"First, are you willing to give us a recorded interview and sign a declaration of intent to testify? We can assure you that you will be taken to a place of complete safety and if necessary, given a new identity and all that would be required for you to start over somewhere fresh."

"Yes," he nodded. "Vazien effectively ended my life back on Maltak, so I'm willing to take the risk. I'm just drifting here anyway, it's a job not a career. I lost my independence, my home, my friends, family, and even my world when he did this to me," he indicated his useless left arm. "I'm more than willing to risk the rest of this useless carcass."

I indicated to Tinnias, who switched on my data recorder, then I went through the usual preliminaries before allowing Umboi to tell us his tragic story.

"Please tell us how you came into contact with Ambassador Vazien."

"Nine years ago, I owned my own gun manufacturing company. I invented many new types of gun, some of which are still in general use, one of them by your very own law enforcement agency. The Listrop Laser rifle, you know it?"

"I have two in my personal armoury," I said.

"I invented that. Anyway, bragging aside, I stumbled upon an idea for a weapon that could use a focused beam of sound waves rather than bullets or lasers. It would be far less damaging upon impact and the beam would travel further, making the weapon effective at longer distances, thereby making it safer for soldiers in the theatre of war, or law enforcers on the streets. I decided to attend a conference and trade show; I used to go to these events regularly. They kept me in touch with other gun makers and potential customers and kept my company name out there and visible. At this particular event, I hinted at having invented a weapon that uses a totally new kind of ammunition that would turn the arms world upside down. I guess I went to town on the advertising, as Ambassador Vazien showed a great deal of interest."

"How did he become involved?"

"He pressed me about the new gun. He told me he could finance its production, for a half share in the profits and his company name sharing space with mine on the weapon itself."

"What was the name he gave for his company?"

"Qelmid Lod Arms."

"And you agreed to his proposal?"

"I showed initial interest, but I didn't give him a definite agreement. He said we should have a formal meeting to discuss things, and he would bring his company guys along to make sure everything he promised was legal, and I was to bring the plans of the weapon so he could take a look to make sure it was worth his time and money. I finally decided not to go forward with the partnership and he seemed fine about it. We shook hands and parted ways and I was happy. Six months later, the Shocker 350 comes out on general sale, manufactured by Qelmid Lod Arms. It was my gun. I bought one and took it apart to compare it with my plans. It's definitely my design. I did some research and found that his company guys were in fact his gun designers, who had memorised my plans and recreated them. He had gone and had it patented under his own name. That gun made him a fortune."

"What did you do when you discovered all this?"

"I called him up and told him what I thought of him. I told him I was going to make sure as many people as possible knew what he'd done. Also, I reminded him I still had the original dated plans and said I was going to put the whole saga on to the galactic web for everyone to see."

"How did he react to that?"

"He laughed and hung up on me. A week later, I was leaving the factory late one evening when I was set upon by four men, dragged into a hover vehicle and driven for almost an hour into the countryside. They told me to keep my mouth shut or it would be sewn shut, that my body would be sent, piece by piece, to various members of my staff and my friends. They stripped me naked and beat me with metal bars. I went blind in my left eye and lost the use of my left arm. On Maltak, we are all left handed, the rare right handers that are born are considered to be marked by a demon from our religious teaching. We never use our right hands, for to do so is said to invite the demon close. Without the use of my left arm, I couldn't eat, wash, dress myself, nor even clean myself after going to the bathroom. No one spoke to me, shops refused to sell me their goods, public transportation refused me a ride, kids wrote obscene things on my house walls with animal waste, women spat at me in the street. I eventually found myself one dark moonless night, standing on the central handrail of the Kandiro Road Bridge. As I was about to jump, my last thought was to despair at how Vazien had so easily won. That changed me. I realised that the only way I could win over Vazien was to live, to have a life, to not die quietly, to wait for the time when the universe deems me worthy of justice."

"Are you willing to sign a declaration of intent to testify?"

"Yes."

Tinnias switched off the data recorder and I bagged and tagged the declaration, then thanked him.

"You are worthy of justice," I said. "The time is now."

"Thank you, and good luck."

"Someone will call you later today to confirm everything we've told you about witness safety, and to let you know what will happen when the time comes. Here's my card, call me anytime if you're worried or have questions."

"We have to get him," I said as I flew us back to the battle cruiser and swiped at the moisture on my cheek.

Tinnias squeezed my shoulder and sighed. "The wanton cruelty of some people never ceases to amaze me. I just don't understand the need to be so cruel in pursuit of power over others."

"These people have all suffered so much at his hands. If we fail to get justice for them, it'll be a while before I can sleep at night." I sniffed as I brought the ship down onto a pad in the shuttle bay.

"We won't fail," Tinnias assured me. "One way or another, we'll get justice for them." He looked at me for long seconds, held my gaze with his big brown eyes and I understood. "Preshul Malmack," he whispered. This Sigma phrase meaning The Silent Footfall, symbolises that time of ultimate desperation, when as law enforcers we've failed to bring the very worst of criminals to justice for whatever reason. It is very rare but we know it happens from time to time. On dark nights in quiet alleyways, justice is meted out to those responsible for the most heinous of acts but whom we failed to bring in to the formal system. The cases of Preshul Malmack have their signs that we recognise, left by law enforcers for other law enforcers to find so that the case quickly ends up at the bottom of some dusty box in the cold case section of the file archive. I've never had cause to take part, but I've heard the words whispered, seen the glances of one law enforcer to another, the nod of understanding in response, and turned my face away. Today it was my father whispering those words and me who nodded in response. Vazien would be brought to justice, I gave my word to the universe and wiped at my cheek, angry that a man might bring me to Preshul Malmack after all these years."

We met Vincent, Kyle, and Byron in the corridor as we made our way back to the Obs Room. They were smiling and laughing, which lifted my spirits. Man, it was so good to get back to my love. They saw me, and their smiles fell away.

"Sam? What's up Bro?" Byron said, wiping my cheek.

"What happened down there?" Kyle said.

Tinnias sighed again. "It's one never ending trail of cruelty and suffering. That guy down there was driven almost to suicide. How the fuck he held on I'll never know. Some folks are so strong. I'm in awe of their courage."

Vincent looked at Tinnias. "Are you okay? We're here if you need to vent, I mean it."

"Vazien's men took him out to the middle of nowhere, stripped him naked, then beat him so bad he went blind in one eye and lost the use of his left arm. They're all left handed where he's from and they have this religious thing that says right handers are marked by a demon, so no one can use their right hand for anything. This guy went from a successful self made man with his own company, to not being able to feed himself or clean himself after using the bathroom. His neighbours shunned him, wrote obscene things about him on his house wall, spat at him in public, all because he could no longer use his left hand and wasn't allowed to use his right. So now he works reception in a hotel and no doubt feels like a shit for using his right hand because he has no choice. How the fuck are we meant to go home to our nice homes and nice families and nice lives and not feel guilty? Can you tell me that because I sure as hell don't know?" He thumped the wall and banged his forehead against it several times in anger and frustration.

He turned, leaned against the wall and ran both hands through his hair. "I'm sorry, I lost it there for a minute."

"Dad, no. Don't apologise for anything." I hissed. "Don't you dare."

"Hey, hey," Kyle snapped, going over to Tinnias and grasping his hand in his own. "You're working to get justice for them, every day. You've left your family and your job to be here to help Sam bring this asshole down. You're hearing first hand how many lives he's ruined. You're listening to it, thinking about it, dealing with it, all the time, both of you. You damn well fucking lose it whenever you need to and don't apologise for it, ever." He gave Tinnias' hand a heavy squeeze before letting it go.

"Thank you, guys," Tinnias said. "Let's go get a drink huh?"

Everyone fell silent after Tinnias and I told them of our conversation with Umboi. No one spoke for several seconds until Jam addressed me quietly.

"Sam? I don't suppose you'd know to what extent this man's arm and eye are damaged?"

Hope leapt into life within my breast as I gaped at him. "No but I could find out. It would be no trouble to go back down there and ask him."

"How about if I were to come with you with a mobile scanner. It wouldn't take more than a minute or two to find out how much help I could be, if any."

"We'll come too," Vincent said and Kyle nodded.

"You're not leaving me out," Byron said.

"Nor me," Toma added.

"Okay then, let's go," Tinnias said. "I'll call him as we're on our way. I'll say there's a couple more questions we forgot to ask, and say we're bringing the guy who can confirm details of witness safety."

"Son?" Lomas said. "Make sure he knows that he will be able to remain safe with us for as long as necessary, at no cost whatsoever. He will be a welcome guest for as long as he needs."

"I will, father."

Tinnias put his Unicom away as I lowered the nose and headed down through the atmosphere. "He's going to wait in reception for us."

The Drycenians got a few stares as we made our way through crowds towards the hotel, but no one bothered us. Those over large yellow eyes are magnificent, hypnotic, they hold you, and people obviously noticed them. I saw Umboi sitting by a window and waved. He got up and came over, a little surprised by the number of people we had with us.

"Don't be alarmed," I smiled. "Can we talk somewhere private and I'll explain everything?"

We managed to squeeze into Umboi's small room. "I'm sorry there isn't enough proper seating for this number of people."

"Oh I'm quite happy on the floor," Toma announced and flopped down, his back propped against the wall. Byron joined him. Umboi stared at Toma, having been the only Drycenian to have spoken.

"Do I have the pleasure of Drycenian company in my humble accommodations?"

"You do," Toma said, standing and offering his hand, which Umboi shook. "My name is Toma and I am here representing His Majesty King Lomas VII, who insists that I make it clear to you that when the time comes, you will be joining us for the duration of any trial that may be happening in connection with this awful business brought about by Ambassador Vazien. I give you his Majesty's personal assurance that there is no safer place existing, than within the confines of our battle cruisers. No one will get to you while you are our guest. I have also been told to assure you that if things don't go as we wish, you will be given a new identity, all the papers, a job, a home, and everything you need in order that you are able to start afresh, safe from harm."

"Well, thank you, very much," Umboi replied, somewhat taken aback.

Jam stepped forward. "Hello Umboi, my name is Jam and I'm his Majesty's personal physician and ship's doctor. When I heard about your medical problems, I insisted Sam and Tinnias bring me down to see if there is anything I can do to aid you."

"I've seen lots of doctors and they all say I've lost the nerves in my arm and my eye only has forty percent vision, they're useless now. You could cut the arm off if you like, it gets in the way somewhat."

"Allow me to indulge my curiosity for a minute, would you? Just sit comfortably." Taking hold of his mobile scanning device, he ran it up and down Umboi's arm, shoulder, chest, and back for several minutes, while we sat in silence. He then looked into his eyes through a special gizmo with a red light at the end. Finally he put it away and smiled. "I can give you ninety percent use of the arm back in seven days, eight at the most, and eighty five percent vision in the eye within a month."

Silence ensued, during which Umboi stared at Jam, and Jam stared back. Disbelief and shock on one face, confidence and compassion on the other. Emotion then exploded from Umboi as his good hand went to his mouth and sobs filled the air around us. Vincent put an arm around his shoulders and squeezed. Toma sat beside him.

"Is this true?" Umboi asked. "Please don't joke about it."

"He's the best doctor in this entire galaxy," Toma said. "No one else is entrusted with our sovereign's health and that of his children. If he says you'll be back to normal, then you'll be back to normal."

"Can you take some time off?" Jam asked.

"If I'm getting my arm back, they can shove their job. With my left arm I can pray to my deity again without shame and know he'll answer. I can even go home and ask forgiveness from my friends and neighbours. Maybe start my business again."

"Then pack your stuff," I smiled.


Umboi was introduced to Klackan, who invited him to share his quarters so they would both have someone to talk to who was in a similar situation. Umboi happily agreed and once he'd unpacked, Jam made sure he was comfortably ensconced within the medical bay. I went to see him as Jam prepared to work on him, wished him well, and promised to visit regularly.

"Don't worry about a thing," I said. "You're in the very best hands."

That evening, after our daily sparring session and sauna, I realised that I was due for a night off the pills and would have to sleep. My heart sank. I had got into a routine of taking a two hour nap each day while Byron was at work and it seemed to help. I didn't get the nightmares, or at least if I did, I didn't remember them as I was so tired that my mind wasn't able to hold onto the memories. I decided that I would continue in this fashion rather than do the three days straight and four hour sleep routine. I was so far into my thoughts that I didn't see Vincent coming at me and I fell to the floor in an inelegant heap.

"Oh shit, I'm so sorry, Bro," he said and helped me up.

"It was my fault," I replied. "I was miles away."

"You're not on top form these days, Bro," Kyle said. "This case must be taking too much out of you."

"I'm sorry, maybe I should let you two spar alone. I'm probably holding you back just now."

"Don't be silly," Vincent said. "It's the only way you can let off steam while on board."

He had a point and it hadn't occurred to me that here was an ideal opportunity for me to work out the emotional trauma left by the nightmare, otherwise I'd be seeing the three of them for years into my future, in my mind's eye. By the time we stopped, Vincent had a split lip and Kyle would no doubt have a black eye in the morning.

"Jeez, Bro," Vincent said, dabbing at his lip. "I thought you said you were holding us back."

"Well you said let off steam," I replied.

"There's a lot of steam in that head of yours," Kyle said, gingerly touching his eyebrow.

"You have no idea," I muttered.


Another two days went by and my contact finally called me.

"Kami, I was getting worried."

"Sorry, Sam. I had a problem getting her Unicom bugged. She has a sophisticated security setup and it took a while to penetrate."

"What did you find?"

"You'll never guess who she's been in contact with."

"The leader of Gaht by any chance?"

"Umm no, good god why would you suggest that."

"Oh," I exclaimed. "Then who?"

"A law enforcer from Tyrrin 4"

"Oh shit, not Tip," I said.

"The name is Commander Ranil Taiko. Does that mean anything to you?"

"Taiko? Yes, I know who he is. So she's called him?"

"Half a dozen times, yes. She mentioned you and your father a few times, discussed somewhere they referred to as, 'the port complex,' which was the source of some obvious anger on her part. It seems something was arranged to happen there but it went wrong somehow."

"That's true," I said. "It did."

"So you understand what that's about?"

"Yeah."

"Okay, good. She also talked about the possibility of blackmailing someone she keeps referring to as, that dark haired little shit cop. I'm guessing she means you, since you're after her."

"Yes, that's most likely to be me. No matter, I've been called many things worse than that. What's this about blackmail? Anything more on that?"

"Well, it's a bit delicate really."

"I need to know, Kami, don't be shy now."

"She called you an interfering shit who prefers cock to what she referred to as, a real woman."

"That's also true. By the way, any idea why she's been doing all this? Has she given any reasons or hinted at a cause for her angst?"

"Only that it's her father at the root of it, something he did a while back that impacted negatively on her. She's not forgiven him and wants revenge. From listening to her calls, I'd say she's trying to frame him for something, and I'd hate to be the one to tell her but she's wasting her time. He's too powerful and crazy, she'll never get anywhere near."

"I agree totally. Listen, I really appreciate this. You've validated what I already thought was going on. Thank you so much. Say hi to the family from me."

"So she did sell us out to Belotan," Tinnias said.

"Well technically no. She sold us out to Taiko, who sold us out to Belotan. They didn't know that he was already in the know and was okay about us, shit, even we didn't know at that point."

"So we can assume Taiko is in with Vazien, that much is obvious," Byron said.

"We can safely assume so, yeah," I nodded.

"And Taiko is also in with Belotan. I wonder if Vazien knows."

"That would be interesting to know," I sniggered.

"What else did she say?" Tinnias asked.

"She calls me, 'that dark haired little shit cop,' and 'an interfering shit who prefers cock to a real woman.'"

Everyone laughed and the mood lightened a little. "Now we just have to decide what to do next," I said. "Do we call her, visit her, leave her alone, go to Donaldson, or what?"

"We could call her," Lomas suggested. "She might take the opportunity of getting to her father by using the legal system. Maybe she doesn't know the extent of her father's reach and influence, she might have no idea how many people he's got on his payroll."

"Maybe if she did," Byron said, "she would realise how much danger she's in by taking him on the way she's doing."

"Or she could just be a crazy bitch with a death wish," Kyle said.

"There is always another option," Jam said, having wandered in quietly. We all looked and waited for one of his famous revelations. "We could go and have a chat with her husband in prison."

"That's a wonderful idea," Vincent said.

"Oh, Sam, Kyle said, "we must do that, it's a great idea.

"I agree," Tinnias said. "Wholeheartedly."

"Okay, let's do it," I said. "Where is he? Does anyone know?"

"Umm yeah, I know where he is," Byron said, giving Vincent a look of concern. "I looked it up the other day when researching Olendra."

"What?" I said. "What was that look about?"

"Come on Bro," Vincent said quietly, "out with it. Is he somewhere I'd recognise?"

"He's in the brand new facility on Steran 3's Moon."

"Vincent got up and left the room. Kyle and I looked at each other and ran after him.

"Oh shit," Kyle hissed. "Not there, anywhere but there." We caught up with him and found him sitting down, back leaning against a door to a storage room, his head in his hands.

"What's wrong," I said.

"It's where Cryo Stasis was," he said.

"But I thought that place had a complete meltdown when you escaped."

"It did, that's what allowed me to escape."

"And I heard they rebuilt a new facility from scratch."

"They did."

"So nothing of Cryo Stasis will be there, except a horrific memory, which you can expunge by returning a free man, legally and rightfully, with friends by your side."

He stood. "Thank you, both of you."

Kyle looked at me and smiled. "You're amazing, Sam."

"I'm sorry guys," Vincent said as we returned to the Obs Room. "That was something of a shock, but it's fine."

"You needn't go anywhere near the place," Lomas said. "Sam and Tinnias can go alone, they'll be perfectly safe in a prison facility."

"I have to," Vincent said. "Ghosts to lay to rest and shit like that."

"Okay, then let's be off to Steran's Moon," Lomas said. "Deep Space Refuelling Station Kilo 18 is right nearby there, so we can stop there and use a shuttle for the short hop to the moon."

"You can shop for some clothes, Sam," Byron said.

"Something that doesn't make you look like an off duty law enforcer, if at all possible," Tinnias said.

Byron and I roared with laughter. "See, I told you," I said.


I dumped my purchases down on the bed and smiled. "That's more money spent on clothes in one shopping trip than in the last few years put together," I said. "You are a bad example."

He sniggered. "You won't have to shop for clothes for a couple of years now. You should thank me really."

"That's true," I nodded. "I can't argue with that. Thanks for your help, my love."

"You're welcome," he grinned.

I had begun to notice Vincent's demeanour changing as we got nearer to our destination, and I guessed it was due to the memories he carried of his time in Cryo Stasis which used to stand on the same spot as the new facility we were due to visit the next day. I asked him about the place, his escape, and the meltdown and by reliving those memories with me, he was able to get rid of a lot of emotion left over from that time.

"Are you worried about seeing this man tomorrow, Sam," Vincent asked, when his emotion was spent and he felt balanced.

"No, why do you ask?"

"You just seem a bit quiet, like you're nervous."

I smiled. "Well I have got something on my mind but I'm not too worried about the interview. He'll either talk or he won't and even if he doesn't, we won't have to worry about him telling Vazien or Olendra because prisoners at Steran aren't allowed calls."

"That's useful," Kyle said.

"Very useful," I nodded. "It means I can put the pressure on a bit without having to worry about the daughter getting her heavies on to us. Of course there's always the possibility that Vazien has insiders at the facility, but that's a risk we're just going to have to get used to taking as I don't believe the extent of his eyes and ears will ever be truly known."

"What are you hoping to learn from him?" Kyle asked.

"Anything we don't already know, I guess. Any more information about what Vazien is up to would be welcome, especially if he is willing to testify. Remember, he's probably not guilty of embezzlement. That was probably set up by Vazien due to him going back on the business deal. If we can prove his innocence, we could win ourselves a favour from him. Even Olendra might decide we're not her enemies after all."

"Then she might decide to talk to you about her father," Vincent added and I nodded.

"Yes, that would be great, but probably a little too much to ask of the universe in one go."

I put some coffee on and thought about the interview the next day. Falco Lorland was an unknown quantity to me but being married to a Vazien gave me good enough reason to be wary. I was so deep in my thoughts that I failed to hear Vincent talking to me.

"Huh?" I said, turning around to face him. "Sorry, I was miles away."

"I just wondered what was on your mind," Vincent said.

"Oh nothing that won't sort itself out in time."


After our workout and shower, we all sat in the Obs Room and discussed the coming interview with Falco Lorland. Byron found us a photograph, business history, social gossip, and his pre intake psyche evaluation from the Steran Facility. The report didn't reveal anything extraordinary. He was a normal guy with too much money, a trophy wife, and a lust for business success. He was regarded by the social press as a good looker and had many rich girlfriends in previous years. He had a rather high opinion of himself, regarded himself as a bit of a celebrity, but in my opinion, he was obviously compensating for something with his slightly over the top nature.

"We won't have to worry about him telling Olendra or Vazien," Tinnias said. "Inmates at Steran aren't allowed calls, so unless Vazien has insiders there, he shouldn't find out for a good long time."

"How should we approach him?" I asked.

"It depends on his character," Tinnias said. "If he's the meek type, then a little push will soon have him doing what we want, but if he's super confident, then the soft approach might be better."

"We won't know till we meet him and find out his personality. "I said. "We could do the pushy pushy like we did with that guy from galactic vidicom, remember?" I raised my arm over my head and Tinnias roared with laughter.

"Oh, man I thought I was gonna bust a gut. That was the funniest shit ever. Noticing everyone's bemused expression, I explained.

"It was during the Rime business. We were struggling with the case and then, quite suddenly, we thought we'd got the guy. His basement was a charnel house, you've never seen such a hellish sight, honestly. We arrested the guy and did the formal interviews etcetera, but it seemed he was holding out on us. So I …" I began but Tinnias burst out laughing again.

"Sam here, asks him how, if he wasn't responsible for the basement, did blood end up on the ceiling. He then gets up and demonstrates this old horror movie chopping scene. Jeez I almost peed my pants. His lawyer went purple with rage."

"It was probably in the worst taste imaginable, but in this job, you have to take the joy where you find it."

"Son, I got a lot of joy out of that, I tell you now."

## CHAPTER THIRTY

Once the laughter had died down, Klackan spoke up. "Can I make a suggestion?"

"Of course," I said. "Join in the debate anytime, Bro."

"Lorland is a business man, right?" I nodded. "That means he's going to be used to working in a hierarchy, and those higher up the chain will get more of his respect than those insects at the bottom."

"Agreed," I nodded.

"So, if Tinnias pushes the, I'm the big boss man, thing a little bit, Lorland might look up to him, naturally regard him as worthy of a bit more respect than you, and he might just talk."

"Hey that's not a bad idea," I said. "After all, those of a higher position tend to automatically receive more respect, whatever business they're in, not just law enforcement."

"That's a very good idea," Tinnias agreed. "Okay, I'll do the talking, insect," he looked down his nose at me and everyone laughed.


I smoked on the balcony in our room and enjoyed the floral aroma as the void of space spread out all around me. No matter how many times I experienced this, I would never get used to being able to stand on a balcony of a space ship without a suit on. I was truly in awe of the Drycenians' technology. Arms encircled my waist and I felt Byron's cheek against my own.

"I like your dad, he's a really funny guy. Easy to talk to like a regular guy. He's so perfect for you. The perfect father for you. The universe did a good job finding him."

"I knew I was going to like him from the very first day I met him, when I joined the agency as a rookie detective. In the twenty years I've worked for him, he's only yelled at me four times."

Before Byron could reply, there was a knock on the door and he went to answer it to find Jam there. He joined us on the balcony, then accepted a cigarette from me.

"How long have you been taking Wide Awake, Sam?"

I heard Byron gasp in shock beside me and I blushed. I knew I couldn't deny it, Doc Jam would have all the medical equipment to prove me a liar.

"Oh, my love," Byron hissed. "Please say it's not true."

I leaned over and kissed him, then looked at Jam and sighed. "Since the day after the bomb scare. I'm not a life long junkie or anything. It's only until this case is finished."

"But why?" Byron asked.

"Because of the nightmares. I get more stress from them than I do from using Wide Awake, and I do take care to have a two hour nap every day while you're at work."

"How many times have you had the nightmares?" Jam asked.

"The night of the bomb scare it was five times. I had one on Glarian as well."

"Five times in one night?" Jam asked, his eyes wide with shock. I nodded. "Shit. No wonder you started taking that stuff. You're a cop so I don't need to lecture you about how totally illegal it is, but I do have to insist on taking it off you."

"Can't you hold off until this case is done?" I asked.

"No, but I can give you something else far less likely to kill you."

"Doc ..." I began but he cut me off.

"No, Sam. You died the other day, if you remember. The monitors registered nothing but a flat line. You died because you chose not to come back. It took Ren a week to find you and bring you back and now you're leaping right back to the edge of the pit again. You've been in the tank once, it won't work a second time. You only get one go so next time you go dancing with death and he wins, you won't be coming back and Byron will be left all alone, again. How dare you put him in that position? How dare you put me in a position of losing a patient someone close to me loves, and having to live with it and lose his friendship as well? How fucking dare you?"

"I'm sorry. I know very little about the medical side of it. It seems the more I try to do the right thing here, the worse I do the wrong thing."

"The more you try to do the right thing?" he continued, still yelling. "The right thing? Don't make me laugh. How can playing games with your life ever be the right thing?"

"Maybe the same way lying to me was the right thing," I yelled back. "Maybe the same way violating me by putting a tracker inside me was the right thing. Maybe doing the unsavoury things is the only way to save a situation, a life. Maybe you'll fail to stop someone's spirit being broken, maybe your own will be broken instead, but maybe, just maybe, it's the only way to try. Believe me, I know. I'm sorry I broke your rules, I truly wish I didn't feel the need but as someone important once told me, there's more than just myself to consider now. I'll go get the bottle."

"Don't leave me," Byron hissed.

I returned to his side and kissed him. "Five minutes, my love. I promise you I'll return within five minutes. I said I wouldn't desert you ever again and I meant it. One day you'll find you can trust me and we'll celebrate that day."

Four minutes later, I handed Doc Jam one of my three bottles of Wide Awake.

"What are the nightmares about?" Jam asked.

"None of your fucking business," I snapped, then immediately regretted it. "I'm sorry for my words, that was uncalled for. I don't want to discuss them right now, they're very personal and nothing will be gained by giving anyone the gory details."

"I forgive you, absolutely. We're all grown men here; we can disagree without it being a life changing event. I must destroy these, but I give you my word I won't tell anyone about this. When you're ready to deal with the nightmares, I'm here for you."

"How did you know?" I asked.

"Your BioMed alerted me to a dangerous substance in your bloodstream and one look at your eyes told me you were on something. It didn't take too much work to find out what it was. I know quite a few chase, catch, and deliver guys take it from time to time, but they are neither my friends nor my patients. Have you taken one today?"

I nodded. "Yes, just after lunch."

"Okay, that was, about seven hours ago? Eight?"

"About that, yeah."

"Right, I have a shot for you if you permit."

"Sure, knock yourself out," I replied, sliding my shirtsleeve up.

"The shots will affect the Thalamus inside your brain and make it temporarily unable to make you remember any dreams. I'll have one for you each night, so come visit me before you go to bed."


"Good morning, Commander Vaylo," the warden said as he greeted Tinnias.

"Morning, Warden. This is Detective Sinclair-Vaylo. Thank you for allowing us to speak with Prisoner Lorland at such short notice."

"Not at all, it's no trouble. Good morning Detective. You wouldn't happen to be related, would you? Same name and all that."

"We are," I nodded.

"And who might umm …" he began but frowned as he looked at Vincent. "Oh my. You're him, aren't you? Vincent Domenico if I remember rightly."

"I am he," Vincent said.

"Oh, Mr Domenico," the warden said, taking Vincent's hand. "I do apologise for the treatment you received at the hands of other members of the judiciary and prison system. This must be a painful visit."

"Thank you, it's healing actually. The best way to deal with painful stuff is meet it head on."

"The previous facility was an awful place and we all deeply regret that whole sorry business. So many died needlessly. I know they were prisoners, some of them the worst of humanity, but I don't believe in execution and it hurts me to think the system I work for made such a mistake. I'm so glad you survived to escape and get cleared."

"Thank you for your words, warden," Vincent replied quietly. "This is my blood brother, Kyle Polt."

"Welcome," he smiled, shaking Kyle's hand. "Now, prisoner Lorland. This way, gentlemen. I'm afraid I'm only permitted to allow the law enforcement personnel in to meet with the prisoner, but you two can watch from the viewing room."

"No problem," Kyle replied.

Tinnias and I were shown into an interview room, where we sat and waited for the prisoner to be brought in. He was a good looking man, taller in the flesh than his photo makes him appear, and he offered us his hand, which we both shook.

"Commander Vaylo," Tinnias said. This is Detective Sinclair-Vaylo. Thank you for agreeing to talk to us."

"You have identification I presume," he said.

"We do. You want to see it? The warden has already seen it, but it's your right so here you are." We handed our ID's over and waited while he perused them. Eventually, he gave them back and looked Tinnias in the eye.

"You were convicted of embezzlement and sentenced to eight years, correct?" Tinnias asked.

"Correct."

"So you had no defence? No one working for you during the case?"

Lorland frowned. "Of course I did. Why ask me that?"

"I'm just wondering why you allowed yourself to be jailed for something you didn't do."

"What the fuck?"

"Well you're obviously innocent. I'd like to know why you didn't prove it and prevent a jail sentence."

Lorland looked at me as if to say, 'is he crazy or something, buddy?' and then looked back at Tinnias. "We did the best we could but the prosecution was better on the day. Shit happens."

"So it was sheer bad luck?"

"Yeah, I guess you could call it that."

"And it had nothing whatsoever to do with the fact that selling or merging of a company is forbidden while the company owner is incarcerated in prison?"

"What the hell?" he snapped, banging the table with both fists.

"So it wasn't just because it was the only thing you could think of to prevent Vazien getting his filthy mitts on your company?"

Lorland stared at Tinnias and Tinnias stared back. Lorland then stared at me and I returned the stare. Then he sighed deeply and ran both hands through his hair. "Oh fuck," he hissed.

"Falco," I said quietly. "We're here because we need your help. You, like so many others, are a victim of that asshole and we want him. You might be able to help us get him, but you have to trust us and talk to us."

"He's a dangerous man," Falco said.

"Oh we know," I said. "Danger runs in the family it seems. Your wife tried to have us killed a couple of weeks ago. I believe I'm that, 'dark haired little shit cop,' she speaks of."

"That sounds just like her. She was hoping that if some cops were roughed up a bit, law enforcement would have Vazien put away. She's been on about it for ages, since well before I came here."

"She has no idea what danger she put herself in by doing that," I said. "Vazien will be incensed if he ever finds out that was her plan."

"That was the other reason I didn't fight the conviction too hard," Falco said. "In here I'm not only safe from Vazien getting my company, but I'm safe from her. She wanted to pretend she'd killed me so she could pin it on him, before she tried it on you two. She was going to actually shoot me to make it look real. I was to beat her up so she could accuse Vazien of hitting her when she came home unexpectedly and found him carrying my body to his hover truck to dispose of. Apparently there are a couple of cops she said she could bribe to say she found me dead after I'd argued with Vazien about him wanting my company. She's crazy with lust for vengeance, it's turned her mind. I didn't believe that my death would be a pretence. I'm sure she would've really killed me. I wish I'd never got involved with her, but she seemed so sweet and normal. Never trust a woman, Detective, I mean it."

"I hear you," I said and almost laughed.

"Will you help us, Mr Lorland," Tinnias said. "It's probably safer that you remain in here until after we get Vazien dealt with. Once he and his daughter are out of the way, I give you my word we will make sure your case is re-evaluated so you can get back to your company. That way, Olendra and Vazien won't get suspicious. They won't know you're talking to us and you'll be safe here."

"Okay, what do you need from me?"

"We need a recorded statement, and a signed declaration of intent to testify. When we're ready to deliver the evidence into the hands of the appropriate authority, you and all the other testifiers will be given formal interviews to validate the information you give in the statement you make today."

"Yes, I'll do whatever you want. I'm sick of this. I want to go back to the way it was before any of this shit happened. I want to be a workaholic again with no time for women, a penchant for expensive wine, and a liking for the odd recreational drug now and then."

"Thank you, Mr Lorland," I said. "Can you start by telling us your full name, occupation, age, and address of your home and business."

When we had thanked Falco Lorland and said our goodbyes, I learned that the warden had given Vincent a tour of the new facility and he reappeared red eyed but smiling.

"How did it go?" I asked him as Kyle hugged him.

"It's fine," he replied. "The old place has completely gone now."

"That's great," I smiled. "I'm happy to hear that."

"Well done for doing that, Son," Tinnias said to Vincent as we boarded my ship for the short hop back to the battle cruiser. "You don't need that shit anymore."

"It seems like a lifetime ago," Vincent remarked. "Like it was someone else y'know?"

"That's because you've left it behind and it can't connect with you anymore," Kyle said.

"All that's left to do now is collate everything, do the report, then find Donaldson and see if he's interested," Tinnias said. "Unless there's anything we've missed."

"Nothing I can think of," I replied. "We've no more testifiers, so we need to evaluate what we have and decide whether we think it's enough to secure a conviction."

After lunch, Tinnias and I settled down in my ship to collate all our interviews and evidence and write an official report to go with it. Every interview and piece of evidence was explained as fully as we were able. Details of possible further evidence and where to find it was laid out with as much accuracy as possible. Names and addresses of any other relevant people or potential interviewees, together with as much detail as we had on how they might relate to the case, were listed. Vincent and Kyle's details were listed also, as they were present at the Niruvan compound, when I was shot, and when we were abducted in the Deep Space Refuelling Station. We took recorded interviews from them to document the event and wrote our own statements to add to them. Toma, Byron, and the troopers who were with us in the Gaht compound and the shooting of me were interviewed and added to the file. Three hours later, we sealed the file and stashed it away in the evidence cubby hole on my ship, then went to get a drink and have a smoke.

"Okay, we're done," Tinnias said. "Now we need to find Donaldson."

"He's on Vendala 4 attending a conference," Byron said.

"Oh is he?" I said and looked at Tinnias, who grinned and sniggered. I couldn't help but laugh at the memory of the one and only time I'd met a Vendalan. Tinnias was with me as we welcomed a party of military personnel to Headquarters back home on Sigma Prime. They were from the IGMF and stopped on Sigma to refuel and have a couple of days rest before continuing their long journey. Three of them were Vendalan and they made quite an impression wherever they went. The Vendalans are famous for being blessed with great beauty and the men have a flurry of spots down each side of their neck, across their shoulders, down their spine to their ass, and down the centre of their chest to their navel. Wherever they go, these men are a draw and I had to admit that I understood why. It was the first time I found another man attractive. I was so captivated by one of them, that Tinnias stepped in front of me to block my view.

"Sam, you're staring."

"Yeah," I replied, leaning to see around him.

He leaned with me. "Staring at another man like a lovesick kid."

"Huh? Oh, yeah, sorry. Wow, he's something else, isn't he?" I said and we both burst out laughing.

He often teases me about that episode and we couldn't help ourselves as we sat in the smoking room on the Drycenian Battle Cruiser, we laughed until we both had tears on our cheeks.

"Either of you two feel like sharing?" Lomas asked and I blushed.

"Judging by those red cheeks," Vincent grinned, "I'd say it's most definitely something we all want to hear."

"Have you ever met the Vendalans?"

"We have, of course," Lomas replied. "Very nice and trustworthy people."

"We haven't," Vincent said, looking at Kyle, who shook his head.

"I haven't either," Klackan added.

"I have, a few times," Umboi said.

"They're famous for being gorgeous," I explained as I described their spots. "Wherever they go, those spots are a draw. Whenever you see those 'top ten most attractive races,' polls on the media, they always win."

Lomas was nodding. "A sizeable number of my troopers even became enamoured the first time we hosted a party of them."

"So did I," Jam sniggered. "In my defence, I had to spend a whole two days teaching emergency medical aid to a group of them, one of whom played the body and was stark naked."

Umboi sniggered. "One of our porters at the hotel made a proper fool of himself when a group of them stayed a couple of nights."

"I couldn't help but stare," I said. "I'd never seen anything like that guy. He looked like a god."

"I stepped in front of him, to block his view," Tinnias said. "It was an official meet and greet so I felt we should at least try to be professional. But then, this idiot here just leans to the side to see around me. It was the funniest shit ever."

"Let's hope we can get to see Donaldson on the ANA Liner and not down on the planet," I said and everyone laughed. "I'll no doubt offend someone by laughing if I have to go down there."

"We have a four day journey to Vendala," Lomas announced, "so there's plenty of time to relax."

During those four days, I got the shots from Doc Jam and I found that they did indeed prevent me from remembering my nightmares, at least at night. The problem was that I started getting hallucinations during the day, when my mind relaxed enough and I would see the awful image of the three of them in the cargo bay. I didn't tell anyone of course and Byron started gently pressing me to tell him about them, but I managed to steer him away before he persuaded me. I hoped I would never have to tell him, but quickly realised that I really should.

I used our sparring to let them have my feelings and every day, they left the cargo bay with split lips, black eyes, and one day, two broken fingers had Vincent yelling his head off. I knew they would approach me about it one day and I practiced a series of lies for that very occasion. They finally broached the subject one day in the smoking room when we found ourselves alone.

"Sam?" Vincent asked.

"Yeah?"

"What did we do?"

"Excuse me?" I said and frowned.

"Come on, we're not kids here. What did Kyle and I do? You've never done this to us before." He pointed to his black eye.

"I did offer to let you two spar without me, but you insisted. You said I could let off steam. Everyone aboard looks up to you as some sort of deity, so I thought, well okay then, if he says to let off steam, I'll do just that."

"What the fuck?" Kyle hissed. "Where was that remark born, Sam? Is this because of Vincent hurting you down on Niruvan?"

I burst out laughing. "Don't be wet, that's ridiculous. Of course not. He saved my life and I'm grateful, as I hope Byron is too."

"He is," Vincent replied.

"Well thank you for informing me how he feels about me. Shame he shares so much with you two but if it's what he needs to repair the damage done by my disappearing act and then by being shot in the back like a dog, then I'll not complain and be grateful for what part of him he feels safe giving me. One day maybe, if I work hard and be humble enough, he won't need you two anymore and I'll have all of him again."

Kyle leapt up. "Sam, buddy. Please talk to us about this. You're obviously in pain and we want to help you with it, we love you."

I lit a cigarette and tried to calm down. I felt hands on my shoulders and wanted to shrug them off but I was tired of suffering the results of my own fucked up head. I was happy, I had a new love who completed me, who loved me with all of his being and I was angry that I had allowed nightmares to become tangled up with reality.

"Would it help if you talked to Vincent on his own?" Kyle asked, squeezing my shoulders. "Or me on my own? Whatever you need, please just open up and let us in."

"Or me on my own," Byron said, having entered the room. I held out my arms and he hugged me.

"I'm sorry, it's these fucking nightmares."

"I thought Jam was giving you shots so you can't remember your dreams," Byron frowned.

"He is, but now I get hallucinations during the day. Sometimes its hard to remember they're not true reality. I think I'm going crazy and I'm scared."

Vincent stood. "Right, come on guys, we're going to see Jam right now." He took hold of my hand and dragged me along before I could refuse. Byron held onto the other.

For the next two hours, we sat with Jam and I offloaded everything. The guilt at having run away and the subsequent fear of Byron not trusting me again, my fear of him leaving me because of what I'd done, my feelings of inadequacy and worry that Byron will run off with the Lileans the moment my back is turned, my anguish at dying and leaving him alone, and finally I shared the nightmare images, Laine's admonishment of me, and the scene in the cargo bay. When I was done, I felt empty but free.

"It sounds as if you're finding my lack of need for vengeance harder to take than if I had sought revenge," Byron said and we all nodded.

"Weren't you even a little angry?" Kyle asked him.

"Yes of course, until he came back."

"Then show him now just how angry you felt, how lonely and confused you felt at his desertion of you. Give him those feelings as he's just given you his," Vincent said. Kyle and Jam were nodding furiously.

After a hesitant start, Byron let me have his anger and was soon yelling and crying as it all came tumbling out. Once he was done and my mind knew I had received just punishment I felt so much better.

"Well done, both of you," Jam smiled. "You've both taken that first important and most difficult step towards meeting each other in the middle of that no man's land between what is natural for each of you. Both of you will work on this. Sam, you will be learning that love conquers revenge every time, and Byron, you will learn how necessary it is that you voice your truth. You're both stepping outside of your comfort zones and working on this can do nothing but bring you closer together and give you a deeper bond. You're bridging the gap between our races and our ways. I'm proud of you."


We held a respectful distance back from the ANA Liner and waited while Lomas hailed them.

"ANA Liner, please respond. This is King Lomas VII of the Drycenian Nation and this is my vessel, DBC1. I'm wishing to speak with Michael Donaldson, Head of the ANA, with all urgency. We are sending our identification beacon now."

"We have it, please wait a moment."

"Your Majesty? It's a pleasure to speak with you again."

"Mr Donaldson, I trust you are well?"

"I am, thank you, and yourself?"

"Still trudging on. I'm hoping to persuade you to come and visit with us for an hour or two. We have a problem that you seem to be the only answer for."

"Would a couple of hours from now be acceptable? I have a conference call with someone very important that I can't get out of without starting an inter galactic incident."

"That would be most agreeable Mr Donaldson. We look forward to welcoming you aboard."

It gave us time to grab a bite of lunch before heading to the shuttle bay to greet Donaldson.

"Have you met him, Sam?" Vincent asked.

I shook my head. "No, as we explained, liaison with the ANA is done by those with a much higher salary than me, so I've never had cause to meet him. I've heard through gossip that he's a nice guy though, but then I guess he has to be a nice guy in that job."

"You old cynic," he grinned. "He is nice. He's honest, which always impresses me."

A small and rather dumpy man exited the ANA shuttle and grinned at the sight of Lomas.

"Your Majesty, how wonderful to see you again. You haven't changed a bit."

"You're most welcome," Lomas replied. "This is my son, Toma, my first officer and head of engineering, Commander Byron, Commander Vaylo from the Inter Galactic Law Enforcement Agency, Detective Samelan Sinclair-Vaylo, also from law enforcement, Kyle Polt, and of course you already know Vincent."

"Vincent, how are you?" Donaldson said, his eyes serious suddenly. "You look well and happy."

"I am, thank you. I owe you a debt Mr Donaldson, I haven't forgotten."

Donaldson shook his head. "No, Vincent. You did me an honour. You gave me the chance to not be ashamed any more. You owe me nothing."

"Now, Mr Donaldson," Lomas said. "Let's go and find some refreshments and we'll tell you why we've asked to see you."

"Sam, Tinnias," Lomas said once we were comfortable, "this is your story so you do the talking or I shall forget something."

I looked at Tinnias, who nodded to me in deference. "Mr Donaldson, we want you to consider bringing a case against Ambassador Vazien."

He almost spat out his drink and gaped at me. "Excuse me?" he said, wiping his shirt.

"We've spent some time gathering evidence and several declarations of intent from potential testifiers, that we feel justifies bringing a case against Vazien."

He looked at me for several seconds before speaking. "I hope part of that evidence proves his arms dealing at long last."

Now it was my turn to gape in astonishment. "You know?"

"Of course I know, I'm the head of the ANA. We can't take it upon ourselves to start gathering evidence. We can only act when approached by the Law Enforcement Agency Representatives. I assume you have a good reason why you're not using your ANA Liaison Officer?"

"Very good," I nodded. "He's a Gaht leak. Not only can we prove his arms dealing, but we can prove illegal mining of a controlled substance, illegal arms dealing to tribal conflicts, desecration of sacred sites and damage to sacred land, embezzling company funds and using Gaht sympathetic banks to hide the money trail, authorizing violence upon various persons who complained or threatened to expose his crimes, espionage on a galactic scale, manufacture of evidence resulting in an innocent man being jailed, attempted murder, including myself and Commander Vaylo, and murder of several persons, including myself and his wife."

He frowned. "Murder of you? Don't you mean attempted murder? You've already included that, have you not? I distinctly heard you."

"He hired a crew of thugs to capture myself, Commander Vaylo, His Majesty, and Toma. He was to kill all four of us. One of them shot me in the back and I was dead for a week before our Doctor brought me back. We have them in our lock up."

"Shit," Donaldson remarked. "Is there anything he hasn't done?"

"There's also evidence in the form of a statement, that his daughter Olendra helped him in the attempted murder of myself and Commander Vaylo."

"What does your evidence consist of?"

"We have data chips, vidicom footage, and declarations of intent from witnesses. It's all here in the file." I handed over the sealed file. "With your authority and resources, you can delve further and find out even more. The file tells you where more evidence and witnesses are likely to be found."

"Give me a couple of days to go over this and I'll return."

"Take all the time you need," Lomas said.

"Those who signed declarations are at very great personal risk if Vazien were to find out about this. Discretion is absolutely paramount," I said.

"We trust you to do the right thing," Vincent remarked and Donaldson looked into his eyes for several seconds.

"Your trust is not misplaced, Mr Domenico."

## CHAPTER THIRTY ONE

After the hectic schedule we had all experienced on our epic evidence gathering journey, the next couple of days felt a little flat. We tried to fill the time while we waited for Donaldson to give us his verdict, but all the time I was very much aware that my time with Byron was approaching its end. He was aware of it too, and as the hours became days, he became more and more emotional at the prospect of having to say goodbye soon. Despite being just as sad about it myself, I had to admit that it did my ego a power of good having someone upset at my leaving them soon. We made promises to get together regularly and agreed that we would soon devote some time to discussing in detail how we might shorten our times apart.

The smoking room was filled with people when the intercom silenced us. "This is Lomas. Donaldson is on his way. Greeting party to the shuttle bay."

"This is it," I said to Tinnias as we all stood. Byron's hand slipped into mine and squeezed. I squeezed back and smiled. "Now would be a good time to find religion and pray."

"Let's hope he's going to take the case eh, Son," Tinnias said.

"If he doesn't, we're seriously fucked," I replied.

"What will you do if he doesn't?" Vincent asked.

"I haven't the faintest idea, Bro, not a damned clue."

"This last few minutes waiting is worse than the last two whole days," Byron remarked and we all sniggered.

Donaldson's shuttle settled down onto a pad and we waited for the bay doors to close and the air to equalize before entering to greet him. Lomas, expert in the art of hiding emotions, swept up to him with a broad smile and welcomed him aboard, before indicating the rest of us.

"You know everyone from your last visit. Come, let's go and find some refreshments."

Donaldson followed Lomas, shaking hands with me on his way out of the shuttle bay. "Hello again, Detective."

"Welcome back, Mr Donaldson," I replied with as relaxed a countenance as I was able to muster.

"I won't keep you waiting, Gentlemen," Donaldson said. "I'm going to take the case."

An audible collective sigh of relief filled the Obs Room. "Thank you so much," I said.

"We're delighted," Tinnias said. "You've no idea how worried we were about how we were to proceed if you said no."

"I think you have a strong case. Your evidence is good, and there is more available once I put the weight of the ANA behind it. What you can do now, if you're agreeable, is collect your witnesses and keep them safe until I call for them to testify. I'll need to know someone's Unicom number so I can get in touch when we need them."

"No problem at all," I said, handing him my card, just as Tinnias also handed his own over.

"I'll also need you both, Mr Domenico and Mr Polt, to testify as you were involved in the attempted murder on Niruvan, the rescue of the detectives from Brakely and his cronies, and the abduction on the refuelling station. I'll also be wanting statements from all who were involved in both events."

"Okay," I nodded.

"I'll also need your Doctor to attend, to validate the information with regard to the murder of Vazien's wife and of yourself."

"Of course, no problem," Jam smiled.

"As for Falco Lorland," Donaldson continued. "I shall be ordering a full investigation into the allegations that sent him to prison, as it is safe to assume that Vazien ordered it. I shall arrange with the Steran facility for you to pick him up and keep him safe alongside your other witnesses. I shall be ordering the arrest and detainment of the Ambassador, his daughter, Olendra, and Commander Ranil Taiko the moment I have full and official statements from all the witnesses."

"Are we to do the interviews," I asked, "or would you prefer to do it?"

"It will save a bit of time if you do them," Donaldson replied. "You do the ones for the witnesses you have, and we'll do any others we find. Call me when they're done and I'll advise you further. It goes without saying that none of this is to leave this room. Vazien is an extremely powerful man with many equally powerful friends. You already have some idea of how long his reach is, but you don't know the full extent of it. The moment he finds out what we're up to, he's going to go mad, so don't blab to anyone, not even family. I suggest you send your families into hiding for the duration, if you have somewhere for them to go."

"Don't worry," Vincent said. "No one will find them were we're going."

"They'll be perfectly safe," Kyle added.

"I can send mine to stay in a witness safety facility on the other side of Sigma," Tinnias said. "They'll be safe there."

"We should talk about what happens in the event that the case fails and Vazien goes free," Donaldson said.

Tinnias and I glanced at each other. "He won't go free, Mr Donaldson," I said.

"We've every faith in the ANA," Tinnias added, having noticed the strange look Donaldson gave me.

"I'll send over some security personnel to collect Brakely and his crew and have them held far away from both Vazien and yourselves. They'll be safe from him, and you'll feel safer with them gone."

The ANA shuttle lifted off the pad and headed out into the void, the huge ANA liner waiting in the distance. Once the bay doors were shut, Lomas turned to us.

"Okay people, I'm going to make some calls and find out which other battle cruisers are around. Once I know where the other ships are, we can formulate a time line which you can use to tell your wives, families, and the other witnesses, when transport will be picking them up for the journey to Drycenia. I said everyone would be kept safe and there's no safer place than there.

"So be ready in four days," I told Preataq Jormla. "Have your pets' necessities packed and look out for a shuttle."

Once the last of the calls were made, Lomas ordered the battle cruiser home to Drycenia, by way of Terramora Prime, Steran 3, Kesh Prime, and Qaigon 7 so that we could pick up the six witnesses who were on our route. We had six days and eleven hours until we said our goodbyes to Vincent and Kyle, who would be remaining with their wives until needed for the trial. I knew that they wouldn't fret, with their wives and children to occupy them, I and all the drama I'd caused would soon become a distant memory. Tinnias and I conducted official interviews with those witnesses we had with us. It would save time when we reached Drycenia so there would only be the four guys from Zibandin left to interview. Tinnias conducted the interviews with Byron, Vincent, Kyle, and all the Drycenians as my friendship with them could be regarded as a conflict of interest and we were not prepared to allow any fuck ups this far along in the process.

I had no intention of leaving Byron, who said we could spend some of the time in the shuttle bay once Tinnias and I had done the interviews with the Zibandin guys and sent all the interview files to Donaldson. He said he would teach me more about maintaining the ship's engines and understanding more how they work, and why they sometimes don't. It would be valuable learning for me and allow me to feel safer when alone out in the void.

"I understand, Son," Tinnias said when we told him. "So long as you agree to come and spend the odd day with the family. They miss you and haven't met Byron yet, so you both owe them some time."

We both nodded. "Absolutely. Won't you be taking them on a tour of Drycenia though? Vincent and Kyle are arranging it for the visitors. Some troopers will be taking a couple of shuttles, for anyone who wants to go."

"Oh yes, and for myself too, I want to see the place. Don't you?"

I hesitated and Byron leapt in. "Yes, I want to show Sam around the place. It'll be just the kind of relaxation we both need."

"That's perfectly fine," Lomas nodded when I told him. "You have the run of the place. Come down whenever you wish and I'll personally give you a tour of the palace."

"Thank you, Sir."

It felt weird when everyone left for the surface of Drycenia, so I packed up all the new clothes I'd bought and found my way to the laundry room. The machines were, of course, written in Drycenian, so a quick call for help on the intercom resulted in the appearance of half a dozen troopers who assisted me in laundering the items. Once clean, I returned them to my ship and put them away in the trunk I use for clothes I buy but don't intend to wear while at work. I couldn't remember the last time it had been this full.

I sat in the cockpit after cleaning my ship from one end to the other. I even removed the bed linen, laundered it, and remade my bunk. The bathroom cubicle and shower sparkled, the windows gleamed, even the glass on the cockpit dials and screens were free of fingerprints and gunk. Once my Nutri Vend and Auto Snack were refilled, I sat down and wondered how the hell I was to make up for all the trouble I'd caused.

"So this is where you're hiding," Byron said, making me jump. "Smells nice in here," he said, giving a long sniff." He kissed me and offered me a beer.

I looked forward to having some proper time alone with Byron, most of which we spent talking. We worked through the emotional legacy of my surprise departure, the nightmares, my death, the drugs I'd taken, and finally reached a place of calm about it all. He didn't hold back his feelings and I tried to understand that love is always greater than the need for revenge. We were finally happy again and looking forward to spending our lives together.

One day, Vincent and Kyle appeared on board with Doc Jam and found us in the smoking room.

"Sam, I meant to tell you before but forgot about it with the drama," Jam said. "We were right about the Transmortal you encountered. Arshad, my spirit friend, told me that as he was connected with you when he died, mind to mind, part of his mind survived inside yours and has been working on you all these years. They did their thing by taking their victims spirit body to the edge of death for a time before bringing it back changed. Because the bit inside you was so small, it couldn't survive when you died, so Ren had to let you over that edge temporarily in order to kill it and free you from its influence."

"So I'm a Transmortal now? But I'm a good guy, despite my recent behaviour."

We all laughed. "You're not one of them as we all knew them, no, but you're bound to have some effects, everyone who encountered them was effected to some degree. I'm going to consult with Arshad. Have you made up with Ren yet?"

I shook my head. "I've not seen him."

"Are your dreams back properly?"

"Yes. Maybe I offended him too much for him to forgive. I could hardly blame him."

"Credit me with some intelligence, Bro." The voice had me spinning around to see Ren standing in the doorway of the smoking room.

"Ren?"

I stood and started towards him but he held out a hand to stop me. "We can't embrace while I'm here in your physical world. We'll have to make do with a hi Bro for now."

"I'm sorry for my angry words, please tell the woman."

"I hear you, Samelan Sinclair, and I forgive you unconditionally." She appeared beside Ren, her red coat contrasting with her silver hair making her a striking woman.

"You got done by those Transmortals, Bro," Ren said. "I had to allow you to pass for just a moment so that the parasite could die and cease its influence on you."

"I know, Jam told me. Has it gone now?" I asked.

He nodded. "Yes, but of course we all know the legacy of their influence."

"So I'm a Transmortal now? But I'm still a nice guy."

"Yes. It was not strong enough to change you completely. In fact, the little change it was able to have, killed it and you're now free of it. You are changed though, but the changes are good ones. Arshad will tell Jam all about it and he'll explain it better than I can. I want to also tell you that you can believe Byron when he says he will never betray you. His love will remain true. You've managed to move past the hurt and guilt, do not go back there again, either of you."

"Thank you so much."

"You have suffered greatly, Samelan," the woman said. "My words caused you some considerable suffering but they were necessary in order that you grow in wisdom. Those words forced you into the darkest region of your mind where you hide those most painful of thoughts and memories. In going there and acknowledging them, you set them free. Do not allow them to return, for they will not serve you positively. You both fully deserve the great and powerful love you are now enjoying. Ren has grown in wisdom too and although his strength deserted him when he knew how you were to be made to suffer, he is now a powerful ally for you. You need never lose faith in him."

"Thank you."

"I'm sorry I couldn't be there," Ren said. "Our bond made me falter when I found out I was expected to cause you some suffering. I am learning here too, not just you."

"Hey, you brought me back from death. That means you never need to apologise for anything, ever. But I know you need to hear the words, so I forgive you unconditionally."

"Now return to your friends and give them the good news," the woman said. "And my name is Laine. The woman makes me sound unfriendly and unapproachable, which I'm obviously not."

It took forty days for Donaldson to call me and tell me a trial had been arranged for thirty days' time. Those forty days were both boring and restful, both at the same time. I spent most of the time with Byron in engineering, helping him out by fetching things, handing him this or that tool, filling out parts manifests, anything that didn't need an engineer's brain. He explained everything he was doing, why he was doing it, and what would happen if he didn't do it.

We got into a habit of going down to visit my family once a week, to have dinner and enjoy just chatting and laughing. They loved Byron immediately and he seemed relaxed and happy in their company. I also visited the witnesses in the houses they'd been allocated and was glad to see them getting along and enjoying their holiday. Byron and I went on the tour with the others and it was lovely to be allowed to explore his home with him. It is a rugged and beautiful world and I felt strangely at home from the first minute I set foot there. We swam in bright blue lakes, marvelled at waterfalls thousands of feet high, hiked through a jungle to listen to ten thousand Singing Pinkas, tiny multi coloured birds, each one with a unique song, who sing at dawn from the treetops, and watched a comet streak past as we lay naked in a grove of Tolom fruit trees in the middle of the night after making love.

Lomas was as good as his word and gave me a tour of his palace and introduced me to his wife and daughter. He then decided to show me around the village and we spent several hours just walking and talking. The Drycenian Royal Village is carved right out of the side of a mountain with only one way in and out, other than by shuttle. It was an eclectic mix of ancient and modern, with circles and spheres the only adornment covering everything. They produce everything their community needs, and with the use of a type of cloning technology, they can reproduce things where they don't have space to produce enough the natural way.

"That way," Lomas explained as we walked through a farm growing vegetables, "we can produce all the food we could ever need but only have to find room to grow a small amount the usual way."

Through the farm, we entered a large plateau on which a herd of animals grazed. At the far end, the mountain rose up and out of sight, thousands of feet above and I noticed what looked like a cave entrance at the end of a short trail that led up the side of the mountain a hundred feet or so.

"Is that a cave over there?" I asked.

"Yes, it's where Vincent, Kyle, and Farra killed the Zaltoid. Its body is still in there, so I ordered it bombed to seal it up so no one can inadvertently resurrect the beast again."

"They told me what happened back then," I said. "What a horrible experience for everyone."

"It was indeed. Come, let's have some refreshment back in my apartments."

"Thank you, Sir," I smiled. "Your home is beautiful, it has a nice feel, good energy."

"How are you coping?" Lomas asked as we walked back to the palace.

"With what?" I frowned.

"With the after effects of the Transmortal."

"Oh, I'm fine, really. Jam told me that I've been changed by it but only in good ways. As with all those affected by them, I'll live much longer and he said I'll probably live as long as you people."

"That's wonderful. Are you happy about it?"

"Yes. It gives me so much more time with Byron. Can I ask you something?"

"Of course, ask anything."

"I know you cared for Byron when his parents died. Thank you for being there for him, you did a wonderful job as stand in parents. Are you happy that he's chosen me?"

"Sam, I couldn't be happier. There was a time when I really thought he had closed off his heart for good and I worried for his mental well being for years, but now he smiles and looks forward to every new day. You are the cause of that change and I am forever in your debt."

"There's no debt amongst friends, Sir," I said and we laughed.


"Lomas told me to give you this," I said holding out a bottle of yellow lake water to Byron. "I have one too and he told me to give you the other one. He filled the bottles himself. It tastes a bit like rank plants but it's not too bad.

"He took you to Yitcheska?"

"Yeah," I nodded. "We walked around, across the plateau to that cave, then he suggested we fly somewhere and gave me directions to this incredible lake with different coloured waters."

"Wow, you're honoured, Sam. Very few outsiders have seen that, in fact I know of only three."

"That would be Vincent, Kyle, and Farra, I presume?"

"No, actually. One was Vaylon Rabramas, another was the Chief Elder of the Mantish Tribe of Xerosia 7, and the third was you, today."

I gaped at him. "Wow, so I really am honoured."

"You are indeed."

"By the way, Byron. There was a signpost at the lake, written in Drycenian, obviously. I asked what it said and Lomas told me to ask you, he said you would tell me all about that."

"Many years ago, when one of Lomas' sons died, he would go and spend many hours at that lake. He said it helped him cope with the grief; the colours reminding him of the joy and beauty his children bring to his life. He had the sign put up when he'd recovered from his grief. It says, 'even amid despair, there is beauty that lifts the soul and cleanses the heart.' I love those words, they're very profound."

"He comes across as a rather eccentric old man but nothing gets by him," I said. "He's as sharp as a razor, that one."

"He knows how we've been struggling and took you there to cheer you up."

"You people are amazing," I said. "I admire you more every single day."

"Dad called and invited us for dinner this evening. I said yes, is that okay?"

"Of course," I smiled, overjoyed at hearing him call Tinnias, Dad. "They love you already and Mom now calls us her boys when she talks about us."

"They're lovely people," Byron grinned. "I'm going to enjoy being connected to your family."

After a wonderful dinner, Tinnias, Byron, and I took an evening walk across the plateau to smoke and have some quiet time. The stars were incredible, the sky, huge from this vantage point and as I looked up into the inky void, I felt small for just a moment. It then struck me like never before, how intricately woven everything is, how deliberate and intertwined. I saw myself, having travelled halfway across the galaxy meeting strangers, all of us with a single united cause, to bring an end to an evil. Now I stood there, looking up into the void, far from home, surrounded by strangers, and felt the weight of my responsibility. I knew in that moment, without a shadow of a doubt, that there is design to everything. Nothing is an accident, nothing a mistake, there is a grand plan after all. I'd been to death and back, been given many more years to live and I knew it was all measured, planned, and watched over by some unknown force of creation.

Once Donaldson gave me the trial date, I told Byron first. He needed to plan the journey so we would know when we needed to leave Drycenia. The trial was being held aboard the ANA Liner and would be surrounded by a fleet of IGMF fighters to ward off any potential trouble, while the Liner swarmed with ANA personnel and military. Vazien would be kept in another ship, moored a half day's travelling time away, his daughter, in another, Taiko in a third, and Brakely's group in another.

Byron worked out that our travelling time would be nine days to the Liner's position, so I called Tinnias. Byron called Lomas and brought him up to speed with the latest details. We agreed that it would be safest for Vincent, Kyle, and my families to remain on Drycenia until the trial was over, after which three battle cruisers would convey them back to their home worlds. This meant that with the travelling time to the liner, and the trial, I would have Byron for at least a couple more weeks.

The night before we were to leave Drycenia, Lomas held a banquet for everyone. We ate too much, drank plenty, laughed a lot, and told many bad taste jokes. Lomas let us smoke outside on the terrace, so we slipped outside every so often. It was a truly lovely occasion despite the gravity of our situation and without exception, every single one of the testifiers had a great time.

The next morning I was up early and went down to help ferry some of the people back to the battle cruiser. I paid my respects to Lomas' wife and thanked her for her hospitality.

"We are in your debt, and happy to be so My Lady."

"It is always a pleasure to have friends visit with us. Please do so again, before too long."

I visited Farra and Kyle's wife, Eyelia and wished them well, then went to say goodbye to Mother and Ambella. To my utter surprise, I became very emotional and it took Mother several minutes to calm me.

I had enjoyed visiting the home of my friends the Drycenians. It is a beautiful world and their way of life, tranquil. If I were to come and live on this world, I know I would be truly happy to do so. As Drycenia vanished into the void behind us, I wondered if Byron would ever bring me back to this haven and its wonderful people. Over the next nine days, we discussed many scenarios for the upcoming trial, all the possible things that could go wrong, and how we might deal with them when, and if, they did. Vincent, Kyle, Byron and I continued with our firearms training, we did many laser battles, played Tapshots, and sparred daily. Byron and I consumed the nights with our love and declarations of our bonding. I was both completely happy and immeasurably sad. Being so totally in love was wonderful, it filled me, completed me, and yet knowing that possibly months of being without him were hurtling towards us, filled me with dread.

The first night of our journey to the liner, I dreamed I was sitting on a hillside with Ren beside me. The view was amazing, I could see for miles. We sat without talking for what seemed like many minutes. I was overjoyed to see my friend again. His presence always made me feel calm and loved.

"I'm so happy to see you again, Ren."

"You have worked hard, I'm proud of you."

"I just hope we've done enough."

"You will soon find out."

"Forgive me for dismissing you like I did, I don't want to offend you ever again."

"Of course I forgive you, and it's impossible for you to offend me, ever. It's okay to be scared, it really is okay."

"My life has changed so completely and so quickly. I can hardly believe it, but it's wonderful," I smiled.

"Your soul is radiant with this new energy," Ren said. "Don't ever try to go back to the old Sam, promise me."

"I promise."

"I need to warn you that the subject of your new love will be brought up during the trial. Vazien will try to use it against you."

"I thought he might," I nodded. "That's why I had Tinnias do the interviews with Byron, Vincent, and Kyle. Just in case he uses my love and our friendships against me."

"That was a good move, my friend. When the subject of love arises, be open and honest when questioned and it will not be a problem."

"I will, thank you for the warning."

"It is normally forbidden for me to give you such information about an upcoming event, but it has been decided that the need to prevent Vazien's evil is worth bending the rules a little."

"Thank you."

"Now there is one more thing I have to tell you. Belotan is to testify against Vazien at the trial."

I was astonished to hear this. "Really? Wow. Why though?"

"He will ask to meet with you and will tell you himself. Now it is time to wake up, Byron is trying to wake you and is getting worried. Wake up now."

I snapped awake and kissed Byron. "Don't worry, Bro, I'm awake and fine."

Donaldson called me to assure me that everything was ready in the ANA Liner. He had decided to engage three judges for the trial, so that no one could be accused of bias.

"I have something to tell you that might surprise you, Detective," Donaldson said when he called me and I remembered my conversation with Ren. "Belotan will be giving evidence for the prosecution."

"Do we know why yet?"

"No, but he wants to meet with you before he gives his evidence. You don't seem surprised."

"I had a hunch this might happen. I'll meet him as soon as I get aboard the liner."

"Okay, you can go ahead and send over the witnesses. We have witness liaison waiting for them. They'll be safe and well looked after, trust me."

"Okay, we're on our way."

We boarded two shuttles for the trip over to the ANA liner, flanked by a pair of fighters for our safety. The battle cruiser was locked down and every single crew member and trooper was heavily armed and waiting at battle stations, just in case. Donaldson was waiting for us and shook hands with every witness, before introducing them to their Witness Liaison Officers who escorted them to a secure waiting area.

"So the race is on at last eh, Detective? How are you feeling? Confident I hope."

"Ask me again after today is finished," I smiled.

Donaldson leaned in close and whispered into my ear. "We'll have him, Sam. As sure as my asshole points downwards, we'll have him."

"Oh please be right," I grinned.

"Now, Detective," he said, stepping back and resuming his usual confident manner. "There are two people here to see you, follow me."

We walked along corridors, Tinnias and I following Donaldson and praying for a successful outcome. He stopped at a door marked, 'Witness Liaison 5' and opened the door.

"Sam, hey, Bro." Tip rushed to me and we man hugged. "How's your neck? You're a member of the most exclusive club in the galaxy now, Bro

"Tip? It's good to see you, man. I'm fine, I don't notice it's there now, I feel totally normal. Are you okay."

"I'm fine. Congratulations by the way, Vincent told me. Where is Byron so I can say hello?"

"He's locking the shuttles. He'll be here shortly. So you've seen Vincent? They know you're here?"

"Yes, we said hello just now."

"You know Belotan is also here?" I said.

He nodded. "Yeah, we said hello."

"Does he know what you were up to?" Tinnias asked.

"Yes I did," Belotan said, emerging from the bathroom and wandering over to shake our hands. "I've known for ages. There are a few of Vazien's insiders at the Tyrrin Headquarters, and one of them told me about Tip. By this time I deeply regretted my association with the Ambassador, so I called Tip and we had a conversation, along similar lines to the one you and I had when I got the word about you and your father at the Niruvan compound."

"So what is your stance on this?" I asked.

"Vazien came to me and suggested we work for our mutual benefit. He would supply arms at a reduced rate and get us the insider knowledge his position gives him, and he'd get the weight and safety offered by an association with Gaht. The problem was that he decided to play us by also forming a similar but secret and financially beneficial alliance with the Dankera Collective. He told them stuff we didn't want them to know, which they paid him for. Yanit found that the quality of the information Vazien was offering soon took a nosedive, so he called me and we talked. He's a nice guy, I respect the man. We both agreed to stop giving Vazien anything of real value, but he became suspicious and that's when he offered me you and your father. When your Drycenian friends called me, we arranged for them to be waiting to ensure your safety."

"We're very grateful to you for being here," I said. "Your testimony will help greatly."

## CHAPTER THIRTY TWO

So the circus began and the ANA went to work, doing what it does so well. The first to be called was Tip, who explained about his undercover work to infiltrate Gaht, the Unicom call from Belotan, and the subsequent events leading from it. He gave his evidence precisely and succinctly, a fine law enforcer and I was proud of having been a part of helping to mould him into the man who stood there, confidently giving evidence in the biggest trial of both our careers. Vazien's defence tried to make it seem as though Tip were a Gaht insider for real, but he and the prosecution produced all the official documentation to prove otherwise.

Next came various people the ANA had found. Bank managers, political interns, secretaries, more neighbours, and various admin staff who all had a reason to hold a grudge against Vazien. From promises of financial gain in payment for 'lost' paperwork, requests for paperwork to be manufactured, to sexual harassment and a couple of rape charges. Two of Vazien's ex bodyguards testified that they had been paid to arrange women for him, and to use force to restrain them if they weren't compliant while he raped them.

Klackan was next and he told his story to a silent court room and I noticed several people dabbing at moist eyes as he told them about his suffering at Vazien's hands. The ANA had managed to find the forensic team who had originally been tasked with investigating the device used in his attempted murder.

"There was a hole as wide as my arm span, right in the gateway of his driveway," the team's supervisor told the court. "There was no way he could avoid it. Bits of it were discovered in gardens four houses down on either side. How he survived I'll never know. It was a miracle, that's what it was. We even found fingerprints on the casing that matched three known employees of Vazien."

The head mechanic at the local hover vehicle repair shop was next and told the court of the damage done to Klackan's bike in the blast. "It was in three main chunks. The front end and handlebars, the middle portion with seat and engine, and the rear portion with the exhausts. Hundreds of little bits flew everywhere, we couldn't hope to find them all. The coolant tank, containing the now illegal Ring Coolant was contained within the middle portion that landed on top of the rider, split open, and dispensed its contents onto his legs. Some of the coolant sprayed all around and to this day, part of the garden in that area is barren. Not even weeds will grow there, it's bare earth."

The doctor who initially examined Klackan was next and told them of his initial findings. "Klackan came into the hospital with crush injuries to the chest and upper legs, many lacerations all over his face and body, sudden onset deafness, and what looked like an allergic rash to the lower legs. Upon further examination of his lower legs, I noticed his pant legs were soaked with something that smelled strongly of animal urine. I had been made aware of the cause of his injuries, so I quickly ascertained the rash was caused by excessive exposure to Ring Coolant. He was treated, recovered well, and was eventually discharged."

Next came the doctor Klackan saw when he became ill later in life. "Klackan came to me with exhaustion, lack of energy, weakness in the legs, breathing difficulties when exerting himself, and weight loss. Upon checking his medical history, I found the report of the injuries he sustained when he drove over a land mine in the driveway of his home. When I read that his legs had been soaked in a full tank of Ring Coolant, I suspected Loigot poisoning and took blood and tissue samples for a full workup. It was confirmed as Loigot poisoning and with the only cure being on Qelashmid Prime, all I was able to do was give him painkillers and a high protein meal supplement. When I saw him, I estimated that he had approximately a year to live."

When the clerk noticed several people openly weeping, he called for a break in proceedings so that everyone could relax and gather their thoughts before continuing. We spent the time in a smoking booth we discovered between two of the witness liaison rooms.

"How's it going, Bro?" Byron asked.

"Klackan was amazing," I said and Tinnias nodded. "He had them openly crying, that's why they called this break."

"You know you've done a good job if you make them cry," Tinnias said and we all risked a laugh.

"Who's going next?" Vincent asked.

"I think the Zibandin guys are next on the list, then Preataq Jormla. That will probably be it for today."

"So why does everyone else have to be here if they won't be going in until tomorrow?"

"It's the rule that all witnesses and testifiers are to be present for the entire trial, unless special dispensation is given."

"I'd much rather be chilling out on the battle cruiser than pacing the room here," Byron remarked.

"You think you've got it bad," I grinned. "We've got to sit through it all in there. At least you can get a drink, a snack, take a shit, fart, and pick your nose whenever you want. We have to sit still and keep quiet or we could halt the whole trial." Everyone laughed and we exchanged a hasty kiss when we heard the call for everyone to reconvene.

The Zibandin tribesmen gave their evidence well. They struggled with emotion as they told of the desecration of their sacred sites by Vazien, the banishment they suffered as a result of working for him, and his abandonment of them once they were forced from their home world by their angry tribal leaders. One of the men told of Vazien's many mistresses, and how he knew one of them as he had wanted her for his own wife.

"We were banished from our home world," one said. "Vazien said we could work for him in his mines but we wouldn't be paid in money, but he would give us a room to sleep in and a meal every day as payment. When we said no, we need money to live, he abandoned us and we were walking on the street, begging and getting food from rubbish bins for many months until a man gave us work at his Tachanium mine. He pays us money, as well as giving us a room and a meal. He is a kind man and we can be proud again and not ashamed."

The ANA called Byron in briefly to explain his findings from the soil sample and he was able to confirm the presence of minute traces of Talisium Dust, a standard constituent of explosives.

"So in your opinion," the defence asked, "how would Talisium Dust get into soil? You may list all the ways you know of."

"From one of two ways," Byron replied. "Either as a direct result of an explosion, or as a result of an accidental spill."

The defence lawyer smiled. "Ahh, so we've no way of knowing if this particular soil sample isn't from such an accidental spill, do we? Aren't you just assuming an explosion took place?"

"No. Talisium Dust particles change upon explosion. One of the molecules, Cadmist, loses one of its nuclei. Unexploded Talisium Dust retains both its nuclei undamaged. As in these photographs," he indicated the display screen, "the Dust in the soil sample from Zibandin had a single nucleus for each Cadmist molecule. That can only happen from explosion. That is neither my opinion nor assumption. It is proven scientific fact."

Preataq Jormla told them of the bombing of his haulage firm after turning down a deal with Vazien, of the overweight shipments, and the penalty notices that mysteriously went away.

"Thirty five people died that day. People who had nothing to do with the deal. One girl was on her third day of work after leaving her education. My company was her first position and she had her whole life ahead of her." He told them how he personally financed the funerals, bought several relatives homes when theirs were repossessed by the banks who owned the finance for them, and how he sold his own home to pay for several employees' medical expenses. The vidicom footage he shot of the crates of guns hidden in the extra compartments of his ships, was shown to the court, as was all footage of conversations and meetings with Vazien, many of which were damning.

To my surprise, Donaldson announced that if everyone was agreeable, they would take another short break and then continue for another few hours. I returned to the witness room with the news.

"How's it going?" Kyle asked.

"The Zibandin guys did well and Preataq Jormla had a couple dabbing at their eyes. Jeez I could murder a coffee."

Vincent handed me a hot drink and a snack and we went next door to eat and smoke.

"You were awesome, my love," I said and hugged Byron.

"Thank you. Who is next up?"

"We only have Doctor Orlan, Umboi, Listler, all of us, and the neighbours left, so then the running order will be up to them. So far, they've sort of kept to a similar time line to the events as they happened. If they continue in the same way, after Umboi is done, we'll have Jam and the business with the exhumation and his wife's murder. Orlan will testify then too. Then it might be Belotan and the Niruvan business, which will mean Tinnias and me, Vincent, Kyle, you, Toma, and whichever troopers were involved, will be called. During that part, they should address the Olendra connection too, as she was involved in that. The Taiko connection will be addressed sometime too. Then we'll have the shooting of me and last, it should be our abduction on the refuelling station. That'll be us finished then, so the defence will be up after that and who knows who they'll call or when."

"So we're here for the duration," Kyle said.

"Yeah, sorry, guys."

"No problem, drink up before it gets cold."

The clerk called everyone back and I kissed Byron, then followed Tinnias back into the courtroom. Umboi had at least a dozen people crying as he told his story. The stolen plans, the secret patent, his abduction and the beating that left him blind in one eye and without the use of his left arm. I heard sobs when he told how he was unable to feed himself, wash, or clean himself after using the bathroom, how the use of the right hand is taken as inviting the demon. When he said how he was ashamed because he couldn't use his hands enough to pray to his deity, I heard more audible sobs. He went into some detail about how his former friends and neighbours spat at him in the street, refused him service in stores, daubed animal waste on his house wall in obscene taunts, and how finally, he almost took his own life by jumping from a bridge.

Orlan came next and told everyone how Vazien persuaded him to supply a phial of the River Fever pathogen, then a little while later, his wife died of River Fever.

Jam was called next and everyone went quiet, interested to look upon another Drycenian. He gave his evidence in his usual confident way, explaining everything so that all could understand, and produced documentation to show the exhumation was done in accordance with all the accepted Law Enforcement Agency regulations, under mine and Tinnias' supervision as per the law requires. Charts and diagrams were produced, showing how the River Fever pathogen works, when infected by ingestion and by injection. No one alive could argue with his evidence. I was proud.

Belotan was called and the Niruvan business was brought up next. He told them how Vazien approached him with a proposition to work together, how he then gave the same deal to the Dankera Collective, his conversation with Yanit, his knowledge of Tip being a law enforcer, and of being tipped off about myself and Tinnias being law enforcers masquerading as homeless street bums. He explained how he was called by Lomas and of their long conversation, which resulted in him deciding to work with us as he was now regretting having had anything to do with Vazien.

"He is dishonest, even to me. He's a crook and I should know, I'm the biggest crook there is. He's reckless and dangerous, kills without a second thought, has no compassion for his fellow man, and thinks nothing of the harm and suffering he causes everywhere he goes. I was a fool to get involved with him, so I welcomed the chance to work with the law enforcers. Yes, I'm a criminal but my workforce like me, that tells you all you need to know."

Captain Listler took the stand and went through the story of his encounter with Vazien, of his being court martialled for cowardice and the ending of his exemplary military career. His witness, Uri Lukin confirmed everything and told how he only survived by hiding amongst the dead bodies of his comrades, and how the fear of further reprisals caused him to change his name and leave his home world, family, job, and friends.

Next came Vazien's neighbours, who gave full details of the rows they heard between Vazien and his wife, his threat to kill her, the offer of a job to Arlat and the subsequent threat to their son, and the burning down of their home.

Lomas was called next and went into detail about his conversation with Belotan, how he was impressed at the man's wit and willingness to work for the right side of the law. Then came Vincent, Kyle, Toma, Byron, and the eight troopers who all gave details of the firefight, and their rescue of Tinnias and me from the Gaht compound. Everyone involved in the Brakely business was called and asked about Brakely and the shooting of me. Byron and each of the troopers involved were called, then Jam came back to explain about my death and resurrection in the tank. It was argued that, as I survived, I couldn't be accusing Vazien of arranging a murder, but Jam showed all the medical readouts to show I was indeed dead for over a week before coming back, and they couldn't argue with his clear medical facts. Next was our abduction in the refuelling station and all involved were called back to give accounts of that episode. Tinnias was called and he gave a full account of our time as street bums, our investigation of the Gaht compound, our trip to Dankera and discovering Commander Ranil Taiko apparently happy to be in the Collective's centre of operations. He told of the secret cameras we installed and pieces of vidicom footage were shown to the court. He told them about the firefight when Vazien visited the compound and our rescue by Vincent, Kyle, and the Drycenians. Our abduction and my murder by Po was told in full detail, as was the abduction on the refuelling station, and finally, he gave a full account of our journey around the galaxy, hunting for witnesses, our interviews with them and the recordings were checked for adherence to regulations.

I was next up. My evidence was the same as Tinnias' had been and I told them everything in as much detail as possible. The interviews, the abduction, the shooting, the Gaht compound, Dankera 7, I didn't miss anything out and by the time Donaldson announced the end of the day's proceedings, Tinnias and I were exhausted. I needed a stiff drink, a meal, a workout, and some serious loving.

The day's events were discussed in detail over dinner and our workout was left for another day.

"What happens tomorrow then, Sam?" Umboi said.

"Tomorrow the defence does its thing. This means they can call any one of us and grill us for however long they like. They will try to discredit your testimony, remember that Vazien can afford the very best defence lawyers available. Every mistake you've ever made in your life will be brought out and aired for the entire court to see and pick through. Think before answering, don't panic, you have all the time you need. That's for everyone by the way, so remember, all of you. Vazien has opted not to give evidence on his own behalf, but he does retain the right to instruct his lawyers to ask whatever questions he wishes, so long as they pertain to the case, or the quality of your testimony. Whenever they step out of line, our lawyers will handle it, so no need to start a row. Leave the arguing to the experts."

"I'm so proud of you, Bro," Byron said as we lay, tired from the day. "I wish I could help more."

"You're helping by being there, you've no idea how much it helps knowing I can come back and be with you."

"Oh I think I've a pretty good idea," he smiled.

"I need to be loved," I said, "right now."

"Sir, yes, Sir," he grinned as he leaned in to me.

We awoke far too early for comfort and it was a quiet and bleary eyed group who gathered for breakfast, then boarded the shuttles for the trip over to the liner for the second day of the trial. Olendra and Falco Lorland were called first, and it quickly became apparent that she was not going to be able to dodge a bullet this time, especially as her father, with all his power, position, and money, couldn't help her.

Commander Ranil Taiko was called next and by the look on his face, he knew he had no hope of avoiding doing some jail time. He surprised everyone by admitting everything right from the start of questioning. I saw Tinnias shaking his head sadly and I understood. With years of work behind him, a position of authority and the respect of many hard working detectives all looking to him for guidance in the never ending job of fighting crime, to throw away such a career was madness.

The defence announced themselves and began their cross examinations. I was called first and was questioned for hours about each interview, each recording, the regulations, each day of our time as homeless street bums, every moment of the abduction. They tried and tried to discredit me but I've been doing this for far too long. I knew what I was doing and answered everything accurately and with as much confidence as I could find. It was while grilling me about the abduction on the refuelling station that they finally decided to kick me in the balls.

"Tell me, Detective. Are you a married man?"

"No, but I am in a committed relationship."

"What are the regulations concerning conflict of interest in criminal cases? You may give us the basics. No need to go into full detail."

"Regulations say that if a law enforcer's family member, close friend, or committed partner are needed as a witness, a conflict of interest can arise if the detective is involved in interviewing him or her. So long as the detective concerned plays no part in the interviewing of the said witness, there is no conflict of interest."

"I request that exhibit 39a be brought to the attention of the court. Could you tell us, Detective, what this document is?"

"It's a witness statement."

"And who is the witness?"

"Commander Byron of Drycenian Battle Cruiser DBC1."

"And who conducted this interview?"

"Commander Vaylo."

"Who happens to be your father, does he not, Detective?"

"He does."

"So is it not true that there is a clear conflict of interest in this statement?"

"No."

"How do you come by that opinion?"

"Commander Vaylo is neither family, close friend, nor committed partner to Commander Byron."

A ripple went around the court and the defence lawyer visibly squirmed before continuing.

"But isn't it true, Detective, that you and Commander Byron are lovers?"

"It is," I nodded. "A very fine lover he is too, take my word for it. Since I played no part in his interview, I fail to understand your point in bringing this up."

More sniggers and a ripple of applause went around the room and Donaldson was reluctantly forced to tell everyone to be quiet. I could tell he didn't want to, his grin told me that. He stopped the proceedings for lunch and told us to reconvene in two hours. Tinnias and I almost ran back to the room and just made it inside before we burst out laughing, Tinnias' guffaws turning his face bright red.

"Oh fuck," he said when he could speak. "Oh fuck that's the funniest moment of my entire life. Son, I love you."

"You don't think I went too far?" I said when I could speak.

"Oh hell no. It would almost be worth him getting off just to have experienced that. Oh I gotta go and pee or I'll wet myself."

"Fancy sharing?" Vincent grinned. Guffaws echoed around the bathroom and we laughed.

The whole room shook with laughter when Tinnias and I had finished explaining, with Tinnias impersonating me in a most hilarious fashion. We were still laughing when there was a knock at the door. I answered to find Donaldson looking serious.

"What's up?" I asked, knowing he was going to ruin everyone's day.

"Can I come in?"

"Of course, sorry. Come in." I stepped aside and let him in.

He stood in the middle of the room and didn't wait to be offered a seat. "Vazien just hanged himself in his cell."

"What the fuck?" I hissed. "That fucking asshole."

"Excuse me for being a bit dim witted," Lomas said, "but shouldn't we be pleased?"

"Well yes, Your Majesty," I said, "but it means he gets off with his crimes. Technically, no one gets justice."

"Why technically? Kyle asked.

"Because there is a law that lets us continue with the trial and convict him posthumously, if everyone wants that. Some may be happy just to be rid of him. It must be unanimous. If you do decide to continue, the defence won't bother to put up much of a fight and we'll be done by the end of the day." I looked around the room. "Okay everyone, talk to me." Within a couple of minutes, Donaldson had been instructed to continue and we all returned to the courtroom. The defence lawyer stood.

"In light of the events of the last two hours, my colleague and I formally retract the Ambassador's defence. We accept his actions as indicative of guilt and will not be adding anything further to the case."

The prosecution lawyer stood. "We accept the statement of our esteemed colleagues and are happy to accept his actions as a statement of guilt. We formally request a posthumous conviction."

"Very well," Donaldson replied. "I call Olendra, Child of Vazien into the court. She entered, her hands and feet cuffed, the yellow overall doing nothing for her femininity. The guards led her to the prisoner's cubicle and locked her inside. Donaldson looked at her gravely. "Olendra, your father's actions have proven his guilt, which in turn, proves yours. You were entirely responsible for the attempt on the lives of two highly respected law enforcers, as well as many Niruvan citizens. When deciding upon your sentence, I have taken your father's suicide and your husbands leaving you into consideration. You will go to Mallisways Penitentiary for seven years. Guards, take her down."

I watched her shuffle from the court and felt sad for her. She was still young and had years of life left in which to achieve her dreams and make a difference, but she chose the wrong path and ended up like this. I shook my head sadly.

"I call Commander Ranil Taiko into the court," Donaldson continued. Taiko entered, his shoulders sagging and I felt bewildered as to why someone of his experience would throw everything away by getting involved with Vazien. His career was over, most likely his marriage too, and his reputation was shattered. "Commander Taiko," Donaldson said. "You voluntarily allied yourself to Ambassador Vazien and the Dankera Collective, an action you knew was in direct violation of law enforcement regulations. In doing so, you were complicit in many crimes, some of which have been laid out in this court yesterday. You threw away an outstanding law enforcement career of some thirty years in your misguided quest for power and wealth. You will not have a comfortable experience in prison, Commander, as I'm sure you are aware. I sentence you to twenty two years in the Steran Secure Facility. Guards, take him down." He was ushered out of the court and I saw Tinnias wipe at his cheek. I took his hand and squeezed.

"I call Carl Brakely into court," Donaldson continued. "Ambassador Vazien, by taking his own life and thereby admitting his guilt, has therefore, proved to this court that he hired you and your crew to abduct and kill Commander Vaylo, Detective Sinclair-Vaylo, His Majesty King Lomas VII, and his son and heir, Toma XIV. Do you wish to plead?"

"Yes, Sir. I admit everything. Now that the Ambassador is dead, he can't hurt anyone anymore. His threats of retribution ensured we were all too scared to go against him or leave his influence and I'll take my punishment and look forward to having a chance to start fresh. I never wanted anyone killed, but he had us all by the balls with threats to our families. I have a daughter of seven, I would sooner kill than let him near her. When my man injured the Commander, I made sure he paid for it, and when he shot Sam, I gave him a good kicking. When I discovered the power and strength the Drycenians had, I decided to ask for their help, they've already told you themselves, hopefully."

"They did, and I take their words on board when I sentence you. I cannot let your actions go unpunished, despite your apparent change of heart. I am prepared however, to give you the benefit of the doubt and cut your sentence to eight years at Shringles Maximum Security Facility. You will be expertly assessed and given skills that will aid you in starting over when your term is served. Do not make me regret my kindness. Guards, take him down."

Each of Brakely's men were called and sentenced to various terms ranging from four to eight years. Finally, Po came in.

"Jaril Poyas. You committed your first murder just a week after your ninth birthday and have ended many more lives since that day. You have been sentenced to death five times in your absence for crimes ranging from violent assault, rape, child abduction, attempted murder, and murder, twenty four that we know of and no doubt many more we don't. You freely admitted to the Drycenian security forces that the only reason you assaulted Commander Vaylo was because he assumed Ambassador Vazien would kill your family and didn't give you the respect you deserve for having done it yourself just weeks before. No sane person will understand your loyalty to the Ambassador, nor the enjoyment you take from maiming, raping, and murdering innocent people. You are to be taken from this court, to an appropriately registered unit where you will be executed according to the statute set by the Inter-Galactic Judiciary. Your ashes will then be scattered on an unnamed barren moon of secret location where we can but hope the vacuum of the universe can, in time, render them clear of your evil. If you have a deity, may they have mercy upon your black soul. Guards, take him down."

I sniffed and felt Tinnias squeeze my hand.

Donaldson continued. "Ambassador Vazien, Child of Konmith, you have been accused and convicted of many terrible crimes. You have caused much suffering to innocent people, some of whom never made it to get justice. Many families mourn for loved ones lost at your hands and far too many will carry painful memories for years into their future. Having admitted your guilt by choosing to take your life, I have no hesitation in convicting you on all counts. Your body will be taken from here, to Laksmay Penitentiary where it will be cremated and your ashes stored for one hundred and seventy eight years. If your relatives wish to retrieve your remains after your sentence has been carried out, they may do so. If not, your ashes will be ejected into the Laksmay system's sun. I now call Falco Lorland into the court."

Falco entered by the main door and walked to the front of the court. "Mr Lorland," Donaldson smiled. "The crime for which you were imprisoned and served eleven years was a total fabrication by Ambassador Vazien. I cannot give you back those eleven years, but I can give you your freedom, free of any stain upon your record. I can also assure you that the services of the ANA lawyers are at your disposal so that you can make a rightful claim for compensation from Vazien's estate. As you have already requested, I grant you an immediate divorce from your wife, Olendra, Child of Vazien and declare that as a convicted criminal, she loses all rights to claim financial aid from you or your company. You leave this court a free man."

Donaldson looked up at the packed court and smiled. "This trial is now ended, and may your gods grant you all peace, however you might choose to worship them."

That's it, folks. That's the story of the most powerfully dangerous criminal I've so far encountered. It's a story of suffering, pain, change, death, and most importantly, love. I travelled further in that case than ever before on a single case, and it was the first time I had my father working with me. So much was changed as a result of that case, for many people and much of it was good change. Klackan and Umboi both got their full health back and were able to return to lives they were proud of, to work they enjoyed, and people they loved. The Drycenians set Preataq up with a new home and enough money to live comfortably and start his own horticulture business. Lomas personally visited the tribes on Zibandin and got his best scientists working on repairing their sacred sites. He told them how brave the tribesmen were to help get rid of the evil man from underground, who was now dead because of their bravery, and they were welcomed back into the arms of their kin. Umboi decided not to return to his home world, so he was set up with a new manufacturing plant on Sigma Prime, where he could design and build arms for law enforcement. Listler was happy working the bar, so the Drycenians bought him a controlling share, a new apartment, and enough money to live comfortably, redecorate and modernize the bar. Lomas personally met with the top brass of the Inter Galactic Military Force and told them everything concerned with Captain Listler's involvement in the incident. His conviction was officially quashed and his previous rank was restored to him. Myself, Tinnias, Byron, Lomas, Toma, Vincent, and Kyle, personally attended the ceremony to watch him receive his insignia, medals, and cap badge.

The nature of Vazien's crimes and of his suicide in prison shocked the entire political community. Systems were put in place to prevent such things happening again, politicians would now be required to be audited regularly, their activities would now be monitored and they would be answerable for every wrong doing.

We had one more week with Vincent and Kyle before our schedule brought us to Lilea. Our last night was filled with laughter, apologies, forgiveness, and promises to keep in touch. It took a couple of weeks to get home to Sigma Prime, during which Doctor Jam gave me some injections that strengthened my bones by adding some kind of alloy to them. He also corrected my eyesight and gave me a telephoto implant like the one he put in Farra's eyes. I can now see things a long way away and by using the muscles around my eyes, I can bring everything closer like a camera. It's weird and amazing. Both Tinnias and I received a BioMed implant and knowing our Drycenian friends are now aware of my location and health is a great comfort. We talked a lot about my initial mistrust of them and much healing took place as my confidence in them grew. I began to open up and allow people in, to start trusting people. They promised to keep in touch with me regularly and Jam told me I would be required to visit them for a few days several times each year, to keep our bonds strong and talk through stuff, as he put it.

Byron and I talked about how we might get to spend time together and Lomas announced that the High Council of Drycenia had asked him to host engineering students three times every year for a month each time. He also confided that Byron's Assistant Chief Engineer, Lish, had been begging for some more responsibility and had requested a transfer in order to get it. By taking regular times off, Byron would not only be getting to spend time to relax and be with me, but he would be helping Lish gain more experience. Since Byron had never taken any time off from his work, he had plenty to call upon whenever he wanted, so we agreed that every time I went home, I'd meet up with the battle cruiser to pick him up and we'd go to Sigma. Then, when I returned to work, I would drop him off first. This meant that we would get at least a month together every eight weeks. He came back home with me when this case finished and we spent many weeks together, sightseeing and relaxing.

So much of me changed, not just my love life. In realising where my identity lay, I became whole for the first time and understood so much of what had gone before. In seeing my true self, I understood how closed and broken I had been without realising it. My old self had served me well for many years and as I felt him changing into the new person I saw in the mirror each morning, I mourned for the loss of him. The mourning was not a painful mourning though, it was a grateful one and I emerged hopeful and optimistic. My new and now longer life had just begun, I had found new love of a strength and depth I never knew existed, but most importantly, I found myself. The time I spent with the Drycenians during this case turned my life upside down in many ways and some of that process was traumatic, as I've described. Listening to it again, it seems as if I spent all my time being a total mess and falling apart, but that would not be accurate. It was a time of great personal change, many changes all happening at once and I will forever be grateful for it

Toma impressed me with his growing wisdom one day, when I saw him tending to some plants in his quarters. In one pot was something that look like a dying twig with no more than half a dozen brown leaves, while in the other was a flowering plant that was covered in beautiful and sweet smelling blossoms. He took a sharp knife and sliced down through the dying one's main stem, almost to soil level.

"Putting it out of its misery?" I sniggered.

"On the contrary, my friend. A poison builds up within this particular plant's stem, a poison that would eventually kill it if left to continue on its damaging path. Through the trauma of cutting it, the poison is set free and this time next year, this plant will become another like that one." He pointed to the beautiful plant and smiled at me.

I understood what he was telling me and thanked him for his wisdom. Never again would I under estimate him. He will be a fine King when the time comes.

Once back home, I found that word of the change to my lifestyle had got around and I found myself talking about it to many people. Even my mountainous friend, Leevine had found out and as I showed Byron around Tunipz, Leevine accepted him like a brother and paid him the highest compliment he was able.

"If anyone ever does you wrong, you tell me and I'll sort them out."

This is Commander Byron of Drycenian Battle Cruiser DBC1 again. The process of relaying the details of this time has been a healing experience for us both. No one is perfect, we all have negative stuff deep down inside that we try to hide, with varying degrees of success. I say this because it occurred to me that relaying this story makes it seem as if Sam was the only one with negative baggage. I don't want anyone to think I'm Mr Perfect because I'm not at all. Both of us had need of healing and both of us benefitted from that healing. Those few days during which Sam died, taught me the value of every moment and the importance of not putting things off for another day. I was not only proud to be involved in bringing this case to the right conclusion, but exhilarated to be working with my brain instead of my hands for a change. I decided to get myself involved in Sam's work much more often and you'll hear about it in future V-Logs. I wish you all happiness and healing. Now back to Sam.

Sam here. I just want to end by urging you all to make an effort to build good memories for the time when they're all you have of someone you love.

This is V-Log reference Q890/M, data log reference point 4136902/627 Detective Samelan Sinclair-Vaylo, signing off.

# THE END

www.ingramcontent.com/pod-product-compliance
Lightning Source LLC
Chambersburg PA
CBHW071639260626
47170CB00001B/166